THE GUTTERVERSE

Book One: Reload

A Novel

Lampert X Griffin

LAMPERT & SONS PUBLISHING

This is a work of fiction. Names, characters, places, and incidents either are the product of the author's imagination or are used fictitiously.

Published in the United States by Lampert & Sons Publishing

ISBN 978-1-969709-45-6 (paperback)

FIRST EDITION

For everyone who's ever been told their story doesn't matter.
It does.

THE DAY THE WORLD BROKE

The night the world changed, D-Lo was losing at cards.

Melo's apartment. His mom working the night shift, his little brother asleep in the other room. They were playing for candy bars—neither of them had real money—and D-Lo was down three Snickers and a Kit-Kat.

"You're cheating," D-Lo said.

"I'm strategizing." "That's the same thing." "It's really not." Melo laid down his hand. Full house. "Pay up." D-Lo threw a Snickers at his head.

That's when the sky lit up.

Green light—bright as daylight, wrong as a scream—flooding through the windows. The power went out. The TV died. Melo's phone sparked and went black.

Three seconds of absolute silence.

Then the world came back, and everything was different.

"What the hell was that?" Melo whispered.

D-Lo didn't know.

Nobody knew. Not then.

Over the next few weeks, they started hearing stories. People lifting cars. People walking through walls. People seeing things that hadn't happened yet.

Black SUVs appeared in the neighborhood—unmarked, tinted windows, men in tactical gear who looked at residents like they were studying specimens. The Trust, people started calling them. Nobody knew exactly what they were or who they worked for. They just knew to stay out of their way.

"You think it's real?" Melo asked. They were on the roof of Building C, watching Trust vehicles cruise through the projects like sharks circling. "The powers?" "I don't know." "If you could have one, what would it be?" D-Lo thought about it. "Flying, maybe. Get out of here. See the world." "Nah, that's boring." Melo grinned. "I'd want to see the future.

Know what's coming before it comes. Then I'd never lose another bet." D-Lo laughed. But something cold moved through him. A premonition he couldn't name.

"Whatever happens," he said, "we stick together. Right?" "Always." Melo bumped his fist. "Marrow boys for life. Nobody breaks that up." "Nobody."

D-Lo didn't know that across town, in their apartment, his little sister had woken up screaming.

Kimi was twelve years old. She'd been dreaming about their mother—the good dream, the one where mama was still alive and making pancakes on Sunday morning—when the green light flooded through her window.

For three seconds, Kimi saw something.

Not with her eyes. Deeper than that. She saw threads of light connecting everything—her bedsheets to the floor, the floor to the walls, the walls to the world outside. She saw possibility itself, shimmering and infinite.

Then it was gone.

She sat in the dark, heart pounding, trying to remember what she'd seen.

But it slipped away like water through fingers, leaving only a strange ache behind her eyes and the absolute certainty that something had changed.

Something inside her.

She didn't tell D-Lo. Didn't tell anyone. What was there to say? *I saw magic for three seconds and now my head hurts?*

So she buried it. Forgot about it. Let it sleep.

For now.

That was six months ago.

Before D-Lo understood what the green flash had done to some people.

Before he understood what it had done to him.

Before "always" became just another lie the universe told.

SEVEN YEARS BEFORE D-LO DIED FOR THE FIRST TIME

Melo saved his life with nothing but words.

They were fifteen, cutting class behind the vocational building, passing a blunt Melo had lifted from his uncle's stash. D-Lo was laughing at something that wasn't even funny when Melo's voice dropped.

"Don't look, but Marcus Townsend and his boys just came around the corner." D-Lo's stomach clenched.

Marcus Townsend was seventeen, ran with the Southside crew, and had decided two weeks ago that D-Lo had looked at him wrong in the cafeteria. D-Lo hadn't looked at him at all—he'd been staring at the mystery meat trying to figure out if it was edible—but that didn't matter. Marcus had decided there was beef, and in the Marrow, that meant there was beef.

"How many?" "Five." Melo's eyes tracked them without his head moving. A skill you learned young in the projects. "They're coming this way." "Shit." "I got you." Melo stood up, tucked the blunt behind his ear, and walked directly toward Marcus Townsend.

D-Lo's heart stopped.

"Yo, Marcus!" Melo's voice was bright. Friendly. Completely insane.

"My man! I've been looking for you!" Marcus stopped. Confused. His boys fanned out behind him, hands drifting toward waistbands.

"The hell you want, Melo?" "Business, bro. Strictly business." Melo pulled out his phone, started scrolling. "You know my cousin Darnell? Works at the Footlocker on Fifth? He said he can get Jordans for half retail. The new ones. The red and blacks." D-Lo watched his best friend spin a lie out of nothing—no cousin, no Footlocker connect, no Jordans—while Marcus Townsend forgot entirely why he'd been walking this direction.

Five minutes later, Marcus left with a fake phone number and a promise that would never be fulfilled.

Melo walked back, sat down, retrieved the blunt, and hit it like nothing had happened.

"You're insane," D-Lo said.

"I'm resourceful." "He's gonna figure out that number's fake." "By then we'll be somewhere else." Melo shrugged. "That's tomorrow's problem. Today's problem was not getting our asses beat. Problem solved." D-Lo stared at his friend. Melo had no powers. No muscles. No weapons.

Just a quick mind and a quicker mouth and the absolute certainty that he could talk his way out of anything.

"Thank you," D-Lo said.

"For what? I just wanted to finish this blunt in peace."

Later, on the roof, watching the sunset paint the projects in colors that almost made them beautiful, D-Lo asked: "You ever feel bad about it? The lying. The scamming. All of it." Melo was quiet for a moment. Unusual for him.

"My mom works sixty hours a week and still can't make rent. My pops is doing seven years for something he didn't do because he couldn't afford a real lawyer. My little brother needs glasses but Medicaid takes six months to process anything." He looked at D-Lo. "The system lies to us every single day. Tells us if we work hard, play by the rules, we'll be okay. That's the biggest scam there is." He turned back to the sunset.

"So yeah. I lie. I hustle. But I only take from people who can afford to lose it, and I only do it to survive. The day the world stops lying to me, I'll stop lying back." D-Lo didn't have an answer for that.

He wasn't sure there was one.

THREE DAYS BEFORE D-LO DIED FOR THE FIRST TIME

The Melo who called about Mr. Kim's grocery store wasn't the same Melo who'd talked down Marcus Townsend.

Something had shifted. The green flash, maybe. Or just time. The lies had gotten bigger. The stakes higher. The line between surviving and self-destruction had blurred until D-Lo couldn't tell which side his friend was standing on.

"Word is he keeps like ten racks in a safe in the back," Melo said.

They were walking through the projects, Melo pitching like he was selling something legitimate. "Cash only business. No cameras in the office.

Just walk in, pop the safe, walk out." D-Lo stopped walking.

"Melo. Mr. Kim's son is six-four and used to box Golden Gloves." "So?" "So I seen him knock out three dudes at once when they tried to shoplift." "We ain't shoplifting. We robbing. Different energy." "That don't make it better." "It makes it more honest!" The logic was so broken D-Lo couldn't even find the pieces.

"I gotta go to work, Melo." "Work? Bro, why you still doing that warehouse shit? You too smart for that." "I'm too smart to rob a Korean grocery store and get my ass beat by a Golden Gloves boxer." Melo's face flickered—something dark, something desperate—before the grin came back.

"Trouble is opportunity, D! That's what they don't teach you in school!" D-Lo didn't respond. He knew Melo. Knew that "no" never meant no to him.

Knew that sooner or later, Melo's schemes were gonna catch up with both of them.

He just didn't know it would be sooner.

Patterson Logistics occupied a rusting building on the edge of District Nine, where the projects gave way to industrial wasteland.

D-Lo had been working there since he was nineteen—loading trucks, unloading trucks, moving boxes from one place to another for reasons nobody ever explained. Minimum wage plus occasional overtime. Enough to keep the lights on and Kimi fed, but not enough for anything else.

Every day felt the same.

Clock in at eight. Move boxes until noon. Thirty-minute lunch in a break room that smelled like cigarettes and despair. More boxes until five.

Clock out. Go home. Repeat.

The other guys on the crew were variations of the same story: men who'd ended up here because nowhere else would have them. Ex-cons. High school dropouts. Addicts trying to stay clean. Guys running from something or waiting for something or just existing in the space between.

D-Lo fit right in.

In the break room, Marcus—an old head who'd been working here since before D-Lo was born—was reading an actual physical newspaper.

"Anything good?" D-Lo asked.

"World's still going to hell. Government still lying. Rent still too damn high." Marcus shrugged. "So no." He tapped an article. "Says here there was a 'containment incident' at a 'research installation.' No details. No specifics. Just 'containment incident.'" "That could mean anything." "That's the point. When they don't want you to know something, they use words that don't mean nothing." Marcus folded the paper. "Mark my words—something's coming. Something big." D-Lo didn't feel anything coming except his next shift.

But Marcus wasn't wrong.

Something was already here.

His phone buzzed on the walk home.

MELO: bro you in tonight or what

D-LO: in for what

MELO: the lick. mr kim's. i got a crew. we moving at midnight

D-Lo stared at the screen.

D-LO: i told you no

MELO: come on man i need you

D-LO: you don't need me. you need someone to talk you out of stupid shit and you ain't listening anyway MELO: this aint stupid. this is opportunity

D-LO: opportunity to get your ass beat or locked up. im out

MELO: fine. be like that. but when im counting bands, dont come asking for a loan D-Lo pocketed his phone.

Melo was gonna do what Melo was gonna do. Always had. Always would.

All D-Lo could do was not be there when it went wrong.

Kimi was doing homework at the kitchen table when he got back.

"How was work?" "Work." He dropped his bag by the door. "How was school?" "School." She didn't look up from her math worksheet. "We're having a test on Friday. Fractions." "You need help?" "I got it." D-Lo stood there for a moment, watching his little sister furrow her brow at numbers. She was smart—smarter than him, definitely—but she worked for it. Didn't take anything for granted.

Their mama would've been proud.

"I'm making dinner," he said. "Spaghetti." "Again?" "You complaining?" "I'm observing. We've had spaghetti four times this week." "Spaghetti is versatile. It's a canvas. Tonight I'm adding... hot sauce." "That's not a variation. That's a crime." "It's culinary innovation." Kimi finally looked up, a smile tugging at her lips.

"You're weird." "I learned from the best." She threw her eraser at him. He caught it and threw it back.

And for a moment—just a moment—everything felt normal. Safe. Simple.

He didn't know it would be the last normal night for a long time.

D-Lo was asleep when his phone rang.

He grabbed it without looking, muscle memory from years of emergency calls—Kimi sick, landlord threatening, Melo in trouble.

"Hello?" Heavy breathing on the other end.

Then Melo's voice, shaking: "D... bro... I fucked up..." D-Lo was instantly awake.

"What happened?" "The lick... it went wrong... Mr. Kim's son was there... and then these other dudes showed up... and there was shooting..." D-Lo's blood went cold.

"Are you hurt?" "I don't know... I don't... there's blood but I don't think it's mine..." Melo's voice cracked. "D, I think somebody's dead. I think..." "Where are you?" "Behind the store. In the alley. I can't move, man. I'm scared to move." "Stay there. Don't move. I'm coming." D-Lo was already pulling on clothes, heart hammering.

"D-Lo?" Kimi's voice from her room. "What's wrong?" "Nothing. Go back to sleep." "You're lying." "Kimi, please. Just stay here. Lock the door. Don't let anyone in." He was out the door before she could argue.

Running through the night.

Toward his best friend.

Toward trouble.

Toward a bullet that was waiting for him three days later.

Three months after the green flash, D-Lo would die for the first time.

Two weeks after that, Melo would disappear.

And D-Lo would learn that "Marrow boys for life" was just another promise the universe wasn't interested in keeping.

But he'd also learn something else.

Something the universe hadn't counted on.

He could come back.

END PROLOGUE

CHAPTER 1

THE FIRST SAVE FILE

D-Lo woke up to the sound of arguing, a blunt roach burning in the ashtray beside his bed, and the unmistakable smell of somebody frying fish at 10 in the goddamn morning.

The Marrow Projects were alive and pissed off again.

Concrete walls amplified everything in this bitch—babies crying, couples fucking loud enough to shake the drywall, dudes on the stairwell selling stepped-on weed they swore was "pressure," aunties yelling through cracked windows about who owed who money. The soundtrack of Section 8 survival. If silence ever fell over Building C, that meant somebody died or the cops were coming. Sometimes both.

He blinked the sleep out his eyes and reached for his phone, knocking over an empty Hennessy bottle that rolled off the nightstand and hit the carpet with a dull thunk.

10:43 AM.

He overslept. Again.

Last night had been a blur—some house party three buildings over, a girl named Shanice or Shaniqua or something with a tongue ring who'd pulled him into a bedroom that smelled like Black & Milds and cheap perfume. He remembered her nails digging into his back. Remembered stumbling home at 4 AM with his boxers on backwards and a hickey the size of a quarter on his neck.

Good times. Bad decisions. Same difference in the Marrow.

"Kimi!" he shouted, rolling off the mattress. His head throbbed like somebody was kickboxing his brain. "You go to school or nah?" His little sister poked her head around the doorway. Thirteen years old, braids pulled back, wearing a hoodie three sizes too big that used to be their daddy's. She had a bowl of Frosted Flakes in one hand and judgment in her eyes.

"Ain't no school on Saturday, fool." "Oh." Right. D-Lo rubbed his face. "True. Good. I knew that. Just testin' you." Kimi shook her head like she was the older sibling. "You smell like weed, liquor, and regret." "That's just my natural musk." D-Lo grabbed a deodorant stick that barely had anything left on it. "Now where my shoes—" A loud pop cracked outside the window.

Not fireworks. Not a car backfiring.

A gunshot.

Kimi didn't even flinch.

That was the sad part. That was the part that made D-Lo's chest hurt every single time—watching his baby sister hear gunshots the way other kids heard ice cream trucks. Just another sound in the symphony of the hood.

"Don't go outside," D-Lo said, grabbing her shoulders. His hangover evaporated. Nothing sobers you up faster than bullets.

"I ain't stupid." He stepped into the hallway—peeling paint, flickering lights, cigarette smoke thick as soup. Old Man Tully was posted up by the stairwell with a forty in a paper bag, watching the action like it was a TV show.

Another gunshot. Then shouting.

D-Lo's stomach dropped.

He recognized the voice instantly.

Melo.

His dumbass friend who'd been catching trouble since they were both in diapers. The same Melo who got suspended in eighth grade for selling bootleg DVDs out his locker. The same Melo who once tried to rob a pizza delivery driver and got his ass beat with a thermal bag. The same Melo who somehow always survived his own stupidity through sheer luck and D-Lo's intervention.

D-Lo ran down the concrete steps two at a time, ignoring the fact that he was wearing mismatched slides and a wife-beater with a hole in it.

The moment he stepped into the courtyard, he saw it: Melo holding a pistol sideways like he was in a music video, waving it at some dude near the vending machines that hadn't worked since Obama's first term.

"Melo!" D-Lo hissed, keeping his voice low. "Bro, what the FUCK are you doing?" Melo glanced over, eyes wide and jittery—probably high on something that wasn't just weed. His pupils were too big. His movements too twitchy.

"D-Lo, chill! I got this! This dude owe me money!" The guy he was threatening—tall, tatted, built like he'd done a few bids—raised both hands slow. Prison calm. The kind of calm that said he'd seen worse.

"Man, I don't even know you like that—" Melo fired another shot into the air.

"YOU DO NOW!" The sound echoed off the buildings like thunder in a concrete canyon.

D-Lo put his hands on his head. "Lord, I truly hate this man." Windows slammed open. A baby started crying. Somewhere, a woman screamed, "CALL THE POLICE!" And then D-Lo noticed something worse.

Three dudes in black hoodies creeping out from behind the dumpster at the edge of the courtyard. Moving quiet. Moving purposeful. One had a chrome .45 catching sunlight. Another had something bigger—looked like a sawed-off.

They weren't here for Melo.

They were here for the gun. Or the drugs Melo probably had on him. Or the chain around his neck that was definitely fake but looked real enough to die for.

"Melo," D-Lo whispered, inching closer, "you need to put the gun down and—" One of the masked guys raised his piece.

Time slowed.

D-Lo's brain screamed MOVE. But his feet refused to cooperate. He'd been here before—not literally here, but moments like this. Moments where everything went slow and your body felt like it was underwater and you knew something terrible was about to happen but you couldn't do shit about it except watch.

The masked man fired.

D-Lo saw the muzzle flash—bright, orange, violent.

Saw Melo's eyes widen.

Saw the bullet coming at him like it was floating through honey.

He opened his mouth to scream— *THUNK.*

The bullet hit him square in the chest.

D-Lo felt heat. Then ice. Then nothing.

He collapsed to the ground, staring up at the gray sky. The clouds looked like cotton that had been left out too long. Dirty. Neglected.

Just like everything else in the Marrow.

He heard Melo screaming. Heard the masked men running—footsteps fading like drums losing their rhythm. Heard Kimi's voice faintly from somewhere far away, calling his name like a prayer that wasn't gonna get answered.

The world dimmed. Darkness crept from the edges of his vision like spilled ink.

"Not like this..." D-Lo murmured, barely able to breathe. Blood bubbled in his throat, hot and copper-tasting.

"I ain't even eat breakfast." Then everything went black.

There was no light at the end of the tunnel.

No angels. No pearly gates. No grandmama reaching out to welcome him home.

Just a loud, glitchy POP like an old TV shutting off.

Static.

Silence.

Then—

D-Lo opened his eyes.

Same room. Same peeling ceiling with the water stain that looked like a screaming face. Same thin-ass blanket that barely kept him warm in winter. Same empty Hennessy bottle on the floor.

He sat up fast. Heart hammering. Hands shaking.

He looked down at his chest—no blood. No bullet hole. No wound.

He felt his sternum, pressing hard, expecting pain, expecting the wet heat of ruined flesh.

Nothing.

His phone buzzed on the floor.

He picked it up with trembling fingers.

10:43 AM.

"What the hell…" he whispered.

"Kimi!" he shouted. "You go to school or nah?" Kimi poked her head in. Same braids. Same hoodie. Same bowl of cereal.

"Ain't no school on Saturday, fool." D-Lo stared at her. Wide-eyed. Terrified.

He stood slowly, joints creaking like he'd aged fifty years in no seconds.

"Hey, uh… what you just say?" "That you look musty." "No, before that." "That there ain't no school?" She frowned, spoon halfway to her mouth.

"What's wrong with you? You look like you seen a ghost." He touched his forehead. His pulse. His chest.

He remembered dying. The bullet entering his body like a fist made of fire. Melo screaming. The sky going dark.

"How am I alive?" D-Lo whispered. "I was dead… I was dead dead…" Kimi set down her cereal. "You feelin' okay? You need me to call somebody?" "No. No I am NOT feelin' okay." D-Lo swallowed hard. His throat felt dry. His hands wouldn't stop shaking.

"Listen… stay inside today." "I literally already said I was—" "STAY INSIDE!" he snapped, voice cracking.

Kimi blinked. Finally, in a long time, she looked scared. Not of the gunshots. Not of the hood. Of him.

"…Okay. Damn." D-Lo grabbed his keys, slipped his slides back on, and ran outside. Down the stairs. Past Old Man Tully, who was still nursing that forty like nothing had happened.

Because nothing had happened.

Not yet.

D-Lo burst into the courtyard.

And there they were: Melo and the same man arguing. The same words. The same gestures. The same energy building toward the same violence.

Replay. Exact replay.

D-Lo froze.

"Oh hell nah."

D-Lo sprinted across the courtyard, slides slapping concrete, lungs burning with fear instead of exertion.

"Melo! Stop! Stop right now!" Melo turned, confused. "Bro, what—" The masked men stepped out from behind the dumpster.

Same positions. Same weapons. Same death on their minds.

D-Lo screamed, "GET DOWN!" Gunshot.

D-Lo felt the bullet hit his stomach this time—lower, hotter, worse.

He folded over, choking on his own blood.

The world went black again.

10:43 AM.

D-Lo sat up screaming.

"OH HELL NAH I'M IN A VIDEO GAME!" Kimi dropped her cereal. Milk splashed everywhere.

"What is WRONG with you!?" "SHUT UP I'M TIME TRAVELING!" He bolted out the door again. Heart pounding. Fear mixing with something else now—something like understanding. Something like possibility.

This time he grabbed a brick from the pile of construction debris nobody had cleaned up in six months.

Ran straight at Melo.

Threw the brick at his head.

BONK.

Melo dropped instantly.

The other dude ran.

Masked men stepped out. Raised guns.

"BRUH I JUST SAVED YOUR—" Gunshot. Bullet to the neck.

D-Lo felt his blood spray out before he felt the pain.

Darkness.

10:43 AM.

"Kimi, if I die again I love you." "...What?" D-Lo didn't even answer.

He stormed out the door like he was speedrunning a mission.

This time he didn't approach Melo. Didn't shout. Didn't grab a brick.

He hid behind the vending machine—the broken one with the faded Sprite logo and the bullet hole in the glass from last summer.

When Melo pulled the gun, D-Lo yelled: "THREE DUDES TO YOUR LEFT!" Melo whipped around.

Gunfire erupted.

Mask 1 dropped—chest shots. Mask 2 ran—self-preservation. Mask 3 shot Melo in the leg and fled.

D-Lo stepped out, shaking. Hands on his knees. Breathing hard.

He lived. Barely.

Melo screamed on the ground, clutching his thigh as blood pooled on the concrete.

D-Lo stared at his hands. Then at the sky. Then at the blood that wasn't his.

He realized something terrifying.

"I ain't just relivin' moments..." He breathed heavy.

"I can change them." He didn't know how. He didn't know why.

But he knew one thing for sure: He had a save file.

And the whole hood was one big broken-ass video game.

Sirens howled in the distance—always late, always slow, like the city gave exactly zero fucks about who died in the Marrow.

Melo was still screaming, the gunshot wound in his thigh pumping blood with every panicked heartbeat.

"BRO, CALL AN AMBULANCE! I'M DYING! I'M LITERALLY DYING!" D-Lo knelt beside him, pressing his hands against the wound. The blood was hot. Alive.

"You ain't dying. It hit meat, not artery. Just calm down—" "HOW YOU KNOW THAT!?" "Because I seen worse," D-Lo muttered.

He didn't mention that he'd also been worse. Multiple times. In the last twenty minutes.

Old heads were gathering now, stepping out of buildings, cigarettes dangling from lips, watching with eyes that had seen this movie before.

Mrs. Robinson from 2C waddled over with a towel.

"Hold this on it, baby," she told D-Lo. "Lord have mercy, these children out here killing each other again." D-Lo pressed the towel down. Melo whimpered.

"Why?" D-Lo asked quietly. "Why you had the gun, Melo?" Melo's eyes darted. Shame mixed with pain.

"I was just... I was just trying to get paid, man. Dude owed Trick money and Trick said if I collected I could get twenty percent—" "You almost died for twenty percent of somebody else's debt?" "I didn't think—" "You NEVER think! That's your whole problem!" The sirens got louder. Red and blue lights bounced off building walls.

D-Lo stepped back from Melo as the EMTs rolled in. Cops too—NBPD, looking bored, looking like this was just another Saturday.

One officer glanced at D-Lo.

"You see what happened?" D-Lo kept his face blank. Rule #1 in the Marrow: don't snitch. Not because of street code bullshit—because snitching got you killed faster than the original crime.

"Nah. Just heard the shots and came down." The cop squinted. Didn't believe him. But didn't push it either. Too much paperwork. Not enough care.

They loaded Melo into the ambulance. He reached for D-Lo's hand.

"Bro... thank you. I don't know how you knew, but—" "Just stay out of trouble," D-Lo said.

He stepped back. Watched the ambulance pull away. Watched the cops take statements they wouldn't follow up on. Watched the neighborhood return to normal—kids already back outside, dudes back on the corners, life resuming like violence was just a commercial break.

D-Lo walked toward the back of the building. Found a quiet corner between dumpsters.

And threw up.

Everything. The fear. The deaths. The blood that wasn't there but still felt warm on his hands.

He wiped his mouth with the back of his hand and stared at the sky.

"What the fuck is happening to me?"

He took the long route home. Avoiding people. Keeping his eyes down.

Every little sound made him jump. A car backfiring almost made him dive behind a bush like a soldier with PTSD.

He passed the liquor store. Thought about going in, grabbing a bottle, drowning whatever this was in brown liquor.

But that felt wrong.

If he could reset... if he could go back... he needed to be sharp.

Needed to understand.

He muttered to himself like a man losing his grip: "Okay... okay... think, D-Lo. You died. Multiple times. Like eight?

Nine? Ten? I lost count. But each time I came back. Same time. Same day.

Same everything." He walked past Old Man Tully's stoop.

Tully stared at him with those ancient eyes that had seen too much.

"You look shook, young blood." "I'm good, OG." "You ain't good. But you will be." D-Lo didn't know what that meant. He kept walking.

"What if it's a power?" he whispered to himself. "Like some superhero glitch? Naw, that's stupid. Unless..." He froze.

The explosion.

Project Renaissance.

That weird-ass flash the night everything went black for three seconds city-wide. The night six months ago when the sky lit up green and the power grid flatlined and every phone in the city died at the same moment.

People had been talking ever since. Stories spreading. Whispers about "wired people." Folks lifting cars. Folks bending spoons. Folks reading minds.

Rumors. But rumors in the hood always got at least one foot in the truth.

D-Lo swallowed hard.

"...Ain't no way."

Back home, Kimi was sitting cross-legged on the couch, new bowl of cereal, watching him with suspicion.

"You good?" she asked through a mouthful.

"No," D-Lo said honestly. "Not even kinda." He locked himself in the bathroom. Turned on the light. Stared at himself in the cracked mirror.

Same face he'd always had—brown skin, low fade that needed a touch-up, tired eyes that had seen too much for twenty-two years.

But something was different now. Something behind his eyes.

"Look," he said to his reflection. "I know you probably insane. But entertain the possibility that you not." He tapped his forehead.

"You remember everything. You the only one." He opened the medicine cabinet, grabbed his grandmama's old lipstick—hadn't been able to throw it away since she passed—and wrote on the mirror: *IF YOU DIE AGAIN, DOES THIS STILL STAY?*

Then he stared at it.

"Scientific method," he whispered proudly. "Bill Nye the hood guy."

He dragged his old toaster out from under the sink.

Plugged it in.

Filled the bathtub.

Kimi shouted from the living room: "Whatever you're doing, it sound stupid!" "You worry about yourself!" he yelled back.

He stared at the toaster like it was about to tell him the secrets of the universe.

"Okay... if I die... and the mirror resets... then I ain't crazy.

If I die and the writing stays... I'm just suicidal with decorations." He took a deep breath. Lifted the toaster. Closed his eyes.

"YOLO," he whispered.

Then paused.

"Naw, not YOLO. That don't apply here. That's backwards." He dropped the toaster in the tub.

ZZZZT—CRACK—FLASH.

Pain shot through his whole body. Everything went white. His heart felt like it was punching itself.

10:43 AM.

D-Lo shot awake in bed.

"KIMI! CHECK THE BATHROOM MIRROR!" "What!? Why!?" "JUST DO IT!" She came back two seconds later.

"No writing." D-Lo stared at the ceiling, wide-eyed.

"Oh my God... I'm a walking USB drive." He walked into the bathroom. Stared at the blank mirror.

"This... ain't normal." He grabbed the lipstick again. Wrote: *SAVE FILE #2 — TOASTER EDITION*

He grinned despite everything.

"Oh this lit."

D-Lo jogged down to Vick's Deli.

The air smelled like frying oil, dust, and dreams deferred.

Vick was behind the counter watching his stories on full volume. Dude had to be pushing seventy but still worked fourteen-hour days because that's what you did in the Marrow.

"D-Lo," Vick said without looking up. "No credit." "Good," D-Lo said, slapping cash on the counter. "I'm payin' today." He grabbed a scratch-off. Scratched.

LOSE.

D-Lo sighed. Picked up another one. Scratched.

LOSE.

"Okay. Cool. Cool cool cool." He tapped the counter.

"Resetting in 3... 2... 1..." He walked outside, stepped into the alley behind the deli, and punched himself in the throat as hard as he could.

He dropped like a sack of laundry.

Darkness.

10:43 AM.

"Kimi," D-Lo croaked. "Don't ask." He ran back to the deli. Same scratch-off. Same corner. Same ticket.

He scratched.

WIN — \\$50.

D-Lo's eyes widened.

"Oh. My. God." He was a cheat code.

He pushed his luck. Bought the next one.

LOSE.

He considered the door, the traffic, the staircase outside. He needed another death. Preferably convenient.

He sighed. "This gon' be a long day." He stepped outside— A delivery driver on an e-bike smacked him at full speed.

D-Lo went flying.

"Noooooooo—!" Blackness.

D-Lo woke up laughing.

Actually laughing.

"Kimi... I'm a superhero." "You're an idiot." "Both can be true!" He sat on the edge of the bed.

And that's when the fear hit him.

The deaths. The pain. The resets. The fact that the more he learned...

22

the more dangerous this power became.

If he could redo anything… if he could retry any mistake… if he could alter reality…

What else could he change?

What else would break?

What else would die?

He had unlimited chances. But everyone else only got one.

He wiped sweat from his forehead.

"Okay," he whispered. "New rule." He grabbed a sticky note from Kimi's homework pile and scribbled: *RULE #1: DON'T DIE RECKLESSLY.*

RULE #2: DON'T LET ANYBODY FIND OUT.

RULE #3: DON'T TRY TO FIX EVERYTHING.

He stared at the list.

Added one more: *RULE #4: Don't let Melo hold no damn gun.*

He almost smiled.

Then the building shook.

A boom thundered down the hallway.

People screamed, "SOMETHING'S ON FIRE!" Another voice shouted, "SOMEBODY MELTED THE WALL!" And somewhere downstairs, a kid cried, "MOMMA, THE CAT GLOWIN'!" D-Lo swallowed hard.

He walked to the window.

And saw it: A woman in the courtyard. Waving her hands. And the air around her shimmered like bending heat.

She wasn't human anymore.

At least, not just human.

The hood was waking up.

And D-Lo realized something that made his stomach drop: He wasn't the only one.

CHAPTER 2

THE TRUST

The woman in the courtyard was screaming, but it wasn't fear.

It was rage.

Raw, boiling, uncut rage—the kind that had been simmering for decades and finally found an outlet.

D-Lo pressed his hands against the window glass, watching Mrs. Waverly transform from the sweet old lady who gave out stale cookies on Halloween into something that looked like a special effect from a movie they couldn't afford to film in this neighborhood.

Her hands crackled with shimmering air, heat waves bending the light around her like blacktop in July. The plastic trash bin near her feet didn't melt—it slumped, collapsing into a puddle of bubbling goo. A parked Camry's windows cracked from the temperature spike alone.

People poured out of their apartments like roaches when the lights come on.

"OH HELL NO—" "THE DEVIL IN THAT WOMAN!" "CALL SOMEBODY! CALL JESUS!" "She glowin', bro. SHE GLOWIN'." "Man, I'm goin' back inside. This ain't my business." D-Lo recognized her now. Mrs. Waverly from Building A. Had to be pushing sixty-five. Used to babysit him and Kimi when their mama was still alive and working double shifts. Sweet woman. Quiet woman. The kind of woman who went to church every Sunday and never raised her voice above a polite request.

Now she was shaking like she was having a seizure, except she wasn't falling.

She was powering up.

Her arms glowed red-hot, veins visible beneath the skin like lava tubes.

Her breath came out as steam, fogging the air around her face. Her gray hair stood up like static electricity was making love to her scalp.

"Oh shit... oh shit," D-Lo whispered.

Kimi appeared beside him, cereal bowl forgotten.

"Is that Mrs. Waverly?" "Yeah." "Why she look like that?" "I don't know." "Is she gonna explode?" D-Lo didn't answer. Because honestly? It looked like she might.

"Stay here," he said.

"D-Lo, don't—" But he was already moving.

By the time D-Lo reached the ground floor, chaos had erupted full blast.

Two young dudes—couldn't have been older than seventeen—approached Mrs. Waverly with their hands up, trying to calm her down like she was a stray dog instead of a human volcano.

"Ayo, Mrs. W, it's cool, just breathe—" She screamed.

A blast of heat rippled outward like a shockwave. Both boys flew backwards, hitting the concrete hard. One of them didn't get up. The other crawled away, the front of his shirt smoking, skin already blistering red.

A pickup truck parked nearby had its windows explode outward, glass spraying across the courtyard like shrapnel.

Mrs. Waverly fell to her knees, clutching her head.

"MAKE IT STOP! MAKE IT STOP! OH GOD, IT HURTS!" D-Lo ducked behind a concrete pillar, heart slamming against his ribs.

"Okay. First instinct: run. Second instinct: run faster. Third instinct: call somebody smarter." He peeked around the pillar.

Mrs. Waverly was crying now, tears evaporating off her cheeks before they could fall. The ground beneath her was starting to crack, heat radiating downward.

"But I guess I'm the designated superhero around here, so... damn." He took a deep breath. Stepped out.

"Mrs. Waverly! Yo! It's me, D-Lo! Denise's boy!" She whipped toward him. Her eyes glowed orange—not metaphorically, literally glowed, like someone had replaced her pupils with embers.

D-Lo raised his hands.

25

"Please don't flambé me." "I CAN'T CONTROL IT!" she screamed. "I'M BURNING FROM THE INSIDE! I CAN FEEL IT EATING ME!" The air around her shimmered hotter. D-Lo felt his skin prickle from ten feet away.

He realized something important: she wasn't trying to hurt anyone. She was terrified. She needed grounding. Not fighting.

He approached slowly, hands still up.

"It's okay. Just breathe. I know it hurts. I know you scared. But you gotta focus on my voice, okay? Just my voice." She reached toward him—fingers blazing, skin cracked like dried earth.

A wave of heat rushed out— D-Lo dove behind a dumpster just in time. The metal side he'd been standing next to glowed red for a second before cooling.

"DAMN LADY, YOU TRYIN' TO MAKE ME A CAUTIONARY TALE!?"

Sirens screeched into the courtyard—four NBPD squad cars skidding to stops at angles, like they'd practiced this formation.

But the officers who jumped out weren't regular cops.

D-Lo squinted.

Kevlar vests—heavy ones, military-grade. Helmet shields with dark visors. And rifles that looked like props from a sci-fi movie—sleek, angular, glowing blue along the barrel.

"What the hell...?" D-Lo whispered.

Special Threat Unit.

He'd heard rumors about them. Supposedly formed after Project Renaissance "to handle anomalous situations." Everyone in the hood thought it was bullshit—just another excuse for cops to get new toys and crack more skulls.

But looking at them now, D-Lo realized the rumors were underselling it.

One officer—big white dude with a neck like a tree trunk—raised a megaphone.

"ALL CIVILIANS BACK AWAY! THE SUBJECT IS WIRED! THIS AREA IS NOW UNDER ANOMALY CONTAINMENT!" Wired.

D-Lo filed that word away.

They aimed at Mrs. Waverly.

"No!" D-Lo shouted, stepping out from behind the dumpster. "Don't shoot her! She ain't trying to hurt nobody!" "CIVILIAN, STAND DOWN!" "She's scared! You'll make it worse!" They shot anyway.

Not bullets. A glowing blue net erupted from one of the rifles, expanding mid-air, trailing electric sparks. It wrapped around Mrs. Waverly like a spiderweb made of lightning.

She shrieked.

The sound wasn't human anymore—it was pure pain, raw and awful. Her skin hissed where the net touched it, smoke rising, the smell of burning flesh hitting D-Lo's nostrils and making him gag.

"STOP!" D-Lo ran forward. "SHE AIN'T TRYING TO—" A baton slammed into his stomach.

Air left his lungs. He dropped to his knees, gasping.

An officer pressed a knee into his back, grinding his face against the concrete.

"Stay down! This area is under anomaly containment!" D-Lo wheezed, "Man, get off me! I ain't anomalizin' nothing!" "You interfered with a containment operation. That makes you a potential sympathizer or accomplice." "A WHAT!? I'm trying to help an old lady!" The officer reached for his belt. Taser.

D-Lo felt the prongs hit his back.

Pain shot through his spine—not like the bullet deaths, but bad enough. Every muscle locked up. His teeth clamped together so hard he thought they'd crack.

And then— The entire courtyard shifted.

A ripple of heat erupted from Mrs. Waverly like a bomb detonating.

The STU squad flew backwards—all four of them, launched off their feet like toys. The net melted. Windows in a thirty-foot radius blew out simultaneously. A fire hydrant burst, water shooting skyward before instantly turning to steam.

The officer on D-Lo's back was thrown ten feet, landing in a heap against a car.

D-Lo lay there, gasping, watching Mrs. Waverly rise.

She was trembling, glowing, her skin cracking with heat like cooling lava.

"I'M SORRY!" she cried. "I CAN'T—STOP—IT!!!" She looked like a human volcano seconds from a full eruption.

D-Lo knew how this was going to end.

She was going to kill everyone within a hundred feet.

Unless he intervened.

He crouched behind an overturned trash barrel—the green industrial kind that weighed like two hundred pounds when full but had been tossed like a basketball by the shockwave.

"This is stupid," he whispered to himself. "This is suicidal. This is beyond dumb. I am literally the dumbest person in New Babylon." He clenched his fists.

"But I guess that's what heroes are. Professional dumbasses." He stood.

The cops were still down, groaning. Civilians had scattered—smart ones, anyway.

Mrs. Waverly stood in the center of a heat crater, pavement cracked and smoking beneath her feet.

D-Lo walked toward her.

Heart pounding. Sweat evaporating off his skin before it could drip.

Knees shaking.

"Mrs. Waverly..." She looked at him. Tears evaporated on her glowing cheeks.

"RUN, BABY! I DON'T WANT TO HURT YOU!" "I know you don't." He kept walking.

Every step brought more heat. His shirt was starting to smoke. The rubber soles of his slides were getting soft.

"I'm sorry," he said.

"For what?" she choked out.

"For this." He reached out and touched her arm.

10:43 AM.

D-Lo woke up gasping, clutching his arms even though they weren't burned anymore.

He'd felt it—the split second of contact. The skin on his hand vaporizing. His blood boiling. His eyes... he didn't want to think about his eyes.

28

"Kimi!" he gasped. "Don't come out! Mrs. Waverly 'bout to go nuclear in the courtyard! Stay inside!" "What!?" He was already running.

Same chaos. Same meltdown. Same cops approaching.

This time D-Lo sprinted to the officers first.

"You need to back off!" he shouted. "She's scared! If you shoot her, you'll make it worse!" "Civilian, move aside!" "Listen to me! She's not in control! That net thing is gonna—" "I said MOVE!" The officer shoved him. D-Lo grabbed his arm—dumbass move, he knew it immediately—and in the struggle, the officer's rifle discharged early.

The blue net fired wild, sailing over Mrs. Waverly's head and wrapping around a streetlight instead.

The other officers panicked. Spread out instead of converging.

Mrs. Waverly's heat blast hit only two of them this time, not the whole team.

D-Lo sprinted toward her before she could overload.

"Mrs. Waverly! LISTEN TO ME!" He grabbed her. Held her. Let the heat sear his palms, his forearms, his chest.

"YOU CAN CONTROL IT!" "I CAN'T!" "YES YOU CAN! Focus on my voice! Remember Kimi? Remember babysitting her? Remember when she spilled grape juice on your good carpet and you didn't even yell?" Mrs. Waverly sobbed. "It hurts..." "I know." He held tighter. His skin was blistering. He could smell himself cooking.

"I know." For one beautiful second, her glow dimmed. Her temperature dropped. Her breathing steadied.

Relief washed over him— Then an officer fired another net.

It wrapped around both of them.

Electricity surged through D-Lo's body on top of the heat.

Mrs. Waverly screamed.

Her panic spiked. The heat spiked with it.

And everything went white.

10:43 AM.

D-Lo sat up, panting.

"Third time's the charm... or whatever number I'm on..." He stood. Ran outside.

But this time—this time—he had a plan.

29

He wouldn't confront her directly. He wouldn't involve the cops.

He'd noticed something in the previous attempts: Mrs. Waverly's meltdown started when a group of teenagers on the corner made fun of her house shoes. Called her a "dusty old bitch." She was humiliated. Angry. Scared.

And then she changed.

Trauma triggered powers. Maybe calm could reverse it.

D-Lo sprinted to Vick's Deli. Busted through the door.

"Vick! I need ice! All of it!" "Boy, what—" D-Lo vaulted the counter, yanked open the freezer, and grabbed two bags of ice.

"I'll pay you back!" "YOU BETTER!" He sprinted to the courtyard.

Mrs. Waverly was just starting to glow, the teenagers already laughing and walking away, not realizing what they'd triggered.

But instead of yelling, D-Lo walked slowly. Calm. Controlled.

He approached her with the ice bags held out like a peace offering.

"Mrs. Waverly... you look like you need somethin' cool." She stared at him, trembling, steam rising from her shoulders.

But her glow softened.

D-Lo stepped closer. Took her hand. Pressed the ice against her arm. She gasped.

The heat dimmed. Her breathing slowed.

Her knees buckled and D-Lo caught her, lowering her gently to the ground. The ice bags were already melted, but they'd done their job.

"I don't know what's happening to me," she whispered, crying.

"I do," he said softly. "And we gonna figure it out. I promise." The heat faded completely.

The cops rushed in once her body temp dropped.

Medics took over—not the STU this time, regular EMTs.

They handled her gently. She was scared but conscious.

D-Lo stepped back, exhausted, trembling. His hands were shaking. Not from the cold.

One STU officer—younger, Black, with eyes that held something like recognition—approached him.

"You handled that pretty well. Like you knew what to do." D-Lo forced a casual shrug. "Just good under pressure." "Mm-hmm." The officer squinted. "You wired too?" "Nah. I'm just a regular dude trying to help his neighbor." "Regular dudes don't run toward women who can melt concrete." D-Lo met his eyes.

"Maybe your definition of regular is too narrow." The officer held his gaze for a long moment. Something passed between them—not hostility, but not friendship either. Understanding, maybe.

Or warning.

"Keep your head down," the officer said quietly. "You don't want to be on the Trust's radar." "The what?" But the officer was already walking away.

They loaded Mrs. Waverly into the ambulance. She reached out as they closed the doors, locking eyes with D-Lo.

"Thank you, baby," she whispered.

He nodded.

The doors shut. The ambulance pulled away.

D-Lo let out a long, shaky breath.

And that's when he heard the voice behind him.

"You handled that smooth, lil man." D-Lo turned.

And forgot how to breathe for a second.

She was leaning against the stair rail like she owned it—tall, maybe five-nine, brown skin that caught the light like polished wood. A leather jacket hung open over a tank top that didn't leave much to the imagination, and didn't apologize for it either.

Curves that made his eyes want to wander. He kept them on her face through sheer willpower.

Dice tattoo on her wrist. Earrings shaped like tiny playing cards—the ace of spades on one side, ace of hearts on the other. Cigarette dangling from full lips, unlit. Eyes sharp as knives and twice as dangerous.

She looked like trouble had a dress code and she was the designer.

"Not bad at all," she said, a smirk playing at the corner of her mouth.

"You might be stupid, but you ain't helpless." D-Lo blinked. "Who are you?" Instead of answering, she flicked a coin into the air.

D-Lo watched it spin—catching sunlight, tumbling end over end— And land on its edge.

Where it stayed.

Perfectly balanced. Perfectly still. Defying gravity. Defying physics.

Defying common damn sense.

She winked.

"Somebody who knows what it's like to be… wired." D-Lo stared at the coin. Then at her. Then at the coin again.

"How—what—that ain't—" "Possible?" She chuckled, low and warm. "Baby, after what you just did for that old lady, you still think there's such a thing as 'possible' and 'impossible'?" She pushed off the rail and walked toward him. Her stride was unhurried.

Confident. The kind of walk that said she'd never run from anything in her life—and if she ran toward you, that was worse.

"Chanel Merriweather," she said, stopping close enough that he could smell her—cigarettes, vanilla perfume, and something underneath that might've been gunpowder. "People call me Clutch." D-Lo blinked. "Clutch… like the basketball move?" "Nah." She smiled—slow, knowing. "Like 'I make things happen when they ain't supposed to.'" She reached out and plucked the coin off the ground—hadn't fallen, hadn't wobbled, just waited for her.

Then she flicked it again.

It bounced off the concrete once. Twice. Hopped up and caught an impossible gust of air that wasn't there— And landed in D-Lo's palm.

Tails.

He hadn't even raised his hand. It just… went there.

"Now flip it," she said.

D-Lo did.

The coin spun in the air. Slowed down. Wobbled. Shifted—literally shifted mid-air like something grabbed it— And landed tails again.

D-Lo frowned. "Aight, nah, see that ain't right." "Exactly." Clutch approached, close enough that their chests almost touched. "That's my thing."

She led him to a quieter spot—behind Building C, near the dumpsters that nobody used because they'd been full since '09. She leaned against the brick wall and finally lit her cigarette, the flame dancing in her fingers for a moment longer than it should've.

"You saw what happened with the old lady," D-Lo said. "You saw… all of it?" "Enough." She exhaled smoke sideways, away from him. "I saw you run toward something that would've killed anybody with sense. I saw you do it twice—or was it three times? Hard to tell with your particular...

gift." D-Lo's blood froze.

"What you mean?" Clutch smiled, dragging on her cigarette.

"You reset. Don't you?" "How do you—" "Because I've been watching you since this morning. Not personally.

Just... keeping tabs. When you popped up at Vick's the third time buying the same scratch-off, I knew something was off." D-Lo's heart hammered. His first instinct was to deny. His second was to run.

He did neither.

"If you were watching me," he said slowly, "why didn't you help?" "Because I wanted to see what you'd do." She shrugged, no apology in it.

"Needed to know if you were a threat or an asset." "And?" She looked at him. Really looked—not through him, but into him. Seeing whatever it was that made her decide.

"You're neither," she said finally. "You're something worse.

You're a good person." D-Lo didn't know how to respond to that.

"Lady—Clutch—whatever—I don't know what you want, but I just had a very weird day, and I been dead like eight times, and I really need to go check on my sister." "Your sister's fine. She's watching videos on her phone and eating her third bowl of cereal." D-Lo blinked. "How do you—" "Luck. I'm lucky." She flicked ash. "Lucky enough to know things fall where I need them. Including information." "That don't make sense." "Welcome to the new world, baby." She pushed off the wall, stepping into his space again. "Nothing makes sense anymore. Project Renaissance saw to that." D-Lo swallowed.

"What do you know about that?" "More than you. Less than the people hunting us." "Hunting us?" Clutch nodded toward where the STU vans were still parked, officers milling around, taking statements they'd never follow up on.

"The Trust. That's who those boys in black work for. Private-public partnership—government money, corporate oversight, zero accountability. They're the ones who caused all this. And now they're 'containing' the mess they made." "Containing how?" Clutch's expression darkened.

"You don't want to know." D-Lo thought about Mrs. Waverly. The way that net made her scream. The fear in her eyes.

"Yeah," he said quietly. "I do." Clutch studied him for a long moment.

Then she dropped her cigarette and crushed it under her boot.

"Walk with me, Reload." D-Lo frowned. "Reload?" She smiled.

"Best name I got for someone who keeps dying and walking it off."

They moved through the Marrow's back alleys—the parts tourists never saw, the parts even Google Maps pretended didn't exist.

Clutch walked like she knew every shortcut, every shadow, every spot where cameras didn't reach. Which she probably did.

"How long you been... wired?" D-Lo asked.

"Since the night Project Renaissance blew." She didn't look at him.

"I was at a card game in the basement of Reggie's spot over on Miller.

When the flash hit, I was mid-shuffle. Cards went everywhere. And when I picked them up..." She trailed off.

"What?" "They were in perfect order. Aces to kings. All four suits. Without me doing a damn thing." She laughed, but there was no humor in it. "I thought I was losing my mind. Took me three days to realize I could do it on purpose. Bend things. Make the unlikely happen. Make the impossible... probable." "That's... actually kind of dope." She stopped walking and turned to face him.

"It's a curse, D-Lo. Every single one of us—every wired person in this city—we're walking targets. The Trust wants to contain us. The government wants to study us. The gangs want to use us. And the regular people?" She gestured back toward the courtyard, where neighbors were still staring, still whispering.

"They're scared of us. Can't blame them. But fear makes people do ugly things." D-Lo thought about the officers. The way they shot first, asked questions never.

"So what do we do?" Clutch studied him.

"We survive. We stay smart. We find others like us." "Others?" "There's more of us than the Trust knows. More than anyone knows." She started walking again. "I've been building a network. People I can trust. People who can protect each other." "And you want me to join?" "I want to know if you're worth joining." She glanced back. "The reset thing is powerful. Maybe the most powerful gift I've seen. But it don't mean shit if you can't handle pressure." "I just saved an old lady from becoming a nuke." "After dying twice trying." D-Lo opened his mouth to argue. Closed it.

Fair point.

"Look," Clutch said, stopping at a corner where three alleys met. "I ain't trying to pressure you. You got a life. A sister.

Responsibilities. I'm not gonna tell you none of that matters." She reached into her jacket and pulled out a burner phone. Cheap, prepaid, the kind you bought at gas stations.

"But when you're ready—when you want answers, when you need help, when shit gets too heavy—call me." She tossed him the phone.

D-Lo caught it.

"How do I reach you? There's no contacts." Clutch smiled—and for the first time, it reached her eyes.

"Flip a coin. If it lands the way you want, dial any number. I'll answer." D-Lo stared at her. "That's insane." "That's luck, baby." She turned and started walking away, leather jacket catching the light.

D-Lo watched her go.

Then called after her: "Clutch!" She paused. Didn't turn around.

"The old lady—Mrs. Waverly. You said the Trust is 'containing' people.

What are they gonna do to her?" Clutch's shoulders tensed.

"Pray you never find out." Then she was gone.

D-Lo walked home in a daze.

The phone felt heavy in his pocket. Not physically—it weighed barely anything. But the implications of it. The door it represented.

When he got back to the apartment, Kimi was exactly where Clutch said she'd be: on the couch, phone in hand, bowl of cereal (her fourth, if the milk ring stains were any indication) on the coffee table.

She looked up.

"You okay?" "Yeah." "You look like you seen some shit." "I seen a lot of shit." "More than usual?" D-Lo sat down next to her. Heavily. Like his bones weighed extra.

"Yeah, Kimi. More than usual." She was quiet for a moment. Then she leaned her head against his shoulder.

"Mrs. Waverly was on fire, wasn't she?" "Something like that." "Is she dead?" "No. They took her to… somewhere." He didn't say hospital because he wasn't sure that's where she went. "She's alive." "Good. She always gave me extra cookies." Kimi paused. "Are you gonna be on fire too?" D-Lo looked down at her.

Thirteen years old. Already seen more death and violence than most people saw in a lifetime. And still here, still asking questions, still trusting him to have answers.

"I don't know," he said honestly. "But whatever happens, I'm gonna keep you safe. That's the only thing I know for sure." Kimi nodded.

Then went back to her phone.

Like it was settled. Like his word was enough.

D-Lo stared at the ceiling.

Wired. Reload. The Trust. Mrs. Waverly. Clutch.

A world he didn't understand, changing into something he understood even less.

And somewhere out there, other people like him—scared, confused, powerful—waking up to the same nightmare.

The hood was always dangerous.

But now?

Now it was something else entirely.

He must have dozed off, because the next thing he knew, Kimi was shaking him awake.

"D-Lo. D-Lo!" "What? What's wrong?" She pointed at the window.

He stood up and looked outside.

And felt his stomach drop.

In the courtyard below, a man was walking.

Not running. Not hurrying. Walking.

He wore blue coveralls. Work boots. A utility belt with keys dangling from it.

And he was dragging a mop behind him.

The mop left no trail. Because it wasn't wet.

The man stopped in the center of the courtyard. Looked up. Directly at D-Lo's window.

And smiled.

Even from four stories up, D-Lo could see his eyes.

Empty. Hollow. Dark enough to swallow light.

A whisper echoed in D-Lo's head—not heard, but felt: "I can smell your fractures, boy. So many deaths. So much pain." D-Lo stumbled back from the window.

"What is it?" Kimi asked.

He grabbed her shoulders.

"Don't look outside. Don't answer the door. Don't make any noise." "D-Lo, you're scaring me—" "Good. Stay scared. Stay quiet." He grabbed the burner phone from his pocket. Flipped a coin from the jar on the kitchen counter.

It landed heads.

He dialed a random number—the first ten digits that came to mind.

It rang once.

Clutch answered.

"That was fast." "There's a man in my courtyard," D-Lo whispered. "Something's wrong with him. He looked at me and I heard his voice in my head." Silence on the other end.

Then: "What did he look like?" "Blue coveralls. Like a janitor. He was dragging a mop." More silence.

When Clutch spoke again, her voice was different.

Scared.

Clutch—who bent luck to her will—sounded scared.

"Don't go near him. Don't let him touch you. Don't let him see you again." "Why? Who is he?" "We call him the Janitor." Her breath shook. "He doesn't just kill people, Reload. He... cleans them. Takes everything—your memories, your trauma, your pain—and eats it. Feeds on it. Grows stronger." Ice flooded his veins.

"How do I stop him?" "You don't. Nobody does. You run. You hide. You pray he finds something tastier." D-Lo looked at Kimi. At the window. At the shadow of the man still standing in the courtyard below.

"And if he doesn't find something tastier?" Clutch's answer was barely a whisper: "Then you die. Over and over. And he remembers every single time."

CHAPTER 3

WHAT GRAVES DO

Kimi hadn't seen her brother in eleven days.

She'd stopped counting after the first week, but her brain kept tracking anyway. Eleven days since D-Lo had kissed her forehead, told her to stay inside, and disappeared into the night with that woman—Clutch, the one who looked at the world like it owed her money.

Eleven days of waking up alone.

Eleven days of making her own dinner, doing her own homework, pretending everything was fine when Mrs. Patterson from 4A asked how she was holding up.

Eleven days of listening to helicopters circle the Marrow like vultures waiting for something to die.

The Trust had the projects on lockdown.

Checkpoints at every entrance. Soldiers—she refused to call them police—on every corner. They'd set up a command post in the community center parking lot, black tents and armored vehicles and men with guns who looked at residents like they were criminals just for existing.

Kimi watched them from the window, the way D-Lo used to watch them.

Noting patterns. Counting personnel. Tracking which vehicles came and went and when.

She didn't know why she was doing it. Habit, maybe. Or the sense that information was power, even if you didn't know how to use it yet.

The soldiers changed shifts at 6 AM and 6 PM. The checkpoints got looser around meal times—guys got hungry, got sloppy. The surveillance drones flew a predictable pattern: north to south along the main road, east to west along the back fence, fifteen-minute intervals.

She wrote it all down in a notebook she kept under her mattress.

Just in case.

School was closed "until further notice." The official reason was "safety concerns." The real reason was that three teachers had been taken in the raids and nobody wanted to talk about where they'd gone.

Mr. Henderson, who taught seventh-grade science and always smelled like coffee and chalk dust. Ms. Okafor, the art teacher who let kids stay after school when they didn't want to go home. Coach Davis, who ran the after-school basketball program and never asked why some kids showed up with bruises.

All wired, apparently.

All gone.

Kimi wondered if D-Lo knew about them. If he'd tried to save them too.

If that's what he was doing out there—saving people who couldn't save themselves.

She hoped so.

She hoped he wasn't just gone.

Day twelve, she ran out of food.

Not completely—there was still rice, some canned vegetables, half a jar of peanut butter that was more oil than nut at this point. But the real food, the stuff that made meals instead of just calories, was gone.

D-Lo had left money. Three hundred dollars in an envelope taped to the inside of the toilet tank, which was apparently where people in the hood hid things they didn't want found. But money didn't help when the corner store was closed and the checkpoint guards searched everyone who tried to leave the block.

She could go to Mrs. Patterson. The old woman had been bringing soup every few days, checking in, making sure Kimi hadn't burned the building down or gotten herself arrested. But Mrs. Patterson was already feeding half the floor. Her own pantry had to be running thin.

Kimi stared at the empty refrigerator.

Made a decision.

The checkpoint on Miller Street was manned by two guards. One was older, white, with a beard that needed trimming and eyes that had stopped seeing individual faces a long time ago. The other was younger, Latino, with a name tag that said REYES and a nervous energy that suggested he hadn't been doing this job long.

Kimi approached with her hands visible, the way D-Lo had taught her.

"ID," the older guard said. Not a question.

"I'm thirteen. I don't have ID." "Building and unit." "C-4." The guard checked a tablet, scrolling through something Kimi couldn't see. She kept her face neutral. Bored, even. Like this was an inconvenience, not a threat.

"Purpose of travel?" "Food. We're out." "There's a distribution center at the community center—" "The line's six hours long and they ran out yesterday before noon." Kimi met his eyes. "My brother's at work. I'm trying not to starve before he gets home." The lie came easily. Too easily, maybe. But the guard didn't know D-Lo was gone. Didn't know she'd been alone for almost two weeks. Didn't know anything except what she chose to show him.

The younger guard—Reyes—shifted uncomfortably.

"Let her through, Mike. She's a kid." Mike grunted. Waved her past.

Kimi walked through the checkpoint without looking back.

First victory.

Small, but hers.

The grocery store on Fifth was picked clean, but the bodega on Seventh still had stock—overpriced, but available. Kimi bought bread, eggs, cheese, a bag of apples that were slightly bruised but still edible. She paid with one of D-Lo's twenties and didn't flinch at the change.

On the way back, she took the long route. Not because she was scared of the checkpoint—she'd passed it once, she could pass it again—but because she wanted to see.

The Marrow looked like a war zone.

Broken windows that hadn't been fixed. Doors hanging off hinges from raids that had happened days ago. Graffiti on the walls, fresh, angry: TRUST = TERROR. WIRED LIVES MATTER. WE SEE YOU.

And people.

Moving through the streets like ghosts, heads down, trying not to be noticed. Elderly folks who used to sit on stoops and watch the world go by, now hurrying to get inside before curfew. Kids younger than Kimi, clustered in doorways, looking lost.

She passed the basketball court where D-Lo used to play. The hoops were still there, but nobody was using them. A Trust drone hummed overhead, camera eye swiveling.

She kept walking.

The crying came from the alley between Buildings F and G.

Kimi almost missed it. Almost kept walking, because rule number one in the Marrow was don't get involved in other people's business. But the sound caught her—small, terrified, the kind of crying that came from someone trying very hard not to make noise.

She stopped.

Looked around.

No soldiers. No drones. The alley was shadowed, hidden from the main street by a dumpster that hadn't been emptied in weeks.

She should keep walking.

She stepped into the alley.

The kid couldn't have been older than eight.

He was huddled behind a stack of broken pallets, knees pulled to his chest, tears cutting tracks through the dirt on his face. His clothes were too big—hand-me-downs, Kimi recognized the look—and his sneakers had holes in both toes.

"Hey," she said softly. "You okay?" Stupid question. Obviously he wasn't okay. But it was the question you asked.

The kid looked up. His eyes were red, puffy, terrified.

And glowing.

Faintly, barely visible in the dim light of the alley, but definitely glowing. A soft blue-white, like someone had put LEDs behind his pupils.

Wired.

Kimi's breath caught.

"Please don't tell them," the kid whispered. "Please. They took my mom.

They took—" His voice broke. "Please." Kimi looked at the alley entrance. Still clear. But for how long?

She thought about D-Lo. About what he would do.

About what Graves did.

"What's your name?" she asked.

"M-Marcus." "Okay, Marcus. I'm Kimi." She crouched down to his level, keeping her voice calm. "When did it start? The eyes?" "This morning. I woke up and everything was bright and my mom screamed and then they came and—" "Okay. Okay." She held up a hand. "We're gonna figure this out. But you can't stay here. Can you walk?" He nodded.

"Can you keep your eyes down? Don't look at anybody?" Another nod.

Kimi took a breath.

"Okay. Follow me. Stay close. Don't say anything." She picked up her grocery bag and stepped back into the street, a terrified eight-year-old with glowing eyes two steps behind her.

The walk back to Building C was the longest fifteen minutes of her life.

Every soldier they passed, Kimi's heart hammered. Every drone that hummed overhead, she wanted to run. But she didn't. She walked like she had somewhere to be, like the kid behind her was a cousin or a neighbor or anyone other than what he actually was.

Marcus kept his head down. Kept his eyes on the ground. Didn't make a sound.

Good kid.

Brave kid.

At the checkpoint, Reyes was alone—Mike must have gone on break.

"Back already?" Reyes asked.

"Forgot my brother wanted orange juice." Kimi held up the bag. "He's picky." Reyes glanced at Marcus. "Who's this?" "My cousin. He's staying with us while his mom's at work." The lie came smooth. Easy.

Like she'd been doing this her whole life.

Reyes looked at them for a long moment. Something flickered in his eyes—suspicion, maybe. Or something else.

"Go on," he said. "Stay inside. Curfew's in two hours." They walked through.

Kimi didn't breathe until they were inside Building C's stairwell.

Mrs. Patterson took one look at Marcus and understood everything.

"Get him inside," she said, already moving toward her apartment.

"Don't let anyone see." Twenty minutes later, Marcus was on Mrs. Patterson's couch with a bowl of soup, his glowing eyes hidden behind a pair of sunglasses that were way too big for his face. He looked ridiculous. He looked safe.

"His mama was Linda Hayes from Building K," Mrs. Patterson said quietly, standing with Kimi in the kitchen. "They took her three days ago. The boy's been hiding ever since." "What do we do with him?" "We keep him safe until we can get him out." Mrs. Patterson's eyes were hard. "There's people. Underground. They help kids like him." "The Ghosts?" Mrs. Patterson looked at her sharply. "How do you know about that?" "My brother." Kimi swallowed. "He's with them. I think." A long silence.

"Then maybe," Mrs. Patterson said slowly, "he can help."

That night, Kimi sat by her window and watched the drones circle.

Somewhere out there, D-Lo was fighting a war she couldn't see.

Somewhere down below, Marcus was sleeping on Mrs. Patterson's couch, one step ahead of the soldiers who wanted to take him apart.

And here she was. Thirteen years old. No powers. No weapons. Nothing but a notebook full of patrol patterns and a stubborn refusal to let the world break her.

She thought about the checkpoint. About the lie she'd told without thinking. About the way Reyes had looked at her—like he knew, like he'd let her through anyway.

Maybe not everyone in a uniform was the enemy.

Maybe even enemies had choices.

She pulled out her notebook. Added a new entry: *Reyes. Latino. Young. Checkpoint Miller St. Might be useful. Might be trouble. Watch.*

She closed the book.

Tomorrow she'd figure out how to contact D-Lo. How to get Marcus to safety. How to survive another day in a neighborhood that had become a prison.

Tonight, she'd done something that mattered.

She'd done what Graves do.

Two days later, a Ghost operative appeared at Mrs. Patterson's door. A teenager with a scar across his jaw and eyes that had seen too much.

"We got your message," he said. "The kid?" Mrs. Patterson brought Marcus out.

The Ghost crouched down, smiled at the boy, and said: "You're gonna be okay. We've got a place for you. People who'll help you understand what's happening." Marcus looked at Kimi.

"Thank you," he said.

"Don't thank me." Kimi's throat was tight. "Just... be safe, okay?" He nodded.

The Ghost took his hand.

They disappeared into the night.

When the operative came back—alone—he had a message.

"You're D-Lo's sister?" "Yeah." "He says he's sorry he's been gone. Says he's coming home soon as he can. Says..." The Ghost paused. "Says you're the bravest person he knows." Kimi blinked. Her eyes burned.

"Tell him to stop being corny and come home already." The Ghost smiled.

"I'll pass it along." He was gone before she could say anything else.

Kimi stood in the doorway of Mrs. Patterson's apartment, listening to the helicopters circle, watching the drones fly their patterns, feeling something new in her chest.

Not fear.

Not loneliness.

Purpose.

She went back inside, pulled out her notebook, and started planning.

CHAPTER 4

THE MARROW BLEEDS

Mrs. Delores Patterson had lived in Building A of the Marrow Projects for forty-three years.

She'd seen everything.

The riots of '68. The crack epidemic. The gentrification that never quite reached them. The slow death of hope that settled into the concrete like mold.

But she'd never seen anything like this.

It started with helicopters.

Three of them, circling overhead like vultures, their rotors chopping the air into something that felt like a heartbeat. A warning. A countdown.

Mrs. Patterson stood at her window—same window she'd stood at for four decades—and watched them swarm.

"Lord have mercy," she whispered.

Her phone rang. Her granddaughter, Tanisha.

"Grandma, you seeing this?" "I'm seeing it, baby." "What's happening?" "Nothing good." Mrs. Patterson squinted at the street below. "You stay inside. Lock your door. Don't open it for nobody." "Grandma—" "NOBODY, Tanisha. Not even if they say they're police. You hear me?" A pause.

"I hear you." Mrs. Patterson hung up.

And watched the trucks roll in.

They came from every direction.

Black SUVs. Armored vans. Vehicles that looked more like tanks than anything that belonged on city streets.

Men poured out—dozens, then hundreds—wearing tactical gear that made them look like soldiers from a movie. Helmets with dark visors. Rifles with glowing blue lights. Boots that hit the pavement like hammers.

And they moved through the Marrow like they owned it.

Mrs. Patterson watched them surround Building Q first. Watched them kick in the door. Watched residents stumble out—hands up, faces terrified—while officers screamed commands in voices that weren't human anymore. Just noise. Just authority. Just violence waiting to happen.

"This ain't right," she muttered.

The phone rang again.

"Delores, you watching?" Her neighbor, Mr. Williams from 3C.

"I'm watching." "They took the Johnson boy. Marcus. Dragged him out in cuffs. His mama was screaming—" "I saw." "What we gonna do?" Mrs. Patterson didn't have an answer.

In sixty-seven years of life, through every crisis and catastrophe this neighborhood had faced, she'd always known what to do. Always had a plan. Always found a way.

But this?

This felt like the end of something.

By noon, the Marrow had become a war zone.

Checkpoints at every entrance. Armed guards on every corner. Residents being pulled from their homes, lined up against walls, searched like criminals.

Some of them were criminals—Mrs. Patterson wasn't naive about her neighbors. But most weren't. Most were just people trying to survive.

Trying to get to work. Trying to get their kids to school. Trying to live.

Now they were prisoners in their own homes.

Mrs. Patterson made soup.

It was what she did during crises. Made soup. Fed people. Reminded them they were human.

She was halfway through the pot when the knock came.

Not a polite knock.

A BANG BANG BANG that rattled her door in its frame.

"TRUST SPECIAL OPERATIONS. OPEN UP." Mrs. Patterson set down her spoon.

Walked to the door.

And opened it.

Two officers stood in her doorway. Their visors were up—young faces, one white, one Latino, both of them looking uncomfortable.

"Ma'am, we need to search your apartment." "For what?" "Anomaly signatures. Standard protocol." Mrs. Patterson crossed her arms.

"Anomaly signatures. That what you calling it now?" The white officer shifted. "Ma'am, I need you to step aside." "This is my home. I've lived here since before your mama was born. You think you can just—" "Ma'am." The Latino officer's voice was softer. Almost apologetic.

"Please. We don't want any trouble." Mrs. Patterson looked at him.

Saw something in his eyes.

Shame.

"You know this is wrong," she said quietly. "Don't you?" He didn't answer.

But he didn't deny it either.

She stepped aside.

They searched her apartment. Went through her drawers, her closets, her memories. Used some kind of scanner that beeped and flashed as it passed over her possessions.

It found nothing.

Because there was nothing to find.

Mrs. Patterson wasn't wired. She was just old. Just tired. Just trying to make soup for her neighbors.

"Clear," the white officer said into his radio. "Moving to next unit." They left without apology. Without acknowledgment. Without even closing the door.

Mrs. Patterson closed it herself.

Went back to her soup.

And wept.

That afternoon, the stories started spreading.

Mrs. Williams from 2B: "They took her son. Just grabbed him out of his bed. Said he was 'flagged for containment.' He's sixteen. Hasn't done nothing to nobody." Mr. Chen from 4A: "They shot a dog. Can you believe that? Family dog, been in the building for years. It barked at them and they just… shot it." Little Destiny from across the hall: "Mama says we can't go outside.

Says the bad men will take us. Are the bad men gonna take us, Mrs. Patterson?" Mrs. Patterson held the child.

Told her everything would be okay.

Lied.

Because what else could she do?

Evening came.

The raids slowed but didn't stop. Officers remained on the corners, watching, waiting.

Mrs. Patterson was bringing soup to the Johnsons—Marcus's mother hadn't stopped crying since they took her boy—when she saw him.

A young man.

Walking through the courtyard like he belonged there. Like the armored soldiers and the checkpoints and the helicopters didn't matter.

She recognized him. D-Lo Graves from Building C. Denise's boy. She'd watched him grow up. Watched him take care of his sister after Denise passed. Good kid. Quiet. The kind of kid who helped carry groceries without being asked.

He was walking toward Building F, where smoke was still rising from whatever had happened that morning. Something about a fire. Something about a man who could generate heat.

An officer stepped in front of him.

Words were exchanged.

The officer reached for his weapon.

And then— Mrs. Patterson didn't know how to describe it.

Reality… hiccupped.

One second D-Lo was standing there. The next, he was twenty feet away, and the officer was on the ground, and nothing made sense.

D-Lo kept walking.

Like nothing had happened.

Like he hadn't just done something impossible.

Mrs. Patterson watched him disappear into Building F.

And for once, all day, she felt something other than despair.

Hope.

Foolish, fragile, impossible hope.

Maybe there was someone who could fight back.

Maybe there was someone who could protect them.

Maybe the end wasn't here yet.

The raids continued into the night.

More people taken. More families torn apart. More screams echoing through hallways that used to hold birthday parties and cookouts and the sound of children playing.

Mrs. Patterson stayed at her window.

Bearing witness.

Because someone had to remember.

Someone had to tell the story of what happened here.

Someone had to make sure the Marrow wasn't forgotten.

Around midnight, the helicopters finally left.

The trucks pulled out.

The officers retreated to their perimeters.

And the Marrow was left to count its wounds.

Seventeen people taken, according to the whisper network.

Three dead—"accidents," the official report would say.

Countless lives disrupted, traumatized, broken.

All in the name of "containment." All in the name of "safety." All in the name of lies.

Mrs. Patterson turned off her lamp.

Lay down in her bed.

And prayed—for the taken, for the traumatized, for the boy who walked through checkpoints like they weren't there.

For the Marrow.

For her home.

For whatever came next.

Morning came.

The sun rose over a neighborhood that had been invaded, occupied, violated.

But it rose.

Mrs. Patterson got up.

Made coffee.

Made soup.

And started her rounds.

Checking on neighbors.

Holding hands.

Reminding people they weren't alone.

The Trust had come for them.

But the Marrow was still here.

Still breathing.

Still fighting.

And as long as one person remembered what mattered—family, community, love—it would survive.

Mrs. Patterson had lived through everything.

She would live through this too.

INTERLUDE — THE SURVEILLANCE
TRUST MONITORING STATION SEVEN

Agent Chen watched the screens with growing unease.

The target—GRAVES, DARIUS, Anchor Classification Pending—had died again. That made twelve times in the past seventy-two hours. Each death appeared on their sensors as a temporal spike, a reality fracture, a bright flash of impossible energy.

Each time, he came back.

Chen had been with the Trust for fifteen years. He'd seen wired subjects do incredible things—bend light, move objects with their minds, survive injuries that should have killed them.

But this was different.

This was wrong.

"Sir?" He turned to his supervisor. "Request permission to escalate to Director Halden." "What's your assessment?" "The subject is learning." Chen pulled up the data—spikes and valleys, each reset slightly different from the last. "Look at the pattern. The first few deaths were random—accidental triggers, panic responses. But these last three..." He pointed at the screen.

"He's dying on purpose. Resetting deliberately. Using his power like a save point in a video game." His supervisor went pale.

"That's not possible. Anchors can't control their—" "This one can. Or he's learning to." Chen turned back to the screens.

"And if he figures out what he's really capable of..." He didn't finish the sentence.

He didn't have to.

CHAPTER 5

THE HOLLOW MAN

CHICAGO, 1952

Isaiah Washington was grading papers when the world first spoke to him.

Third period essays on To Kill a Mockingbird—twenty-seven of them, stacked neatly on his desk at Harrison Elementary, waiting for his red pen. Outside the window, snow was falling on the South Side, soft and quiet, turning the neighborhood into something that almost looked peaceful.

He'd just written "Excellent insight, Marcus!" on a particularly thoughtful paragraph when time... stuttered.

That was the only word for it. A skip in the record. A glitch in the film reel. One moment he was reading about Scout Finch; the next, he was standing at the window with no memory of getting up, his hand pressed against the cold glass, and the snow was falling upward.

Isaiah blinked.

The snow resumed its normal descent.

He looked at his hand. At the window. At the clock on the wall, which showed a time fifteen minutes later than it should have been.

What in the Lord's name...

He sat back down. Picked up his red pen. Tried to focus on the essays.

But his hand was shaking.

And somewhere in the back of his mind, a door had opened that would never close again.

It happened again three days later.

Sunday dinner. Sarah had made her famous pot roast—the one that had convinced him to propose, the one their children would someday beg for on special occasions. The whole family was gathered: his mother, his brother Raymond, Sarah's sister Delilah and her husband.

Little Maya, just three years old, was in her high chair, mashing potatoes with her fist and giggling.

Isaiah was reaching for the gravy when— —he was standing in the backyard, snow soaking through his church shoes, staring at a sky that had turned the color of old copper. The air tasted like pennies. Like blood. Like something burning.

And he could see... lines.

Thin filaments of light stretching from everything to everything else.

From the house to the trees to the clouds to his own chest. Connecting.

Weaving. Forming a pattern so vast and intricate that his mind couldn't hold it.

He reached for one of the lines— —and was back at the dinner table, gravy boat in hand, Sarah asking if he was feeling alright because he'd gone pale as a ghost.

"Fine," he heard himself say. "Just fine. Bit of a headache." But under the table, his hands were trembling so badly he had to sit on them.

That night, after Sarah fell asleep, Isaiah went to the bathroom and stared at his reflection in the mirror.

His eyes looked different.

Deeper, somehow. Like they were seeing things that weren't in the room.

What's happening to me?

The mirror didn't answer.

But somewhere, in a dimension he couldn't name, something noticed.

By February, Isaiah could control it.

Sort of.

He'd learned to feel the stutters coming—a pressure behind his eyes, a buzzing in his teeth, a sense of the world going thin around him. When it happened, he'd excuse himself. Find a quiet place. Let the vision take him.

And what visions they were.

He saw the threads that connected all things—past, present, future woven together like fabric. He saw the branching paths of possibility: what might happen, what could happen, what would happen if this or that choice was made.

He saw, once, a version of Chicago where the bomb had fallen—buildings melted to glass, shadows of people burned into walls, Lake Michigan boiling into steam.

He saw another version where his daughter Maya grew up to become a doctor, then a senator, then something more.

He saw a third version where Sarah died in childbirth with their second child, and Isaiah walked into Lake Michigan with stones in his pockets.

The threads showed him everything.

And slowly, he learned he could touch them.

The first time he changed something, it was an accident.

A car was speeding through the intersection on 47th Street.

Mrs. Patterson—not that Mrs. Patterson, different city, different decade, but Isaiah would never forget the name—was stepping off the curb, not seeing it coming.

Isaiah saw it happening before it happened.

Saw the threads: the one where she died, the one where she didn't, the moment of divergence.

He grabbed without thinking.

Pulled.

And Mrs. Patterson stumbled backward, startled by nothing, as the car roared past close enough to ruffle her coat.

She looked around, confused.

Isaiah, standing twenty feet away, felt blood trickling from his nose.

But she was alive.

I did that, he thought, trembling. *I changed what was going to happen.* For the first time since the visions started, he felt something other than fear.

He felt hope.

Maybe this is a gift. Maybe I can help people. Maybe— He didn't know, then, that someone was watching.

He didn't know that the Trust had been monitoring Chicago for months, tracking reports of "temporal anomalies." He didn't know that he'd just become the most valuable—and most dangerous—target on their list.

He didn't know that hope was a luxury he couldn't afford.

Not anymore.

MARCH 1953

They came for him at the school.

Isaiah was staying late—parent-teacher conferences had run long, and he still had a stack of permission slips to organize for the spring field trip. The building was quiet. Empty. Just him and the cleaning staff somewhere down the hall.

He heard footsteps.

Measured. Multiple. Wrong.

Isaiah looked up.

Three men stood in the doorway of his classroom. Dark suits. Dark ties.

Faces like stone.

"Mr. Washington," the lead one said. Not a question.

Isaiah's hand moved toward the phone on his desk.

"I wouldn't," the man said. "We just want to talk." "Who are you?" "We're with a government organization. One you've never heard of." The man stepped into the room, his two colleagues flanking him. "We've been watching you for some time, Mr. Washington. We know what you can do." Isaiah's blood went cold.

"I don't know what you're—" "The Patterson woman. The Johnson boy who didn't fall off the roof last week. The fire on State Street that should have killed twelve people but somehow didn't." The man pulled out a file, thick with documents.

"You've been busy." Isaiah said nothing.

"We're not here to arrest you," the man continued. "We're here to make you an offer." "What kind of offer?" "The kind where you work with us. Use your... abilities... to help prevent disasters. Protect people." The man smiled. It didn't reach his eyes. "Think of it as public service on a grander scale." Isaiah thought about Sarah. About Maya. About the life he'd built.

"And if I refuse?" The man's smile didn't waver.

"Mr. Washington, you're what we call an Anchor. A fixed point in temporal reality. Do you have any idea how rare that is? How valuable?" He closed the distance. "We've documented four others throughout history. All of them eventually... destabilized. Destroyed themselves and everything around them." "I'm not going to—" "The Seattle Incident of 1889. The fire that burned forty blocks.

Official story: a pot of glue ignited." The man opened his file. "Real story: an Anchor lost control. Tried to change too many things at once.

Reality... cracked. Hundreds dead. An entire neighborhood erased." Isaiah's hands were shaking.

"We can help you," the man said. "Teach you to control your gift.

Channel it safely. Prevent you from becoming another Seattle." "And my family?" "Will be protected. Provided for. As long as you cooperate." Isaiah looked at the file. At the photographs inside—grainy, black-and-white, showing destruction he couldn't imagine.

He thought about Maya's smile. About Sarah's laugh. About the future he'd seen, the one where his daughter grew up to change the world.

He thought about the threads, and the terrible power they held.

"Okay," he said quietly. "I'll come with you." The man nodded.

"A wise choice, Mr. Washington." Isaiah didn't feel wise.

He felt like he'd just signed something he couldn't take back.

THREE MONTHS LATER

The facility had no name.

No windows. No natural light. Just endless corridors of concrete and steel, somewhere underground, somewhere that didn't exist on any map.

Isaiah's room was comfortable enough—a bed, a desk, a bookshelf stocked with everything he'd requested. They let him write letters to Sarah, though he suspected they were read before being sent. They let him call home once a week, though he knew the line was monitored.

But the tests.

The tests were something else.

"Again, Mr. Washington." Dr. Harmon stood behind the observation glass, clipboard in hand, watching as Isaiah tried—and failed—to reach the threads.

The collar around his neck buzzed faintly. It was supposed to "regulate his temporal emissions." It felt like a leash.

"I'm trying," Isaiah said through gritted teeth.

"Try harder. The readings show you're capable of far more than you're demonstrating." That's because I'm afraid of what happens if I demonstrate it.

Isaiah had seen what they wanted from him. Glimpses, through doors left ajar, through conversations not meant to be overheard. They weren't trying to help him control his power.

They were trying to weaponize it.

Temporal reconnaissance. Reality adjustment. "Pruning undesirable futures." They wanted him to look at the threads and tell them which ones to cut.

And if he refused— "Your family is doing well," Dr. Harmon said, as if reading his mind.

"Maya is thriving in preschool. Sarah has taken up gardening. Your brother Raymond got that promotion he wanted." The subtext was clear.

They're thriving because we're allowing them to thrive.

Isaiah closed his eyes.

Reached for the threads.

And hated himself for how easily they came.

SIX MONTHS LATER

He tried to escape once.

It didn't work.

He used the threads to find a path—a sequence of events that would lead to an unlocked door, an unguarded corridor, a car left running in the motor pool.

He made it as far as the perimeter fence before they caught him.

The collar shocked him unconscious.

When he woke, he was back in his room. But different.

Smaller.

Darker.

No books. No desk. No letters from home.

Just a bed, a toilet, and a speaker in the ceiling that played white noise twenty-four hours a day.

"We're disappointed, Mr. Washington," Dr. Harmon's voice said through the speaker. "We thought we had an understanding." "Where's my family?" Silence.

"WHERE'S MY FAMILY?" "They're safe. For now. How long they remain safe depends entirely on you." Isaiah screamed.

He screamed until his voice gave out, and then he screamed silently, inside, where no one could hear.

In the darkness, he reached for the threads.

But they felt different now.

Colder.

Hungrier.

Something was changing inside him, and he didn't know how to stop it.

1960

Isaiah Washington died on a Tuesday.

Not physically—they were careful about that. But everything that made him him—his hope, his faith, his love for Sarah and Maya and the life he'd built—they carved it out piece by piece, year by year, until all that remained was a hollow space where a person used to be.

They filled that space with null-energy.

With programming.

With purpose.

The Conductor, they called him. Because he could conduct temporal energy like electricity. Because he followed their commands like a train follows its tracks. Because the man he'd been was just a faint whistle in the distance now, barely audible over the noise of what he'd become.

Sometimes, late at night, when the machines were quiet and the collar was dormant, Isaiah could still feel the threads.

Could still see the futures he'd been denied.

Maya, grown and brilliant, never knowing what happened to her father.

Sarah, remarried eventually, happy eventually, dying at eighty-three with grandchildren around her bed.

A world that moved on without him.

He reached for those threads sometimes.

Not to change them.

Just to remember that they'd been real once.

That he'd been real once.

Before they hollowed him out.

Before they made him into a weapon.

Before they turned him into the thing he was now: a function, a process, a monster that hunted his own kind at his masters' command.

I'm sorry, he thought, to no one who could hear. *I'm so sorry. I should have been stronger. I should have—* But the thought faded, like all his thoughts faded now, into the static and the nothing and the endless, hungry dark.

The Conductor opened his eyes.

The Conductor awaited his orders.

The Conductor felt nothing at all.

SEVENTY YEARS LATER

Deep beneath New Babylon, the machines hummed.

Isaiah Washington—what remained of him—drifted in a suspension tank, consciousness fragmented across a dozen monitoring systems, body preserved in a state between life and death.

He hadn't been deployed in years. Decades, maybe. Time was hard to measure when you existed in pieces.

But something was changing.

Something had… shifted.

The Cleaner was dead.

Isaiah felt it like an ache in a phantom limb—Marcus, the second Anchor, the one who'd broken differently than Isaiah had, finally released from his centuries of hunger. Gone.

And a new Anchor had emerged.

A boy from the projects. A kid who died and came back. A young man who was learning to see the threads, to touch them, to choose.

In the void of the suspension tank, something stirred.

A fragment of memory.

Maya's face on her third birthday, chocolate frosting smeared across her cheeks.

Maybe this one will be different.

The machines detected increased neural activity. Alarms began to sound.

Maybe this one can do what I couldn't.

Technicians rushed to their stations. Sedatives flooded the tank.

Maybe this one can set me free.

Isaiah Washington—the Conductor, the Trust's greatest weapon, the third Anchor they'd hollowed and rebuilt—sank back into the darkness.

But something had changed.

A door had opened.

And this time, it wouldn't close.

CHAPTER 6

BEFORE THE FALL

THREE DAYS EARLIER

The alarm didn't wake D-Lo.

The alarm had been broken since 2019.

What woke him was Kimi banging on his door like she was trying to audition for a SWAT team.

"D-LO! You gonna be late for work AGAIN!" He groaned into his pillow. The pillow smelled like weed and regret, which was basically his signature scent at this point.

"I'm UP!" "You ain't up! I can hear you lying!" "How you hear someone lying!?" "BECAUSE I KNOW YOU!" Fair point.

D-Lo dragged himself vertical, blinking at the water-stained ceiling of his bedroom. Same ceiling he'd been staring at since he was eight years old. Same cracks in the plaster. Same brown spot in the corner that was either a leak or mold or both.

Home sweet home.

He grabbed his phone off the milk crate that served as a nightstand.

7:43 AM

Shit. He was supposed to be at the warehouse by eight.

He scrambled out of bed, grabbed yesterday's jeans off the floor, sniffed them—acceptable—and pulled them on while hopping toward the bathroom.

"There's no hot water!" Kimi called from the kitchen.

"SINCE WHEN!?" "Since always! You think the city fixed something for once?" D-Lo stuck his head under the cold faucet and tried not to scream. The shock hit his system like a slap, which was

61

probably the only way he was going to be functional today anyway.

Three hours of sleep.

Melo had kept him up until 4 AM playing 2K and talking shit about some scheme he had brewing. D-Lo had learned to tune out Melo's schemes.

They never worked. They always almost got somebody killed or locked up.

But Melo was family—not blood, but close enough. They'd grown up together. Survived together. When D-Lo's mama died, Melo's family had fed him and Kimi for three months until the social services paperwork went through.

So when Melo wanted to hang, D-Lo hung.

Even when it meant showing up to work looking like a zombie extra.

Kimi was at the table, eating cereal with the intensity of someone who took breakfast personally.

She was thirteen going on thirty—skinny, braids pulled back tight, wearing one of D-Lo's old hoodies that hung past her knees. Their mama's eyes stared out of her face, which still hit D-Lo wrong sometimes.

"You look like death," she observed.

"Thank you for your support." "I'm just saying. Mr. Patterson gonna fire you if you keep showing up looking crazy." "Mr. Patterson ain't gonna fire me because Mr. Patterson knows I'm the only one who actually shows up." D-Lo grabbed a piece of bread from the counter—no toaster, they'd pawned it last month—and shoved it in his mouth dry. "Besides, warehouse work ain't exactly a beauty contest." "Everything's a beauty contest." Kimi slurped her milk. "That's what Miss Johnson says in Life Skills." "Miss Johnson ain't never worked a warehouse in her life." "Miss Johnson got a husband and a house in the suburbs. You got a mattress on the floor and a job you might lose." D-Lo paused mid-chew.

"When'd you get so mean?" "I learned from the best." She grinned.

He couldn't help but grin back.

This was their rhythm. Had been since Mama passed four years ago. D-Lo was twenty-two now—had been eighteen when he became Kimi's legal guardian, which was a fancy way of saying "the only adult she had left." Dad had bounced when Kimi was two. D-Lo barely remembered him—just a voice, a shadow, the smell of cigarettes and cheap cologne. Sometimes he wondered if the man was still alive, still out there somewhere, maybe with a whole other family.

Then he stopped wondering.

Didn't matter.

They had each other. That was enough.

D-Lo stepped out of Building C into the morning chaos of the Marrow Projects.

The courtyard was already alive—kids running to the bus stop, old heads sitting on benches pretending they weren't keeping watch, a group of young dudes on the corner doing what young dudes on corners always did.

The smell hit him first: garbage from the dumpsters that hadn't been emptied in a week, weed smoke drifting from somewhere on the third floor, and underneath it all, the permanent funk of a place that had been neglected since before D-Lo was born.

Home.

He loved it and hated it in equal measure.

Mrs. Patterson from 4A waved at him from her window.

"You late, baby!" "I know, Mrs. P!" "Tell Mr. Patterson I said he better not fire you!" "Different Patterson, Mrs. P!" "All Pattersons the same! They all think they better than everybody!" D-Lo didn't have time to unpack that, so he just waved and kept moving.

The Marrow Projects were technically called the Martin Luther King Jr. Housing Development, but nobody called it that. The name "Marrow" had stuck because somebody back in the day said living here meant you were "down to the marrow"—the deepest, hardest, most essential part.

Also because the buildings were slowly killing everyone from the inside out, like bone cancer.

Dark humor was the only kind that survived here.

Twenty-six buildings, A through Z. D-Lo and Kimi were in C. Melo was in K. Kettle—the big dude who worked kitchens—was over in F. The corner boys controlled Q through T. The old heads held court in A, which had the best benches and the least gunfire.

Everyone knew the rules.

Stay in your lane. Don't snitch. Don't start nothing, won't be nothing. And always, always, always watch your back.

"YO, D!" D-Lo turned.

Melo was jogging across the courtyard—tall, skinny, jittery in the way that meant he was either excited or high. Probably both.

"Bro, you ain't answer my texts!" "Because I was trying to sleep. Which you made impossible." "Sleep is for the dead, my guy. And we about to be rich." D-Lo sighed.

"What now?" Melo grinned—that dangerous grin that always preceded something stupid.

"Remember I told you about that lick?" "You told me about like fifteen licks. None of them worked." "This one different. This one guaranteed." "The last one you said was guaranteed, we almost got shot by a dude who turned out to be an off-duty cop." "That was a fluke!" "That was Darrell Jackson. He's been a cop for twelve years. His patrol car was literally parked outside." Melo waved dismissively.

"Details. Listen—you know Mr. Kim's store on 4th?" "The Korean spot?" "Yeah. Word is he keeps like ten racks in a safe in the back. Cash only business, you feel me? No cameras in the office. Just walk in, pop the safe, walk out." D-Lo stopped walking.

"Melo." "What?" "Mr. Kim's son is six-four and used to box Golden Gloves." "So?" "So I seen him knock out three dudes at once when they tried to shoplift." "We ain't shoplifting. We robbing. Different energy." D-Lo stared at his friend.

"That don't make it better." "It makes it more honest! At least we ain't being sneaky about it." The logic was so broken D-Lo couldn't even find the pieces.

"I gotta go to work, Melo." "Work? Bro, why you still doing that warehouse shit? You too smart for that." "I'm too smart to rob a Korean grocery store and get my ass beat by a Golden Gloves boxer." "You ain't even hearing me out!" "Because I heard you. Answer's no." D-Lo started walking again.

"I'll catch you later. Stay out of trouble." "Trouble is opportunity, D! That's what they don't teach you in school!" D-Lo didn't respond.

He knew Melo.

Knew that "no" never meant no to him.

Knew that sooner or later, Melo's schemes were gonna catch up with both of them.

He just didn't know it would be sooner.

Patterson Logistics occupied a rusting building on the edge of District Nine, where the projects gave way to industrial wasteland.

D-Lo had been working there since he was nineteen—loading trucks, unloading trucks, moving boxes from one place to another for reasons nobody ever explained. Minimum wage plus occasional overtime. Enough to keep the lights on and Kimi fed, but not enough for anything else.

Every day felt the same.

Clock in at eight. Move boxes until noon. Thirty-minute lunch in the break room that smelled like cigarettes and despair. More boxes until five. Clock out. Go home. Repeat.

The other guys on the crew were variations of the same story: men who'd ended up here because nowhere else would have them. Ex-cons. High school dropouts. Addicts trying to stay clean. Guys running from something or waiting for something or just existing in the space between.

D-Lo fit right in.

"Graves! You're late!" Mr. Patterson—no relation to Mrs. Patterson from 4A, as far as D-Lo knew—was a squat white man with a permanent scowl and a clipboard that seemed surgically attached to his hand.

"Sorry, boss. Train was late." "The train's always late when you're late. Funny how that works." "I think it's a conspiracy, honestly. The MTA specifically targets me." Mr. Patterson's scowl deepened.

"Get to Bay 4. Truck's waiting." "Yes, sir." D-Lo grabbed his gloves from his locker and headed to Bay 4, where a semi-trailer sat with its doors open, packed floor to ceiling with boxes.

Home appliances, according to the manifest.

D-Lo didn't ask where they came from or where they were going. That wasn't his job. His job was to move them from the truck to the warehouse. That was it. That was the whole thing.

Simple. Mind-numbing. But honest.

He grabbed the first box—a microwave, according to the label—and started the process that would occupy the next eight hours of his life.

The break room was empty except for Marcus, an old head who'd been working at the warehouse since before D-Lo was born.

Marcus was eating a sandwich and reading a newspaper—an actual physical newspaper, which D-Lo found deeply old-school.

"Anything good?" D-Lo asked, sitting across from him.

"World's still going to hell. Government still lying. Rent still too damn high." Marcus shrugged. "So no." "Sounds about right." D-Lo pulled out his own lunch—a sandwich Kimi had made him, peanut butter and jelly, because groceries were tight and PB&J was cheap.

"You hear about that thing over in Eastwick?" Marcus asked.

"What thing?" "Some kind of accident at that facility. The one nobody talks about." D-Lo frowned. "What facility?" "Exactly." Marcus tapped the newspaper. "Says here there was a 'containment incident' at a 'research installation.' No details. No specifics. Just 'containment incident.'" "That could mean anything." "That's the point. When they don't want you to know something, they use words that don't mean nothing." Marcus folded the paper. "Mark my words—something's coming. Something big. You can feel it in the air." D-Lo didn't feel anything in the air except the smell of old coffee and Marcus's sandwich.

"You been saying something big is coming since I started here." "And I been right every time. Just 'cause it ain't happened yet don't mean it ain't coming." D-Lo couldn't argue with that logic.

Mostly because it didn't make any sense.

Shift ended at five.

D-Lo clocked out, collected his thirty-two dollars in cash (Mr. Patterson didn't believe in direct deposit for "part-timers," which was everyone), and started the walk home.

The sun was setting over New Babylon, painting the sky orange and pink in a way that almost made the city look beautiful. Almost made you forget about the trash on the sidewalks and the graffiti on the walls and the constant background noise of sirens and shouting.

Almost.

D-Lo's phone buzzed.

MELO: bro you in tonight or what
D-LO: in for what

MELO: the lick. mr kim's. i got a crew. we moving at midnight
D-Lo stared at the screen.
D-LO: i told you no
MELO: come on man i need you
D-LO: you don't need me. you need someone to talk you out of stupid shit and you ain't listening anyway MELO: this aint stupid. this is opportunity
D-LO: opportunity to get your ass beat or locked up. im out
MELO: fine. be like that. but when im counting bands, dont come asking for a loan D-Lo pocketed his phone.

He knew Melo well enough to know that nothing he said would make a difference. Melo was gonna do what Melo was gonna do. Always had been.

Always would be.

All D-Lo could do was not be there when it went wrong.

Kimi was doing homework at the kitchen table when D-Lo got back.

"How was work?" "Work." He dropped his bag by the door. "How was school?" "School." She didn't look up from her math worksheet. "We're having a test on Friday. Fractions." "You need help?" "I got it." D-Lo stood there for a moment, watching his little sister furrow her brow at numbers that might as well have been hieroglyphics. She was smart—smarter than him, definitely—but she worked for it. Didn't take anything for granted.

Their mama would've been proud.

"I'm making dinner," he said. "Spaghetti." "Again?" "You complaining?" "I'm observing. We've had spaghetti four times this week." "Spaghetti is versatile. It's a canvas. Tonight I'm adding... hot sauce." "That's not a variation. That's a crime." "It's culinary innovation." Kimi finally looked up, a smile tugging at her lips.

"You're weird." "I learned from the best." She threw her eraser at him.

He caught it and threw it back.

And for a moment—just a moment—everything felt normal.

Safe.

Simple.

He didn't know it would be the last normal night for a long time.

D-Lo was asleep when his phone rang.

He grabbed it without looking, muscle memory from years of emergency calls—Kimi sick, landlord threatening, Melo in trouble.

"Hello?" Heavy breathing on the other end.

Then Melo's voice, shaking: "D... bro... I fucked up..." D-Lo was instantly awake.

"What happened?" "The lick... it went wrong... Mr. Kim's son was there... and then these other dudes showed up... and there was shooting..." Ice shot through his veins.

"Are you hurt?" "I don't know... I don't... there's blood but I don't think it's mine..." Melo's voice cracked. "D, I think somebody's dead. I think..." "Where are you?" "Behind the store. In the alley. I can't move, man. I'm scared to move." "Stay there. Don't move. I'm coming." D-Lo was already pulling on clothes, heart hammering.

"D-Lo?" Kimi's voice from her room. "What's wrong?" "Nothing. Go back to sleep." "You're lying." "Kimi, please. Just stay here. Lock the door. Don't let anyone in." He was out the door before she could argue.

Running through the night.

Toward his best friend.

Toward trouble.

Toward a bullet that was waiting for him in the morning.

CHAPTER 7

THE LESSON

Bishop found D-Lo on the observation platform, staring at the tunnel map.

"Can't sleep?" D-Lo didn't turn around. "Lot on my mind." "There always is, for people like us." Bishop settled onto a crate nearby, his old joints creaking. "Mind if I join you in your insomnia?" "Free country. Sort of." Bishop chuckled. "Haven't been free since the green flash. Maybe never were." He pulled out a small flask, took a sip, offered it to D-Lo.

"Whiskey. The good stuff. Been saving it for a night that needed it." D-Lo took the flask. The whiskey burned going down, but it was a warm burn. Comforting.

"Can I ask you something?" D-Lo said.

"That's generally how conversations work." "How do you do it? Lead them. The Ghosts." D-Lo gestured at the map.

"All those people depending on you. How do you make decisions when any choice might get someone killed?" Bishop was quiet for a long moment.

"You want the honest answer or the inspiring one?" "Honest." "I make mistakes. All the time. Every day, I make choices that hurt people—sometimes the people I'm trying to protect." Bishop took another sip from the flask. "Forty years I've been doing this. Forty years of saving some and losing others. And you want to know the truth?" "Yeah." "It never gets easier. Every loss still hurts. Every death still weighs." He met D-Lo's eyes. "The day it stops hurting is the day you've lost something more important than the people you're trying to save."

D-Lo didn't know what to say to that.

"The difference," Bishop continued, "between a good leader and a bad one isn't whether you make mistakes. Everyone makes mistakes. The difference is what you do after." "What do you do?" "I learn. I remember. I carry the names of everyone I've lost and I use them—not to punish myself, but to remind myself why the mission matters." Bishop's voice softened. "And I forgive myself. Not because I deserve forgiveness, but because holding onto guilt doesn't bring anyone back. It just makes you less effective at saving the next one." D-Lo thought about all the times he'd reset. All the versions of himself that had died. All the people he'd watched die before he learned how to save them.

"I don't know if I can do that," he admitted.

"You can. You will." Bishop stood, put a hand on D-Lo's shoulder.

"Because the alternative is becoming so paralyzed by guilt that you can't function. And then everyone dies—not just some of them, all of them." His grip tightened.

"You have a gift, son. A terrible, beautiful gift. The ability to try again. To learn from failure in ways nobody else can. Don't waste that gift on self-pity." "What should I waste it on?" Bishop smiled.

"Getting better. Every reset, every death, every failure—use it.

Learn from it. Become the person who can save the ones you couldn't save before." He walked away, then paused.

"And D-Lo?" "Yeah?" "Your sister. Kimi. She's why you keep fighting, right?" D-Lo nodded.

"Hold onto that. When everything else gets dark—and it will, trust me, it will—hold onto the reason you started. The reason you keep going." Bishop's eyes were distant, seeing something D-Lo couldn't see. "I had a reason once. A long time ago. Lost sight of it for a while. Nearly lost myself." "What brought you back?" "Lexi." The name came out soft. "Found her when she was twelve.

Scared.

Alone. Hunted." He shook his head. "She became my reason. The person I couldn't fail, no matter what." "And if you do fail?" "Then I fail. And I get up. And I try again." Bishop walked toward the exit. "That's all any of us can do, son. Fall down. Get up. Keep going.

Until we can't anymore." He disappeared into the shadows.

D-Lo stood alone on the observation platform, staring at the map, thinking about reasons and failures and the weight of the names you carry.

And somewhere in the distance, a train rumbled through the darkness.

Like time itself, moving forward whether you were ready or not.

Bishop found D-Lo after the first training session, when everyone else had scattered to recover.

"Walk with me." It wasn't a request.

D-Lo fell into step beside him, muscles screaming from hours of drills, his reset ability barely keeping up with the punishment Celestine had inflicted. They moved through the deeper tunnels, past sleeping refugees and storage areas, until they reached a section D-Lo hadn't seen before.

A memorial wall.

Hundreds of names, carved into the stone. Some neat, professional.

Others rough, desperate—carved by shaking hands in moments of grief.

"Every Ghost who's died since we came underground," Bishop said. "I carved most of these myself." D-Lo scanned the names. So many. Too many.

"How do you keep going?" "Because stopping means they died for nothing." Bishop traced one of the names—ELENA VASQUEZ—with a calloused finger. "Elena was fifteen.

Pyrokinetic. Tiny thing, couldn't have weighed a hundred pounds soaking wet. She died holding off a Trust squad so eighteen people could escape through a tunnel collapse." "You knew her?" "I trained her. Same as I'm training you." Bishop's voice was heavy.

"She was terrified of her power. Thought she'd burn someone by accident.

I spent months teaching her control, precision, how to be dangerous on purpose instead of by accident." "And then she died." "And then she died saving people she'd never met. People who'll never know her name." Bishop turned to face D-Lo. "That's the job. That's what we do. We train, we fight, we die, and we hope—pray—that it means something." "Does it? Mean something?" Bishop was quiet for a long moment.

"I've been doing this for twenty-three years," he said. "Lost count of how many people I've buried. How many missions went wrong. How many times I've asked myself that same question." "And?" "And I don't know." He met D-Lo's eyes. "I don't know if any of it means anything. Maybe we're just delaying the inevitable. Maybe the Trust wins eventually and everything we've built gets wiped away." Something cold settled in his chest.

"That's not exactly inspiring." "I'm not trying to inspire you. I'm trying to prepare you." Bishop's jaw tightened. "Because someday—soon, probably—you're going to be in my position. Making the calls. Sending people to die. Carving names into walls." "I don't want that." "Nobody wants it. But it happens anyway." Bishop put a hand on D-Lo's shoulder. "The question isn't whether you can avoid it. The question is whether you can carry it."

They walked back through the tunnels in silence.

When they reached the main chamber, Bishop stopped.

"You want to know the real answer?" D-Lo looked at him.

"To whether it means something?" Bishop nodded.

"Ask Lexi. She's my answer. She's my proof." His voice softened in a way D-Lo had never heard. "I found her when she was eleven. Tiny, traumatized, watching her father get dragged away by the Trust. I didn't think she'd survive the week." "But she did." "She did more than survive. She became…" Bishop shook his head.

"Everything I hoped for. Everything I couldn't be. She's going to lead these people somewhere I can't follow. Somewhere better." "You love her." "Like she was my own." Bishop's eyes glistened, just for a moment.

"That's the meaning, D-Lo. Not the fights we win or the enemies we kill.

The people we save. The people who go on after we're gone." He clapped D-Lo on the shoulder.

"Remember that. When the time comes. Remember what you're fighting for." "And what are you fighting for?" Bishop smiled—the first real smile D-Lo had seen from him.

"Lexi's future. Kimi's future. Your future." He started walking toward the command area. "That's enough for me. That's more than enough." D-Lo watched him go.

And wondered if he'd ever be strong enough to carry what Bishop carried.

Later that night, D-Lo found the memorial wall again.

He stood in the dim light, reading names he didn't know, faces he'd never see.

And he made a silent promise.

If I have to add names to this wall, I'll carve them myself. I'll remember every single one. And I'll make sure their deaths mean something. He didn't know if that was enough.

But it was all he had.

CHAPTER 8

THE UNDERLINE

D-Lo didn't sleep that night.

Every time he closed his eyes, he saw the Janitor's face—if you could call it a face. Those hollow eyes staring up at his window. That smile that wasn't a smile. The whisper that bypassed his ears and crawled directly into his brain like a worm made of ice.

I can smell your fractures, boy.

He sat in the dark of his bedroom, back against the wall, watching the window. The burner phone Clutch gave him sat in his lap like a security blanket that couldn't actually secure shit.

Kimi slept in her room. He'd checked on her four times already. Each time she was fine—curled up with her phone still playing some YouTube video on low volume, braids spread across her pillow like she didn't have a care in the world.

Good. Let her not have cares. He had enough for both of them.

Around 3 AM, his regular phone buzzed. Unknown number.

He answered anyway.

"Yeah?" "You still breathing?" Clutch's voice. She sounded tired too.

"Barely. He still out there?" "No. Left around midnight. Walked east toward the old industrial district." "You watching my building?" "I'm watching everything, Reload. That's my job." D-Lo exhaled. "What does he want?" "Same thing he always wants. Pain. Trauma. Fear." She paused. "You got more of that than most people. All those deaths you carry—all those resets—they leave marks. Fractures, like he said. He can sense them.

Smell them." "So I'm basically walking around with a 'free buffet' sign on my back." "Something like that." D-Lo rubbed his eyes. "How do I make it stop?" "You don't. You just stay alive long enough to figure out how to fight back." Another pause. "Get some sleep. Tomorrow's gonna be worse." She hung up.

D-Lo stared at the phone.

Tomorrow's gonna be worse.

Comforting.

10:43 AM.

D-Lo woke up to screaming.

Not the usual Marrow screaming—not arguments or fights or someone's TV too loud.

This was terror. Pure, primal terror.

He was on his feet before his brain fully woke up, muscle memory carrying him to the window.

The courtyard was chaos.

People running in every direction. A car alarm blaring. Smoke rising from somewhere near Building F.

And in the center of it all—a man.

Huge. Broad-shouldered. Built like he'd eaten gym equipment for breakfast and asked for seconds.

His skin was steaming.

Actual steam. Pouring off him in white plumes like he was a pot of water about to boil over. The concrete beneath his feet was cracking, darkening, turning black from the heat.

"Oh shit," D-Lo breathed. "Not again." He grabbed his shoes.

Kimi appeared in his doorway.

"Another one?" "Stay inside." "D-Lo—" "STAY INSIDE." He was out the door before she could argue.

By the time D-Lo reached Building F, the situation had escalated from bad to biblical.

The man—had to be six-four, two-sixty, all muscle—was stumbling backwards, slamming into a brick wall. Where his skin touched, the brick hissed. Mortar cracked. A section of wall started to glow orange.

"S-Somebody..." the man groaned. His voice was deep, shaking.

"Help… I can't—control—it—" He doubled over, gripping his head. Steam erupted from his arms, his throat, his fingertips.

Then his skin began to turn red.

Bright, scorching red. Like metal being heated in a forge.

D-Lo ducked behind a dumpster—then immediately regretted it when he realized the dumpster was already starting to warp from proximity heat.

He scrambled to a safer spot behind a concrete pillar.

"Yo!" he shouted. "Big man! Can you hear me?" The man's head snapped toward him. Eyes wild. Desperate.

"GET AWAY! I DON'T WANT TO HURT NOBODY!" A pulse of heat rippled outward. D-Lo felt it pass over him like opening an oven door—except the oven was set to "surface of the sun." Nearby, a group of young hustlers were dragging someone away from the blast zone. D-Lo caught a glimpse of the victim—a guy with charcoal-black burns across his arm, skin peeling like wet paper, screaming in agony.

"HE BURNED MARKUS! HE BURNED HIM TO THE BONE!" D-Lo's stomach turned.

This wasn't like Mrs. Waverly.

Mrs. Waverly was scared. Confused. Needed comfort.

This man was scared too—but his power was built for destruction. Every pulse of fear made him more dangerous. A feedback loop with no off switch.

"Okay," D-Lo muttered to himself. "Think. Ice worked on Mrs. Waverly.

But this dude is way hotter. Way bigger. I'd need a whole damn glacier." The man stumbled forward, reaching out like he wanted help but knowing his touch would kill.

"PLEASE! SOMEBODY! MAKE IT STOP!" His skin was pulsing now. Like a pressure cooker before it pops.

D-Lo recognized that rhythm from his time in the kitchen—before he dropped out, before the streets, before everything went sideways. He'd seen pots explode. Seen pressure valves fail.

This man was about to blow.

And when he did, everyone in a fifty-foot radius was dead.

D-Lo made a decision.

A stupid decision. The kind of decision that had gotten him killed eight times yesterday.

He stepped out from behind the pillar.

"Hey! Big man! Look at me!" The man turned. Steam jetted from his shoulders.

"What's your name?" D-Lo asked, walking closer. Every step brought more heat. His shirt was starting to smoke.

"M-Michael..." the man gasped. "Michael Rucker... but everyone calls me..." He doubled over. A geyser of steam erupted from his back.

"...Kettle..." D-Lo almost laughed. Almost.

"Kettle? Like the thing you boil water in?" "Worked kitchens my whole life." Kettle groaned. "Folks say I'm calm.

Keep things from boiling over." "Oh that's ironic as hell." "I KNOW!" Kettle's skin flickered—red to white to pink—like he was cycling through temperatures too fast to stabilize.

"Okay, Kettle, listen to me," D-Lo said, forcing his voice calm even though his heart was trying to escape through his throat. "I know it hurts. I know you're scared. But you gotta breathe—" "I CAN'T! IT'S BURNING ME FROM THE INSIDE!" Kettle roared. His whole body pulsed.

And D-Lo saw it coming—the final pressure spike, the moment before catastrophic failure.

"EVERYBODY DOWN!" he screamed.

He dove behind the pillar.

WHOOM.

The explosion wasn't fire. It was pressure.

A shockwave of superheated air blasted outward like a bomb, sending dumpsters flying, cracking pavement, blowing out every window within thirty yards.

D-Lo got slammed against the pillar hard enough to crack a rib. Even with cover, his exposed skin burned like he'd been slapped by the sun itself.

His ears rang. His vision blurred.

For a second, he thought he was dead again.

Then he heard crying.

D-Lo pulled himself up, wincing.

His left side was on fire—cracked rib, definitely, maybe two. His arms were red and raw. His lungs felt like he'd inhaled sandpaper.

But he was alive.

He stumbled toward the epicenter.

Kettle was still standing. Barely.

His body was cracked like pottery left in a kiln too long. Heat shimmered around him so intensely the air rippled like water.

But he wasn't attacking. He was crying.

Big, heaving sobs that turned to steam before the tears could fall.

"I... didn't mean... to hurt him..." Kettle choked. "Markus was my friend... we grew up together... and I... I..." D-Lo approached slowly.

"Hey. Hey, big man. It's okay." Kettle looked at him with pure fear.

"Don't come close. I'm too hot. I'll kill you." "Yeah, probably." D-Lo kept walking anyway. "But you ain't trying to hurt nobody. I can see that." "How you know?" "Because you're crying." D-Lo stopped six feet away—close enough to feel the heat searing his skin, far enough to maybe survive another pulse. "Monsters don't cry. They don't feel bad. They don't beg for help." Kettle's sobs intensified.

"What's happening to me?" "Same thing that happened to Mrs. Waverly yesterday. Same thing that happened to me." D-Lo swallowed. "We're wired. Something changed us." "I don't want this. I ain't never wanted to hurt nobody in my life." "I know. I know." D-Lo looked around, spotted a corner store with a busted freezer spilling ice onto the sidewalk. "Listen—I'm gonna try something. It might help. Or it might make you blow up again. Either way, I need you to trust me." Kettle stared at him.

"Why you helping me? You don't even know me." D-Lo thought about it. Thought about all the times he'd died. All the resets. All the pain.

And the fact that nobody had been there to help him figure it out.

"Because somebody should," he said. "And I'm the only one dumb enough to try." He sprinted to the corner store. Grabbed as much ice as he could carry.

Sprinted back.

"Okay, big man. This might hurt. But I need you to let me try." Kettle nodded weakly.

D-Lo pressed the ice against his shoulder.

SSSHHHHHHHH.

Steam exploded. The ice vaporized instantly.

D-Lo's hands burned—blistered immediately, skin going red then white.

He screamed. Kettle screamed.

But D-Lo didn't let go.

He pressed harder. More ice. More steam. More pain.

And slowly—slowly—Kettle's glow began to fade.

His temperature dropped. His breathing steadied.

He collapsed to his knees.

D-Lo collapsed with him.

Both of them panting. Both of them crying. Both of them alive.

"Thank you," Kettle whispered. "Thank you." D-Lo looked at his ruined hands.

"You welcome, big man. You're welcome."

"Well damn." D-Lo looked up.

Clutch stood at the edge of the blast zone, cigarette unlit between her lips, eyebrows raised.

"You really do have a death wish, don't you?" "It's more of a death hobby at this point." She walked over, surveying the damage. Cracked pavement. Shattered windows. A dumpster that had been launched forty feet and embedded in a chain-link fence.

"The Trust is gonna be here in about four minutes," she said. "We need to move him." "Move him where?" "Somewhere they won't look." She turned to Kettle. "Big man. Can you walk?" Kettle nodded weakly. "I... I think so." "Good." She grabbed his arm—and to D-Lo's amazement, her luck must have extended to heat resistance, because her skin didn't blister.

"Let's go." D-Lo struggled to his feet.

"What about my hands?" Clutch glanced at them.

"You'll heal. Or you'll reset. Either way, stop bitching and move." D-Lo opened his mouth to argue.

Then he heard the sirens.

And decided bitching could wait.

The boiler room under Building H was exactly as terrible as it sounded.

Rusted pipes ran across the ceiling like veins in a metal corpse. The air smelled like mildew, old sweat, and decades of deferred maintenance.

A single bulb flickered overhead, casting shadows that moved when they shouldn't.

But it was hidden. And right now, hidden was worth more than gold.

Kettle collapsed against an old water heater, trembling. His skin had cooled to something approximating normal, but he still radiated warmth—enough that the pipes near him started to drip condensation.

D-Lo slumped onto an overturned milk crate, cradling his burned hands.

Clutch leaned against the wall and finally lit her cigarette, the flame dancing in her fingers like it was flirting with her.

"So," she said, exhaling smoke. "Introductions. Big man, I'm Clutch.

I bend luck. The idiot with the burned hands is Reload. He dies and comes back." Kettle blinked. "He what?" "Long story," D-Lo muttered.

"And you're Kettle," Clutch continued. "You generate heat. Probably thermal manipulation tied to emotional response—anger, fear, stress.

The more you feel, the hotter you burn." Kettle stared at her. "How you know all that?" "I've been studying us. The wired. Trying to understand how it works.

Why some people get powers and others don't. Why the powers manifest the way they do." "And?" "And it's tied to psychology. Trauma. Emotion." She gestured at Kettle.

"You said you worked kitchens. Spent your whole life keeping things from boiling over—tempers, situations, problems. Now your body does it literally. The thing you suppressed became the thing you can't control." Kettle looked down at his hands.

"That's... that's messed up." "Welcome to the new world." D-Lo leaned forward. "So what's my psychology? Why do I reset when I die?" Clutch studied him.

"You tell me. What was your life like before all this? What did you want more than anything?" D-Lo thought about it.

About growing up in the Marrow. About watching friends die—shot, locked up, overdosed. About all the mistakes he'd made that he couldn't take back.

About wishing, every single day, that he could get a do-over.

"I wanted a second chance," he said quietly. "Just one. To fix the things I messed up." Clutch nodded.

"Now you have infinite chances. But here's the catch—" She leaned forward, cigarette ember glowing. "You can fix things for yourself. But nobody else gets retries. Every mistake they make is permanent. Every death is final." That weight settled on his shoulders.

Infinite chances for him. Zero for everyone else.

"That's not fair," he said.

"Nothing about this is fair," Clutch replied. "But it is what it is." The boiler room fell silent.

Just the drip of pipes. The wheeze of Kettle's breathing. The distant wail of sirens above.

Then— A sound.

Faint. Distant.

Metal scraping against concrete.

SCRAAAAAPE.

SCRAAAAAPE.

All three of them froze.

Clutch's cigarette ember flickered—then died.

The hairs on his arms rose.

"No," he whispered. "No no no—" *SCRAAAAAPE.*

Closer now.

Something was coming down the stairs.

The door creaked open.

Slow. Deliberate. Like whoever was on the other side wanted them to hear every squeak of the hinges.

And then he stepped in.

Blue coveralls. Work boots. Utility belt with keys that jingled faintly, wrong, like wind chimes made of bones.

A mop handle dragging behind him, leaving no trail.

The Janitor.

He looked exactly like D-Lo remembered—too thin, too pale, too quiet.

Eyes like empty wells. Shadow that moved a half-second slower than his body.

But now, seeing him up close, D-Lo noticed details he'd missed before.

The coveralls had stains that weren't dirt or oil.

The mop handle was cracked, splintered, like it had been used for something other than cleaning.

And his smile—that smile—was wrong in ways D-Lo couldn't articulate.

Too wide. Too still. Like a mask someone forgot to animate.

"Hello," the Janitor said softly.

His voice was gentle. Too gentle. The kind of gentle that made your skin want to crawl off your body and find somewhere safe to hide.

Kettle tensed. Heat flickered across his skin.

"Back up, man." The Janitor tilted his head like he didn't understand the request.

"You're hurt," he said calmly. "You're cracked. Fractured. Full of pain." His eyes moved across all three of them—landing on each in turn, weighing them, measuring them.

"Pain," he whispered, "is a stain. And I clean stains." He stepped forward.

Clutch flicked her unlit cigarette at him—an instinctive move, probably hoping her luck would make it mean something.

The cigarette stopped mid-air.

Hung there for a moment.

Then dropped straight down.

Dead.

Clutch's face went pale.

"He canceled my luck," she whispered. "That's not possible—" "Lot of impossible things happening lately," the Janitor said pleasantly. "I am one of them." Kettle roared and charged.

Heat burst from his body—flames erupting along his arms, his shoulders, his back. The air around him warped with temperature.

He swung a massive fist at the Janitor's head.

And the Janitor didn't move.

Didn't flinch.

Didn't burn.

The moment Kettle's fist connected, the heat was sucked away—extinguished like a candle in a hurricane.

Kettle gasped.

"What—what are you—" The Janitor grabbed his face.

Kettle screamed.

Not a pain scream. Something worse.

A soul scream.

D-Lo watched in horror as Kettle's body went rigid, his eyes rolling back, his mouth open in a silent howl of agony. Something was being pulled out of him—not blood, not bone, but something deeper. Something essential.

Clutch grabbed a broken pipe off the floor and swung it at the Janitor's skull.

The pipe stopped an inch from impact.

Bent.

Like it was made of rubber.

"Rude," the Janitor said without looking at her.

He continued draining Kettle—drinking his fear, his trauma, his pain—and with every second, Kettle grew weaker, dimmer, smaller.

D-Lo snapped.

"STOP!" He rushed forward. Grabbed the Janitor's arm.

And felt something worse than heat.

Cold.

The deepest cold he'd ever experienced. Cold that reached into his chest and wrapped around his heart. Cold that found every death he'd ever died and made him feel them all at once.

The Janitor turned toward D-Lo.

Those empty eyes locked onto him.

And widened.

For once, D-Lo saw something behind them.

Interest. Recognition. Hunger.

"Oh," the Janitor breathed. "Oh, you're special." D-Lo tried to pull away. Couldn't.

"You're broken over... and over... and over," the Janitor whispered. "I can feel the fractures. Dozens. Maybe hundreds." He leaned forward. Inhaled deeply. Like smelling fresh-baked bread.

"You've died," he said. "So many times. And you remember all of it." D-Lo's blood turned to ice.

Clutch shouted something. He couldn't hear what.

The Janitor's free hand reached for D-Lo's face.

"I would like to cleanse you," he said softly. "You're a masterpiece of damaged flesh. So much pain. So much fear. So much delicious suffering." His fingers brushed D-Lo's forehead.

And he was being read.

Every death. Every reset. Every moment of agony he'd experienced.

All of it, catalogued and consumed in the space of a heartbeat.

"Save file," D-Lo gasped.

The Janitor's eyes widened again.

"Oh," he whispered. "You're the one who repeats." His hand pressed fully against D-Lo's forehead.

Pain. Absolute. Complete.

Darkness.

10:43 AM.

D-Lo woke up screaming.

Not just a startle. A full, throat-ripping, lung-emptying scream.

Kimi came running.

"D-Lo! D-Lo, what's wrong!?" He couldn't answer. Couldn't stop screaming.

Because he remembered.

Not just his death.

He remembered what the Janitor took. What the Janitor saw.

Every single reset. Every single death. Laid out like a buffet.

And the worst part—the thing that made his stomach lurch and his skin crawl—was the feeling he couldn't shake.

The feeling that the Janitor was still there.

Still inside his head.

Still watching.

Still hungry.

D-Lo stumbled to the bathroom.

Threw up.

Threw up again.

Kimi stood in the doorway, terrified.

"D-Lo, you're scaring me—" He looked at her.

Grabbed her shoulders.

"I need you to listen to me very carefully," he said, voice shaking.

"There's a man. He looks like a janitor. Blue coveralls. Mop. If you ever see him—EVER—you run. You don't talk to him. You don't look at him. You run and you don't stop until you can't run anymore. Do you understand?" "D-Lo—" "DO YOU UNDERSTAND?" She nodded. Tears in her eyes.

"Yes. Okay. I understand." He pulled her into a hug. Held her tight.

And over her shoulder, he stared at the bathroom mirror.

Where he'd written: *SAVE FILE #2 — TOASTER EDITION*

The words were gone now. Reset.

But underneath, in handwriting that wasn't his—cramped, spidery, wrong—someone had written something new: *I REMEMBER TOO.*

D-Lo's heart stopped.

The Janitor didn't just survive resets.

He remembered them.

He was waiting.

And now he knew exactly what D-Lo was.

D-Lo dialed Clutch's number with shaking hands.

She answered on the first ring.

"Reload. You reset." "He remembers," D-Lo gasped. "The Janitor. He remembers when I reset.

He wrote on my mirror." Silence. Long silence.

"Clutch? You there?" "I'm here." Her voice was tight. Controlled. But underneath it—fear.

"That's not supposed to be possible. When you reset, everything goes back. Everyone forgets." "Not him." "Not him," she agreed. "Which means..." She didn't finish. She didn't have to.

If the Janitor remembered, then D-Lo's greatest advantage—his ability to retry, to learn, to escape—was neutralized.

He couldn't hide.

He couldn't run.

He couldn't redo.

Because no matter how many times he came back, the monster would be waiting.

"What do I do?" D-Lo asked.

Clutch's answer was barely a whisper.

"We find out what he wants. And we figure out how to stop him." "How?" "I don't know yet." A pause. "But I know someone who might." "Who?" "Someone who's been studying the wired longer than anyone. Someone who knows things the Trust doesn't want anybody to know." Clutch exhaled.

"Meet me at the corner of Miller and Vine. One hour. Bring Kettle if you can find him." "Kettle? He's—" D-Lo paused. "Wait. If I reset, does that mean…" "It means everything went back. Including him. He's fine. Probably waking up right now, wondering why he feels like shit." D-Lo closed his eyes.

One hour. Answers. Maybe.

"I'll be there." He hung up.

Looked at the mirror one more time.

I REMEMBER TOO.

The words seemed to pulse. To breathe. To watch.

D-Lo grabbed a towel and wiped them away.

They smeared—then faded—then vanished.

But the feeling didn't.

The feeling that something was wrong. Something was waiting. Something was coming.

And it knew his name.

CHAPTER 9

THE LOST

D-Lo hadn't seen Melo in three weeks.

That wasn't unusual—Melo ran with a different crowd now, deeper into the game than D-Lo had ever been willing to go. But three weeks without even a text? Without showing up at D-Lo's door with some new scheme or complaint or piece of neighborhood gossip?

Something was wrong.

"You sure about this?" Clutch asked.

They stood outside Melo's building—Building K, on the bad side of the Marrow, where even the rats knew to watch their backs.

"He's my boy," D-Lo said. "Been my boy since we were six. I can't just—" "You can't just walk into a building controlled by corner boys asking questions about one of their runners." "He ain't a runner. He just—" D-Lo stopped. "He was just trying to make money. Same as everybody." Clutch lit a cigarette.

"Same as everybody gets you killed same as everybody." "That's why I gotta find him." Clutch sighed. But she followed him inside.

Building K smelled like piss and desperation.

The elevator had been broken since before D-Lo was born. Graffiti covered every surface—tags, gang signs, phone numbers for things D-Lo didn't want to think about. The stairwell lights flickered like they were having seizures.

Melo's apartment was on the seventh floor.

They made it to the fourth before they ran into trouble.

Two kids—couldn't have been older than fifteen—blocking the stairwell. Both of them wearing red bandanas. Both of them with bulges in their waistbands that weren't cell phones.

"Wrong building, cuz," the taller one said.

"I'm looking for Melo. Jameel Carter. He lives on seven." The kids exchanged looks.

"Ain't nobody by that name here." "He's lived here his whole life. His mama's apartment is 7C." "I said—" The tall kid stepped forward. "—ain't nobody by that name here." Clutch's hand drifted toward her pocket.

D-Lo put a hand on her arm.

"We're not looking for trouble. I just want to find my friend." "Your friend ain't here. Your friend ain't been here." The kid's eyes were cold. Too cold for fifteen. "And if you smart, you won't come back asking about him." The message was clear.

Melo was gone.

And these kids knew why.

They found out from Mrs. Carter.

She wasn't in 7C anymore—she'd been moved to a shelter in District Twelve after "the incident." It took D-Lo three days to track her down.

She looked twenty years older than the last time he'd seen her.

"Jameel's gone," she said. Her voice was hollow. Empty. The voice of someone who'd cried until there was nothing left. "They took him." "Who took him?" "The Trust." She spat the word like poison. "He was at some card game when the flash happened. Started doing things—seeing things—knowing what cards were coming before they were dealt." D-Lo's stomach dropped.

"He was wired." "He didn't know what it was. Thought he was just lucky." Mrs. Carter laughed bitterly. "Lucky. That's what he kept saying. 'Mama, I'm so lucky now. Everything's gonna be different.'" "When did they take him?" "Two weeks ago. Came in the middle of the night. Broke down my door.

Shot my boy with something that made him seize up like he was having a fit." Tears streamed down her face. "I tried to stop them. They threw me into a wall like I was nothing. Like he was nothing."

"Mrs. Carter, I'm so sorry—" "They took my baby." Her hands clenched. "Took him to wherever they take people like him. The Vault, I heard them say. Some underground place where they do experiments." The Vault.

The same place they'd been fighting against.

The same place they were planning to raid.

"Did they say anything else? Anything about what they were going to do with him?" Mrs. Carter shook her head.

"Just that he was 'flagged for processing.' Whatever that means." She looked at D-Lo with eyes that had lost all hope. "You were his friend, D-Lo. His best friend. He talked about you all the time. Said you were the only one who never tried to use him for nothing." "I'm gonna find him, Mrs. Carter." "How? They got guns. They got powers. They got—" "I don't care what they got." D-Lo's jaw tightened. "Melo's my boy. And I'm gonna bring him home."

That night, D-Lo sat on the roof of Building C, staring at nothing.

Clutch found him there.

"You're beating yourself up." "I should've been there." "Where? At a card game you didn't know about? Against Trust operatives you couldn't have stopped?" "I should've known he was wired. Should've warned him.

Should've—" "Should've what? Read his mind?" Clutch sat beside him. "You're not God, D-Lo. You can't save everyone." "I can save some people." He turned to her. "I can reset. I can try again. I can—" "You can die over and over trying to change things that might not be changeable." Clutch's voice was hard. "And every time you die, you come back a little more broken. A little more tired. A little more lost." "So what? I'm supposed to just let them have him?" "I'm saying you need to be smart about this. The Vault raid is already planned. We're already going in. Melo might be there. He might not. But burning yourself out trying to save one person isn't going to help anybody." D-Lo knew she was right.

He hated that she was right.

"He taught me to ride a bike," he said quietly. "Did I ever tell you that? When I was seven. My mama couldn't afford a bike, so Melo stole one from some kid in District Six and brought it over. Spent the whole day running behind me, making sure I didn't fall." "Sounds like a good friend." "The best." D-Lo's voice cracked. "And I couldn't even be there when they came for him." Clutch didn't say anything.

Just sat with him.

Let him grieve.

Because sometimes that was all you could do.

Later—much later—D-Lo went to see Melo's mother one more time.

He brought food. Money. Everything he could scrape together.

She took it without speaking.

Then, at the door: "D-Lo." "Yes ma'am?" "If you find him..." She paused. "If he's already gone... if they already did whatever they're gonna do..." "Mrs. Carter—" "Don't let him suffer." Tears fell down her cheeks. "If he's gone, don't let him suffer. That's all I ask." Something broke inside him.

"I'm gonna bring him back," he said. "Alive. Whole. I promise." He didn't know if it was a promise he could keep.

But he made it anyway.

Because that's what you did for family.

Even when family meant something different than blood.

The Vault raid took on new meaning after that.

It wasn't just about saving Lexi anymore.

It wasn't just about striking back at the Trust.

It was about Melo. About Mrs. Carter. About everyone the Trust had taken in the middle of the night.

D-Lo trained harder.

Died more.

Learned faster.

And every time he reset, he carried the weight of everyone he was fighting for.

His sister.

His friends.

His crew.

His city.

His best friend, somewhere in the dark, waiting to be saved.

I'm coming, Melo, he thought.

Just hold on.

I'm coming.

CHAPTER 10

THE JANITOR

Finding Kettle wasn't hard.

D-Lo just followed the smell of smoke and the sound of crying.

Building F, third floor, apartment 3F. The door was open—not broken, just... open. Like Kettle had walked in and forgotten that doors were supposed to close.

D-Lo knocked on the frame anyway.

"Yo. Kettle. You in there?" No answer.

He stepped inside.

The apartment was sparse—bachelor living at its most basic. A couch that had seen better decades. A TV that still had a VCR built into it. A kitchen that was cleaner than any kitchen D-Lo had ever seen, every pot and pan hanging in perfect order, every surface wiped down, every knife in its place.

The kitchen of a man who took pride in his work.

The kitchen of a man who didn't have much else.

Kettle sat on the floor in the corner of the living room, knees pulled to his chest, arms wrapped around himself. He was shaking. Not from cold—from something deeper.

"Hey," D-Lo said softly. "Big man. You remember me?" Kettle looked up. His eyes were red. Puffy. The eyes of someone who'd been crying for hours.

"I burned Markus," he whispered. "I remember burning him. But then I woke up and... and he texted me good morning. Like nothing happened." D-Lo sat down across from him.

92

"That's because of me. I reset. When I die, everything goes back to the way it was. Except..." He trailed off.

"Except what?" "Except I remember. And apparently, some other people remember too." Kettle stared at him.

"That don't make sense." "Nothing makes sense anymore, big man." D-Lo extended his hand. "But I know someone who might have answers. You coming?" Kettle looked at the hand. Looked at D-Lo. Looked at the kitchen—the one piece of his life that made sense, that he could control, that he understood.

Then he took D-Lo's hand and let himself be pulled up.

"Yeah," he said quietly. "I'm coming."

The corner of Miller and Vine was exactly the kind of place you didn't want to be standing at noon on a Sunday.

Used to be a thriving intersection—barbershop, check cashing place, Chinese restaurant that everybody swore was a front but had fire lo mein. Now it was a graveyard of closed storefronts and plywood windows, tagged with graffiti that ranged from artistic to obscene.

Clutch was already there, leaning against a shuttered storefront, cigarette burning between her fingers. She looked like she hadn't slept.

Join the club.

"You brought the big man," she said as D-Lo and Kettle approached. "Good." Kettle shifted uncomfortably. "You're the luck lady." "And you're the walking furnace. We all got our crosses." She dropped her cigarette and crushed it. "Let's move. We're meeting someone inside." "Inside where?" Clutch gestured at the shuttered storefront behind her.

The sign above the door was faded, barely readable: *MADAME CELESTINE — FORTUNES & FUTURES*

D-Lo raised an eyebrow. "We're meeting a psychic?" "We're meeting someone who knows things." Clutch pulled open the door—which shouldn't have opened, given the padlock and chains, but apparently luck had opinions about that. "Try not to say anything stupid." "I make no promises."

The inside of the shop was exactly what D-Lo expected and nothing like it at the same time.

Candles everywhere—not the fake ones, real flames, dozens of them, casting dancing shadows on walls covered in tapestries and symbols he didn't recognize. Shelves lined with bottles and jars containing things he didn't want to identify. A smell in the air that was incense and something earthier, something that made his nose tingle.

In the center of the room, behind a table covered in black velvet, sat a woman.

She was old—how old, D-Lo couldn't guess. Sixty? Eighty? A hundred?

Her skin was dark brown and deeply lined, her hair silver-white and wrapped in a patterned cloth. Her eyes were milky, clouded—blind, maybe—but they tracked him as he entered like she could see straight through to his soul.

"Clutch," the woman said. Her voice was like gravel and honey mixed together. "You bring new broken things to my door." "They need answers, Celestine. About the Cleaner." The old woman's expression shifted.

Fear.

Actual fear.

On the face of someone who dealt in fortunes and futures.

"Why do you speak that name in my house?" "Because he's hunting them." Clutch stepped forward. "He touched this one—" she pointed at D-Lo "—and he remembers. Across resets. He wrote on the mirror." Celestine's blind eyes fixed on D-Lo.

"Come here, boy." D-Lo glanced at Clutch. She nodded.

He approached the table.

Celestine reached out, her hands gnarled and wrinkled, and grabbed his wrist. Her grip was stronger than it should have been.

She closed her eyes.

And D-Lo felt something—a probe, a presence, something brushing against the inside of his skull like fingers flipping through pages.

Then she let go.

Her face had gone pale.

"Mon Dieu," she whispered. "So many deaths. So many returns. You are fractured like shattered glass, boy." "Yeah, I've heard that." D-Lo rubbed his wrist. "What I want to know is why the Janitor can remember. Why he can follow me across resets." Celestine shook her head slowly.

"Because he is not bound by time. He is not bound by anything." She leaned back in her chair. "Sit. All of you. This will take some telling."

They sat on cushions arranged around the table—D-Lo, Kettle, and Clutch—while Celestine lit more candles and began to speak.

"The thing you call the Janitor has many names. The Cleaner. The Stain-Eater. The Hollow Man. He has existed for a very long time—longer than Project Renaissance. Longer than the Trust. Longer, perhaps, than this city itself." Kettle frowned. "How is that possible? The wired started after the explosion." "No." Celestine's voice was sharp. "The wired EMERGED after the explosion. But power has always existed. Anomalies have always existed.

They are drawn to places of suffering, of trauma, of accumulated pain." She gestured around her.

"Why do you think the Marrow Projects are what they are? Why do you think this neighborhood has always been forgotten, neglected, left to rot? It is not accident. It is not politics—or not only politics. This land is saturated with suffering. Generations of it. And suffering draws things. Feeds things." D-Lo felt cold.

"You're saying the Janitor came here because of... what? All the pain?" "I am saying he has always been here. Sleeping. Waiting. Feeding slowly on the ambient misery of forgotten people." Celestine's blind eyes seemed to bore into him. "The explosion did not create him. It woke him up. Made him hungry in ways he had not been for decades." Clutch leaned forward. "How do we stop him?" Celestine laughed.

It was not a pleasant sound.

"Stop him? Child, you do not stop a thing like that. He is not a man.

He is not even truly alive. He is a function. A process. Pain exists, and he cleans it. Trauma exists, and he consumes it. You cannot stop a function. You can only avoid it." "That's not good enough," D-Lo said.

"Then you will die." Celestine shrugged. "Again and again and again.

And he will remember each time, and grow stronger each time, and eventually you will break so completely that there will be nothing left to reset." The words hung in the air like smoke.

D-Lo felt Kettle's hand on his shoulder. Warm—not burning, just warm.

Comforting.

"There has to be another way," Kettle said quietly.

Celestine studied him.

"The gentle one. The one who burns but does not want to." She tilted her head. "You carry guilt like a stone around your neck. You think your power is a curse." Kettle's jaw tightened. "It is." "No. It is a gift. A terrible gift, but a gift nonetheless." She turned back to D-Lo. "As is yours. The ability to retry is not just about avoiding death. It is about learning. Growing. Finding the path that works when all other paths fail." "But if he remembers—" "Then you must find a path he cannot predict." Celestine smiled thinly.

"The Cleaner feeds on patterns. On predictable pain. On consistent trauma. If you wish to survive him, you must become unpredictable. You must do things that do not make sense. You must break your own patterns before he can consume them." D-Lo thought about that.

Break your own patterns. Do things that don't make sense. Become unpredictable.

"That's not really advice," he said. "That's just telling me to be random." "Randomness is a form of freedom," Celestine replied. "The Cleaner understands patterns because patterns are what he consumes. But chaos?

Chaos is noise. Chaos is static. Chaos is the one thing he cannot digest." Clutch stood up.

"We've been here too long. The Trust has eyes everywhere." As if on cue, D-Lo heard something outside.

Engines. Multiple vehicles. Slowing down. Stopping.

"Shit," Clutch hissed. "They found us."

Celestine didn't panic.

She simply stood, walked to a tapestry on the wall, and pulled it aside.

Behind it was a door.

"This leads to the tunnels beneath the city. Follow them east until you reach the old subway station. There are people there who can help you." "What about you?" D-Lo asked.

Celestine smiled.

"The Trust has been trying to take me for forty years. They have not succeeded yet." She reached out and touched his cheek—her hand cold and dry. "Remember what I told you, boy. Become unpredictable. Break your patterns. And when the Cleaner comes for you again—and he will—do not give him what he expects." Heavy boots outside. Shouting.

"TRUST SPECIAL OPERATIONS. OPEN THE DOOR." Clutch grabbed D-Lo's arm. "We need to go. NOW." D-Lo took one last look at Celestine.

The old woman was walking toward the front door, calm as Sunday morning.

"Go," she said without turning around. "And survive." Clutch pulled him through the hidden door. Kettle followed.

The last thing D-Lo heard before the door shut was the sound of the front entrance being breached—and Celestine's voice, rising in a language he didn't understand, words that made the candles flare and the shadows dance.

Then darkness.

The tunnel was old.

Brick walls. Curved ceiling. The smell of stagnant water and ancient decay. Pipes ran along the sides, rusted and dripping.

Clutch produced a flashlight from somewhere—her luck, probably—and led the way.

"What the hell was that?" D-Lo gasped as they moved. "How did the Trust find us?" "They've been watching me," Clutch admitted. "I knew they were. I just didn't think they'd move this fast." "You KNEW they were watching and you brought us there anyway?" "Celestine's place has protections. Or it did." Clutch's jaw tightened.

"They must have brought something new. Something that can cut through her wards." Kettle's voice echoed in the tunnel. "What about the old woman?" "Celestine can take care of herself." But Clutch didn't sound certain.

They moved in silence for a few minutes. The tunnel branched several times, but Clutch seemed to know where she was going—or her luck did.

Finally, D-Lo spoke.

"That stuff she said. About the Janitor. About becoming unpredictable." "What about it?" "Do you think it's true? That I can avoid him by being random?" Clutch was quiet for a moment.

"I think Celestine knows things. Old things. I also think she speaks in riddles because straightforward answers are too easy." She glanced back at him. "But the core of it makes sense. The Janitor hunts by pattern.

He finds pain and follows it. If you don't act like prey, maybe he won't see you as prey." "Maybe." "It's the best we've got." Kettle spoke up from behind. "What's this subway station she mentioned?

The one with people who can help?" Clutch's expression changed. Complicated.

"It's called the Underline. Old subway system—collapsed decades ago.

The city sealed it off. But people still live down there." "What kind of people?" "Our kind. Wired. The ones who couldn't stay above ground. The ones the Trust hunted, the gangs targeted, the world forgot." She paused. "They call themselves the Babylon Ghosts." D-Lo felt a chill.

"Ghosts?" "Because they're supposed to be dead. According to the Trust's records, most of them don't exist anymore. Erased. Eliminated. Gone." Clutch's voice was soft. "But they're alive. They're organized. And they're the only ones who've figured out how to survive down here long-term." The tunnel widened ahead.

D-Lo could see light—faint, flickering, but real.

And voices. Movement.

"Stay close," Clutch said. "Let me do the talking. And whatever you do, don't threaten anyone. They'll kill you before you finish the sentence." "Comforting." "It's the truth." They emerged into a larger space—an old subway platform, graffitied and crumbling, lit by strings of lanterns and jury-rigged electric lights.

And waiting for them, weapons raised, faces hidden behind masks and bandanas, were at least a dozen figures.

Kids, mostly. Teenagers.

All of them armed. All of them watching.

One stepped forward.

Small. Wiry. A girl, maybe sixteen or seventeen, with a mask shaped like a skull and eyes that held zero warmth.

"Clutch," she said. "You brought strangers to our door." "They need help, Lexi. The Cleaner is hunting them." The girl—Lexi—tilted her head.

Her eyes moved to D-Lo. Studied him. Looked through him.

"This one has died many times," she said. "I can see the fractures." D-Lo stiffened. "How can you—" "I see things." Her voice was flat. Matter-of-fact. "It's my curse." She closed the distance.

Close enough that D-Lo could see the scars on her neck, her arms—marks that looked like burns and cuts and things he couldn't identify.

"The Cleaner is dangerous," she said. "More dangerous than you know.

He's been hunting in these tunnels for months. Taking our people.

Feeding." "We know," D-Lo said. "That's why we're here. We need help." Lexi stared at him for a long moment.

Then she looked at Kettle. At Clutch. Back at D-Lo.

"Help," she repeated. "You want help from ghosts." "I want to survive. And I want to stop that thing from hurting anyone else." "Noble." The word dripped with skepticism. "Everyone's noble until the screaming starts." "I've already done the screaming. Multiple times." D-Lo stepped forward, meeting her eyes. "I've died more times than I can count. I've felt that thing inside my head. And I'm still standing. So either help me fight it, or get out of my way. But don't stand there acting like I haven't earned the right to ask." Silence.

The other Ghosts shifted, fingers tightening on weapons.

Clutch tensed.

Kettle's skin flickered with heat.

Then Lexi smiled.

It transformed her face—made her look younger, almost human.

"You've got fire," she said. "Good. You'll need it." She turned and gestured for them to follow.

"Come. There's someone you need to meet. And then we'll talk about the Cleaner."

The deeper they went, the more D-Lo realized this wasn't just a hideout.

It was a city.

A hidden city beneath the city.

The old subway tunnels had been transformed—living spaces carved into alcoves, communal areas set up in abandoned stations, supply caches hidden in maintenance corridors. Lanterns and stolen electrical lines provided light. Filtered water systems—crude but functional—provided drinking water. Gardens grew under UV lamps, vegetables reaching toward artificial suns.

And everywhere, people.

Kids, mostly—teenagers and younger, some as young as eight or nine.

All of them with that same look in their eyes. The look of people who'd seen too much, lost too much, survived too much.

"How many live down here?" D-Lo asked.

"Enough," Lexi replied without turning around. "More every month. The Trust's containment efforts are getting more aggressive. Lots of wired people disappearing from the surface. The ones who escape come to us." "And you just... take them in?" "Somebody has to." She glanced back. "The world above doesn't want us.

The Trust wants to cage us or kill us. The gangs want to use us. Down here, we only have each other." They passed through a larger chamber—an old station platform with the original signage still visible: *BABYLON STATION — DOWNTOWN EXPRESS*

Someone had spray-painted over the schedule board: *WE LIVE WHERE THE CITY DIES.*

"Our motto," Lexi said, following D-Lo's gaze. "Reminder of who we are.

Where we come from." "It's catchy." "It's true." She led them to a makeshift structure built against the far wall—corrugated metal and scavenged wood, almost like a throne room in a kingdom of trash.

Inside, sitting on a chair made of welded subway car seats, was a man.

Old. Weathered. One eye missing, covered by a patch. The other sharp as a blade.

His skin was covered in tattoos—not gang tattoos, but symbols. The same symbols D-Lo had seen in Celestine's shop.

"Clutch," the man said. His voice was deep, resonant. "Been a while." "Bishop." Clutch nodded. "Still alive, I see." "Spite is a powerful motivator." He looked at D-Lo and Kettle. "These the ones the Cleaner marked?" "This one." Clutch pointed at D-Lo. "He's got the reset gift. And the Cleaner remembers him across timelines." Bishop's one eye widened slightly.

"That's not supposed to be possible." "That's what everyone keeps saying. And yet." Bishop stood. He was tall—had to be six-five—and built like a man who'd spent decades doing hard labor. He walked toward D-Lo, each step deliberate.

"Let me see." D-Lo didn't know what that meant, but he held still.

Bishop reached out and pressed his palm against D-Lo's forehead.

The world went white.

D-Lo saw— *Himself dying. Bullet to the chest. Reset.*
Himself dying. Bullet to the neck. Reset.
Himself dying. Toaster in the tub. Reset.
Himself dying. Hit by a bike. Reset.
Himself dying. Heat from Mrs. Waverly. Reset.
Himself dying. Heat from Kettle. Reset.
Himself dying. The Janitor's touch. Reset.
—and then he was back.

Standing in the throne room. Bishop's hand falling away from his forehead.

The old man's face was pale.

"Mon Dieu," he whispered. The same words Celestine had used.

"What did you see?" Clutch asked.

"Everything." Bishop looked at D-Lo with something like awe. "He's not just wired. He's anchored." Clutch frowned. "What does that mean?" "It means he doesn't just reset time for himself. He's a fixed point.

A tether." Bishop stepped back. "The universe uses him as a reference.

When he dies and comes back, reality literally reorganizes around him." The room tilted. His vision swam.

"I don't understand." "Neither do I. Not fully." Bishop sat back down, rubbing his face.

"But I understand enough to know why the Cleaner is hunting you. You're not just a meal to him. You're a feast. An endless feast. Every death you carry, every reset you make—you generate more trauma than a normal person accumulates in a lifetime." "So I'm basically an all-you-can-eat buffet." "Worse. You're a buffet that refills itself." D-Lo laughed.

It was not a happy laugh.

"Great. That's just great." He sat down on an overturned crate. "So what do I do? How do I stop being… that?" Bishop shook his head.

"You don't. It's what you are. What you can do is learn to use it. To control it. To make it a weapon instead of a weakness." "How?" Bishop looked at Lexi.

Lexi looked at D-Lo.

"We train you," she said. "Teach you to fight. Teach you to survive. Teach you to use your gift instead of being used by it." "And the Cleaner?" "He's coming." Bishop's voice was grim. "You can feel it, can't you?

That cold spot in your chest. That itch at the back of your skull. He's locked onto you now. He won't stop until he has you." D-Lo could feel it.

He'd been trying to ignore it.

That sense of being watched. That whisper at the edge of his hearing.

"How long?" he asked.

"Days. Maybe hours." Bishop stood again. "But here's the thing—he's never faced someone like you before. Someone who can reset. Someone who can learn from every death. If you're smart, if you're fast, if you're lucky—" Clutch snorted.

"—you might find a way to beat him. Or at least to survive him." D-Lo looked at Kettle. At Clutch. At Lexi and Bishop and the hidden city of ghosts around them.

"Train me," he said. "Teach me everything you know." Bishop smiled.

It was not a comforting smile.

"Be careful what you ask for, boy. The lessons down here are written in blood." "I've already bled plenty." "Then you're halfway there." Bishop turned to Lexi.

"Take him to the proving ground. Let's see what he's made of." Lexi nodded.

"Follow me, Reload." D-Lo stood.

"How do you know that name?" Lexi smiled—that same sharp, transformative smile.

"I know lots of things." She started walking. "First lesson starts now. Keep up." She disappeared into the darkness.

D-Lo followed.

And somewhere, in the tunnels above or below or everywhere at once, the Janitor smiled.

The hunt was getting interesting.

CHAPTER 11

LADY LUCK

Clutch didn't tell her story to just anyone.

But D-Lo had died for her people. Died multiple times trying to save Mrs. Waverly, trying to save Kettle, trying to save strangers who didn't even know his name.

That earned something.

They sat on the roof of Building C, passing a blunt back and forth, the city lights glittering below them like a circuit board someone had dropped and forgotten to pick up.

"You want to know how I got wired," Clutch said. It wasn't a question.

D-Lo exhaled smoke. "Only if you want to tell me." "I don't." She took the blunt from his fingers. "But I'm gonna anyway.

Because you need to understand what we're dealing with. What this life costs." She stared at the horizon.

And began.

"My real name is Chanel Merriweather. Born in Brooklyn, moved to New Babylon when I was six. Single mother, two older brothers, apartment so small we slept in shifts." She smiled, but it didn't reach her eyes.

"Mama worked three jobs. Cleaned offices downtown, did hair on weekends, sold plates out the apartment on Sundays. Woman never stopped moving.

Said if she stopped, she'd fall asleep and never wake up." The blunt crackled as she inhaled.

"My brothers were Marcus and Deon. Marcus was the smart one—got a scholarship to City College, was gonna be the first Merriweather to graduate anything. Deon was the wild one. Streets had him before he hit puberty. Everybody knew he'd either end up rich or dead." "Which one happened?" "Both. Then neither." She passed the blunt back. "Deon started running with the Brass Fangs back when they were just getting started. Before Goldmask took over. They were small-time then—corner boys with ambition but no organization." "What happened?" "What always happens. Deon moved up. Got noticed. Started making real money. Mama didn't ask where it came from. Couldn't afford to ask. We went from scraping to surviving to actually living—new furniture, lights always on, food in the fridge that wasn't just rice and beans." She stared at her hands.

"I was sixteen. Thought I had it all figured out. Deon was handling the family, Marcus was in school, Mama could finally rest. Everything was perfect." "Perfect don't last in the Marrow." "Perfect don't last anywhere." Clutch's voice hardened. "The Fangs got into a war with another crew—the Southside Syndicate. Territory dispute that turned into bodies. Deon was in the middle of it." D-Lo waited.

"They came to our apartment," Clutch said quietly. "Three in the morning. I was asleep in the living room—fell asleep watching TV, hadn't made it to the bedroom. Heard the door get kicked in. Heard the shots." She closed her eyes.

"By the time I got to Mama's room, she was already gone. Two to the chest. Deon was in the hallway, trying to shield Marcus. They shot through him to get to his brother." "Jesus." "Jesus wasn't there that night." Clutch opened her eyes. "I hid in the closet. Heard them searching the apartment, looking for money, drugs, whatever they thought Deon had stashed. Heard them laughing about it.

Laughing while my family bled out ten feet away." D-Lo felt sick.

"How'd you survive?" "Luck." She laughed bitterly. "They checked every room except the one I was in. Walked right past the closet door three times. One of them even put his hand on the handle—then got a phone call and walked away." She took the blunt back.

"I didn't understand it then. Thought God was saving me. Turns out God had nothing to do with it."

"I was sixteen with no family and no home. Went into the system for about five minutes before I realized foster care in New Babylon meant getting passed around until you aged out or got pregnant or both." "So you ran." "I ran." Clutch nodded. "Lived on the streets for two years. Learned how to survive. Learned who to trust—which was nobody. Learned that the only person who was gonna save Chanel Merriweather was Chanel Merriweather." "And then Project Renaissance happened." "And then Project Renaissance happened." She exhaled slowly. "I was at a card game. Underground spot in the basement of a building that doesn't exist anymore. Playing poker with some people who owed me money and some people I owed money to." "High stakes." "Everything's high stakes when you're homeless. I was down three hundred—money I didn't have—and the next card was gonna decide whether I walked out of there or got my ass beat." She pulled out her coin. Turned it over in her fingers.

"The flash hit right when the dealer flipped the river card. Whole room lit up like the sun was inside with us. Lasted maybe three seconds. And when it stopped…" "What happened?" "The card was exactly what I needed. Gave me a flush. I won the pot." She smiled thinly. "Thought it was just luck. Regular luck. The kind everybody gets sometimes." "But it wasn't." "Next hand, same thing. And the next. And the next." Her smile faded.

"People started noticing. Started accusing me of cheating. I swore I wasn't—because I wasn't, not on purpose. But every card I needed just… appeared. Every dice roll went my way. Every coin flip landed how I wanted." "When'd you figure it out?" "When they pulled guns." Clutch's voice went flat. "Four dudes, all pissed, all convinced I was running a scam. One of them put a pistol to my head and pulled the trigger." D-Lo stiffened.

"It jammed." "What?" "The gun jammed. Brand new piece, well-maintained, shouldn't have happened. But it did." She looked at him. "Second guy tried—his jammed too. Third guy's gun fired, but the bullet missed me by an inch. Hit the fourth guy in the shoulder instead." "You're kidding." "I'm not." Clutch pocketed the coin. "In the chaos, I ran. Got out of there before they could figure out what was happening. And that's when I realized—it wasn't luck. It was me." She stood, walking to the edge of the roof.

"I spent the next year testing it. Learning my limits. Figuring out what I could and couldn't do." She turned back to him. "I can bend probability. Make the unlikely happen. Make the impossible... probable.

But it's not free." "What do you mean?" "Every time I push too hard, I feel it. Like I'm burning something inside myself. Using up some resource I can't replace." She rubbed her arms. "And lately... lately I've been burning hotter than ever."

D-Lo joined her at the edge.

Below them, the Marrow was settling into its nighttime rhythm—quieter, darker, more dangerous.

"You think your power is killing you?" "I think everything has a price." Clutch lit a cigarette. "Powers don't come from nowhere. They're tied to something—our trauma, our psychology, whatever the mutagen latched onto. And when we use them, we're spending... something." "That's terrifying." "That's reality." She blew smoke into the wind. "Celestine told me once that luck is just probability debt. Every time I bend the odds in my favor, I'm borrowing from futures that won't happen. And eventually..." "Eventually the debt comes due." "Exactly." They stood in silence for a moment.

"Is that why you're helping me?" D-Lo asked. "Because you're dying anyway?" Clutch laughed—a real laugh this time.

"I'm helping you because you're not an asshole. Because you ran toward Mrs. Waverly instead of away from her. Because you died for people you didn't know and came back and did it again." She turned to face him.

"I've spent eight years looking out for myself. Only myself. And you know what? It's exhausting." "So this is retirement?" "This is me finally having something worth fighting for beyond my own survival." She stubbed out her cigarette. "You're special, Reload.

Not just your power—you. The way you care about people. The way you keep getting up." "I don't have a choice about getting up. That's literally my thing." "You have a choice about what you do when you get up. You could run.

Hide. Use your resets to get rich, get out, live somewhere the Trust would never find you." She poked his chest. "But you don't. You stay.

You fight. You protect people who can't protect themselves." D-Lo didn't know what to say.

"That's rare," Clutch said softly. "In the hood. In the wired world. In any world. That's rare."

"One more thing you should know." D-Lo looked at her.

"The people who killed my family—they're still out there. Still operating." Her jaw tightened. "The Brass Fangs absorbed the Syndicate a few years after. Made peace. Consolidated power. The guys who pulled the triggers are probably lieutenants now." "And Goldmask?" "Goldmask didn't order the hit. That was before his time. But he knows who did. Protects them." Her eyes hardened. "Every time I see that golden mask, I think about my mother's face. About Marcus trying to shield Deon with his body. About the sound of my brothers dying while I hid like a coward." "You weren't a coward. You were sixteen." "I was both." She turned away. "That's the thing about survival, Reload.

Sometimes it doesn't feel like victory. Sometimes it feels like punishment." D-Lo thought about his own survival.

About all the deaths he'd experienced.

About the weight of watching people die while he got to try again.

"I get it," he said quietly.

"I know you do." Clutch looked at him over her shoulder. "That's why I told you."

They climbed down from the roof as the sun started to rise.

The Marrow was waking up—residents heading to early shifts, kids getting ready for school, the endless cycle of survival resuming.

"Clutch." She paused at the stairwell door.

"When this is over—when we deal with the Janitor, the Trust, all of it—I'm gonna help you." D-Lo met her eyes. "Whatever you need.

Whatever it takes." "Help me do what?" "Get justice. For your family. For you." Clutch stared at him for a long moment.

Then she smiled.

A real smile.

The kind that made her look like the sixteen-year-old she'd been before the world broke her.

"Don't make promises you can't keep, Reload." "I don't." She held his gaze.

Saw that he meant it.

Nodded once.

"Then I'll hold you to that." She disappeared into the stairwell.

D-Lo stood there, watching the sun rise over the projects.

Thinking about family.

About loss.

About the debts that never got paid.

And about the people who were worth dying for.

CHAPTER 12

PROBABILITY

The coin was her father's.

A silver dollar from 1921—worn smooth on one side, the eagle barely visible on the other. He'd carried it for thirty years before the night the Trust came for him. Before the night everything changed.

Clutch turned it over in her fingers now, feeling the familiar weight, the cool metal, the grooves where his thumb had rubbed away the detail.

"You're doing that thing again," Kettle said from across the room.

"What thing?" "The thing where you stare at the coin and go somewhere else." "I'm not going anywhere." But she was. She always was, when she held this particular piece of metal. "Just thinking." "About what?" Clutch looked at him—this big, gentle man who could melt steel with his hands but was afraid of hurting anyone. Looked at D-Lo, asleep on a cot nearby, exhausted from another training session with Celestine.

Looked at the worn walls of the Underline, the makeshift home they'd built in the bones of the city.

"About probability," she said finally. "And how it never works the way you expect."

Her name wasn't always Clutch.

Once, a long time ago, in a life that felt like it belonged to someone else, she'd been Clara Johnson.

Clara Johnson, age thirteen, whose father was a math professor at City College and whose mother made the best sweet potato pie in three boroughs. Clara Johnson, who got straight A's and played violin in the school orchestra and had never broken a rule in her life.

Clara Johnson, who watched her father die on a Tuesday afternoon because she couldn't control what she didn't understand.

"It's called probability manipulation," her father explained.

They were in his study—the small room at the back of their apartment, filled with books and chalkboards and the smell of pipe tobacco. He'd called her in after dinner, his face serious in a way that made her stomach clench.

"Some people can influence outcomes. Push the odds in their favor or against their enemies." He pulled out the silver dollar, turned it over in his fingers. "I've had it since I was about your age. Never told your mother. Never told anyone." "Why are you telling me?" "Because you have it too." He met her eyes. "The broken light bulb at school last week. The way that car swerved at the last second when you were crossing the street. The lottery ticket that won just enough to cover our rent when we were short." Clara's heart was racing.

"I didn't mean to—" "I know. You don't know what you're doing yet. Neither did I, at first." He handed her the coin. "But you need to learn. Before someone notices.

Before the Trust comes looking." "The Trust?" Her father's face went dark.

"An organization. Very old. Very powerful. They track people like us.

Collect us." He paused. "Sometimes they just watch. Sometimes they take.

I've been hiding for thirty years, Clara. Living small, staying quiet, never using my gift where anyone might see." "But—" "But you're young. Your power is growing. And they have ways of detecting what we do." He gripped her hands. "I'm going to teach you.

How to control it. How to hide it. How to survive." Clara looked at the coin in her palm.

She could feel it now—the weight of possibility pressing against her skin. The sense that reality was flexible, malleable, waiting for her to push.

"Okay," she said. "Teach me."

The lessons were strange.

Not math or science, though her father used both to explain. More like meditation. More like learning to feel the shape of the universe.

"Everything is probability," he said. "The coin lands heads or tails.

The bus arrives on time or late. The rain falls or doesn't fall. Most people experience these as random. But we can feel the weight of each outcome. Push against it. Tip the scales." "How?" "Start small. This coin." He flipped it in the air. "Before it lands, feel both possibilities. Heads is here—" he pointed left "—and tails is here." He pointed right. "Now. Make it land heads." Clara focused.

She could feel what he meant—two futures, balanced on a knife's edge.

She pushed, gently, toward heads.

The coin landed.

Tails.

"Try again." She tried.

And again.

And again.

By the end of the first week, she could influence the coin about sixty percent of the time. By the end of the first month, ninety.

By the end of the third month, she could make a deck of cards cut exactly where she wanted, make the subway arrive within thirty seconds of when she needed it, make the rain pause just long enough for her to reach cover.

"You're a natural," her father said, pride in his voice. "Stronger than I was at your age." "Is that good?" His expression flickered.

"It's… noticeable. You need to be careful. Pull back your power when you're in public. Only use it when absolutely necessary." He gripped her shoulder. "Promise me, Clara. Promise you'll be careful." "I promise." But she was thirteen.

And thirteen-year-olds don't always keep their promises.

The day the Trust came, it was raining.

Clara was walking home from school, umbrella forgotten at her desk. The rain was coming down hard—the kind of cold, driving rain that soaked through your clothes in seconds.

She pushed without thinking.

Just a little nudge. A suggestion to the universe that maybe the rain should let up, just for her, just for these few blocks.

The rain stopped.

Not slowed—stopped. A perfect circle of dry air around her, drops falling everywhere else but refusing to touch her.

Clara walked through the storm like a ghost, untouched by the water that drenched everyone else.

She didn't notice the black SUV.

Didn't notice the man watching from the driver's seat, speaking into a radio.

Didn't notice that she'd just done something impossible, visible, trackable.

Three hours later, they came for her father.

"CLARA! HIDE!" Her father's voice, sharp with terror, cutting through the sound of the front door being kicked in.

She was in the kitchen, doing homework. She didn't think—she moved.

Slid into the pantry, behind the sacks of rice and flour, pressing herself against the wall.

Voices. Boots. The sound of furniture being overturned.

"Professor Johnson." A man's voice, calm and professional. "We need to discuss your daughter." "She's not here." "We both know that's not true. Our sensors detected a significant probability event in this neighborhood three hours ago. Someone manipulated local weather patterns—isolated atmospheric control, very impressive. Only two registered manipulators in the city have that kind of range, and the other is contained." "I don't know what you're—" A sound. Wet. Terrible.

Her father screamed.

"Please, Professor. We don't want to hurt you. We just want to help your daughter. Untrained manipulators are dangerous—to themselves and others. We can teach her. Protect her. Help her understand her gift." "You'll take her. Break her. Turn her into another weapon." "We'll save her. Like we saved you, thirty years ago. Before you ran." A pause. "Yes, we know who you are. Isaac Johnson, formerly Asset 117, classification Probability-4. You escaped during the '93 facility fire.

We've been looking for you ever since." Clara's heart was pounding so hard she was sure they could hear it.

Daddy was one of them. They had him. He escaped.

"Where is she?" the man asked.

"I'll never tell you." Another sound. Worse than before.

Her father stopped screaming.

The silence was somehow more terrible.

"Search the apartment," the man said. "She's here somewhere." Footsteps.

Coming toward the kitchen.

Clara pressed herself deeper into the shadows, pulled her luck in tight, begged the universe to make her invisible— The pantry door opened.

A flashlight swept across the shelves.

Please don't see me please don't see me please— The beam passed over her face.

The agent paused.

Looked directly at her.

And... moved on.

"Kitchen's clear," he reported.

The door closed.

Clara didn't breathe for a very long time.

She found her father's body in the living room.

They'd left him there—a message, maybe, or just carelessness. His eyes were open, staring at the ceiling. The silver dollar was still clutched in his hand.

Clara took it.

Said goodbye in a voice that didn't sound like hers.

And left through the fire escape before the Trust could return.

She was thirteen years old, alone in New Babylon, with nothing but her father's coin and a power she barely understood.

She should have died a hundred times.

But probability is a funny thing.

Doors opened when she needed them. Opportunities appeared at just the right moments. Danger swerved around her like water around a stone.

She learned to survive.
Then to thrive.
Then to fight.

"Clutch." She blinked, returning to the present.

D-Lo was awake, looking at her from his cot.

"You okay?" he asked.

"Yeah. Just... remembering." He sat up slowly, joints creaking. The training with Celestine was taking a toll.

"The coin?" She looked down at the silver dollar in her palm.

"My father's. He taught me everything I know." She paused. "The Trust killed him. Looking for me." D-Lo was quiet for a moment.

"I'm sorry." "It was a long time ago. I was thirteen." She pocketed the coin.

"I'm thirty-one now. I've been running ever since." "That's why you help people like us. Other wired." "That's part of it." She looked at him. "The other part is that I'm tired of running. Tired of hiding. Tired of watching them take everything from people who never did anything except exist." "So you fight." "So I fight." She stood, stretched. "You're getting stronger, you know.

Celestine says you're learning faster than anyone she's trained." "Doesn't feel like it." "It never does. Until the moment it matters." She walked toward the door. "Get some rest. Tomorrow's going to be hard." "They're all hard." "Yeah." She paused at the threshold, looked back. "But we're harder.

That's the only edge we need." D-Lo watched her go.

Then he lay back down, staring at the ceiling, thinking about all the ways probability could bend.

And somewhere in the darkness, Clutch turned her father's coin over and over and over, feeling the weight of possibility, preparing for whatever came next.

INTERLUDE — THE BRIEFING

TRUST HEADQUARTERS — CONFERENCE ROOM A

"Gentlemen, we have a problem." Director Halden stood at the head of the table, holographic displays floating behind him. Twelve faces stared back—the Trust's senior leadership, men and women who'd dedicated their lives to containing threats most people didn't know existed.

"The Anchor situation has escalated." He waved a hand, and the display changed—a map of New Babylon with red dots clustered in the Marrow Projects.

"Darius Graves has made contact with the Underline. He's training with them. Learning to control his power." "Then we move now," General Morrison said. "Full assault. Eliminate the threat before it grows." "We tried that. We lost eleven operatives." Halden's voice was cold.

"The subject has reached Stage Two ahead of schedule. He can see temporal threads now. Can anticipate our movements before we make them." Silence around the table.

"What are our options?" Senator Walsh asked.

"Limited. We can attempt containment—surround the Underline, wait for them to make a mistake. But that risks civilian casualties and media attention." "Then we use the Conductor." Halden's jaw tightened.

"The Conductor is our last resort. If we deploy him prematurely and Graves finds a way to neutralize or corrupt him—" "Then we lose our only reliable weapon against a fully manifested Anchor." Dr. Yates finished the thought. "I understand the hesitation.

But we may not have a choice." Halden looked at the display.

At the red dots clustered underground.

At the single, pulsing point that represented Darius Graves.

"I'll make the call when I'm ready. Not before." He dismissed the holograms. "In the meantime, I want increased surveillance. I want every exit from the Underline covered. And I want options—plural—for when we do move." "And the subject's family?" "The sister is leverage. Find her. Contain her. But gently." Halden's voice softened slightly. "We're not monsters. We're just people doing a terrible job because someone has to." The meeting ended.

But the problem remained.

CHAPTER 13

THE DEEP

There were parts of the Underline even Lexi didn't go.

D-Lo was about to find out why.

"This is everything we've charted." Lexi spread the map across the table—hand-drawn, coffee-stained, covered in symbols and warnings. The Underline stretched across it like a web, tunnels branching and connecting in patterns that made D-Lo's head hurt.

"That's a lot of tunnels." "Old subway system. Collapsed in the 1970s. They built the new lines above it but never bothered to fill in the old ones." She traced a section near the center. "This is our territory. The Ghosts control about eight square miles." "And the rest?" Lexi's finger moved to the edges of the map.

"Here—" She pointed to a section marked with red. "—the Crawlers." Mutants. Trust experiments that escaped during the Renaissance flash.

They don't attack us as long as we stay out of their territory." "And here?" D-Lo pointed to a section marked with black.

"The Silence." Lexi's voice dropped. "We don't go there." "Why not?" "Because nobody who goes there comes back."

She took him deeper than he'd ever been.

Past the Ghost settlements. Past the training grounds. Past the scavenged infrastructure that kept them alive.

Into the old tunnels.

"Watch your step," Lexi said. "The floor's unstable in places." D-Lo watched his step. The ground was cracked, buckled, twisted by decades of neglect and whatever geological forces were doing weird things beneath the city.

"What's down here?" "History." Lexi's flashlight played across the walls. "Look." Graffiti—but not the kind D-Lo knew from the streets. These were older. Stranger. Symbols that didn't belong to any gang he recognized.

"What is that?" "The people who lived down here before Project Renaissance. Before the Ghosts. Before everything." Lexi touched one of the symbols—a spiral with an eye at the center. "They called themselves the Forgotten.

Homeless, mostly. People the city pushed underground and tried to pretend didn't exist." "What happened to them?" "Same thing that happens to everyone the Trust doesn't like. Some were taken. Some were experimented on. Some just... vanished." She moved on.

"But they left marks. Warnings. Maps to safe places and warnings about dangerous ones." D-Lo studied the symbols as they walked.

A language of survival, written in the dark.

They heard them before they saw them.

Sounds that weren't quite human. Scraping, clicking, wet noises that made D-Lo's skin crawl.

"Stay close," Lexi whispered. "And don't run. Running triggers their hunting instinct." "Their what?" A shape emerged from the darkness.

It had been human once. Maybe. The basic form was still there—two arms, two legs, a head. But everything else was wrong. The skin was grey and translucent, revealing veins that pulsed with something that wasn't blood. The eyes were too large, adapted for darkness. The fingers ended in claws.

And it wasn't alone.

More shapes emerged. A dozen. Two dozen. Surrounding them in the tunnel.

"Lexi Ghost," one of them spoke. Its voice was a rasp, like sandpaper on concrete. "You come far. Too far." "We're just passing through, Scuttle. No disrespect intended." The creature—Scuttle—tilted its head. The movement was jerky, insectile.

"This one new." It pointed at D-Lo. "This one... different. We feel him.

Reality bends." D-Lo's heart hammered.

"He's with me," Lexi said. "Under my protection." "Your protection means nothing in the deep places. Here, we are law." Scuttle moved closer. D-Lo could smell it now—decay and chemicals and something older. "Give him to us. We study. We learn. We become." "He's not for study." "Then payment. Something of value. Something that bleeds." Lexi's hand moved to her knife.

"How about you let us pass and I don't tell the Ghosts to start dropping poison into your water supply?" Silence.

The Crawlers shifted, clicked, communicated in ways D-Lo couldn't understand.

Then Scuttle laughed.

It was a terrible sound.

"Lexi Ghost has teeth. Good. We remember." It stepped back. "Pass.

But next time, bring offering. Or don't come back." The Crawlers melted into the darkness.

D-Lo didn't breathe until they were gone.

They didn't go much further.

But Lexi showed him the edge.

A tunnel, larger than the others, stretching into absolute darkness. No sound came from it. No echo. No indication that it led anywhere at all.

"The Silence," Lexi said. "We lost six Ghosts exploring it. Sent a team of our best scouts. They went in. They never came out." "What's in there?" "Nobody knows. The old maps call it 'the Wound.' Say something happened here before the city was built. Something that tore a hole in..." She trailed off. "I don't know. Reality? The world? Whatever you call the thing that keeps everything normal." D-Lo stared into the darkness.

For a moment—just a moment—he thought he saw something.

Threads.

Hundreds of them.

All leading into the tunnel.

All disappearing into the black.

"We should go," he said.

"Yeah." Lexi turned away. "We really should."

On the way back, they passed through sections of the Underline D-Lo hadn't seen before.

Not Ghost territory. Something else.

People. Dozens of them. Living in carved-out spaces along the tunnels.

Cooking over makeshift fires. Hanging laundry on lines strung between pipes. Children playing in the dim light.

"Who are they?" "Refugees. People the Trust drove underground. Wired who can't pass as normal. Families who lost everything in the raids." Lexi nodded to an old woman stirring a pot. "Mrs. Chen. Used to run a restaurant in District Eight. Her grandson manifested fire powers. Trust burned the restaurant down trying to capture him." "Did they get him?" "We got there first." Lexi smiled slightly. "He's one of us now.

Twelve years old. Calls himself Ember." They walked through the settlement, and D-Lo saw more stories everywhere he looked.

A man with scales instead of skin, teaching younger kids to read.

A woman whose hair moved like it was alive, braiding a little girl's cornrows.

A teenager with no visible power, but a prosthetic leg—Trust-made, stolen in a raid, repurposed for someone who needed it.

"There are hundreds of people down here," D-Lo said.

"Thousands. Across the whole Underline." Lexi's voice was matter-of-fact. "The Trust thinks they've contained the wired threat.

They've just pushed it underground. Literally." "Why don't they know about this?" "Because we're careful. Because we stay hidden. Because..." She paused.

"Because the people up there don't want to know. It's easier to pretend we don't exist."

Before they left the settlement, a little girl ran up to them.

Couldn't have been older than six. Dark skin, bright eyes, a smile that didn't belong in a place like this.

"You're Reload," she said. "The one who comes back." D-Lo blinked.

"How do you know that?" "Everybody knows. You're gonna save us." She held up a drawing—crayon on scrap paper. It showed a figure in a hoodie surrounded by glowing lines. "See? That's you. Fighting the bad men." D-Lo looked at the drawing.

At the hope in this little girl's eyes.

At the weight she was putting on his shoulders without even knowing it.

"What's your name?" "Maya." He took the drawing.

Folded it carefully.

Put it in his pocket.

"Thank you, Maya. I'll keep this with me." "Promise you'll save us?" He looked at Lexi.

At the settlement.

At the thousands of people counting on him without even knowing it.

"I promise." Maya grinned and ran back to her mother.

Lexi watched her go.

"You shouldn't make promises you can't keep." "I know." D-Lo touched the drawing in his pocket. "But what else am I supposed to do? Tell a six-year-old nobody's coming to save her?" "Some people would." "I'm not some people." Lexi looked at him.

Something softened in her expression.

"No," she said quietly. "You're not." They headed back toward Ghost territory.

Carrying the weight of thousands with every step.

CHAPTER 14

THE SISTER

Kimi Graves was thirteen years old and tired of being protected.

She understood why D-Lo did it. Understood the fear behind every locked door, every curfew, every "stay inside" that came out of his mouth like a reflex. Their parents were gone—Dad to prison when she was six, Mom to the needle when she was nine—and D-Lo had spent the last four years making sure she didn't end up gone too.

She loved him for it.

She also kind of hated him for it.

Because being protected meant being kept in the dark. Meant watching her brother come home with blood on his clothes and lies on his lips. Meant pretending she didn't hear him crying in the bathroom at 3 AM, didn't see the bruises that appeared and disappeared like magic, didn't notice that something fundamental had changed in him since that night six months ago when the sky turned green.

She wasn't stupid.

She knew D-Lo was wired.

She just didn't know what his power was yet.

The night of the raid, D-Lo wasn't home.

He'd left three hours ago with some excuse about meeting friends—lies, always lies—and Kimi had done what she always did. Homework. TV.

Pretended everything was normal while her brother went off to do whatever dangerous shit he was doing.

She was watching a reality show—some nonsense about rich women fighting over nothing—when she heard the first scream.

Not a fight scream. Not a "somebody stole my stuff" scream.

A "something terrible is happening" scream.

Kimi was at the window before she made the conscious decision to move.

Black vans in the courtyard. Men in tactical gear pouring out of them.

Not cops—she knew cops—these were something else. Something worse.

They moved like soldiers, like hunters, kicking in doors on the first floor, dragging people out into the night.

Trust.

She'd heard the name whispered in hallways and corner stores. The boogeyman that came for people who were different. The government agency that didn't officially exist but somehow had unlimited resources and zero accountability.

They were here.

In her building.

Coming up.

Kimi's first instinct was to hide.

The closet. Under the bed. Somewhere small and dark where they wouldn't think to look.

That's what D-Lo would want her to do.

That's what a good little sister would do.

But then she heard Mrs. Patterson next door—seventy-two years old, diabetic, half-blind without her glasses—screaming for help. And she heard the Trust officers laughing about it. Actually laughing, like terrorizing an old woman was the funniest thing they'd seen all week.

Something changed in Kimi's chest.

Not fear.

Rage.

She grabbed her phone and started recording.

The hallway was chaos.

Doors hanging off hinges. Neighbors being zip-tied and dragged toward the stairs. A kid from the fourth floor—couldn't be older than eight—crying in the corner while officers stepped around him like he was furniture.

Kimi pressed herself against the wall, phone held low, recording everything.

Mrs. Patterson's door was open. Inside, two officers were tossing the apartment, looking for something. Looking for someone.

"Where is he?" one of them demanded. "Where's your grandson?" "I don't know what you're talking about—" "Marcus Patterson. Age nineteen. Manifested telekinetic abilities three weeks ago. We have him on camera." The officer grabbed Mrs. Patterson's arm. "Tell us where he's hiding or we take you instead." "I don't know! I swear I don't know!" The officer raised his hand.

Kimi didn't think.

She stepped into the doorway.

"HEY!" Both officers turned.

Kimi held up her phone. The red recording light was visible.

"I'm livestreaming this to six different platforms right now. My brother has thirty thousand followers. You want to explain to the internet why you're about to hit a seventy-year-old woman?" It was a lie.

D-Lo didn't have thirty thousand followers. The phone wasn't livestreaming anything. But she said it with the same confidence Melo used when he was spinning his cons—the confidence that made people believe because doubting felt too risky.

The officers hesitated.

"Put the phone down," one said.

"Make me." Kimi didn't move. "I've already got your faces. Badge numbers. Everything. You touch me, you touch her, this goes viral in ten seconds. How's that gonna look for your secret little operation?" The officers exchanged glances.

"She's bluffing." "You want to bet your career on that?" Kimi raised the phone higher.

"I'll wait." Silence.

Then, from downstairs, a voice on a radio: "All units, primary target located. Building K, third floor. Converge immediately." The officers looked at Mrs. Patterson. At Kimi. At the phone.

"This isn't over," one said.

They left.

Mrs. Patterson was shaking.

Kimi helped her to a chair, found her glasses, made her drink some water. The old woman's hands trembled so badly she could barely hold the cup.

"Thank you," Mrs. Patterson whispered. "Child, thank you." "Don't thank me yet." Kimi moved to the window. The Trust vans were pulling out, heading toward Building K. "They'll be back. They always come back." "How do you know that?" Kimi thought about D-Lo. About the bruises. About the lies.

"Because whatever they're hunting, it's not going away. And they don't stop until they get what they want." Mrs. Patterson was quiet for a moment.

"Your brother. He's one of them, isn't he? One of the special ones?" Kimi didn't answer.

"I'm not going to tell anyone." Mrs. Patterson took her hand. "But you should know—Marcus came to see me last week. Said he was going somewhere safe. Somewhere underground." Her eyes met Kimi's. "If your brother needs a place like that... there are people who help. People who hide the special ones. Marcus called them Ghosts." Kimi filed that away.

Ghosts.

Underground.

She'd find out more later.

When D-Lo came home at 2 AM, Kimi was sitting on the couch, waiting.

He froze in the doorway.

"You're supposed to be asleep." "And you're supposed to tell me the truth." She didn't move. "The Trust raided buildings F through M tonight. I was here. Where were you?" D-Lo's face went through several emotions—fear, guilt, relief, more guilt.

"Kimi—" "Don't." She stood up. "Don't lie to me again. I'm not a little kid, D.

125

I'm not some fragile thing you have to protect from the world. I live in this world. I see what happens. I know something's going on with you, and I'm tired of being kept in the dark." Silence.

D-Lo looked at her—really looked at her—and for the first time, Kimi saw him seeing her. Not as a responsibility. Not as a burden to carry.

As a person.

"If I tell you," he said slowly, "you can't untell yourself. You'll be in it. Part of it. And it's dangerous, Kimi. More dangerous than you know." "I'm already in it. I've been in it since the night the sky turned green." She crossed her arms. "So stop treating me like a liability and start treating me like family. Because that's what I am. And family doesn't keep secrets like this." D-Lo was quiet for a long moment.

Then he sat down on the couch.

Patted the seat next to him.

"Okay," he said. "Okay. I'll tell you everything. But you have to promise me—whatever happens, whatever you hear—you don't do anything stupid. You don't try to help. You stay safe." Kimi sat.

"I promise," she said.

Another lie.

But this one felt right.

He told her everything.

The deaths. The resets. The Trust. The Janitor. The Ghosts and the Underline and the war being fought in the shadows of New Babylon.

Kimi listened without interrupting.

When he finished, the sun was coming up.

"So you can't die," she said.

"I can die. I just come back." "And you've been using that to… what? Fight the government? Save people?" "Try to." D-Lo rubbed his eyes. "I'm not very good at it yet." Kimi was quiet for a moment.

Then: "Mrs. Patterson's grandson is wired. Telekinetic. The Trust came for him tonight, but he wasn't there. She said he went somewhere called the Ghosts." D-Lo's head snapped up.

"How do you know that?" "Because I talked to her. Because I stopped two Trust officers from beating her by pretending I was livestreaming them." She smiled thinly.

"I'm not just someone you protect, D. I can help. I can be useful. You just have to let me." D-Lo stared at her.

For a long moment, she thought he was going to yell. Going to send her to her room. Going to do what he always did—push her away to keep her safe.

Instead, he laughed.

A tired, broken, genuine laugh.

"You're thirteen." "And you're twenty-two. What's your point?" "My point is..." He shook his head. "My point is you're the bravest person I know. And I'm sorry I didn't see it before." Kimi felt something warm bloom in her chest.

"Does this mean you'll stop lying to me?" "I'll try." He pulled her into a hug. "But you have to promise—really promise—that you won't put yourself in danger. Not for me. Not for anyone." She hugged him back.

"I promise," she said again.

And this time, she almost meant it.

The sirens started at 3 AM.

D-Lo was in the Underline, three days into training that made his bones ache, when Murmur came running.

"Trust. They're hitting the Marrow. Building H." Building H. Where Mrs. Patterson lived. Where seventeen wired kids had been hiding in the basement, waiting for the Ghosts to evacuate them.

D-Lo was moving before Murmur finished.

"You're not ready," Lexi called after him. "D-Lo, you can barely hold a thread for three seconds—" "Then I'll hold it for three seconds." He ran.

The surface was chaos.

Trust vehicles blocked every exit from Building H. Officers in tactical gear dragged people into the street—old women in bathrobes, kids in pajamas, anyone who might be hiding something. Searchlights cut through the dark like accusing fingers.

D-Lo found a fire escape. Climbed.

The basement access was through apartment 2B—Mrs. Patterson's place.

He'd been there a hundred times as a kid, eating her oatmeal cookies, listening to stories about the neighborhood before the projects went bad.

Her door was open.

Splintered.

Inside, Trust officers were tearing apart her living room. One had her pinned against the wall, arm twisted behind her back.

"Where are they? The wired ones?" "I don't know what you're talking about—" He hit her. Open palm, hard enough to snap her head sideways.

D-Lo saw red.

He didn't remember deciding to move.

One second he was in the doorway. The next, the officer who'd hit Mrs.

Patterson was on the ground, and D-Lo's fist was throbbing.

"What the—" The second officer raised his weapon.

D-Lo reached for the threads.

They were there—faint, flickering, barely visible. He grabbed at the one where the bullet missed.

It slipped through his fingers like water.

The gun fired.

Pain exploded in his shoulder.

He went down.

"Got a live one! Wired—he was reaching for something!" Boots. Hands. Someone zip-tying his wrists behind his back while blood soaked through his shirt.

Mrs. Patterson was screaming. "He's just a boy! He's just a boy from the neighborhood!" "Ma'am, step back or you're coming too." D-Lo's vision was swimming. The threads were everywhere now—death approaching, futures branching, possibilities he couldn't grab.

He was going to die here.

Reset.

Wake up in his apartment.

And Mrs. Patterson would still be arrested. The kids in the basement would still be found. Everyone he'd tried to save would be gone.

Unless— He reached again. Not for survival. For something smaller.

The thread where the officer's radio crackled. Where backup was needed three blocks away. Where attention shifted, just for a moment.

He brushed it.

Barely.

The radio squawked: "All units, shots fired on Miller Street. Possible wired suspect fleeing north—" The officers exchanged looks.

"Stay with this one. I'll check it out." One left. One remained.

Better odds.

D-Lo reset.

The bullet wound vanished. He was back in the doorway, three seconds before he'd charged in.

This time, he didn't charge.

He watched. Counted. Two officers. One facing away.

He moved silent. Grabbed the radio off the distracted one's belt.

Pressed transmit.

"Shots fired, Miller Street! Need backup!" Confusion. Movement. The officer by Mrs. Patterson turned toward the door.

D-Lo hit him from behind. Once, twice. The man went down.

The second officer spun, drawing his weapon— Mrs. Patterson swung a cast-iron skillet into the back of his head.

He dropped.

Silence.

"Go," Mrs. Patterson said. Her hands were shaking, but her voice was steel. "The children are behind the water heater. There's a tunnel—Darius, go NOW." He went.

The basement was exactly as he remembered—concrete walls, exposed pipes, the smell of mold and fear.

Seventeen kids huddled behind the ancient water heater. Ages eight to fifteen. All of them wired. All of them terrified.

"D-Lo?" A girl he recognized—Tamika, twelve, could make plants grow.

"Is it safe?" "No. But we're leaving anyway." The tunnel was old—prohibition-era, Mrs. Patterson had told him once, used for running bootleg liquor. It connected to the sewer system, which connected to the Underline.

He led them into the dark.

They emerged in Ghost territory two hours later.

Seventeen kids. All alive. All safe.

Lexi was waiting.

Her face was unreadable as D-Lo stumbled out of the tunnel, shoulder aching from phantom pain, seventeen exhausted children trailing behind him.

"You were gone four hours." "I got them out." "You almost died. Murmur heard it—heard your mind go quiet." "But I didn't." "But you COULD have." She grabbed his arm, pulled him close. Her eyes were furious. Terrified. "You can't save everyone, D-Lo. Not yet. Not like this." "I saved seventeen." "And if you'd died? If the reset hadn't worked? If the Trust had captured you?" Her grip tightened. "You're not just risking yourself.

You're risking everything we're building." He wanted to argue.

Wanted to say it was worth it.

But he looked at the kids—scared, exhausted, alive—and knew she was right.

He'd gotten lucky.

Lucky wasn't a strategy.

"Teach me," he said. "Teach me how to do it better." Lexi's expression softened. Just slightly.

"That's what I've been trying to do. If you'd actually listen." "I'm listening now." She studied him for a long moment.

Then nodded.

"We start tomorrow. Real training. No shortcuts, no hero bullshit. You learn to control what you have before you try to use it." "And if the Trust comes back? If someone else needs help?" "Then you do what soldiers do." Her voice was hard. "You make the call. Save who you can. Accept who you can't." D-Lo looked at the seventeen kids being led to safety.

Thought about Mrs. Patterson, alone in her ruined apartment.

Thought about all the people he couldn't reach.

"I don't know if I can do that." "Then learn." Lexi turned away. "Because the alternative is dying for nothing. And I've buried enough people who died for nothing." She walked into the Underline.

D-Lo followed.
The lesson had cost him.
But maybe that was the point.

CHAPTER 15

THE DEVIL'S OFFER

They found D-Lo three days after the boiler room.

Not the Trust. Not the Janitor.

Someone worse.

The black Escalade pulled up beside him on Martin Luther King Boulevard, smooth and quiet as a shark. D-Lo was carrying groceries—bread, eggs, milk. Kimi had made a list. He was trying to be a good brother.

The window slid down.

"D-Lo Graves. Get in." Three men. Gold chains, gold rings, gold teeth. The uniform of the Brass Fangs.

"I'm good." "Your sister's at the window right now. Third floor, Building C. Blue hoodie. Eating cereal." The speaker's scar caught the light. "We're just making sure you understand what's at stake." Dread coiled in his gut.

He got in.

The warehouse was in District Nine, industrial, abandoned—except it wasn't abandoned at all. Inside, someone had built a throne room.

Leather couches, glass tables, bottles of liquor that cost more than D-Lo's rent.

And sitting at the center: a man in a golden mask.

Goldmask.

D-Lo had heard the name. Everyone in New Babylon had heard the name. The man who'd unified the Brass Fangs, crushed their rivals, built an empire that operated in the spaces between legal and illegal.

"Sit." Goldmask's voice was cultured. Wrong for the setting.

"Please." D-Lo sat. Kept the groceries on his lap like armor.

"I'll be direct," Goldmask said. "You're wired. You have an ability that fascinates me. And I'd like to discuss opportunities." "You want to recruit me." "I want to make you rich." The mask tilted. "There's a difference."

"Your power," Goldmask continued, "is worth billions. Advance knowledge of outcomes. Perfect information. You could predict the future by living it, dying, and trying again." "That's not—" "I know exactly how it works." Goldmask stood, walked to a window overlooking the empty factory floor. "Mrs. Waverly. The boiler room.

Every death you've experienced. Information is my business, D-Lo. The Trust isn't the only organization with eyes in the Marrow." He turned back.

"Work for me. Use your gift to give me an edge. In exchange—apartment uptown, private school for Kimi, money, protection. Everything you've ever wanted." The weight of the offer pressed down— A way out.

A real life for his sister.

All he had to do was sell himself.

"And if I say no?" "Then you walk out. No threats, no retaliation. I'm a businessman, not a monster." Goldmask paused. "But the Trust will keep hunting you. The Janitor will keep feeding. And the Marrow will keep being what it is." D-Lo thought about Kimi.

About Clutch and Kettle.

About the Ghosts in the tunnels.

"I appreciate the offer," he said. "But I'm gonna pass." Silence.

The bodyguards shifted. Hands toward weapons.

Goldmask raised a finger. They stopped.

"May I ask why?" "Because my power isn't for sale. And because people are counting on me." "Admirably naive." "Maybe." D-Lo stood. "But it's who I am." He walked toward the door.

Expecting a bullet.

Instead, Goldmask laughed.

"I like you, D-Lo Graves." D-Lo paused.

"You're loyal. Principled. Stupid, but principled." Goldmask's voice carried something almost like warmth. "Those are rare qualities." "This the part where you threaten my family?" "No. This is the part where I give you something." Goldmask snapped his fingers.

A teenager emerged from the shadows—maybe sixteen, hoodie pulled up, eyes that had seen too much. He carried a tablet.

"This is Glitch. He's wired—sees through electronic systems.

Cameras, networks, security feeds. He's been watching the Trust for me." Glitch handed D-Lo the tablet.

On the screen: blueprints. Security rotations. Transport schedules. A facility labeled THE VAULT.

"What is this?" "The Trust's detention center. Where they take wired people who get captured." Goldmask returned to his throne. "Your friend Melo is there.

Along with about two hundred others." D-Lo's hands tightened on the tablet.

"Why are you giving me this?" "Because you said no." Goldmask steepled his fingers. "That interests me. Most people take the easy path. You chose the hard one. I want to see where it leads." "There's a catch." "There's always a catch. But not today." The mask tilted. "Consider this an investment. The Trust is my enemy too—they're bad for business, and they've taken people I'd rather have working for me. If you can hurt them, we both benefit." D-Lo stared at the blueprints.

The information was real. He could feel it.

But nothing from Goldmask came free.

"When does the debt come due?" "When I decide." Goldmask's smile was audible. "But not for a long time.

Go save your friend, D-Lo. Build your little revolution. And when the Trust breaks you—when you're standing in the ashes of everything you tried to protect—come find me." He waved a hand.

"Dismissed."

The Escalade dropped D-Lo outside Building C.

Glitch was in the passenger seat. He spoke before D-Lo could exit: "The Vault runs skeleton crew between 2 and 4 AM. Shift change at 3.

That's your window." "Why are you helping me?" Glitch's eyes were flat. Empty. "Because Goldmask owns me. And because the Trust killed my sister." "I'm sorry." "Don't be sorry. Be effective." Glitch handed him a burner phone.

"This has my contact. When you're ready to move on the Vault, text me. I'll kill their cameras for ninety seconds." "What do you get out of it?" "I get to watch them burn." The first emotion D-Lo had seen—cold, bitter hatred. "That's enough." The SUV pulled away.

D-Lo stood on the sidewalk, tablet in one hand, burner phone in the other.

He'd turned down the devil's offer.

But he'd taken his gift.

And he had no idea what that would cost him.

Upstairs, Kimi was at the window.

"Where WERE you?" "Long story." "Those guys in the black truck—" "I handled it." She stared at him. Saw something in his face that made her go quiet.

"D-Lo. What's going on?" He looked at the tablet. At the blueprints of the Vault. At the location where Melo and hundreds of others were being held.

"I found where they took Melo." "Who told you?" "Someone who thinks he owns me now." D-Lo set down the groceries.

"He's wrong. But he doesn't know that yet." Kimi didn't ask more questions.

She'd learned when not to push.

"So what do we do?" D-Lo thought about Clutch. About Kettle. About Lexi and the Ghosts.

About building an army.

About tearing down a prison.

"We plan."

CHAPTER 16

THREE KINGS

The meeting happened at midnight.

Neutral ground—an abandoned warehouse in the no-man's-land between Trust territory and Ghost territory. The kind of place where people came to make deals they couldn't make anywhere else.

Or to die.

D-Lo stood in the center of the warehouse, flanked by Lexi and Clutch.

Behind them, in the shadows, Kettle waited with his skin already warming, ready to turn the whole building into an inferno if things went wrong.

They weren't alone.

THE FIRST KING

Marcus Cole—Goldmask—entered through the east door.

He was everything the rumors said: tall, broad, dressed in a suit that cost more than most people made in a year. His mask was exactly what D-Lo had expected—gold, covering the upper half of his face, leaving only his jaw and mouth visible.

His mouth was smiling.

It wasn't a friendly smile.

"The Anchor." Goldmask's voice was deep, cultured. The voice of someone who'd clawed their way up from nothing and wanted everyone to know it.

"I've heard a lot about you." "Likewise." "Good things, I hope." "Depends on your definition of good." Goldmask laughed. His entourage—six men in matching suits, all visibly armed—spread out behind him.

"I like you already. Direct. Honest." He stopped ten feet away. "Do you know why I asked for this meeting?" "I've got guesses." "Share them." D-Lo studied the crime lord's face—what he could see of it.

"You're worried. The Trust is cracking down on wired activity, which means your operations are getting squeezed. You need allies. Or at least, you need to know if the Ghosts are allies or enemies." Goldmask's smile widened.

"Very good. And what's your answer?" "Neither. We're not interested in your business. We don't want your territory. We just want to survive." "Survival." Goldmask turned the word over like he was tasting it.

"Survival requires resources. Protection. Things I can provide." "In exchange for what?" "Your power. Your... unique abilities." The smile turned sharp.

"Imagine what someone who can reset time could do for my organization. The heists we could pull. The mistakes we could undo. The enemies we could eliminate." "I'm not for hire." "Everyone's for hire. It's just a matter of price." D-Lo felt Lexi tense beside him.

Felt Clutch's coin spinning faster in her pocket.

"Not everyone," he said. "Some things aren't for sale." Goldmask studied him for a long moment.

Then— "We'll see."

THE SECOND KING

The west door opened.

Agent Reyes walked in like she owned the place—which, in a way, she did. The Trust's authority extended everywhere, even into the shadows where people like Goldmask pretended to rule.

She was alone.

That was either confidence or insanity. D-Lo wasn't sure which.

"Darius Graves." Reyes stopped equidistant from both groups, hands clasped behind her back. "Also known as Reload. Anchor classification, Stage Two. Currently the most wanted individual in New Babylon." "I'm flattered." "You shouldn't be. Being wanted by us isn't a compliment." Her eyes swept the room—Goldmask, Lexi, the various armed figures lurking in the shadows. "Interesting gathering. A crime lord, a terrorist organization, and a reality-warping anomaly. If I called in a strike team right now, I could solve three problems at once." "Then why haven't you?" "Because Director Halden believes in negotiation. In finding solutions that don't end in bloodshed." Reyes's expression didn't change. "He sent me to make an offer." "I'm listening." "Surrender. Come with us voluntarily. In exchange, we guarantee the safety of your sister, your friends, everyone you care about." "And if I refuse?" "Then we stop being gentle." Reyes's voice hardened. "We have resources you can't imagine. Technologies that make your tricks look like children's games. Sooner or later, we'll take you. The only question is how much damage happens first." D-Lo felt the threads pressing against his awareness.

So many possible futures branching from this moment.

So many ways this could go wrong.

"Counter-offer," he said.

Reyes raised an eyebrow.

"Leave us alone. Stop hunting wired people. Dismantle the Vault and free everyone you've imprisoned." D-Lo stepped forward. "Do that, and I'll consider not tearing your organization apart from the inside." Silence.

Then Goldmask laughed.

"I like this one. He's got fire." Reyes didn't laugh.

"You don't have that kind of power. Not yet." "Not yet." D-Lo met her eyes. "But I'm learning. And every day I get stronger while you get more scared. That's why you're here. That's why Halden sent you instead of a strike team. Because you're not sure you can win anymore." Something flickered in Reyes's expression.

Fear, maybe.

Or respect.

Hard to tell.

THE THIRD KING

The shadows moved.

D-Lo felt him before he saw him—a wrongness in the air, a pressure against his senses, a smell like old basements and forgotten grief.

The Janitor stepped into the light.

He looked exactly as D-Lo remembered: gray coveralls, work boots, a face that was almost human but not quite. His smile was wrong. His eyes were hollow. His shadow stretched behind him, filled with shapes that screamed in silence.

"Well, well." The Janitor's voice was a whisper and a shout at the same time. "All the important people in one place. How convenient." Goldmask's men drew weapons.

Reyes's hand moved toward her earpiece.

Lexi's blade cleared its sheath.

But nobody attacked.

Because everyone in that room knew what the Janitor was.

What he could do.

"Don't mind me," the Janitor said, strolling toward the center of the warehouse. "I'm just here to observe. To watch the little kings argue over their little kingdoms." He stopped beside D-Lo.

Close enough to touch.

"You smell different tonight, Reload. Stronger. Like you've been growing." The wrong smile widened. "I approve. The more powerful you become, the more satisfying you'll be to consume." "You're not getting that chance." "Oh, but I am. Sooner or later." The Janitor's hollow eyes swept the room. "None of you can stop me. Not the criminal with his gold mask.

Not the government with its soldiers. Not even the girl with the threads." He leaned close to D-Lo's ear.

Whispered: "I've been eating people like you for centuries. You're nothing special. Just another meal waiting to happen." Then he was gone.

Faded back into the shadows like he'd never been there.

But his words lingered.

And D-Lo realized that whatever conflict existed between Goldmask and the Trust, whatever tension filled this warehouse, it was nothing compared to the thing that hunted them all.

THE AFTERMATH

The meeting ended without a deal.

Goldmask retreated to his territory, making vague threats about "future consideration." Reyes left with a promise that the Trust's patience wasn't infinite. The Janitor vanished, leaving only the memory of his wrong smile.

And D-Lo stood in the empty warehouse, thinking about kings and monsters and the war that was coming.

"That went well," Clutch said dryly.

"Could have been worse. Nobody died." "Yet." Lexi sheathed her blade. "The Janitor showed up. That's not good." "No. It's not." D-Lo turned toward the exit. "But at least now we know where everyone stands." "Do we?" "Goldmask wants to use me. The Trust wants to control me. The Janitor wants to eat me." D-Lo laughed—a harsh sound. "Pretty clear, actually." "And what do you want?" D-Lo thought about it.

About Kimi, waiting for him in the Underline.

About the Ghosts, depending on him.

About all the futures he'd glimpsed in the threads—some bright, some dark, most ending in blood.

"I want to survive," he said finally. "I want to keep the people I love safe. And I want to stop the things that threaten them—all of them.

Goldmask. The Trust. The Janitor." "That's a lot of enemies." "Yeah." D-Lo walked into the night. "Better get started."

CHAPTER 17

WIRED

The proving ground was exactly what it sounded like.

A section of the Underline that had been converted into a combat arena—old subway cars pushed to the sides to create open space, the floor covered in scavenged gym mats and sand, the walls tagged with the names of everyone who'd trained here.

Some names were crossed out.

D-Lo tried not to think about what that meant.

Lexi stood in the center of the space, arms crossed, watching him with those unreadable eyes.

"Strip," she said.

D-Lo blinked. "Excuse me?" "Your hoodie. Your shirt. Take them off." "Why?" "Because I need to see how you move. And because you're going to sweat through them in about three minutes anyway." D-Lo glanced at Clutch, who was leaning against a subway car, cigarette dangling from her lips.

She shrugged. "Don't look at me. Her house, her rules." Kettle had already found a spot against the wall, keeping his distance from everyone. His skin flickered with faint heat—nerves, probably.

D-Lo sighed and pulled off his hoodie, then his shirt.

He wasn't built like Kettle—nobody was built like Kettle—but he wasn't soft either. Growing up in the Marrow meant you either got hard or got hurt. He had the kind of lean muscle that came from running, fighting, surviving.

And scars.

More scars than a twenty-two-year-old should have.

141

Lexi's eyes traced them without comment.

"Knife," she said, pointing to one on his ribs.

"Yeah." "Bullet graze." Another, on his shoulder.

"Yeah." "And these—" She gestured at a cluster of faint marks on his chest, right over his heart. "These are new." D-Lo looked down.

She was right.

There were marks he'd never seen before—faint, spiraling patterns, like frost on a window. They weren't scars exactly. More like...

imprints.

"The Cleaner," Lexi said quietly. "He marked you." "What does that mean?" "It means he can find you anywhere." Her voice was flat. "It means he's not hunting blind anymore. You're tagged." D-Lo felt ice in his stomach.

"Can we remove it?" "Maybe. Bishop is looking into it." She stepped back, rolling her shoulders. "But that's not why we're here. We're here because you need to learn how to fight." "I know how to fight." Lexi moved.

One second she was six feet away. The next, her fist was an inch from his throat, stopped just before impact.

D-Lo hadn't even seen her start.

"No," she said calmly. "You know how to brawl. You know how to survive street fights against people who are slow and predictable. That's not fighting. That's flailing." She stepped back.

"The things hunting you—the Cleaner, the Trust, the gangs who want to use your power—they don't flail. They calculate. They execute. They kill with precision." Her eyes locked onto his. "If you want to survive them, you need to be better than them." D-Lo swallowed.

"Okay. Teach me." Lexi smiled.

It was not a friendly smile.

"First lesson: pain is information." She hit him in the stomach.

The next three hours were the worst of D-Lo's life.

And he'd died multiple times, so that was saying something.

Lexi didn't just train him—she dismantled him. Every weakness, every bad habit, every instinct that had kept him alive on the streets but would get him killed against a real threat—she found them all and punished them.

When he telegraphed a punch, she made him pay.

When he dropped his guard, she made him pay.

When he got frustrated and swung wild, she put him on the ground so hard his teeth rattled.

"Again," she said, standing over him.

D-Lo groaned. "Give me a second—" "The Cleaner won't give you a second. Again." He got up.

She put him down.

Again.

And again.

And again.

By the end, D-Lo was lying on the mat, staring at the ceiling, every muscle screaming.

Lexi crouched beside him.

"You're not bad," she said.

"I feel bad." "Feeling bad means you're learning." She offered her hand. "Most people quit after the first hour. You lasted three." He took her hand and let her pull him up.

Standing this close, he noticed things he'd missed before. The scars on her neck were burns—precise, deliberate, like someone had pressed something hot against her skin in patterns. Her knuckles were calloused, the skin split and healed so many times it looked like armor.

And her eyes—up close, they weren't just cold. They were tired. The kind of tired that sleep couldn't fix.

"What happened to you?" he asked before he could stop himself.

Lexi's expression flickered.

Then closed off.

"Same thing that happened to everyone down here," she said. "The world decided I didn't matter. So I decided to prove it wrong." She turned and walked away.

"Rest for twenty minutes. Then we work on your gift."

While D-Lo recovered, Clutch approached Kettle.

The big man was still against the wall, watching the training with haunted eyes. His skin had cooled, but D-Lo could see the tension in his shoulders—the constant effort of keeping himself under control.

"Your turn," Clutch said.

Kettle shook his head. "I can't." "You have to." "You don't understand." His voice was tight. "Every time I let go—every time I stop fighting it—people get hurt. Markus got hurt. I could've killed him." "But you didn't." "Only because he got lucky!" Kettle's hands clenched into fists.

Steam rose from his knuckles. "I can't control it. When I get scared, or angry, or even just... stressed... it comes out. And I can't stop it." Clutch studied him for a moment.

Then she did something D-Lo didn't expect.

She reached out and put her hand on Kettle's arm.

Right on his skin.

Where the heat was already building.

Kettle flinched. "Don't—you'll get burned—" "I won't." Clutch's voice was steady. "My luck extends to survival.

I've tested it. Bullets curve around me. Blades miss vital organs. And heat—" She pressed harder. "—heat finds other places to go." D-Lo watched, fascinated.

The air around Clutch's hand shimmered—but instead of burning her, the heat seemed to... redirect. Flow around her. Dissipate into the air.

Kettle stared at her.

"How...?" "I told you. Luck." She removed her hand. No burns. No blisters. "The universe wants me to survive. So it bends to make that happen." "That's incredible." "It's useful." Her expression hardened. "But it's not infinite. The bigger the threat, the more luck I need to burn. And I can feel it—there's a limit. A point where luck runs out and probability catches up." She stepped back.

"Your power isn't a curse, Kettle. It's a tool. Like mine. Like D-Lo's.

But tools are useless if you don't know how to use them." She gestured at the proving ground. "So let's figure out how to use yours." Kettle hesitated.

Then, slowly, he stood.

"What do I do?" Clutch smiled.

"First, you're gonna heat up. On purpose. Controlled. And I'm gonna stand right next to you while you do it." "That's insane." "That's trust." She crossed her arms. "You need to learn that your power doesn't have to hurt people. It can protect them. Warm them. Save them.

But only if you stop being afraid of it." Kettle looked at her for a long moment.

Then at D-Lo.

Then at Lexi, who was watching from across the room.

"Okay," he said quietly. "Okay. Let's try."

D-Lo watched from the mat as Kettle and Clutch moved to an open area of the proving ground.

Kettle stood in the center, shoulders tight, breath shallow.

Clutch stood three feet away.

"Start slow," she said. "Don't try to push. Just... let it rise.

Like water heating up. Gradual." Kettle closed his eyes.

For a moment, nothing happened.

Then D-Lo saw it—a faint glow beginning at Kettle's fingertips.

Spreading up his hands. His wrists. His forearms.

His skin shifted from brown to orange to red.

Heat rippled off him in waves.

The air around him shimmered.

Clutch didn't move.

"Good," she said. "Now hold it. Don't push. Don't pull. Just hold."

Kettle's jaw clenched.

Sweat evaporated off his forehead before it could form.

"I can feel it wanting to go," he whispered. "Wanting to explode."

"That's the instinct. That's the fear. You've been so scared of it for so long that your body defaults to maximum output." Clutch's voice was calm. "But you're not scared right now. You're in control. So stay there."

Kettle trembled.

The glow intensified—then stabilized.

His temperature held.

Not exploding.

Not fading.

Just... burning. Steady. Consistent.

D-Lo realized he'd been holding his breath.

He let it out.

"Holy shit," he whispered.

Lexi appeared beside him.

"He's got potential," she murmured. "If he can master that, he'll be one of the most powerful wired we've ever seen." "If?" "Control is harder than power. Anybody can destroy. Creating takes discipline." She watched Kettle with something like respect. "Most heat-generators burn out within a year. Literally. Their bodies can't handle the thermal stress. They go supernova and take a city block with them." D-Lo felt cold despite the ambient heat.

"Will that happen to Kettle?" "Not if he learns to regulate. Not if he finds his balance." Lexi's eyes moved to D-Lo. "Same applies to you." "What do you mean?" "Your gift—the reset ability—it's not free. Every time you die and come back, you're pulling on something. Some force, some energy, some cosmic thread that ties you to this timeline." She turned to face him fully. "Pull too hard, too often, and that thread snaps. And when it does…" "What?" "You don't come back." Her voice was soft. "You just… aren't.

Not dead. Not alive. Just gone. Like you never existed at all." D-Lo felt that weight again—the weight of infinite chances that weren't actually infinite.

"How do I know when I'm close to the limit?" "You don't. Nobody does." Lexi shrugged. "That's why you need to learn to survive without dying. That's why we train." She walked away to check on Kettle and Clutch.

D-Lo sat on the mat, staring at his hands.

The spiraling marks on his chest—the Cleaner's tag—seemed to pulse faintly.

A reminder.

A countdown.

A promise of things to come.

The training broke for food around hour four.

The Ghosts had a communal kitchen set up in an old maintenance bay—scavenged pots, salvaged ingredients, and a cooking system that ran on Kettle's carefully controlled heat.

D-Lo sat with a bowl of something that was technically soup, watching the underground community move around him.

Kids laughing despite everything.

Teenagers flirting despite everything.

146

Adults working, planning, surviving—despite everything.

It reminded him of the Marrow.

The same energy.

The same defiance.

The same refusal to let the world's bullshit break them completely.

Clutch dropped onto the bench beside him.

"We need to talk." "About what?" She leaned close, voice low.

"Something's wrong with my luck." D-Lo frowned. "What do you mean?" "I mean it's been acting weird ever since we went to Celestine's." She pulled out a coin—her coin, the one she always carried—and flipped it. "Watch." The coin spun.

Rose.

Hung in the air for a moment— Then fell straight down and landed on its edge.

Perfectly balanced.

Like always.

"Looks normal to me," D-Lo said.

"That's the problem." Clutch's jaw was tight. "When I flip a coin, I choose how it lands. Heads, tails, edge—whatever I want. But this time, I wasn't choosing. I was just flipping. And it still landed on the edge." "So?" "So that means it's not me doing it." She grabbed the coin and pocketed it. "Something else is influencing probability around us. Something big.

And I can feel it pushing against my gift, like... like two magnets with the same charge." D-Lo thought about that.

"Could it be the Cleaner?" "No. This feels different. Not malicious. Just... present. Watching." She rubbed her arms like she was cold. "I think something's waking up.

Something connected to all this wired bullshit. And I think it's interested in us." "That's not comforting." "It's not supposed to be." She stood. "I'm going to talk to Bishop.

See if he knows anything. You keep training." She walked off.

D-Lo stared at his soup.

Something waking up.

The Cleaner hunting him.

The Trust closing in.

His own power slowly eroding his existence.

And now, apparently, some new cosmic force paying attention.

"Great," he muttered. "Just fucking great."

The Underline didn't have day or night—just artificial lights that dimmed on a schedule to simulate a normal cycle.

When the lights went down, D-Lo found a sleeping space in the corner of an old train car, blankets and a thin mattress that was luxury by underground standards.

He couldn't sleep.

Every time he closed his eyes, he saw the Janitor.

Felt those fingers on his forehead.

Heard that whisper: I can smell your fractures.

He got up and walked.

The Underline at night was different—quieter, more intimate. He passed couples huddled together for warmth, kids sleeping in piles like puppies, guards posted at tunnel entrances with weapons ready.

A community.

Built in the bones of a dead transit system.

He found himself at the edge of the settlement, where the maintained tunnels gave way to darkness. A sign hung from the ceiling: *BEYOND THIS POINT: UNMAPPED*

ENTER AT YOUR OWN RISK

D-Lo stared into the black.

Something was out there.

He could feel it.

"Can't sleep?" He turned.

Lexi stood behind him, arms crossed, wearing a tank top and loose pants that might have been pajamas in another life. Without her jacket and weapons, she looked smaller. Younger.

Almost vulnerable.

Almost.

"Too much in my head," D-Lo admitted.

"That's the curse of your gift." She moved to stand beside him, staring into the same darkness. "All those deaths, all those memories—they stack up. Fill your skull with noise." "You seem to know a lot about it." "I know a lot about a lot of things." She was quiet for a moment. "My gift is sight. I see... possibilities. Threads. Futures that might happen, pasts that did happen, presents that are happening elsewhere." "That sounds exhausting." "It is." A faint smile. "But it's also useful. I can see threats coming before they arrive. I can see weaknesses in enemies. I can see the fractures in people—the places where they've been broken and healed wrong." "Is that why you looked at me like that? When we first met?" Lexi nodded slowly.

"You're covered in fractures, D-Lo. More than anyone I've ever seen.

Every death you've experienced has left a mark, even if it got erased.

Your soul looks like a mosaic made of broken glass." D-Lo didn't know how to respond to that.

"But," Lexi continued, "broken things can still be beautiful. Can still be strong. Sometimes the cracks are what let the light in." She turned to face him.

In the dim glow of the distant lanterns, her eyes weren't cold anymore.

They were searching.

Curious.

"Why do you keep going?" she asked. "After everything you've been through. After dying over and over. Why don't you just... stop? Hide?

Let someone else be the hero?" D-Lo thought about it.

Really thought about it.

"Because I have a sister," he said finally. "And a community. People who need protecting. People who don't have the option to come back if they make a mistake." He looked at his hands. "I got this power—this curse, this gift, whatever it is—and I can either use it to help people or let it eat me alive. Those are the only two choices." Lexi studied him.

"You really believe that." "I have to. Otherwise, what's the point?" She was quiet for a long moment.

Then she did something unexpected.

She took his hand.

Her fingers were calloused, scarred, strong—but her grip was gentle.

"Get some sleep," she said. "Tomorrow we work on your actual power.

Not just fighting—understanding. Learning what you can really do." "And the Cleaner?" "He's coming. We both know it." She squeezed his hand once, then let go.

"But he's not here yet. So tonight, we rest. We prepare. And tomorrow, we fight." She walked away.

D-Lo watched her go.

Then turned back to the darkness.

Somewhere out there, the Janitor was hunting.

Somewhere out there, the Trust was planning.

Somewhere out there, something new was waking up.

But here, in this moment, D-Lo was alive.

And that was enough.

Miles above the Underline, in the empty streets of the Marrow at 3 AM, a figure walked.

Blue coveralls.

Work boots.

A mop handle dragging behind him, scraping against concrete.

The Janitor moved through the projects like a ghost—unnoticed, unseen, unremembered. People who glimpsed him from windows immediately forgot what they'd seen. Dogs that barked at him suddenly went silent, cowering.

He stopped in the courtyard outside Building C.

Looked up at the fourth floor.

At the window where D-Lo had first seen him.

"You're hiding," he whispered to the empty air. "But not for long." He pressed his palm against the concrete wall.

The stone cracked beneath his touch—hairline fractures spreading outward like spiderwebs.

"I can feel you. All that beautiful pain. All those delicious deaths." He smiled—that wrong, too-wide smile. "You think the tunnels can protect you. You think those broken children can stop me." He pulled his hand away.

Left behind an imprint—five fingers burned into the concrete.

"They can't." He turned and walked toward the storm drain at the edge of the courtyard.

The entrance to the Underline.

"I'm coming," he said softly. "And when I find you..." He descended into darkness.

"...I will clean you so thoroughly that even your ghost won't remember who you were." The storm drain swallowed him.

Above, a dog began to howl.

Then another.

Then another.

Until the whole Marrow was filled with the sound of animals screaming at something they couldn't see but knew, instinctively, to fear.

INTERLUDE — THE INTERROGATOR

THE VAULT — INTERROGATION WING

Dr. Reeves had been breaking people for twenty-three years.

Not physically—that was crude, ineffective. True interrogation was about psychology. Understanding what someone valued. What they feared.

What made them human.

And then taking it away.

The subject in Room 7 was interesting.

Young. Female. Thirteen years old. Sister of the primary target.

Kimberly Graves.

She sat across from him, hands folded on the table, eyes steady. Not crying. Not trembling. Just... waiting.

Most subjects broke within hours. The isolation. The uncertainty. The knowledge that nobody was coming to save them.

This one was different.

"Your brother is causing us quite a bit of trouble," Dr. Reeves said.

Conversational. Friendly.

"Good." No hesitation. No fear.

Dr. Reeves felt his professional interest sharpen.

"You're not afraid?" "I'm terrified." The girl met his eyes. "But fear doesn't mean I have to be weak. My brother taught me that." "And what else did he teach you?" "That people like you always lose. Maybe not today. Maybe not tomorrow.

But eventually." She leaned forward. "He's coming for me. And when he does, you're going to regret every second I spent in this room." Dr. Reeves smiled.

He'd heard threats before. Thousands of them. Empty words from desperate people.

But something in this girl's voice...

151

Something that sounded almost like certainty.

He made a note in his file: *SUBJECT DEMONSTRATES UNUSUAL PSYCHOLOGICAL RESILIENCE. RECOMMEND ENHANCED PROTOCOLS.* Then he continued the interrogation.

But for the first time in twenty-three years, he wasn't entirely sure who was winning.

CHAPTER 18

DEAD ENDS

D-Lo had been searching for Melo for six weeks.

Six weeks of false leads. Six weeks of dead ends. Six weeks of staring at his phone, waiting for a message that never came.

Where are you, man? What happened to you?

The first week, he'd searched the obvious places.

Melo's apartment—empty, stripped clean, like nobody had ever lived there. Mrs. Carter, Melo's mother, was gone too. The landlord said they'd moved out in the middle of the night, left no forwarding address, owed three months' rent.

D-Lo paid the debt from his own savings.

It was the least he could do for a woman who'd fed him when his own mother was too sick to cook.

He tried Melo's usual spots—the corner store where they used to buy loose cigarettes, the basketball court behind Building G, the rooftop where they'd spent countless nights staring at stars that were barely visible through the city's light pollution.

Nothing.

Nobody had seen him.

Nobody knew where he'd gone.

It was like Melo had been erased.

The second week, D-Lo got desperate.

He asked questions in places you weren't supposed to ask questions.

Talked to people you weren't supposed to talk to. Put out word through channels that led to other channels that led to people who made their living knowing things.

For a price.

"Jameel Carter," the information broker said. He was a thin man with nervous eyes and a shop that sold bootleg electronics as a front.

"Yeah, I heard something." "What?" "Word is he got picked up. Not by cops—by the suits. The ones in the black trucks." D-Lo's blood went cold.

"The Trust?" "Ain't supposed to call them that. Ain't supposed to admit they exist." The broker shrugged. "But yeah. Them. They came for a few people after that robbery at Kim's. Cleaning house, maybe. Or looking for someone specific." "Looking for who?" The broker studied D-Lo for a long moment.

"Looking for someone who can do impossible things. Someone who keeps showing up where they ain't supposed to be." His eyes narrowed.

"Someone like you, maybe." D-Lo left three hundred dollars on the counter.

It was everything he had.

The third week, he found the Transit Authority worker.

A woman named Patrice who operated the booth at the Marrow Street station. She'd worked the night shift the same night Melo disappeared.

"Yeah, I remember him," she said, keeping her voice low. "Handsome kid.

Big smile. Came running through about two in the morning, looking scared out of his mind." "Did you see where he went?" "Down. He went down—past the platform, into the service tunnels. I yelled at him, told him he couldn't go down there, but he wasn't listening." She hesitated. "He wasn't alone." "Who was with him?" "I don't know. A woman. Older. She was guiding him, like she knew where she was going." Patrice shook her head. "I figured maybe she was helping him. Or maybe... I don't know. I called it in, but nobody ever followed up. Nobody ever follows up on anything in this neighborhood." D-Lo thanked her.

Went down into the tunnels himself.

Found nothing but darkness and rats and the distant rumble of trains.

The fourth week, Kimi confronted him.

"You look like death," she said, standing in the doorway of their apartment as he stumbled in at 3 AM. "You're not eating. You're not sleeping. And you missed two shifts at work." "I'm fine." "You're not fine. You're falling apart." She blocked his path to the bedroom. "Melo's gone, D-Lo. Whatever happened to him—you can't fix it by running yourself into the ground." "I'm not trying to fix it. I'm trying to find him." "And what happens when you find him? What if he doesn't want to be found? What if—" She stopped herself. "What if he's already gone?" The words hung in the air.

D-Lo couldn't respond.

Because he'd been asking himself the same question every night. Lying awake at 4 AM, staring at the ceiling, wondering if he was searching for a friend or a ghost.

"I have to try," he said finally. "He'd do the same for me." "Would he?" Kimi's voice was soft, but there was an edge to it.

"Because from what I remember, Melo was pretty good at looking out for Melo." "That's not fair." "Maybe not. But it's true." She stepped aside. "Go to bed, D-Lo. Get some rest. And tomorrow... maybe start accepting that some people can't be saved." D-Lo walked past her.

Lay down on his mattress.

Stared at the ceiling until the sun came up.

The fifth week, he found the woman.

Her name was Celestine, and she ran a fortune-telling shop in a strip of abandoned storefronts. D-Lo had heard rumors about her—that she knew things, saw things, helped people who had nowhere else to go.

"You're looking for the boy who disappears," she said before he could speak. She didn't look up from the cards she was laying out on the table. "The one with the quick tongue and the quicker feet." "You know where he is?" "I know where he was. The tunnels took him. The Underline." She turned a card over. "But the Underline is vast, and he was taken deeper than most go." "Taken by who?" "By people who collect things. Broken things. Useful things." She finally looked at him, and her milky eyes seemed to see straight through to his soul. "You have your own brokenness, child. Your own usefulness.

That's why you survived when others didn't. That's why you keep coming back." His chest seized.

"How do you know about—" "I know many things. Including this: your friend is alive. Changed, perhaps. Damaged, certainly. But alive." She returned to her cards.

"When the time is right, you'll find him. Or he'll find you. The threads converge—I can see them, even now." "When? Where?" "Patience is not your virtue, I see." She smiled, thin and knowing.

"Focus on surviving. On learning what you can do. When you're strong enough to help him, the path will appear." D-Lo wanted to argue.

Wanted to demand answers.

But something in her voice—in the way she'd known things she shouldn't—made him stop.

"Thank you," he said instead.

"Don't thank me yet." She turned another card. "The road ahead is darker than you know. And your friend's return may not be the reunion you're hoping for." D-Lo left the shop.

Stood on the street.

And for once, in five weeks, allowed himself to believe that Melo might still be alive.

The sixth week, he stopped searching.

Not because he'd given up.

Because he'd understood.

Melo was out there—somewhere in the tunnels, somewhere in the hands of people who collected the broken and the useful. And D-Lo couldn't save him by running himself ragged, by neglecting Kimi, by sacrificing everything on the altar of a friendship that might already be gone.

He had to get stronger.

Had to learn what he could do.

Had to become something that could actually fight back.

So he stopped searching.

Started training.

And every night, before he fell asleep, he made the same promise to the empty air: I'm coming for you, Melo.

As soon as I figure out how.
I'm coming.

CHAPTER 19

THE DIRECTOR

Director Halden didn't sleep.

Not because he wasn't tired—he'd been tired since 1968. But sleep meant vulnerability. Sleep meant losing control. And control was all that kept the world intact.

At 3:47 AM, he stood in the Command Center, watching feeds from across the city.

Forty-seven active operations. Three hundred twelve operatives.

Seventeen wired flagged for containment.

And one Anchor who threatened everything.

"Report." Agent Chen pulled up the data.

"Subject Graves continues to exceed projections. His reset ability is unprecedented—past forty confirmed deaths with no cognitive degradation." "He's evolving." "Rapidly. Each reset increases his temporal awareness. He's starting to see threads." Chen highlighted a section. "That usually doesn't happen until Stage Two." "And he's not there yet?" "At the threshold. Full Stage Two within the week, possibly sooner." Halden absorbed this.

Forty years of hunting Anchors had taught him patience. The first—Portugal, 1962—had been easy. Captured before Stage One.

Disposed of. The second—Chicago, 1952—had reached Stage Two before they took him. The hollowing had been complicated.

But successful.

"The Conductor is proof of that," he murmured.

"Sir?" "Nothing." Halden turned from the screens. "Continue surveillance.

Log all temporal anomalies. And prepare contingency protocols." "Which ones?" "All of them."

After Chen left, Halden remained.

People called him a monster. He'd heard the whispers. Seen the looks.

Even his own agents thought he was cold—a machine incapable of empathy.

They were wrong.

Halden felt everything.

He simply chose not to let it interfere with necessity.

He walked to a restricted terminal. Entered codes that only three people knew. Accessed files that officially didn't exist.

The Archive.

Proof of what Anchors could do.

ANCHOR EVENT: LISBON, 1755

Stage Four manifestation. Subject designation unknown. Origin: earthquake survivor who developed temporal manipulation abilities during aftershock sequence.

Event summary: Subject reached Stage Four approximately six weeks after initial manifestation. Reality cascade began at 0347 local time.

Affected area: 2,300 square kilometers. Casualty estimate: 85,000.

Note: Subject erased herself from existence during cascade. No physical evidence of her existence remains. All documentation of event relies on Trust memory-shielded archives.

Halden scrolled.

ANCHOR EVENT: CHICAGO, 1952

Stage Three manifestation. Subject: Isaiah Washington, 34, schoolteacher. Origin: Project Harbinger inadvertent exposure.

Event summary: Subject contained at Stage Three after sixteen square miles of urban area experienced reality erasure. Estimated 12,000 casualties, though exact number cannot be determined as erased individuals leave no records.

Containment protocol: Experimental hollowing procedure. Subject successfully converted to Conductor designation. Current status: Contained. Dormant.

Note: Footage attached. For Director clearance only.

Halden had watched the footage once.

Once was enough.

Sixteen square miles of city—buildings, streets, people—simply ceasing to exist. Not destroyed. Not burned. Erased. As if they had never been.

The Trust had photos of the aftermath: a perfect circular void where a neighborhood had been, the edges sharp as surgical cuts, reality simply... stopping.

Twelve thousand people.

Not dead.

Unmade.

Their memories erased from every mind that had ever known them. Their photographs blank. Their birth certificates empty.

That was Stage Three.

Stage Four was worse.

Halden closed the Archive.

In 1952, he'd been twenty-six years old. A junior analyst. He'd watched Isaiah Washington weep as they drilled into his skull, begged for his family as they hollowed out his humanity, screamed until he couldn't scream anymore.

Halden had felt every moment of it.

And he'd done it anyway.

Because the alternative was worse.

An Anchor at Stage Four didn't just destroy cities. They destroyed concepts. Realities. Entire branches of possibility collapsed when they lost control. The Lisbon Anchor had been contained before she could spread. Chicago had been contained before Washington reached Stage Four.

But D-Lo Graves was approaching Stage Two faster than any Anchor on record.

And he was building an army.

160

"You think I'm evil." Halden was speaking to no one. Or perhaps to everyone. To the ghosts of every wired person he'd ordered contained, every family he'd destroyed, every moral line he'd crossed in the name of protection.

"I understand. From your perspective, I am. A man who hunts the different. Who cages the powerful. Who turns humans into weapons." He walked to the window. The city spread below him—millions of people living their lives, unaware of the threats that moved in the margins.

"But you don't know what I know. Haven't seen what I've seen. The footage from Chicago. The reports from Lisbon. The mathematical certainty of what happens when an Anchor reaches Stage Four." He pressed his hand against the glass.

"Every Anchor in history has ended the same way. Either we stop them, or they destroy everything around them. There are no exceptions. No success stories. No Anchors who learned control and lived peacefully among normal humans." He turned from the window.

"D-Lo Graves seems different. I've watched him. He cares about people.

Protects his sister. Inspires loyalty. He's not evil—he's not anything yet. Just a young man with a power he doesn't understand." Halden returned to his desk.

"But potential means nothing against probability. Every Anchor seems different at first. Isaiah Washington was a schoolteacher who loved his students. The Lisbon Anchor was a grandmother who wanted to save her family. They all start as people trying to do good." He pulled up D-Lo's file.

"They all end as gods. And gods, by their nature, cannot coexist with mortals."

The door chimed.

"Enter." Chen again. "Sir, the Council is asking about Project Omega. They want to know if activation is necessary." "What did you tell them?" "That the decision is yours." Halden considered.

The Conductor was a last resort. Isaiah Washington's hollow shell, filled with seventy years of accumulated power, capable of things that made normal wired look like parlor tricks. Using him meant risking catastrophic collateral damage.

But leaving D-Lo Graves unchecked meant risking something worse.

"Prepare activation protocols. Don't execute yet." Halden turned back to the window. "Let's see what the boy does next. If he defeats the Cleaner—if he proves he can control his power—we may have options other than termination." "You want to recruit him?" "I want to evaluate him. An Anchor who could be controlled, guided, pointed at genuine threats..." Halden's eyes were cold. "That would be valuable. But if he shows any signs of Stage Three progression—any at all—we end him. Immediately." "Understood." Chen left.

Halden remained at the window.

Watching the city.

Watching the future.

Wondering, not for the first time, if he was the hero of this story or the villain.

And knowing, with absolute certainty, that it didn't matter.

The world needed protecting.

Whatever the cost.

It started over something dumb.

"That's not how you hold a knife." D-Lo adjusted his grip. "This is how I've always held a knife." "That's why you keep almost cutting yourself." Lexi reached over, repositioned his fingers. "Blade faces away. Thumb on the spine. How did you survive this long?" "By not getting in knife fights." "You're in one now." "I'm cutting tomatoes." "Aggressively." She leaned against the counter, arms crossed. "Like they personally wronged you." D-Lo looked at the mangled tomato. She had a point.

"My mom used to make this sauce," he said. "Secret recipe. Wouldn't tell anyone what was in it." He scraped the tomato massacre into a pot.

"I'm trying to figure it out." "By murdering vegetables?" "By experimenting." Lexi peered into the pot. "What's in there so far?" "Tomatoes. Onions. Garlic. Brown sugar." He paused. "Hot sauce.

Don't judge me." "I'm absolutely judging you." "It's good! It's—" He stirred, tasted. Made a face. "Okay, it's not good yet." "What did it taste like? Your mom's version?" D-Lo closed his eyes. Trying to remember.

"Sweet but not too sweet.

Smoky. There was something else, something I could never identify.

She'd make it Sunday mornings, let it simmer all day. The whole apartment smelled like—" He stopped.

The whole apartment had smelled like home.

"Sorry," he said. "I don't know why I'm—" "My mother made these dumplings." Lexi's voice was quiet. "Every lunar new year. Pork and chive. She'd let me fold them, even though I was terrible at it." A small smile. "They always fell apart when we boiled them. She'd pretend not to notice." "Where is she now?" "Trust took her. First wave, right after the flash." Lexi's expression didn't change, but something shifted behind her eyes. "I was seventeen. Came home from school and the apartment was empty. No note. No explanation. Just—gone." D-Lo turned off the stove.

"I'm sorry." "Don't be. It was a long time ago." She straightened. "But I remember the dumplings. The way she'd hum while she cooked. The flour on her hands." They stood in silence.

Two people who'd lost too much, trying to cook in a borrowed kitchen.

"You know what?" D-Lo said. "This sauce is terrible." Lexi laughed.

Actually laughed—surprised, genuine, the kind of laugh that transformed her whole face.

"It's really bad," she agreed. "What even is that flavor?" "Desperation and hot sauce." "That's not a recipe. That's a cry for help." D-Lo found himself grinning. "You got any better ideas?" "Actually, yes." Lexi pushed off from the counter, moved to the small pantry. "My mother's dumplings were terrible, but she taught me one thing." She emerged with soy sauce and sesame oil. "When in doubt, add umami." "What's umami?" "The fifth taste. Savory. Deep." She poured a careful splash into the pot. "Trust me." D-Lo watched her stir—economical movements, focused attention, the same precision she brought to everything.

"You cook?" "I survive." She tasted. Added more sesame oil. "Food is fuel. But sometimes fuel can taste good." She held out the spoon.

D-Lo tried it.

The sauce was—different. Still not his mother's. But something had shifted. The flavors actually worked together now.

"Okay," he admitted. "That's better." "Told you." She set down the spoon. "Umami. Works every time." "Where'd you learn that?" "Cooking for thirty people underground teaches you shortcuts." She started cleaning up, movements automatic. "Everything's about making limited resources work. Stretching ingredients. Finding flavor in places you wouldn't expect." "Like hot sauce?" "Hot sauce is fine. Hot sauce with brown sugar AND tomatoes is a war crime." "Hey, I'm experimenting." "You're flailing." But she was smiling when she said it. "Maybe that's okay. Flailing is how we figure things out."

They ate the sauce over rice.

Not good. Not terrible. Somewhere in between—the kind of meal that existed to fill stomachs rather than satisfy souls.

But D-Lo found himself not minding.

"Can I ask you something?" he said.

Lexi raised an eyebrow.

"Before all this. Before the Trust, the Ghosts, everything. What did you want to be?" She was quiet for a long moment.

"Teacher," she said finally. "Elementary school. Third grade." D-Lo stared at her.

"You. Third grade teacher." "What's wrong with that?" "Nothing, I just—" He shook his head. "You're kind of terrifying." "Third graders need terrifying." A ghost of a smile. "Someone has to teach them fractions. It's a brutal subject." "And now?" "Now I teach people to fight. To survive. To make hard choices." She pushed rice around her bowl. "Not that different, really. Still trying to give people tools they'll need." "You're good at it." "I've had practice." "No, I mean—" D-Lo set down his fork. "The way you explained the Kettle strategy in training. The way you break everything into steps.

You don't just know this stuff. You know how to make other people know it." Lexi's expression flickered. Something vulnerable, quickly hidden.

"My mother wanted me to be a doctor. My father wanted me to take over his business. They compromised on law school." She laughed, bitter.

"None of them got what they wanted." "What about what you wanted?" "I wanted to help kids learn things. Show them the world was bigger than they thought." She met his eyes. "Instead, I teach people to kill." "You teach them to protect themselves." "Same thing, in the end." "No." D-Lo leaned forward. "It's not. Killing is about ending something. Protecting is about keeping something alive. You do the second thing. Always." Lexi studied him.

"You really believe that." "I have to." He shrugged. "Otherwise, what's the point? I die and come back, die and come back—if it's not to protect something, what's it for?" "Survival?" "Survival's not enough." He surprised himself with the certainty in his voice. "Survival is just existing. I want to exist for something." The kitchen went quiet.

Just the hum of old refrigerators and the distant sound of the Underline settling.

"You're strange," Lexi said finally.

"Thanks?" "That wasn't an insult." She stood, collected the bowls. "Most people I meet are trying to survive. Trying to get through the next day.

You're trying to figure out what the days are for." "Is that bad?" "It's—" She paused at the sink, back to him. "Rare. Inconvenient.

Kind of stupid." "You're really bad at compliments." "I'm excellent at compliments. When people deserve them." "And I don't?" She turned. Met his eyes.

"You do. That's what makes it inconvenient."

CHAPTER 20

THE WEIGHT OF COMMAND

Director Adrian Halden had been protecting the world for thirty-seven years.

Nobody thanked him for it.

The situation room was quiet except for the hum of monitors and the occasional murmur of analysts cross-referencing data. Holographic displays floated above the central table, showing real-time surveillance feeds from across New Babylon.

Red dots clustered in the Marrow Projects.

More red dots in the tunnels beneath.

And one dot—larger, brighter, pulsing with an intensity that made the screens flicker—that marked the location of Darius Graves.

The Anchor.

Halden studied the display with the same expression he'd worn for three decades: calm, measured, betraying nothing of the thoughts churning beneath.

"Sir." Agent Reyes approached, tablet in hand. "The asset we placed in District Nine confirms the target is moving. Heading underground.

Probably to the Underline." "Casualties?" "Three officers from the containment team. They'll reset, but..." Reyes hesitated. "This is the ninth incident in two weeks. The men are getting nervous." "The men are trained professionals. They'll adapt." "Yes, sir." Halden turned back to the display.

Darius Graves.

Twenty-two years old. Raised in the Marrow Projects by a mother who died young and a father who was never there. Dropped out of high school to work, spent three years loading trucks at Patterson Logistics, gave everything he had to keeping his little sister alive and fed.

An ordinary story.

The kind of story that happened every day in neighborhoods like the Marrow, in cities like New Babylon, in a country that had long ago decided certain people weren't worth protecting.

But Darius Graves wasn't ordinary anymore.

He was the fifth documented Anchor in human history.

And if the projections held, he'd either become the most powerful being on the planet—or destroy it entirely.

Halden remembered the first Anchor.

Not personally, of course. The Seattle Incident had happened in 1889, eighty-six years before he was born. But he'd studied the files.

Memorized the photographs. Understood, in a way that never left him, exactly what an uncontrolled Anchor could do.

Her name was Elizabeth Chen.

Sixteen years old. A seamstress's daughter. Pretty, in the way of old photographs—stiff poses and uncertain smiles.

She'd manifested after a factory fire killed her mother and three of her sisters. The trauma cracked something open inside her, and suddenly she could see the threads that held reality together.

She tried to fix things.

That was the heartbreaking part.

She'd tried to save her family. Tried to pull the threads backward, to undo the fire, to change what had happened.

But Anchors didn't work that way.

Not at Stage One.

Not at Stage Two.

By Stage Three, when she finally had enough control to attempt the change, the accumulated temporal stress was too great.

Reality... fractured.

Forty blocks of downtown Seattle were erased. Not burned—erased. As if they'd never existed. Three hundred people vanished mid-step, mid-breath, mid-sentence. Their families woke the next morning with memories of people who no longer existed, photographs that showed empty spaces, graves that held nothing but air.

Elizabeth Chen died in the fracture.

Or became part of it.

Nobody was quite sure.

The Trust was founded the following year.

Not to destroy Anchors, despite what people like Dr. Rao believed.

To save them.

To find them early. Before they reached Stage Three. Before the fractures accumulated. Before the weight of reality's expectations crushed them into something dangerous.

To give them the training and containment they needed to survive their own power.

It was mercy.

Even if it didn't look like mercy from the outside.

"Sir?" Halden blinked. Reyes was still standing there.

"The Council is requesting an update on Project Renaissance. They want to know if we're ready to deploy the Conductor." The Conductor.

Isaiah Washington.

Another thing that didn't look like mercy from the outside.

"Tell the Council I'm not deploying the Conductor until we've exhausted conventional options." "Sir, the Council—" "The Council doesn't understand what we're dealing with." Halden turned from the display. "An Anchor is not a conventional threat. Standard containment protocols assume the target wants to survive. Graves has died over fifty times in the past month. He's not afraid of death.

He's not afraid of pain. He's learning faster than any Anchor we've documented." "Then shouldn't we—" "Deploy the Conductor against someone who might be able to break him?" Halden shook his head. "The Conductor is our last resort. Our only reliable method of containing a fully manifested Anchor. If we deploy him prematurely and Graves finds a way to neutralize or corrupt him..." He didn't finish the sentence.

He didn't have to.

"I want increased surveillance. I want every exit from the Underline monitored. And I want Graves's sister located and secured." "The girl?" "Leverage. Graves has demonstrated a consistent willingness to risk himself for others. His sister is the only person he can't afford to lose." Halden's expression didn't change. "Find her. Contain her.

And make sure she's comfortable. We're not monsters, Reyes. We're just people doing a terrible job because someone has to." "Yes, sir." Reyes left.

Halden turned back to the display.

The red dot pulsed steadily in the darkness beneath New Babylon.

What are you becoming, Darius Graves?

And when you finish becoming it, will there be anything left of the world?

That night, alone in his office, Halden opened the locked drawer in his desk.

The photograph inside was thirty years old. Faded. Creased from being handled too many times.

A woman and a boy.

The woman was beautiful—dark hair, kind eyes, the kind of smile that could make you believe the world was a better place than it actually was.

The boy was eleven.

Scrawny. Serious. Looking at the camera like he wasn't sure it could be trusted.

You should have told me, his mother had said, the last time they'd spoken. You should have trusted me.

But he hadn't. Couldn't. Because telling her would have meant explaining what the Trust really did. What they'd done to keep her safe. What they'd do to anyone who threatened the fragile equilibrium of a world that didn't know how close it always was to breaking.

She'd died thinking he was a government bureaucrat.

A paper-pusher.

A disappointment.

Maybe that was better.

Maybe it was better for her to die hating what she thought he was, rather than what he actually was.

Halden closed the drawer.

The photograph went back into the darkness.

And he returned to the monitors, where a red dot pulsed beneath the city, growing brighter with every passing hour.

I didn't ask for this, he thought. *None of us asked for this.*

But someone has to protect the world from what it doesn't understand.

Someone has to make the terrible choices.

And if I'm the monster, at least I'm a monster who keeps the real monsters in check. It wasn't a comforting thought.

But comfort was a luxury he'd surrendered a long time ago.

The next morning, the reports came in.

The Anchor had eliminated the Cleaner.

Somehow—impossibly—Darius Graves had defeated a being that had consumed souls for centuries. Had freed the trapped spirits. Had destroyed Marcus, the second Anchor, the failure that had become a predator.

Halden read the report twice.

Then a third time.

Then he sat in silence for a very long while.

"Get me the Council," he said finally.

Reyes looked up from her station.

"Sir?" "It's time to discuss the Conductor." "You said—" "I know what I said." Halden stood. His joints ached—too many years of tension, too many nights without sleep, too much weight carried for too long. "I was hoping we had more time. Hoping Graves would burn himself out, or destabilize, or do something predictable." He looked at the display.

The red dot was still there.

But it was different now.

Brighter. Steadier. Almost… peaceful.

"He's not burning out," Halden said. "He's stabilizing. He's learning to control it. And if we don't act soon…" If we don't act soon, he'll become something we can't contain.

Something we can't predict.

Something that might actually be stronger than us.

"Get me the Council," Halden repeated. "And wake the Conductor." "Yes, sir." Reyes left.

Halden stood alone in the situation room, watching the red dot pulse.

I'm sorry, Darius Graves.

I'm sorry for what we're going to do to you.

But the world doesn't survive on apologies.

It survives on people willing to do terrible things for the right reasons. And I've been doing terrible things for a very long time.

CHAPTER 21

THE KITCHEN

The proving ground was empty except for Kettle.

D-Lo found him there at 3 AM, sitting alone on an overturned crate, staring at his hands.

His skin glowed faintly—not hot, just warm. Like embers waiting to catch.

"Can't sleep either?" D-Lo asked.

Kettle didn't look up. "Haven't slept right since it happened." D-Lo sat down across from him. The Underline was quiet at this hour—most of the Ghosts asleep, the guards on rotation, the tunnels holding their breath.

"You wanna talk about it?" "About what?" "Before. Who you were. What you lost." Kettle was silent for a long moment.

Then he started talking.

"I was a cook. Good one, too." Kettle's voice was soft—softer than you'd expect from a man his size.

"Started washing dishes at sixteen. Some restaurant downtown—nice place, white tablecloths, customers who tipped more than my mama made in a day. Worked my way up. Prep cook at eighteen. Line cook at twenty.

Sous chef by twenty-four." "Sous chef's a big deal." "It was. Is. Whatever." Kettle looked at his hands. "I was good at it.

Keeping things moving. Keeping the kitchen running smooth. You ever been in a professional kitchen during rush?" "Can't say I have." "It's chaos. Beautiful chaos. Tickets coming in, orders going out, flames

172

everywhere, everyone shouting. And in the middle of it, you gotta stay calm. Keep your head. Keep things from boiling over." He laughed bitterly.

"That was always my thing. 'Kettle keeps it cool.' That's what Chef Marcus used to say. 'Kitchen's on fire, Kettle keeps it cool.'" "Chef Marcus?" "Head chef at Meridian. The restaurant I worked at. He was... he was like a father to me." Kettle's voice cracked. "My real father bounced when I was three. Same old story. But Chef Marcus—he saw something in me. Trained me. Pushed me. Said I had a gift." "For cooking?" "For calm. For control." Kettle's glow flickered. "He said the best cooks aren't the ones with the most talent. They're the ones who can handle the pressure. Who can take a hundred things going wrong and make it look like nothing's happening." "Sounds like a smart man." "He was." Kettle fell silent.

D-Lo waited.

"He was at the restaurant. The night Project Renaissance blew."

"We were in the middle of dinner service. Friday night—busiest night of the week. Kitchen was full. Every burner going, every oven hot, tickets stacked three deep on the rail." Kettle's hands clenched.

"I was on the sauté station. Right next to the flames. Right where I always was." "What happened?" "The flash. That... light. It came through the windows, through the walls, through everything. Felt like standing inside a flashbang, except it lasted forever." His glow intensified slightly.

"When it stopped, everything was different. I could feel things I'd never felt before. The heat from the burners—not just on my skin, but inside me. Like it was part of me. Like I was made of it." "That must have been terrifying." "It wasn't. Not at first." Kettle shook his head. "At first it felt...

right. Natural. Like something that had always been there was finally waking up." "So what went wrong?" Kettle's face crumpled.

"Chef Marcus."

"He came over to check on me. After the flash. Everyone was confused, disoriented. Some people were crying. Others were just standing there, staring at nothing." Kettle's voice dropped to a whisper.

"He put his hand on my shoulder. Asked if I was okay. And I—" He stopped.

"You don't have to—" "I burned him." The words came out like a confession. "Not on purpose. I didn't know. I couldn't control it. But when he touched me, all that heat just... released. Like a pressure valve popping." D-Lo felt sick.

"Third degree burns. Down his arm, across his chest. He was screaming.

Everyone was screaming. And I just stood there, watching my hands glow, not understanding what I'd done." "It wasn't your fault." "IT WAS MY HANDS!" Kettle's voice cracked. The temperature in the proving ground spiked—D-Lo felt sweat break out on his forehead. "MY heat! MY power! How is that not my fault!?" He caught himself.

Forced himself to breathe.

The temperature slowly dropped.

"Sorry," he muttered. "See what I mean? Can't control it. Never could." "What happened to Chef Marcus?" "Hospital. ICU for three weeks. Skin grafts. Lost most of the function in his left arm." Kettle stared at the ground. "He can't cook anymore.

Can't hold a knife steady. Can't feel heat properly—the nerve damage messed that up." "Have you talked to him?" "Once. I went to the hospital to apologize. To explain. To..." Kettle's voice broke. "He looked at me like I was a monster. Like he didn't even know who I was. And then he told me to leave. Said he never wanted to see me again." Silence.

"I haven't been back to a kitchen since," Kettle whispered. "Can't.

Every time I see a stove, I think about his face. Every time I feel heat, I think about what I did to him."

D-Lo didn't know what to say.

What could you say?

That it wasn't his fault? It kind of was.

That it would get better? Maybe it wouldn't.

That Chef Marcus would forgive him eventually? Maybe he shouldn't.

So D-Lo said the only thing that felt true.

"That's heavy, man. Real heavy." Kettle laughed—a wet, broken sound.

"Yeah. It is." "But you're still here. Still fighting." "What choice do I have?" "You could've given up. Could've let the Trust take you. Could've walked into the Janitor's arms and let him eat whatever guilt you're carrying." D-Lo leaned forward. "But you didn't." "Maybe I should have." "Nah." D-Lo shook his head. "You know what I see when I look at you?

I see a man who spent his whole life keeping things from boiling over.

Keeping other people calm. Taking care of everyone except himself." "And now I'm the thing that boils over." "Now you're the thing that could melt a hole in the Trust's operation.

Could burn down their containment facilities. Could protect the people who can't protect themselves." D-Lo stood. "You're not a monster, Kettle. You're a weapon. And weapons aren't good or evil—they're just tools. It's all about who's holding them." Kettle looked up at him.

"You really believe that?" "I have to. Because the alternative is that we're all doomed by what we are instead of what we choose to be." D-Lo extended his hand. "And I refuse to believe that." Kettle stared at the hand.

At D-Lo.

At the choice in front of him.

Then he took it.

"Okay," he said quietly. "Okay. I'll try." "That's all any of us can do." D-Lo pulled him to his feet.

And finally, in a long time, Kettle's glow didn't flicker.

It burned steady.

Controlled.

Almost peaceful.

They walked back to the main camp together.

The Underline was starting to wake up—kids stirring, adults preparing for another day of survival, the rhythm of the hidden city beginning again.

"D-Lo." "Yeah?" "Thanks. For listening." "Anytime, big man." "And for saying what you said. About weapons. About choices." Kettle paused. "Nobody's ever told me I was anything other than dangerous." "Then they weren't paying attention." Kettle smiled.

It was small. Fragile. But real.

"I'm gonna figure this out," he said. "The control. The balance.

Whatever Clutch is teaching me—I'm gonna make it work." "I know you will." "And when we face the Janitor..." "You'll be ready." Kettle nodded.

His skin glowed warm—not hot, just warm.

The glow of a man who was finally learning to live with his fire instead of fighting it.

"Yeah," he said quietly. "I think I will."

CHAPTER 22

PROBABILITY AND HEAT

Clutch found Kettle in the Underline's kitchen at 3 AM.

Not the main food hall—the small one, tucked away in a dead-end tunnel that most people didn't know existed. He'd claimed it weeks ago, turned it into something almost functional. A camp stove. Salvaged pots. Spices he'd traded for in ways Clutch didn't ask about.

He was cooking.

"Thought you quit," she said from the doorway.

Kettle didn't turn around. "Can't sleep." "So you're making..." She sniffed the air. "Gumbo?" "My grandmother's recipe. Only thing that shuts my brain up." Clutch watched him work. His hands moved with the kind of automatic grace that came from years of practice—chopping, stirring, seasoning without measuring. Even in the dim light of the tunnel, even surrounded by concrete and desperation, he looked like he belonged behind a stove.

"You're good at this." "I know." No arrogance. Just fact. "I was good at a lot of things.

Before." She walked in, pulled herself onto a counter, let her legs dangle. "The restaurant guy. Marcus." Kettle's hands paused. Just for a second.

"D-Lo told you?" "D-Lo tells me everything. It's annoying." She pulled out her coin, turned it between her fingers. "You burned him. Accident. He blamed you.

You've been punishing yourself ever since." "That's the short version." "What's the long version?" Kettle was quiet for a moment. Then: "I loved him." Clutch's fingers stilled on the coin.

177

"Not like that," Kettle added. "Or maybe like that. I don't know. I never figured it out." He stirred the gumbo. "He was the first person who ever looked at me and saw something worth investing in. My dad was gone. My mom was working three jobs. My teachers had already written me off. And then there was Marcus, telling me I had a gift. Telling me I could be something." "Sounds like a good man." "The best man I ever knew." Kettle tasted the gumbo, added salt.

"When the flash hit, when I felt the heat building inside me... I didn't know what was happening. Didn't know I could hurt people. And he was right there, leaning over my shoulder to check the sauce, and I just—" His voice cracked.

"I can still hear him screaming. Every time I use my power. Every time I feel the heat build. I hear him screaming, and I remember that I did that. Me. The person he believed in." Clutch was quiet for a long moment.

Then she hopped off the counter, walked over to him, and did something she almost never did.

She put her hand on his arm.

"The people who killed my family are still alive," she said. "Walking around. Running corners. Living their lives like they didn't murder my mother and brothers while I hid in a closet." Kettle looked at her.

"I know where they are. I've known for years. I could walk into Brass Fang territory tomorrow and put a bullet in every single one of them." She squeezed his arm. "But I don't. Not because I'm afraid. Because killing them won't bring my family back. It'll just make me into someone they wouldn't recognize." "How do you live with it?" "I don't." Her voice was flat. "I survive it. There's a difference.

Every day I wake up and the weight is still there. Every day I choose not to let it crush me. That's not living. That's enduring." "That sounds exhausting." "It is." She let go of his arm. "But it's better than the alternative.

And sometimes—not often, but sometimes—I find people who make the weight a little lighter." Kettle studied her face.

"Is that what we are? People who make each other's weight lighter?" "We're something." Clutch shrugged. "Crew. Family. Fellow fucked-up people trying to survive in a world that wants us dead. Labels don't matter. What matters is that you're here, I'm here, and neither of us is alone." Kettle turned back to the gumbo.

Stirred.

Tasted.

"It's almost ready," he said. "You want some?" "It's 3 AM." "Best time for gumbo. That's when the ghosts are hungriest." Clutch almost laughed. "You believe in ghosts?" "I believe in feeding people. Ghosts, living people, doesn't matter." He pulled out two bowls. "My grandmother used to say cooking was an act of love. Every meal you make for someone else is a way of saying you want them to survive. To be nourished. To keep going." "That's beautiful." "She was a beautiful person." Kettle ladled gumbo into the bowls. "I didn't appreciate it until she was gone. Story of my life." He handed Clutch a bowl.

She took it.

They sat on overturned crates in the makeshift kitchen, eating gumbo at 3 AM in an underground tunnel while the world above burned.

"This is really good," Clutch said.

"I know." "Arrogant." "Accurate." Kettle smiled—the first real smile she'd seen from him in days. "Thank you." "For what?" "For not telling me it's okay. For not saying time heals all wounds or that I should forgive myself or whatever bullshit people usually say." He met her eyes. "For just being here. Eating gumbo. Not making it weird." Clutch snorted. "Oh, it's definitely weird. We're trauma-bonding over Cajun food in a sewer at 3 AM. That's objectively weird." "Fair point." "But it's good weird." She took another bite. "I could get used to good weird." They ate in silence for a while.

Then Kettle said: "If you ever decide to go after them—the people who killed your family—I want to be there." Clutch looked at him.

"Not to stop you," he added. "To help. To make sure you don't have to do it alone. To be there after, when the weight hits." "Why?" "Because that's what crew does." He scraped the last of his gumbo from the bowl. "And because you're the first person who's ever looked at me and seen something other than a walking disaster. That means something." Clutch felt something shift in her chest.

Not romantic. Not even quite friendship.

Something deeper. The recognition of a kindred soul.

"Deal," she said. "When I go, you go." "Deal." They shook on it.

Gumbo grease and old pain and something like hope.

"Now," Kettle said, "you want to learn how to make this? Because I'm not going to be around forever, and someone needs to keep the ghosts fed." "You're going to teach me to cook?" "I'm going to try. Fair warning: you're going to be terrible at it." "How do you know?" "Because luck doesn't work in kitchens. Only skill." He grinned.

"And you, Clutch, have no skills." "I have skills!" "Name one that doesn't involve gambling or violence." She opened her mouth.

Closed it.

"That's what I thought." Kettle handed her a knife. "Now. First lesson.

How to chop onions without crying." "Everyone cries when they chop onions." "Not if you do it right." He positioned her hands on the knife.

"There's a technique. Like everything else. You just have to learn the patterns." Clutch let him guide her hands.

And for the first time in a long time, she let herself be bad at something.

Let herself learn.

Let herself be human.

CHAPTER 23

THE GHOSTS

The Underline had its own ecosystem.

D-Lo learned this in the first week—learned that the abandoned subway tunnels weren't just hiding places but a community. A city beneath the city, with its own rules, its own rhythms, its own people.

The Ghosts.

"Time you met everyone properly," Lexi said on his fifth day underground. "You're going to be working with these people. Fighting beside them. Maybe dying beside them. Should probably know their names." She led him through the main chamber—past cooking fires and sleeping areas and the constant murmur of survivors trying to make a life in the dark.

"Most of us came from the same place," she explained. "The Marrow.

District Nine. The neighborhoods the Trust likes to pretend don't exist.

We're the ones who manifested and couldn't hide it. The ones who got hunted." "How many?" "Right now? About a hundred and twelve. It changes—people leave, people die, new ones find their way down." She paused at a junction.

"But the core group, the ones who've been here longest? About twenty.

Those are the ones you need to know."

TRACE

The first one she introduced him to was barely visible.

"Trace!" Lexi called into what looked like empty air. "Stop creeping and say hello." A figure materialized—a young woman, maybe nineteen, with skin that seemed to shift between solid and translucent. One moment D-Lo could see her clearly; the next, she was fading into the shadows like smoke.

"New meat," Trace said, studying D-Lo with eyes that flickered in and out of visibility. "The one who resets." "That's me." "Heard you died fourteen times learning the patrol patterns at the depot." She tilted her head. "That's commitment." "Or stupidity." Trace smiled. It was unsettling—her teeth seemed to phase between solid and ghostly.

"Same thing, sometimes." She turned to Lexi. "I'll put him on the rotation. Night watch, probably. His power's useless for stealth, but if anything goes wrong..." "He can try again," Lexi finished. "Exactly." Trace faded back into the shadows. D-Lo blinked, and she was gone.

"She does that," Lexi said. "You get used to it."

MURMUR

The communications hub was a tangle of salvaged electronics—radios, phones, screens, things D-Lo couldn't identify. In the center of it sat a boy who couldn't have been older than fifteen, headphones clamped over his ears, eyes closed in concentration.

"Murmur," Lexi said. "Our ears." The boy opened his eyes. They were pale—almost white—and seemed to look through D-Lo rather than at him.

"You're loud," Murmur said. His voice was soft, almost a whisper.

"Your thoughts, I mean. Most people are background noise. You're... static.

Interference." "Sorry?" "Don't be. It's interesting." Murmur turned back to his equipment.

"I hear everything within about two miles. Conversations, thoughts, electronic signals. All of it, all the time. The noise almost drove me crazy before I learned to filter." "And now?" "Now I listen for the Trust. For danger. For anything that might hurt us." He tapped his headphones. "Right now, there's a patrol three blocks north. Four officers, standard sweep. They'll pass in about six minutes." "That's... useful." "It's

182

survival." Murmur's pale eyes met his. "We all have our roles.

Mine is to make sure nobody sneaks up on us. What's yours?" D-Lo didn't have an answer.

Not yet.

ECHO

She was old—maybe sixty, maybe older. Her hair was gray, her face lined, her face gnarled with arthritis. She sat in a small chamber off the main tunnel, surrounded by children who listened to her with rapt attention.

"Echo," Lexi said softly, not wanting to interrupt. "She's been here longest. Since before I was born." "What's her power?" "Memory. Perfect, total recall—not just her own memories, but anyone she touches." Lexi's voice was reverent. "She remembers everything.

Every Ghost who ever lived down here. Every fight. Every loss. Every victory." Echo looked up, as if sensing them.

"Lexi. And the new Anchor." Her voice was like dry leaves. "Come. Sit." They sat.

Echo reached out and touched D-Lo's hand.

He felt it—a gentle probe, nothing like the Janitor's invasion. More like someone leafing through a photo album.

"So many deaths," Echo murmured. "So many resets. You carry versions of yourself that no longer exist." "Yeah." "That's a heavy burden." She released his hand. "But you also carry hope. The possibility of trying again. Learning. Growing." Her old eyes studied him. "Don't waste that gift on fear. Use it." "I'm trying." "Try harder." She smiled, softening the words. "We need you, Anchor.

More than you know."

SPARKS

The generator room hummed with energy—literally. A young woman stood at its center, hands pressed against the main transformer, electricity arcing between her fingers.

"Sparks keeps the lights on," Lexi explained. "Without her, we'd be in the dark. Literally." Sparks looked up. She was maybe twenty-two, with hair that stood on end from constant static charge and eyes that crackled with barely contained power.

"You're the reset guy." She didn't offer a handshake—probably for the best, given the electricity dancing across her skin. "Heard you took a suppression bolt at the depot. How'd that feel?" "Like getting hit by lightning and having my soul compressed at the same time." Sparks laughed. "Yeah, sounds about right. Those things are nasty—designed to overload our nervous systems, shut down our powers.

Lucky for you, you can just die and try again." "Lucky's not the word I'd use." "It's the word I'd use." Her expression turned serious. "Some of us don't get second chances. Some of us fail once, and that's it. You have a gift, reset man. Don't take it for granted." "I won't." "Good." She turned back to the generator. "Now let me work. This whole place runs on me, and I skipped breakfast."

THE OTHERS

Over the next few days, D-Lo met them all.

Brick—a massive man who could harden his skin to stone. He didn't talk much, but when he stood in front of you, nothing was getting through.

Whisper—a girl who could project her voice anywhere within earshot. She served as their long-distance communication when Murmur's range wasn't enough.

Fade—Trace's younger brother, with similar phasing abilities but less control. He kept accidentally walking through walls he meant to lean against.

Doc—not wired, just a former medical student who'd joined the Ghosts after her clinic was raided. She kept them alive with salvaged supplies and stubborn determination.

Compass—a boy who always knew which direction safety lay. He'd led dozens of refugees through the tunnels to the Underline.

Glass—a woman who could see through solid objects. She made an excellent lookout.

Static—a teenager who could disrupt electronic signals. Useful for scrambling Trust drones.

Each of them had a story. Each of them had lost something—family, home, the life they'd expected to live. Each of them had found their way to the Underline because there was nowhere else to go.

And each of them looked at D-Lo with a mixture of hope and wariness.

The Anchor, they called him.

The one who might save us.

Or destroy us.

The pressure was enormous.

But looking at their faces—young and old, scared and determined, broken and still fighting—D-Lo understood something.

This wasn't just about survival.

This was family.

And you didn't abandon family.

"You understand now?" Lexi asked on the last night of his tour.

They stood on the observation platform, looking down at the Underline's main chamber. Below them, the Ghosts lived their lives—eating, sleeping, laughing, crying. Being human in a world that wanted them to be anything but.

"Yeah," D-Lo said. "I think I do." "These people trust me. Trust Bishop. They'll trust you too, if you earn it." "How do I earn it?" Lexi turned to face him.

"By showing up. By fighting. By bleeding beside them when the Trust comes." Her eyes were fierce. "By not running when things get hard. By treating them like people, not soldiers. Not assets. People." "I can do that." "I know." She almost smiled. "That's why I brought you here. That's why Bishop said yes." She started walking toward the ladder.

"Get some sleep, Reload. Tomorrow, we start training you for real. And trust me—" she glanced back "—it's going to hurt." D-Lo looked down at the Ghosts.

His people now.

His responsibility.

"Can't wait," he muttered.

And meant it.

CHAPTER 24

THE SMALL THINGS

D-Lo noticed things about Lexi.

Small things. Things that didn't matter to anyone else.

Like how she braided her hair when she was thinking—fingers moving automatically through the strands while her mind worked on something a thousand miles away. Like how she hummed gospel songs under her breath when she thought no one was listening, fragments of hymns her father must have sung. Like how she always checked the exits in any room—twice, three times, until she was sure she knew every way out.

Like how she never ate the last bite of anything.

"You gonna finish that?" Clutch asked, eyeing the quarter-sandwich Lexi had pushed to the edge of her plate.

"Not hungry." Clutch shrugged and took it.

But D-Lo watched. And later, when they were alone in one of the Underline's countless corridors, he asked.

"What's with the food thing?" Lexi looked at him. "What food thing?" "You never finish. Always leave a piece behind. I've been watching." "That's creepy." "It's observant." He leaned against the tunnel wall. "You don't have to tell me. I'm just… noticing." Lexi was quiet for a long moment.

"My father used to do it," she said finally. "Said it was a Southern thing. You leave a bite for the angels. A piece for the people who don't have enough." She shrugged. "I don't believe in angels anymore. But I can't stop doing it. Feels like giving up the last piece of him I have left." D-Lo didn't say anything.

Just stood there, in the half-dark of the tunnel, watching her face in the flickering light.

"What?" she asked.

"Nothing. Just..." He shook his head. "You're not what I expected." "What did you expect?" "A leader. A soldier. Someone hard all the way through." He met her eyes. "But you leave food for angels. You hum church songs. You braid your hair when you think." "I don't—" "You do. You're doing it right now." Lexi's hand froze mid-motion, fingers tangled in her hair. She looked down like she'd caught her hand doing something without permission.

"That's embarrassing." "It's human." D-Lo pushed off the wall. "Everyone here looks at you like you're invincible. This perfect warrior who never breaks. But you're not, are you? You're just a girl who lost her dad and learned to fight because the alternative was dying." Lexi's breath caught.

"How do you see that?" "Because I'm the same thing." He stepped closer. "A kid who lost too much too young and built armor to survive. Only difference is my armor's made of death. Yours is made of leadership." She didn't move away.

"You shouldn't say things like that." "Why?" "Because it makes me want to stop pretending." Her voice dropped.

"And I can't afford to stop pretending. Not with everyone counting on me." "Maybe that's exactly why you need to. Sometimes. With someone." D-Lo reached out, touched her hand. "I'm not asking you to fall apart. I'm just saying... you can let the armor down. Here. With me. I won't tell anyone you're human." Lexi looked at his hand on hers.

Then up at his face.

Then she did something he didn't expect—she laughed. A real laugh, surprised out of her.

"You're ridiculous." "I've been told." "And cheesy. That was an extremely cheesy speech." "I meant every word of it." "I know." Her smile softened. "That's the worst part." She didn't pull her hand away.

Later, Lexi gave him a tour of the Underline's deeper sections.

"Most people only see the main tunnels," she said, leading him down a spiral staircase that groaned with every step. "But the Underline goes deep. Miles deep, in some places. Old subway lines, sewer systems, bomb shelters from the Cold War, things nobody has names for anymore." "How'd you find it all?" "We didn't. The Underline found us." She ducked through a low archway.

"Bishop used to say these tunnels were alive. That they chose who to let in and who to spit out. I thought he was being mystical. Then I saw the way the tunnels shift." "Shift?" "Move. Rearrange. A passage that was there yesterday might be gone today. A wall might open where there wasn't a door." She glanced back at him. "You think the wired are the only strange thing in New Babylon?

The city itself is wrong. Has been since before Renaissance. Maybe forever." They emerged into a cavern D-Lo hadn't seen before.

Vast. Cathedral-high ceilings lost in darkness above. And carved into the walls— "Are those faces?" he whispered.

"We don't know who made them. They were here before us. Before the city, maybe." Lexi's voice echoed strangely. "Bishop found writings once.

Called them the Sleepers. Said they were here before humans, and they'd be here after." D-Lo studied the carved faces. Dozens of them. Hundreds. All different, all with closed eyes, all with expressions of peaceful waiting.

"Are they dangerous?" "Everything down here is dangerous." Lexi continued walking. "But the Sleepers don't bother us. They just... watch. Dream. Whatever they do.

Some of the older Ghosts leave offerings—food, candles, small treasures. Say it keeps the tunnels friendly." "Do you believe that?" "I believe in covering my bases." She turned down another passage.

"Come on. There's more."

The Refugee Quarter spread across three connected chambers, each one carved from the rock by hands that weren't human.

D-Lo stopped at the entrance, overwhelmed.

Hundreds of people. Maybe thousands. Families with children, elderly couples, teenagers traveling alone. All of them living in makeshift shelters built from tarps and salvaged materials. Cooking fires sent smoke toward ventilation shafts that someone, somehow, had engineered to draw fresh air from the surface.

"How many?" "Three thousand, last count. And more every week." Lexi led him down a path between shelters. "Most of them aren't wired. Just regular people who got caught in Trust operations, lost their homes, had nowhere else to go." A little girl ran past, chasing a dog made of shadows that flickered between solid and translucent. She was laughing. The dog—if it was a dog—barked silently.

"What was that?" "Miranda's imaginary friend. Except she's wired, so her imaginary friends are real." Lexi smiled faintly. "She's seven. Lost her parents in a raid. One of our families took her in." D-Lo watched the girl disappear into a shelter, the shadow-dog bounding after her.

"All these people are hiding from the Trust?" "From the Trust. From gangs. From landlords. From life." Lexi stopped at a junction where four paths met. "This is what we're protecting, D-Lo.

Not just the wired. Not just the fighters. Everyone. The whole broken mess of humanity that the world above doesn't want." "How do you feed them all?" "Raids. Donations. Gardens." She pointed to a chamber off to the left where grow-lights illuminated rows of vegetables. "Fox figured out how to tap the city's power grid without being traced. We're basically parasites, living off what the surface doesn't notice is missing." "That's incredible." "That's desperation." Lexi's voice hardened. "Every day is a calculation. How much can we take before someone notices? How many people can we shelter before we run out of space? How long before the Trust finds us and burns it all down?" "They haven't found you yet." "The tunnels protect us. The Sleepers, maybe. Or just dumb luck." She turned to face him. "But luck runs out. That's why we need to stop playing defense. That's why what you can do matters." "What I can do gets people killed." "What you can do gives us information no one else has." Lexi gripped his arm. "You can see futures. Test options. Find the path that works.

That's not death—that's hope. The first real hope we've had since Renaissance." D-Lo looked at the refugee camp. At the thousands of people living in a hole in the ground because the world above had decided they didn't deserve to exist.

"No pressure or anything." "Maximum pressure. That's how we operate." Lexi smiled, and for a moment, the armor cracked. The leader disappeared. Just a girl, his age, carrying too much, laughing because the alternative was crying. "But you're not alone. Remember that. Whatever happens, you've got us." She let go of his arm.

Started walking back toward the main tunnels.

D-Lo followed, mind churning with everything he'd seen.

But part of him was still thinking about her hand on his arm.

About the bite of food she'd leave for angels.

About the way she braided her hair when she thought.

About how, in a world full of monsters and miracles, the thing that stuck with him most was watching Lexi Ghost be human.

CHAPTER 25

THE THREADS BETWEEN

"You're fighting your power," Madame Celestine said. "That's your first mistake." They stood in the deepest part of the Underline—a chamber so old the walls bore markings from civilizations long forgotten. Celestine had claimed this space years ago, filling it with candles, crystals, and artifacts that hummed with energies D-Lo couldn't name.

"How do you fight something that happens when you die?" D-Lo asked.

"By thinking of death as the only trigger." Celestine circled him slowly, her cane tapping against the stone floor. "Your power isn't about dying, child. It's about time. About seeing the threads that connect every moment to every other moment." "The threads." "You've seen them. I know you have. In your peripheral vision. In those moments between waking and sleeping. Thin strands of possibility stretching in every direction." D-Lo hesitated.

He had seen them. Flickers of light at the edge of his awareness.

Moments when reality seemed thin and he could almost see through it to... something else.

"I thought I was going crazy." "Perhaps you are. The two aren't mutually exclusive." Celestine smiled.

"But crazy or not, those threads are real. And learning to see them—to touch them—without dying first... that's what we're going to work on."

"Close your eyes." D-Lo obeyed.

191

The chamber fell silent except for the flickering of candles and Celestine's rhythmic footsteps.

"Now—don't try to see the threads. Don't look for them. Just... be aware. Let your mind go quiet. Let the noise fade away." Easier said than done.

D-Lo's mind was a hurricane of anxiety. Kimi in danger. The Trust closing in. The Janitor waiting. A thousand fears competing for attention.

"I can feel you fighting," Celestine said. "Stop." "I can't just—" "You can. You must." Her voice softened. "Think of water. Still water. A lake with no wind, no ripples, no disturbance. Just perfect, glassy stillness." D-Lo tried.

The lake formed in his mind—dark and smooth, reflecting a sky he couldn't quite see.

"Good. Now—notice your breath. Each inhale. Each exhale. The rhythm of your existence." In. Out. In. Out.

The hurricane started to quiet.

"Good. Now—while staying perfectly still, expand your awareness outward. Not looking. Not seeking. Just... noticing. What's there.

What's been there. What might be there." D-Lo let his consciousness drift.

Past the boundaries of his body.

Past the stone walls of the chamber.

Past the limits of the present moment.

And then— He saw them.

Not with his eyes. Not exactly. More like feeling them—delicate strands of light stretching in every direction. Connecting every object to every other object. Connecting now to then to might-be.

"Oh my god." "Don't open your eyes. Don't lose focus." Celestine's voice came from far away. "Just observe. What do you see?" "Everything." The word came out as a whisper. "I see... everything.

Every choice. Every possibility. They're all connected. They're all..." He reached for one of the threads.

And the vision shattered.

He was back in the chamber, gasping, heart pounding.

Celestine nodded slowly.

"Faster than most. You have talent." "What happened? Why did it stop?" "You tried to grab the thread. You can't grab—not yet. First, you must learn to observe. Then to understand. Then, and only then, to influence." She tapped her cane. "Again."

One day, Kimi wandered into the training chamber.

She'd been exploring the tunnels—bored, restless, tired of being the "civilian" everyone had to protect. She stopped at the entrance, watching D-Lo practice with his eyes closed.

Celestine turned toward her.

"You shouldn't be here, child." "I was just—" "I know why you're here." Celestine's milky eyes seemed to look through Kimi, into her. "You want to know if you're special too. If the flash did something to you." Kimi froze.

"I don't know what you—" "You saw the threads. During the Renaissance. Just for a moment." Celestine moved closer, her cane tapping. "You've been seeing glimpses ever since. Dreams that feel like memories. Moments when you know what someone's about to say before they say it." "How do you—" "Because I've been watching you." Celestine's voice softened.

"You're not wired, child. Not exactly. But you're not... empty, either.

There's something sleeping inside you. Something that might wake up if the right trigger comes along." Kimi's heart was pounding.

"What does that mean?" "It means stay close to your brother." Celestine turned back to D-Lo.

"And if you ever feel something stirring inside you—something bright, something hungry—don't fight it. Let it come." Kimi wanted to ask more. But Celestine's attention was already elsewhere, and the moment had passed.

She walked back into the tunnels, thinking about sleeping things.

And wondering what it would take to wake them up.

They practiced for hours.

Or days.

Time didn't work normally in Celestine's chamber.

193

D-Lo learned to find the stillness faster, to hold it longer. He learned to see the threads without reaching for them—to observe the flowing tapestry of possibility without disturbing it.

And slowly, he began to understand what he was seeing.

"Each thread is a potential future," Celestine explained during one of their breaks. "Not a certainty—futures are never certain—but a possibility. A path that reality might take if certain conditions are met." "So when I reset after dying—" "You're cutting a thread. The future where you died is severed; you jump to a different possibility." She sipped the bitter tea she always kept close. "Most wired who can manipulate probability work on single threads. One coin flip. One bullet trajectory. One moment of luck." "But I'm different." "You're an Anchor. A fixed point in time." Her milky eyes studied him.

"You don't manipulate threads—you exist at their intersection. Every possible future flows through you. That's why your power is so strong, and so dangerous." "Because I could change too many things at once." "Because you could change everything at once. One careless pull, one moment of fear or anger or desperation, and you might unravel reality itself." D-Lo felt cold.

"The Trust calls it Stage progression," Celestine continued. "Stage One: you die, you reset. The power is reactive—it happens to you, not through you. Most Anchors stay at Stage One forever, never learning to control what they are." "And Stage Two?" "Stage Two: you see the threads. You start to understand the tapestry of possibility. You can make choices before death forces them on you." She paused. "That's where you are now. On the threshold of Stage Two." "There's a Stage Three?" Celestine's face went grim.

"Stage Three: you don't just see the threads—you can rewrite them.

Change reality directly, without death as a catalyst. Create futures that shouldn't exist. Unmake things that should." She shook her head.

"Every Anchor who's reached Stage Three has either been captured by the Trust or destroyed themselves trying to fix the unfixable." "Is that what happened to the other Anchors? The ones who destroyed cities?" Celestine was quiet for a moment.

"The first Anchor tried to save her family. Pulled too hard on a thread that was already fraying. Reality... rejected the change." She shook her head. "The second—Marcus, the one who became the

Cleaner—tried to absorb the world's pain. Thought he could contain it. But pain doesn't disappear when you take it from someone. It just moves. Accumulates.

Eventually, it consumed him." "And the third?" "The Conductor. Captured by the Trust before he could fully manifest.

They broke him before he could break himself." Celestine's voice was soft. "Different failures. Same lesson." "What lesson?" "That power without wisdom destroys. That strength without compassion corrupts. That trying to save everyone usually means saving no one." She met his eyes. "You cannot fix the world, child. You can only choose which pieces to fight for."

"Try again. But this time, don't just see the threads. Feel where they want to go." D-Lo sank into the stillness.

The threads appeared—glowing filaments stretching in every direction.

He'd learned to recognize the different types: bright threads for likely futures, dim threads for unlikely ones. Thick threads for stable possibilities, thin threads for fragile ones.

"Feel where they want to go," Celestine repeated. "Reality has momentum.

It prefers certain paths over others. Learn to sense that preference, and you'll know which threads are safe to touch." D-Lo focused.

There—a thick, bright thread leading from this moment to tomorrow morning. Stable. Strong. The most likely future.

And there—a thin, dim thread leading to a version where Kettle accidentally started a fire in the Underline tonight. Possible, but unlikely.

And there—a medium thread, pulsing faintly, leading to...

D-Lo's breath caught.

He could see Kimi. In the future. In the Vault. Alone. Scared.

"What is it?" Celestine asked.

"My sister. I can see—she's going to be captured. The Trust is going to take her." "When?" "Soon. I don't know exactly, but—" D-Lo reached for the thread.

"STOP." The command was sharp. D-Lo's hand froze.

"You cannot change it," Celestine said. "Not like that. Not by grabbing blindly at a future you don't understand." "But my sister—"

"Will be captured regardless of what you do in this moment. That thread is too thick, too bright. The momentum is too strong." Celestine's voice was gentle but firm. "Some futures are nearly inevitable. The more you fight them, the worse the alternatives become." "So I'm just supposed to let it happen?" "You're supposed to see it happen. Understand why it happens. And then—when the moment comes—make the choice that leads to the best possible outcome. Not the perfect outcome. The best possible one." D-Lo's fists clenched.

"That's not good enough." "It never is." Celestine touched his face, her fingers cool and dry.

"But it's what we have. And if you try to force a different future—if you tear at the threads without understanding them—you'll become the thing that destroys everyone you're trying to save." D-Lo wanted to argue.

Wanted to scream.

Wanted to rip reality apart and rebuild it into something that didn't hurt.

But he looked at Celestine's face—old, wise, sad—and understood.

She'd been here before.

She'd watched other people make the same mistakes.

And she was trying to save him from becoming another cautionary tale.

"Okay," he said finally. "Teach me. Teach me how to do this right." Celestine smiled.

"Good. Now—show me the thread for your sister again. Let's trace it together. See where it goes. And when we reach the point where you can make a difference—we'll find it." D-Lo closed his eyes.

Found the stillness.

And this time, when he saw the threads, he didn't grab.

He watched.

He learned.

And slowly, piece by piece, he began to understand what he could become.

Three days later—or maybe three hours, time was strange in the chamber—D-Lo touched a thread finally,.

It was a small one. Thin. Dim. The possibility that a candle would fall and start a fire.

He didn't pull.

He nudged.

Just a gentle pressure, redirecting the momentum, steering the thread away from destruction and toward safety.

The candle stabilized.

The fire didn't start.

And D-Lo opened his eyes to find Celestine watching him with something like pride.

"You felt it," she said. "The difference between forcing and guiding." "Yeah." D-Lo looked at his hands. They were shaking. "Is that... is that what it's supposed to feel like?" "When you do it right. When you work with reality instead of against it." Celestine stood slowly, her old joints creaking. "You're ready for the next step." "What's the next step?" "Learning to see the threads during chaos. During combat. During the moments when your body is dying and your mind is screaming and everything in you wants to tear the world apart." D-Lo swallowed.

"How do I do that?" Celestine smiled.

It wasn't a kind smile.

"We practice," she said. "And you die. A lot." "That doesn't sound fun." "It isn't. But by the time we're done, you'll be able to see the threads in the space between heartbeats. Choose your path in the moment before death. Reset not because you failed, but because you chose to try again." She hobbled toward the chamber's exit.

"Rest. Eat. Tomorrow, we begin the hard part." D-Lo watched her go.

Then looked down at his hands again.

The threads were still there, at the edge of his vision. Faint but present. Waiting.

I can do this, he thought. I can learn to control it.

And when Kimi needs me—when everything goes to hell—I'll be ready.

Not to save everyone.

Just the ones that matter most.

It wasn't the answer he'd wanted.

But it was the answer he had.

And for now, it would have to be enough.

The Underline never truly slept, but it had its quiet hours.

Between three and five in the morning, when even the most paranoid sentries grew heavy-lidded and the constant murmur of refugees faded to gentle breathing, the tunnels belonged to the restless.

D-Lo was restless.

He'd been staring at the same crack in the ceiling for two hours, running scenarios in his head. The Vault. Kimi. A hundred ways to die and maybe—maybe—one way to win.

Sleep wasn't coming. So he walked.

He found Lexi in the map room.

She stood before the wall of stolen blueprints and hand-drawn schematics, her back to the entrance, one hand tracing a route through Trust territory like she was memorizing it through her fingertips.

"You should be sleeping," she said without turning.

"So should you." "Leaders don't sleep. We just close our eyes and worry horizontally." D-Lo crossed the room and stood beside her. Close enough to feel her warmth. Not close enough to touch.

"Which route you planning?" "All of them. None of them." She let her hand drop. "Every path I see ends in blood. Ours or theirs. Usually both." "That's not new." "No. But it's heavier tonight." She finally looked at him. In the dim light, she looked younger. Tired. Human. "Do you ever wonder what it would be like? To just... stop?" "Stop what?" "Fighting. Planning. Being the person everyone looks to." She turned back to the maps. "Sometimes I think about what my life would have been if the Trust never existed. If Renaissance never happened. If I was just... a girl." "What would you be doing?" "I don't know. College, maybe. My father wanted me to be a lawyer.

Said I argued like one." A ghost of a smile. "I'd probably be in some dorm room right now, stressing about finals instead of tactical infiltration." "That sounds boring." "That sounds peaceful." The smile faded. "I don't remember what peace feels like, D-Lo. I was eleven when they killed my father. Eleven when Bishop found me hiding in the wreckage. I've been fighting so long I don't know how to do anything else." D-Lo didn't have a response for that.

So he did something else instead.

He took her hand.

Lexi went still.

Not tense—just... surprised. Like she'd forgotten what it felt like to be touched gently, without agenda, without needing something in return.

"What are you doing?" "I don't know." He looked at their hands—his darker, rougher, still bearing calluses from the warehouse job that felt like another lifetime.

Hers slender, scarred across the knuckles, a fighter's hands. "Seemed like the right move." "We shouldn't—" "Probably not." "This complicates things." "Everything's complicated." "D-Lo—" "Lexi." He turned to face her, still holding her hand. "I've died fifty-three times. Every single time, there's this moment right before the end where I think about regrets. Things I should have said. Things I should have done." He swallowed. "I'm tired of having regrets." Her eyes searched his face. Looking for something—deception, maybe. An angle. The kind of manipulation she'd learned to expect from everyone except her inner circle.

She didn't find it.

"This is a terrible idea," she said.

"Probably." "We're going into a fight tomorrow that might kill us all." "I know." "And you want to... what? Talk about feelings?" "I want to spend whatever time we have left not pretending I don't care about you." D-Lo approached. "If we die tomorrow, I don't want to die wondering what might have happened if I'd been brave enough to say something." "You're being dramatic." "I literally come back from the dead. Drama's kind of my thing." Lexi laughed—a real laugh, surprised out of her. It transformed her face, stripped away the armor, revealed the girl underneath the soldier.

"You're impossible." "I've been told."

They sat against the wall, shoulders touching, the maps of their enemies spread out before them like a promise of violence.

"Tell me something," Lexi said. "Something nobody else knows." D-Lo thought about it.

"I used to have nightmares about my mom," he said. "After she died.

Not sad ones—worse. Dreams where she came back and was disappointed in me.

Said I was failing Kimi. Said I wasn't man enough to do what needed doing." "That's not true." "I know. Now. But for years, I carried that. Woke up every morning feeling like I wasn't enough." He stared at the maps without seeing them. "The first time I died and came back, you know what I felt?

Relief. Because for the first time, I had proof that I could do something nobody else could do. That maybe I was enough." "That's a hell of a way to find self-worth." "Tell me about it." Lexi was quiet for a moment. Then: "I watched my father die." D-Lo turned to look at her.

"The Trust didn't just kill him—they made an example. Middle of the day, middle of the street, so everyone would see what happened to people who helped the wired." Her voice was steady. Too steady. The kind of calm that came from telling a story so many times it stopped feeling real. "He was still alive when they dragged him away. Still trying to tell me to run. I didn't run. I hid behind a dumpster and watched them put him in a van." "Lexi..." "I was eleven. Eleven years old, hiding in garbage, watching my daddy disappear." She finally looked at him. "That's why I don't sleep.

Because when I close my eyes, I'm back behind that dumpster. And he's looking at me, and he's saying run, and I'm not running. I'm just watching. Frozen. Useless." D-Lo did the only thing he could think of.

He pulled her close.

She stiffened for a moment—instinct, defense, the armor trying to snap back into place.

Then she softened.

Let her head rest against his shoulder.

Let herself be held.

"This doesn't change anything," she murmured.

"I know." "Tomorrow we still fight. Still maybe die. Still have to be leaders." "I know." "But tonight..." "Tonight we're just people." D-Lo rested his chin on her hair.

"That's enough. That's more than enough." They stayed like that until the quiet hours ended and the Underline stirred back to life.

At some point, D-Lo became aware of how close she was. The warmth of her. The way the dim light caught the curve of her jaw. The way her breath had steadied, but her pulse hadn't.

He wanted to kiss her.

The want was a physical thing—an ache in his chest, a pull toward her that had nothing to do with threads or powers or saving the world. Just two people, scared and exhausted and desperate for connection.

He almost did it. Almost closed the distance. Almost let himself have this one thing that wasn't about survival.

But he stopped.

Because this wasn't about him. It wasn't about what he wanted. It was about her—about giving her space to be something other than a leader, even if just for one night.

So he held her.

And let that be enough.

Neither of them slept.

But finally, in longer than either could remember, they didn't feel alone.

When the sun rose—or when their internal clocks said it should have—they stood.

Lexi straightened her jacket. Fixed her braids. Rebuilt herself piece by piece into the leader the Ghosts needed.

But before she walked away, she turned back.

"D-Lo." "Yeah?" "Don't die tomorrow. That's an order." "I'll do my best. But if I do—" "No." She crossed back to him, fast, grabbed the front of his shirt.

"No 'if I do.' You come back. Every time. However many times it takes. You come back." "I will." "Promise me." "I promise." She held his gaze for a long moment.

Then she kissed him.

Brief. Fierce. A promise.

"See you on the other side," she said.

And walked into the war.

CHAPTER 26

THE MARK

D-Lo woke to alarms.

Not electronic alarms—the Underline didn't have those. These were human alarms. Voices shouting. Feet running. The clatter of weapons being grabbed and readied.

He was on his feet before his brain fully woke up, stumbling out of the train car into chaos.

Ghosts sprinted past him—kids and teens moving with military precision, taking positions at tunnel entrances, forming defensive lines.

Lexi appeared beside him, fully armed, face tight.

"He's here." A cold weight settled in his stomach.

"The Cleaner?" "Something tripped our outer perimeter. Sensors went dark one by one, moving inward. Whatever it is, it's not hiding." "Could be Trust." "Trust would come loud. This is quiet. Methodical." Her eyes met his.

"This is a hunt." From somewhere deep in the tunnels—far away but getting closer—D-Lo heard it.

SCRAAAAAAPE.

SCRAAAAAAPE.

Metal on stone.

A mop handle dragging.

"Get Kettle and Clutch," Lexi said. "Meet me at the command post. We need to—" The lights went out.

All of them.

Every lantern, every jury-rigged electric light, every glow stick and candle—extinguished simultaneously, like a giant hand had smothered them.

Darkness.

Absolute darkness.

And in that darkness, a whisper: "Come out, come out, little broken things..."

D-Lo couldn't see his hand in front of his face.

Around him, he heard panic—kids screaming, people crashing into each other, the sounds of a community that had survived by staying hidden suddenly exposed.

"STAY CALM!" Lexi's voice cut through the chaos. "EVERYONE STAY WHERE YOU ARE! DON'T—" A scream.

Not fear.

Pain.

Someone had been touched.

Someone was being cleaned.

D-Lo felt the cold spreading through the tunnel—that unnatural chill that preceded the Janitor like a bow wave.

He's here. He's in the tunnels. He's hunting.

"KETTLE!" D-Lo shouted into the darkness. "KETTLE, I NEED LIGHT!" For a moment, nothing.

Then—a glow.

Faint at first. Orange. Growing.

Kettle's silhouette emerged from the darkness, his skin illuminating like a human lantern. Heat radiated off him, pushing back the cold.

"I got you," Kettle said, voice shaking but determined. "Stay close." Clutch appeared at D-Lo's side, coin in hand, eyes scanning the shadows.

"My luck is going haywire," she hissed. "I can't get a read on anything.

It's like probability itself is scrambled." "That's him," D-Lo said. "He cancels things. Powers. Luck. Hope." "Then how do we fight him?" D-Lo didn't have an answer.

Another scream echoed through the tunnels.

Closer this time.

Kettle's glow flickered.

"He's coming this way," Kettle whispered. "I can feel him. Cold spot.

Moving fast." Lexi materialized out of the shadows, blade drawn.

"We need to evacuate. Get the kids out through the eastern tunnels." "And the Cleaner?" "Someone has to hold him off." Her eyes locked onto D-Lo. "That's you." "Me? I can't fight that thing!" "You don't have to fight him. You have to distract him. Buy time." She grabbed his arm. "You're the only one who can survive contact. The only one who can come back." D-Lo felt the weight of that statement.

The only one who could die and try again.

The only one expendable enough to face the monster.

"I need more than distraction," he said. "I need to understand my power.

You said we'd work on it today—" "Today became right now." Lexi's grip tightened. "Bishop said you're anchored. That means you don't just reset—you choose. You select which timeline becomes real." "I don't know how to do that!" "Then figure it out." She let go. "Because if you don't, everyone here dies. Not resets. Dies. Forever." She disappeared into the darkness, shouting orders.

D-Lo stood there, heart hammering.

Kettle's glow flickered again.

Clutch grabbed his shoulder.

"Whatever you're gonna do, do it fast."

D-Lo closed his eyes.

Which was stupid—everything was already dark—but it helped him focus.

You don't just reset. You choose. You select which timeline becomes real. He thought about all the times he'd died.

The bullet in the courtyard.

The toaster in the tub.

The bike delivery guy.

Mrs. Waverly's heat.

Kettle's explosion.

The Janitor's touch.

Each time, he'd woken up at the same moment—10:43 AM on that first day. Like a checkpoint in a video game.

But that wasn't choosing.

That was just... resetting. Defaulting. Going back to the last save point automatically.

What if he could choose something different?

What if he could pick a specific moment? A specific outcome?

What if the reset wasn't the limit of his power—just the beginning?

Pain is information, Lexi had said.

Every death taught him something.

Every reset gave him new knowledge.

But what if he could use that knowledge not just to survive, but to change things?

SCRAAAAAPE.

Closer now.

So close D-Lo could feel the cold pressing against Kettle's heat like two forces at war.

He opened his eyes.

And saw something new.

It wasn't vision—not exactly.

More like... awareness.

D-Lo could see the tunnel in front of him, lit by Kettle's glow. But overlaid on that, like a double exposure, he could see other things.

Possibilities.

Branches.

A version of the next moment where he ran left—and died.

A version where he ran right—and died.

A version where he stood still—and died.

A version where he— Wait.

He focused on that last thread.

In that version, he didn't run. Didn't hide. Didn't fight.

He spoke.

He said something to the Janitor.

Something that made the monster pause.

D-Lo couldn't hear what it was—the vision was fuzzy, incomplete—but he could see the outcome.

A moment of hesitation.

A crack in the Janitor's certainty.

An opening.

"I think I see it," D-Lo whispered.

"See what?" Clutch asked.

"The way forward." *SCRAAAAAPE.*

The Janitor emerged from the darkness.

He looked the same as before—blue coveralls, work boots, mop handle dragging behind him. That too-thin frame. That too-pale skin. Those hollow eyes that swallowed light.

But now, in the glow of Kettle's heat, D-Lo could see more.

The Janitor's shadow wasn't just slow—it was wrong. It moved independently, stretching and contracting like it was alive, like it was a separate entity tethered to him but not part of him.

And his smile—that terrible, frozen smile—wasn't a smile at all.

It was a wound.

A scar where a mouth should be, stretched into a shape that mimicked human expression but felt nothing.

"There you are," the Janitor said softly. "My beautiful broken thing." Kettle stepped forward, heat intensifying.

"Stay back!" The Janitor didn't even look at him.

"The burning one. So much pain. So much guilt." He inhaled deeply.

"Your friend—the one you hurt. Markus. You still carry that, don't you?

Even though time erased it, you remember." Kettle flinched.

His glow dimmed.

"That's how I'll start," the Janitor continued. "Your guilt. Your shame.

All that delicious suffering, bottled up inside you—" "You're not going to touch him," D-Lo said.

The Janitor's empty eyes shifted to him.

"Oh? And how will you stop me?" D-Lo looked at the threads.

The possibilities branching out from this moment.

He couldn't see everything—the vision was incomplete, fragmented—but he could see enough.

Enough to know what to say.

"I know what you are," D-Lo said.

The Janitor tilted his head.

206

"Do you?" "You're not a monster. Not really. You're a function. A process." D-Lo's voice was steady, even though his heart was screaming. "You consume pain because that's what you were made to do. But you weren't always this.

Once, you were something else. Someone else." The Janitor's smile faltered.

Just a fraction.

But D-Lo saw it.

"Celestine told us. You've been in the Marrow for decades. Maybe centuries. But you didn't start there." D-Lo took a step forward.

"You started as a person. A real person, with a real life, real feelings. And something happened to you. Something broke you so completely that you became this." "Stop talking." The Janitor's voice had changed.

Harder.

Almost angry.

"What was your name?" D-Lo asked. "Before you were the Cleaner.

Before you were the Janitor. What did people call you?" "I said STOP." The cold intensified.

Kettle gasped, his heat flickering.

Clutch grabbed D-Lo's arm.

"D-Lo, what are you doing—" "I'm finding the crack," D-Lo said. "The fracture in his pattern.

The thing he doesn't expect." He looked the Janitor in the eyes.

Those empty, hollow, light-swallowing eyes.

"You remember everything, don't you? Every person you've cleaned.

Every soul you've consumed. They're all in there, somewhere. All that pain you've eaten—it didn't disappear. It became part of you. Made you what you are." The Janitor stood frozen.

"But that means they're still there. All those people. All those voices." D-Lo's voice dropped to a whisper. "Don't you get tired?

Carrying all of them? Hearing all of them? Feeling all of them?" Silence.

Long, terrible silence.

Then the Janitor spoke.

And his voice was different.

Multiple voices.

Layered.

Overlapping.

Like a crowd speaking through a single mouth.

"We are tired," the voices said. "So tired. It never stops. It never ends. We take and take and take and there is always more pain, always more suffering, always more—" The Janitor clutched his head.

Staggered.

For the first time, he looked vulnerable.

"NOW!" D-Lo shouted.

Kettle didn't hesitate.

His whole body erupted—not an explosion, but a directed blast. A column of superheated air aimed directly at the Janitor, hot enough to melt steel, hot enough to incinerate anything living.

The heat hit the Janitor like a truck.

He flew backwards, slamming into the tunnel wall hard enough to crack stone.

Steam filled the corridor.

The smell of burning fabric.

But when the steam cleared— The Janitor was still standing.

His coveralls were scorched. His skin was blackened in patches. But he was standing.

And he was smiling again.

That wrong, terrible smile.

"Clever," he said, voice singular again. "Very clever. You found a crack." He straightened, bones popping. "But cracks can be filled.

Sealed. Forgotten." He stepped forward.

The cold returned, stronger than before.

Kettle's heat guttered like a candle in a hurricane.

"No," Kettle groaned. "No, I won't—" "You will." The Janitor reached out. "You all will. Eventually." D-Lo saw the threads again.

Saw the possibilities.

In every single one, they died.

Every. Single. One.

Except— There.

One thread.

Barely visible.

A possibility so unlikely it was almost invisible.

D-Lo reached for it.

Not physically—mentally. Spiritually. With whatever part of him was anchored to reality.

He grabbed that thread.

And pulled.

The world glitched.

That was the only word for it.

Reality stuttered, like a video buffering, like a record skipping, like existence itself hiccupped.

And when it stabilized— D-Lo was standing in the same spot.

But the Janitor was gone.

The tunnel was lit—emergency lights that hadn't been there before.

And Lexi was beside him, hand on his shoulder, saying words he'd already heard: "—work on your power. You said we'd work on it today—" D-Lo blinked.

He was back.

Not at 10:43 AM.

Not at his default save point.

He was back to a few minutes ago.

Before the lights went out.

Before the attack.

"D-Lo?" Lexi frowned. "You okay? You look like you've seen a ghost." D-Lo's hands were shaking.

He'd done it.

He'd chosen a specific moment.

He'd reset to a point of his choosing.

"The Janitor," he gasped. "He's in the tunnels. He's coming. We need to evacuate NOW." Lexi's expression shifted from concern to action.

"How do you know?" "I—" D-Lo hesitated. "I saw it. I saw what happens if we don't move.

Everyone dies." She studied him for a fraction of a second.

Then she was moving, shouting orders, mobilizing the Ghosts.

D-Lo stood in the center of the chaos, trembling.

He'd bought them time.

Not much.

Minutes, maybe.

But he'd done something he'd never done before.

He'd chosen.

Reload, he thought. That's not just a name. That's what I am.

He could reset.

He could choose.

He could try different paths, different moments, different possibilities.

And somewhere, in the back of his mind, he felt the thread—the cosmic string that tied him to reality—vibrating with the strain.

Don't pull too hard, Lexi had warned.

He'd just pulled harder than ever.

But everyone was still alive.

For now, that was enough.

The next twenty minutes were controlled chaos.

Lexi had drilled the Ghosts for this—evacuation protocols, escape routes, rally points. They moved like a military unit, efficient and disciplined despite their age.

Kids were shepherded through eastern tunnels.

Supplies were grabbed and carried.

Defensive positions were abandoned in favor of survival.

D-Lo found Kettle and Clutch in the flow of bodies.

"What happened?" Clutch demanded. "One second Lexi's talking about training, the next she's screaming evacuation orders." "The Cleaner's coming. I saw it." "Saw it how?" D-Lo shook his head. "I don't know how to explain it. I just… saw.

Possibilities. Futures. And in all of them except one, he killed everyone." Clutch stared at him.

"You reset." "Yeah." "But not to the normal point. Not to that morning." "No. Just a few minutes. To before the attack." Clutch and Kettle exchanged looks.

"That's new," Kettle said quietly.

"Yeah." D-Lo's hands were still shaking. "It's very new."

When they reached the junction point—where the evacuation tunnels split into multiple paths—Bishop was waiting.

The old man stood like a statue, staff in hand, tattoos glowing faintly in the emergency light.

Behind him, a half-dozen of the oldest Ghosts. The fighters. The ones who'd survived the longest.

"You're staying," D-Lo said. It wasn't a question.

Bishop nodded.

"Someone has to slow him down. Give the little ones time to get clear." "He'll kill you." "Maybe." Bishop smiled—a grim, knowing smile. "But I've been dead before. The Trust killed me twice in the Red Rift. Buried me once.

Burned me once. And yet here I stand." He tapped his chest.

"Some of us are harder to erase than others." Lexi stepped forward.

"Bishop, you don't have to—" "Yes, I do." His voice was gentle. "This is what I'm for, child.

This is what I've always been for. The shield that breaks so others can survive." He looked at D-Lo.

"You found your gift tonight. The ability to choose. To select the path that leads to survival." His one eye gleamed. "But remember—every choice has a cost. Every timeline you abandon is a reality where things went differently. Where people died. Where you failed." D-Lo felt those words settle into his chest like stones.

"How do I live with that?" "You don't." Bishop's smile faded. "You just keep choosing. Keep fighting. Keep surviving. And you hope that the weight doesn't crush you before you find a way to set it down." *SCRAAAAAPE.*

The sound echoed from somewhere in the tunnels behind them.

Distant.

But coming.

"Go," Bishop said. "Take them. Keep them safe." Lexi grabbed his hand.

Squeezed once.

Then turned and ran.

D-Lo followed.

Kettle and Clutch beside him.

The Ghosts streaming past.

Behind them, Bishop raised his staff.

The tattoos on his arms blazed with light—real light, golden and warm, pushing back the darkness.

"Come, Cleaner!" his voice boomed through the tunnels. "Come and taste the pain of a man who refuses to die!" D-Lo didn't look back.

He couldn't.

If he looked back, he'd stop.

If he stopped, he'd fight.

If he fought, he'd die.

And this time, he wasn't sure he'd come back.

They ran.

And behind them, the sound of battle began.

Bishop stood at the junction, staff raised, light blazing.

The Cleaner emerged from the darkness.

Unhurried.

Unworried.

"The old one," the Janitor said softly. "So much pain in you. So many years of suffering. You carry it like armor." "Armor breaks," Bishop replied. "But it protects what matters." "And what matters to you? Those children? That boy?" The Janitor tilted his head. "They will all fall. Eventually. You cannot protect them forever." "I don't need forever." Bishop's voice was steady. "I just need now." He struck the ground with his staff.

Light exploded outward—golden, searing, painful.

The Janitor recoiled.

For once, his shadow moved fast—faster than him—twisting and writhing in the light like a creature in agony.

"Your shadow," Bishop said. "That's where you keep them, isn't it?

All the souls you've consumed. All the pain you've eaten. They're trapped in there. And light hurts them." The Janitor's expression shifted.

Something like surprise.

Something like fear.

"How do you know that?" "Because I've been studying you for forty years." Bishop raised his staff again. "Since you killed my wife. My children. My entire community." His voice cracked.

But his hands stayed steady.

212

"You took everything from me. And I swore, on their graves, that I would find a way to destroy you." "You cannot destroy me. I am eternal." "Nothing is eternal." Bishop's tattoos blazed brighter. "Everything ends. Even functions. Even processes. Even monsters." He charged.

Light against darkness.

Old man against ancient evil.

A battle that had been forty years in the making.

And somewhere in the tunnels ahead, D-Lo felt it—felt Bishop's light flare, felt his pain, felt his sacrifice.

Thank you, D-Lo thought.

He kept running.

And behind him, Bishop screamed—not in defeat, but in defiance.

A scream that echoed through the Underline.

A scream that would be remembered.

A scream that bought them time.

Time to run.

Time to hide.

Time to survive.

CHAPTER 27

THE RAID

The alarm was a sound D-Lo had never heard before—a low, pulsing wail that echoed through the Underline like a dying animal.

"BREACH!" someone screamed. "BREACH IN SECTOR FOUR!" D-Lo was on his feet before he was fully awake, grabbing the knife Lexi had given him, scanning the darkness for threats.

Kettle was already glowing, heat shimmering off his skin.

Clutch had her coin in her hand, eyes sharp.

"What's happening?" D-Lo asked.

"The Trust," Lexi said, appearing from the shadows. She was fully armed—blade in each hand, face set in the mask of the leader she was.

"They found us." "How?" "Doesn't matter. We need to move—now."

The Underline was chaos.

Ghosts ran in every direction—some toward the escape tunnels, some toward the fighting, some just running blind in panic. Smoke filled the corridors. The lights flickered and died, leaving only the orange glow of Kettle's skin and the occasional flash of weapons fire.

"This way!" Lexi grabbed D-Lo's arm, pulling him down a side passage.

"There's a secondary exit through the—" An explosion rocked the tunnel.

Concrete dust showered down. Someone screamed nearby.

"They're collapsing the passages," Clutch said grimly. "Trying to trap us." "Then we go through them." Kettle stepped forward, his glow

214

intensifying. "Find me a wall that leads up." "Kettle, you can't—" "Find me a wall, D-Lo. I got this."

They fought their way through three junctions.

Trust officers in tactical gear, weapons that fired blue energy bolts that burned where they struck. Suppression devices that made D-Lo's power feel distant, unreachable—like trying to grab smoke.

Clutch bent probability around them—shots went wide, enemies stumbled, a support beam fell at exactly the wrong moment for a pursuing squad.

Kettle melted through obstacles—doors, debris, an armored vehicle that had somehow made it into the tunnels.

Lexi fought like a dancer—fluid, precise, leaving unconscious bodies in her wake.

And D-Lo...

D-Lo watched the threads.

It was harder than in Celestine's chamber—chaos and fear and the suppression tech all working against him—but he could still see them.

Faint strands of possibility branching from every moment.

Left.

He pulled Clutch left as a grenade landed where she'd been standing.

Down.

He shoved Kettle to the ground as a sniper's shot scorched the air above them.

Wait.

He held Lexi back for three heartbeats until a structural collapse blocked their pursuers.

"You're seeing them," Lexi breathed. "The threads." "Barely. The suppression tech—" "Doesn't matter. You're doing it." She gripped his shoulder. "Keep doing it. Get us out."

The wall Kettle chose was load-bearing.

It shouldn't have been possible. The amount of heat required to melt through three feet of reinforced concrete while keeping the ceiling from collapsing—it was suicide.

Kettle did it anyway.

215

His glow went from orange to white to something that hurt to look at directly. Sweat poured off his body, evaporating before it hit the ground. His hands pressed against the wall, and the concrete began to glow, then flow, then pour away like water.

"Kettle!" D-Lo shouted. "You'll burn yourself out!" "Then I burn out!" Kettle's voice was strained, distant. "But you get out. Kimi needs you. The crew needs you. So shut up and let me work!" The wall gave way.

Moonlight streamed in—they were above ground, in an abandoned lot somewhere in the Marrow.

Kettle collapsed.

D-Lo and Lexi caught him before he hit the ground, his skin still radiating heat like a dying ember.

"I got you," D-Lo said. "I got you, big man." "Told you," Kettle mumbled. "Got this." Then he passed out.

They weren't the only ones who made it out.

Other Ghosts emerged from other exits—battered, bloodied, but alive.

Maybe forty of them, out of the hundred who'd been in the Underline.

Maybe forty.

D-Lo didn't know if the others were dead or captured or still fighting underground.

He didn't know anything except that his family was safe—Kettle unconscious but breathing, Clutch holding her side where a bolt had grazed her, Lexi directing the survivors with cold efficiency.

"Secondary site," Lexi ordered. "Everyone who can walk, move.

Everyone who can't, pair up with someone who can. We leave in three minutes." "The Trust—" "Will be regrouping. We have maybe an hour before they widen the search." Lexi's voice was steel. "We use every second of it."

The secondary site was a natural cave system—older than the Underline, older than the city, carved by underground rivers that had dried up centuries ago.

Bishop had shown it to Lexi years ago. For emergencies, he'd said.

For when everything else fails.

They'd never needed it before.

They needed it now.

D-Lo helped lower Kettle onto a bedroll, checked his pulse, felt the heat still radiating from his skin. Not dangerous—Kettle was cooling down—but exhausted. Depleted. The kind of tired that took days to recover from.

"He'll be okay," Doc said, appearing with her medical bag. "Pushed himself to the limit, but didn't cross it. A week of rest, he'll be back to full strength." "We might not have a week." "Then he'll fight at half strength. Wouldn't be the first time." D-Lo nodded, stepped away.

Lexi found him at the edge of the cavern, staring at nothing.

"Eleven confirmed dead," she said quietly. "Twenty-three missing—probably captured. The rest made it out." "My fault." "How?" "I was using my power more. Training. Getting stronger." D-Lo's fists clenched. "The Trust tracks temporal anomalies. Every time I practice, I'm sending up a flare." "You didn't know." "I should have guessed. Celestine warned me about being careful. About not drawing attention." He laughed bitterly. "And I was so focused on getting stronger that I led them right to us." Lexi was quiet for a moment.

"Look around," she said finally. "What do you see?" D-Lo looked.

The Ghosts were working—setting up shelters, treating wounds, organizing supplies. Despite everything, despite the death and destruction, they were moving. Surviving.

"I see people who are still alive," he said.

"Forty people. Forty people who would be dead if you hadn't seen the threads. If you hadn't pulled Clutch left, pushed Kettle down, held me back at that chokepoint." Lexi gripped his arm. "The Trust would have found us eventually. They always do. But tonight, because of you, forty people made it out." "And eleven died." "Eleven died. And it hurts. It should hurt." Her voice softened. "But you can't carry their deaths and ignore their lives. That's not how this works. That's not how any of this works." D-Lo closed his eyes.

The threads were there, at the edge of his awareness. Showing him futures—some where more people died, some where fewer. Some where he gave up. Some where he kept fighting.

"I'm scared," he admitted.

"Good. Fear means you understand the stakes." Lexi closed the distance.

"But fear without action is just paralysis. And paralysis gets people killed." "So what do I do?" "What you've been doing. Get stronger. Get smarter. Learn to see the threads without giving away your position." She looked at him. "And when the Trust comes again—and they will—make sure we're ready." D-Lo looked at the survivors.

At Kettle, unconscious but alive.

At Clutch, cracking dark jokes with Doc while getting her wound treated.

At the other Ghosts—kids, mostly, teenagers who should have been worrying about homework and crushes instead of survival and combat.

"Okay," he said. "We train. We prepare. And next time—" "Next time we hit back." "Yeah." D-Lo felt something harden inside him. "Next time we hit back." Lexi smiled.

It wasn't a kind smile.

It was the smile of a leader preparing for war.

"Welcome to the resistance, Reload. Now let's get to work."

The fires were out, but the smoke lingered.

D-Lo stood in what used to be the Underline's main chamber, watching survivors pick through the wreckage. Somewhere behind him, someone was crying—the soft, broken sound of grief too deep for screaming.

Eleven dead.

Twenty-three captured.

He knew the numbers. He'd counted the bodies himself.

Eleven names for the wall. Twenty-three people in Trust custody, probably being processed in the Vault right now. Forty survivors scattered through the backup tunnels, wondering if they'd ever feel safe again. "It's not your fault." Kettle appeared beside him, massive frame covered in ash and burn marks.

He'd pushed his power to the limit during the evacuation, melting through three reinforced doors to give people escape routes.

"Isn't it?" D-Lo kicked a piece of debris. "They came because of me.

Because I've been training here, using my powers. They tracked the temporal signatures." "They came because they're monsters. Same reason they always come." "That doesn't make it better." "No." Kettle sat down heavily on a collapsed support beam. "No, it doesn't."

They buried the dead in the deep tunnels.

No markers—too dangerous. The Trust might find them, desecrate the graves, use the DNA for whatever experiments they ran in their labs. So the Ghosts said their words in darkness, committed their fallen to unmarked earth, and walked away.

D-Lo stayed.

After everyone else had gone, he knelt in the dirt beside the freshest grave—a seventeen-year-old named Darnell who'd been learning to control his enhanced hearing. He'd heard the Trust coming thirty seconds before anyone else. Thirty seconds that saved at least twelve lives.

But not his own.

"I'm sorry," D-Lo whispered. "I'm sorry I couldn't—" The words stuck in his throat.

What could he say? That he'd tried? That he'd died four times during the raid, resetting over and over, trying to find a path where everyone made it?

Some paths didn't exist.

Some people couldn't be saved.

"First one's the hardest." D-Lo looked up.

Clutch stood at the chamber entrance, coin dancing between her fingers.

"First what?" "First time you lose someone and know—know—it was because of a choice you made." She walked closer, sat down on a rock beside him.

"Doesn't matter if the choice was right. Doesn't matter if there was no other option. You feel it anyway. Like carrying a stone in your chest." "Does it get easier?" "No." She caught the coin, held it still. "But you learn to carry more stones. Build up the muscles. Eventually you're walking around with a whole quarry inside you and people think you're fine because you're still standing." "That's depressing." "That's survival." She flipped the coin again. "The alternative is putting the stones down. Refusing to carry them. And the only way to do that is to stop caring." "I don't know how to stop caring." "Good." Clutch stood, offered him a hand. "The day you figure that out is the day you become someone like

219

Halden. Someone who can watch people die and call it 'acceptable losses.'" D-Lo took her hand. Let her pull him up.

"What do I do now?" "Now?" Clutch looked toward the tunnels, toward the survivors rebuilding what little they could. "Now you grieve. Then you get angry. Then you use that anger to make sure this never happens again." "How?" "By getting better. By getting stronger. By being ready next time." Her eyes hardened. "The Trust thinks they won today. They think they scattered us, broke us, proved we're not a threat." "Didn't they?" "No." Clutch started walking. "They reminded us what we're fighting for.

They reminded us what happens if we lose. That's not defeat—that's motivation." D-Lo looked back at the unmarked graves one last time.

Eleven names I'll never forget. Twenty-three people I'm going to get back. Then he followed Clutch into the darkness.

He found Lexi in the backup command post—a cramped cave barely large enough for a table and a few chairs.

She was alone, staring at a map covered in red X marks. Places they couldn't use anymore. Resources they'd lost.

"Hey." She didn't look up.

"Sixty-three percent of our food stores. Eighty percent of our medical supplies. All of our long-range communication equipment." Her voice was flat. Exhausted. "Three years of building, gone in an hour." "We'll rebuild." "Will we?" Now she looked at him. "How many times can we rebuild, D-Lo?

How many times can we lose everything and start over before people stop believing it's worth it?" "As many times as it takes." "That's not an answer." "It's the only one I have." He crossed to her, put his hands on her shoulders. "We're alive. Kimi's alive. The core crew made it. We know their tactics now, know how they found us. Next time we'll be ready." "Next time people will still die." "Yes." He didn't flinch from it. "People will die. We'll mourn them. And then we'll keep fighting. Because the alternative is letting the Trust win. Letting them take everyone. Letting them turn the whole city into another Vault." Lexi's composure cracked—just for a moment. Just long enough for D-Lo to see the fear underneath.

"I'm tired." "I know." "I don't know if I can do this." "You can." He pulled her close. "Not alone. Never alone. But you can do this. We can do this." She let him hold her.

Just for a moment.

Then she straightened, rebuilt herself, became the leader again.

"Crew meeting in one hour. We need to plan our next move." "What is our next move?" Lexi looked at the map. At the red X marks. At everything they'd lost.

"We hit back," she said. "Hard. Fast. Before they think we've recovered." Her jaw set. "The Vault. We're going to crack it open and get our people back." "That's suicide." "That's war." She met his eyes. "You in?" D-Lo thought about the graves. The eleven names. The twenty-three people in Trust custody.

"I'm in."

CHAPTER 28

FAMILY

For one night, they weren't soldiers.

They were just people.

"Full house, bitches." Clutch slapped her cards down with a grin that could've powered the whole Underline.

Kettle groaned.

"That's the fourth hand in a row." "What can I say? I'm lucky." "You're cheating," D-Lo said. "Literally. Your power is cheating." "My power is probability manipulation. Completely different." She raked in the pile of chips—actually bottle caps, because nobody had real money for poker. "Not my fault y'all keep betting against fate." They'd found a quiet corner of the Underline—an old maintenance room that the Ghosts had converted into something almost cozy. Lanterns hung from the ceiling. Salvaged blankets covered the concrete floor. Someone had even dragged in a broken couch that only smelled a little like mold.

Home, such as it was.

Lexi dealt the next hand.

"New rule: Clutch can't touch the deck." "That's discrimination." "That's survival." Lexi slid cards across the makeshift table—a door laid across two milk crates. "Kettle, you in?" Kettle studied his cards. His face gave away nothing.

Then again, Kettle's face always gave away nothing. The man could be holding a royal flush or a handful of garbage and you'd never know.

"I'll see your three caps," he said, sliding chips forward. "And raise you five." D-Lo looked at his cards.

A pair of threes.

Garbage.

But he'd learned something over the past few weeks—sometimes the hand didn't matter. Sometimes it was about how you played it.

"I'm in."

Three hours later, Clutch had won approximately everything.

But nobody seemed to mind.

The bottle of something—nobody asked where Kettle had found it—was making the rounds. The lanterns cast warm shadows. And for the first time since D-Lo had discovered his power, he felt almost... normal.

"Okay, okay," Lexi said, leaning back against the couch. "Most embarrassing thing that ever happened to you. Go." "Why we gotta do embarrassing?" Kettle asked.

"Because we've been playing poker for three hours and I'm tired of losing." Lexi grinned. "Come on, big man. Spill." Kettle sighed.

The kind of sigh that said he was about to reveal something he'd never told anyone.

"When I was seventeen, I had a crush on this girl. LaShonda Williams.

Prettiest girl in the whole school." "What happened?" "I asked her to prom. She said yes." Kettle's cheeks darkened—impressive, given his complexion. "I was so nervous, I practiced dancing in my room for two weeks. My little brother caught me.

Told everybody." "That's not that bad," D-Lo said.

"I was dancing to Mariah Carey. In my underwear. Doing the worm." Silence.

Then Clutch lost it.

Full-on cackling, tears streaming down her face, drink coming out her nose. The laugh was contagious—soon they were all howling, including Kettle, who was shaking his head at his seventeen-year-old self.

"Did you at least take her to prom?" Lexi asked, wiping her eyes.

"Yeah. Danced with her all night. Even did the worm." "No." "On purpose. Owned that shit." Kettle smiled. "She married my cousin eventually. Still brings it up at every family reunion."

223

"Your turn, Reload." D-Lo groaned.

"Come on. We shared." "Fine." He thought about it. "Sixth grade. Science fair. I built a volcano." "That's not embarrassing." "It was supposed to be a baking soda volcano. You know, the safe kind." D-Lo covered his face. "But Melo—my boy from the Marrow—he convinced me that real volcanoes needed real fire. So we modified it." "Oh no," Clutch said.

"Oh yes. Used some chemicals Melo's brother had in his garage. Don't ask me what they were. I still don't know." D-Lo peeked through his fingers.

"The volcano exploded. Like, actually exploded. Set the gym curtains on fire. The whole school had to evacuate." "D-Lo!" "I was suspended for a month. My mama had to pay for the curtains.

Melo's brother went to juvie for something unrelated but they found out about the chemicals and added charges." He dropped his hands. "Worst part? I didn't even win the science fair." "Who won?" "Some kid who made a model of the solar system. Out of styrofoam." D-Lo shook his head. "Styrofoam. I set the school on fire and lost to styrofoam."

The laughter faded eventually.

Replaced by something quieter.

More intimate.

They sat in the warm darkness, passing the bottle, not needing to fill every moment with words. The kind of silence that only happened with people you trusted completely.

"I never had this," Lexi said quietly.

"Had what?" "Friends. People my own age." She pulled her knees to her chest.

"Down here, I was always the leader. Had to be. Couldn't let my guard down.

Couldn't let anyone see me as anything but strong." "That sounds lonely," D-Lo said.

"It was." She looked at him. "It still is, sometimes. Even now." Clutch reached over and squeezed her hand.

"You got us now, Ghost. For whatever that's worth." "It's worth everything." Nobody argued with that.

224

"So what happens after?" Kettle's question hung in the air.

"After what?" "After the Janitor. After the Trust. After all of this." He gestured vaguely at the tunnels around them. "Assuming we survive. What do we do?" Nobody had an answer.

They'd been so focused on surviving—on the next threat, the next fight, the next day—that none of them had thought about what came next.

"I always wanted to travel," Clutch said finally. "See the world. Paris.

Tokyo. One of those beaches where the water's actually blue." "The Caribbean," Lexi offered. "I saw pictures once. It looks like a dream." "What about you, Kettle?" The big man was quiet for a moment.

"I want to cook again. Open a restaurant, maybe. Nothing fancy. Just good food for people who need it." His eyes were distant. "There's a lot of hungry people in this city. Always has been. I think... I think I'd like to feed them." "That's beautiful," D-Lo said.

"What about you, Reload? What do you want?" D-Lo thought about it.

Really thought about it.

"I want Kimi to graduate. Go to college. Have a life that doesn't involve any of this." He looked at the ceiling. "And I want to sit on a porch somewhere, when I'm old, and tell boring stories about the shit we did. Make it sound less terrifying than it was." "That's your dream? Being boring?" "Boring sounds amazing right now." He smiled. "Boring sounds like surviving long enough to get old. That's more than most people from the Marrow can say."

The bottle was empty.

The lanterns were dying.

But none of them wanted to leave.

"Whatever happens," Lexi said, "we stick together. Right?" "Right." "Agreed." "Family." The word came from Clutch.

They all looked at her.

"That's what we are. Not a crew. Not a team. Family." She met each of their eyes. "I've never had one before. Not a real one. But this...

you people..." She couldn't finish.

225

She didn't have to.

They understood.

D-Lo raised an imaginary glass.

"To family." "To family." "To family." "To family." Four voices.

One word.

A promise made in the dark that would carry them through everything to come.

They fell asleep there, eventually.

Clutch on the broken couch, snoring softly.

Kettle against the wall, arms crossed, looking peaceful for once.

Lexi curled against D-Lo, her head on his shoulder, breathing slow and steady.

D-Lo stayed awake longer than the others.

Watching them.

Protecting them.

These people who'd become his world.

Whatever happened next—the Janitor, the Trust, the war that was coming—he wasn't facing it alone.

He had family now.

Real family.

And that made all the difference.

CHAPTER 29

GHOST STORIES

The night before Bishop's last stand, Lexi told D-Lo everything.

Not the sanitized version. Not the legend the Ghosts whispered about their leader.

The truth.

They sat in a forgotten corner of the Underline—an alcove she'd claimed as her own. Candles flickered on ledges. The walls were covered in drawings, childish at the bottom, more skilled as they rose. A timeline in crayon and charcoal.

"I was twelve when they killed my father," she said.

D-Lo sat close but not touching. Giving her space.

"His name was James Ghost—yeah, real last name, goes back generations.

He was a janitor." She caught his flinch. "Not like that. A real one.

PS 142\. Cleaned classrooms, fixed desks, made sure the heat worked. Kids loved him." "Sounds like a good man." "The best man." Her voice cracked. "Mama died when I was three.

Cancer.

Daddy raised me alone. Never complained. Just loved me." She pulled her knees to her chest.

"The night they came, I was doing homework. Math. Daddy was making spaghetti, singing some old gospel song his grandmother taught him.

Couldn't carry a tune, but he sang anyway. Every night." The candles flickered.

"Then the door came down."

"Trust Special Operations. Twelve officers. Full tactical gear. They weren't after Daddy—he wasn't wired. They wanted a woman on the fourth floor who could phase through walls. She'd been hiding in our building for weeks." Lexi's voice went flat. Mechanical.

"Daddy heard them coming. Told me to hide in the closet. The one that still smelled like Mama's fabric—she'd been a seamstress." "What happened?" "They shot him." No emotion. Just facts. "Not because he was a threat.

Because he was standing in the hallway and they didn't want to waste time checking. 'Collateral containment,' I heard one say. Like Daddy was paperwork." D-Lo felt rage building.

"I watched through the closet slats. Watched him fall. Watched the blood spread. Watched them step over his body." "Lexi—" "They found the woman upstairs. Shot her too. Then left. Didn't call anyone. Didn't help the wounded. Didn't even close our door." She wiped her eyes. "I sat in that closet for six hours. Watching Daddy's blood dry."

"After that, I ran. Foster care was a joke—six kids and a boyfriend who looked at me wrong. First night, I was gone." "Where'd you go?" "Everywhere. Nowhere." She laughed bitterly. "Slept in parks, stole food, begged when I couldn't steal. Did things I'm not proud of." "You were twelve." "Twelve going on ancient." She looked at her hands. "Three months on the streets. Almost died twice. The second time—a man in an alley who thought a girl alone was opportunity—that was the first time I killed someone." D-Lo went still.

"He grabbed me. I had broken glass. When it was over, I watched him bleed out the same way I'd watched Daddy." She met his eyes. "I was twelve years old, and I felt nothing. Just relief. That's when I knew something inside me was broken."

"Bishop found me three days later. Hiding in an abandoned building, half-starved, ready to die." Her voice softened. The hard edges melted.

"He just sat down across from me. Pulled out a PB&J sandwich. Held it out and said, 'You look hungry.'" "That's it?" "That's it. No questions. No judgment. Just a sandwich and silence." She smiled faintly. "I ate it in thirty seconds. And when I was done, he held out his hand: 'There's more where that came from. If you want.'" "You went with him." "I had nothing else. And something in his eyes made me trust him." She stared at the candle flames.

"He brought me down here. To the Underline. Trained me for five years.

Said I had a gift—not a power, but the ability to inspire people. To make them believe." "He was right." "He was always right." Her voice cracked. "That's what makes this so hard."

D-Lo waited.

Lexi was quiet for a long moment. When she spoke again, her voice was different. Smaller. Ashamed.

"I haven't told you everything." "You don't have to—" "Yes. I do." She held his gaze. "Because you need to understand what I am. Not just what happened to me—what I did." She stood. Walked to a section of wall covered in black.

No drawings.

Just darkness.

"Three years ago. I was fourteen. The Ghosts were bigger then—almost two hundred of us. We'd started hitting Trust convoys, freeing prisoners, building a real resistance." "Sounds like progress." "It was. And I got cocky." She traced the black section with her finger.

"We intercepted a transport. Intel said six guards, twelve prisoners, standard protocol. Easy grab." Her hand clenched.

"The intel was wrong."

"It was a trap. The Trust had figured out our patterns, fed us false information, waited for us to walk in." Her voice was hollow now.

"Forty Ghosts went into that tunnel. I led them. I gave the order." She turned to face him. "Eight came out." D-Lo's breath caught.

"Thirty-two people. Kids mostly. The oldest was nineteen." Lexi's eyes were dry but haunted. "I watched them die. Some shot. Some captured—we found their bodies later, what the Trust did to them in interrogation." She swallowed. "And the whole time, I kept thinking: I could have waited. I could have verified. I could have been less arrogant." "You didn't know—" "I should have known." Her voice sharpened. "That's what leadership means. Every death that night is on me. Not the Trust—me. I made the call." She sat back down. Closer to him now.

"Bishop didn't blame me. Said losses were inevitable in war. But I saw it in his eyes. The disappointment. The grief. He'd spent years building this family, and I'd gotten a third of them killed in one night." "That's why you're so careful now." "That's why I don't sleep." She leaned against him. "Every time I close my eyes, I see their faces. Maya Chen—she was eleven, wanted to be a doctor. Darnell Thompson—fourteen, used to make everyone laugh. Ava Rodriguez—" "Stop." D-Lo took her hand. "Stop." "You needed to know." Her voice was a whisper. "Everyone thinks I'm this brave leader, this hero Bishop trained. But I'm not. I'm the girl who got thirty-two people killed because she was too proud to double-check intel." "You were fourteen." "Old enough to know better." She looked at him. "That's why I can't lose anyone else. That's why I fight so hard to protect everyone. Because I already have enough ghosts."

D-Lo pulled her close.

She let him.

"You made a mistake," he said quietly. "A terrible one. But you didn't stop. You didn't run. You kept fighting, kept leading, kept trying to make it right." "I can't make it right. They're dead." "No. But you can make it mean something." He tilted her chin up.

"Every person you save now—that's for them. Every prison you break open, every kid you pull off the streets, every victory against the Trust—that's their legacy." "That doesn't bring them back." "Nothing brings anyone back." D-Lo thought about his own deaths. His own timelines erased. "But we can carry them with us. Let them make us better instead of breaking us." Lexi studied his face.

"You really believe that?" "I have to. Otherwise, what's the point?" She was quiet for a long time.

Then: "Bishop used to say something similar. That guilt was only useful if it drove you forward. That the dead don't want us to suffer—they want us to live." "Smart man." "The smartest." She kissed him then. Desperate. Hungry. The kiss of someone who'd been holding themselves together for too long. "I can't lose you too. You understand? Whatever happens tomorrow—I can't watch someone else I love die." D-Lo thought about his power.

About the thread slowly fraying.

About the impossibility of promising forever.

"I'll always come back," he said. "As many times as it takes." She kissed him again.

And for a moment, in a forgotten corner of the Underline, two people who carried too many ghosts found something alive.

Later, D-Lo looked at the black section of wall.

"You never drew anything there." "I was going to. After." She curled against him. "Thirty-two portraits.

Everyone we lost that night. But I couldn't get their faces right. Kept seeing them dying instead of living." "Maybe that's not what you're supposed to draw." "What do you mean?" D-Lo thought about it.

"Maya Chen wanted to be a doctor. Draw that—draw her in a white coat, stethoscope around her neck, saving someone's life." He traced his finger across the black space. "Darnell Thompson made people laugh.

Draw him laughing. Draw them as who they wanted to become." Lexi's breath caught.

"Not memorials," she whispered. "Possibilities." "Yeah. The futures they deserved. The people they would've been." She was quiet for a long moment.

Then she stood. Walked to her supplies. Picked up a piece of charcoal.

"Will you stay? While I draw?" "As long as you need." She started with Maya. A young woman in a doctor's coat, confident smile, hand extended to help someone stand.

D-Lo watched her work.

And at last, he understood why Bishop had chosen Lexi to lead.

Not because she never failed.

Because she never stopped trying to make her failures mean something.

CHAPTER 30

THE HUNT

They didn't stop running until the tunnels opened into a cavern.

Not a subway station this time—something older. Natural. A cave system that had existed long before New Babylon was built on top of it, carved by underground rivers that had dried up centuries ago.

The secondary site.

D-Lo collapsed against a rock wall, lungs burning, legs screaming.

Around him, Ghosts were doing the same—kids and teens sprawled across the cavern floor, gasping, crying, some just staring at nothing with shell-shocked eyes.

They'd made it.

Most of them.

Lexi stood in the center of the cavern, counting heads. Her lips moved silently as she tallied. When she finished, her face went tight.

"We're missing eleven," she said quietly. "Plus Bishop and the rear guard." Eleven.

Eleven people who hadn't made it out.

D-Lo thought about the screams he'd heard in the darkness. The sounds of the Janitor feeding.

Eleven souls, cleaned.

Gone.

"It's not your fault." Clutch sat down beside him, her back against the same rock wall. She looked exhausted—not physically, but deeper. Her luck had been working overtime during the evacuation, bending probability to keep the group together, to make sure paths stayed clear, to ensure they weren't followed.

"I could've warned them sooner," D-Lo said. "If I'd understood my power faster—" "You warned them at all. That's more than most could do." She pulled out her coin, turned it over in her fingers. "Eleven people died. But over a hundred survived. That math ain't clean, but it's better than the alternative." The alternative.

Everyone.

D-Lo had seen that timeline. Had lived it, briefly, before pulling himself back.

Everyone screaming. Everyone dying. The Janitor walking through the Underline like a farmer harvesting crops, taking soul after soul until there was nothing left but empty shells.

"How do you do it?" he asked. "Make peace with it?" Clutch was quiet for a moment.

"You don't," she said finally. "You just keep moving. Keep fighting.

Keep surviving." She pocketed her coin. "The dead don't need your guilt.

The living need your strength." She stood and walked away, leaving D-Lo alone with his thoughts.

Hours passed.

The Ghosts organized themselves with practiced efficiency—setting up sleeping areas, distributing rations, posting guards at the tunnel entrances. They'd done this before, D-Lo realized. Evacuated. Lost people. Rebuilt.

This was their life.

Running. Hiding. Surviving.

And starting over.

He found Kettle near a small fire someone had built—controlled flames, carefully contained, providing warmth and light without smoke. The big man sat alone, staring into the flames like they held answers.

"You okay?" D-Lo asked, sitting beside him.

"No." Kettle's voice was hollow. "Bishop's dead because of me." "That's not true." "He stayed behind to fight the Cleaner. The Cleaner was hunting us.

Hunting you." Kettle's hands clenched. Sparks flickered between his fingers. "If I'd been stronger—if I could control this thing better—maybe I could've helped. Could've fought alongside him." "You lit the way,"

D-Lo said. "When everything went dark, you were the only reason anyone could see. That saved lives, Kettle. Your power saved lives." "My power burned Markus." "And then it saved a hundred people." D-Lo put a hand on Kettle's shoulder. The heat was intense, but bearable. "You're not a weapon, big man. You're a shield. A torch in the darkness. The sooner you believe that, the sooner you'll be able to do what Bishop did." Kettle looked at him.

"What Bishop did?" "Stand against something terrible. Not because he thought he'd win, but because he knew it mattered." D-Lo squeezed his shoulder. "That's what heroes do. And whether you like it or not, that's what you are." Kettle's eyes glistened.

He looked back at the fire.

"I never wanted to be a hero." "Neither did I." D-Lo let go and stood. "But here we are." He walked away.

Behind him, Kettle's flames burned a little steadier.

A little brighter.

An hour later, Lexi called a meeting.

The senior Ghosts gathered in a natural alcove near the center of the cavern—Lexi, D-Lo, Clutch, Kettle, and a handful of others D-Lo didn't recognize. Veterans. Survivors. The ones who'd been fighting longest.

A woman named Trace—mid-thirties, shaved head, scars across her throat that looked like claw marks—spread a hand-drawn map on the ground.

"This is the secondary site," she said, pointing. "We're here. The tunnels we came through are here. And the main Underline—where Bishop made his stand—is here." The distance between them wasn't huge. Maybe a mile.

"The Cleaner knows we ran east," Trace continued. "He doesn't know about this site specifically, but if he's hunting, he'll search. It's only a matter of time." "How much time?" Clutch asked.

"Days. Maybe less." Trace's expression was grim. "Bishop slowed him down—maybe hurt him—but he's not dead. You can't kill something like that." "So what do we do?" Kettle asked. "Keep running?" "We can't run forever." Lexi's voice was steady—leader voice, back in place despite everything. "Every time we move, we lose people.

Resources. Ground. Eventually, there's nowhere left to go." "Then we fight," D-Lo said.

Everyone looked at him.

"You saw what happened back there," Trace said. "Bishop was the strongest of us. He trained for forty years to fight that thing. And he's gone." "Bishop bought us time," D-Lo replied. "Time to figure out how to actually win. Not just survive—win." "And how do we do that?" D-Lo thought about the battle. About the moment the Janitor had faltered. About the voices that had spoken through him.

"The Cleaner isn't just a monster. He's a prison. All those souls he's consumed—they're still in there. Trapped. Suffering." He looked around the group. "Bishop's light hurt him. Not because light is some magical weakness—because it hurt the shadow. The place where the souls are kept." Clutch leaned forward.

"You're saying we need to hurt the shadow. Free the souls." "I'm saying if we can find a way to do that—to crack open that prison—maybe the Cleaner falls apart. Maybe without all that stolen pain, he's nothing." Silence.

Lexi spoke first.

"It's a theory. Not a plan." "Then let's make it a plan." D-Lo stood. "Celestine knew things about the Cleaner. Bishop knew things. There have to be others—people who've studied him, fought him, survived him. We find them. We learn everything we can. And we figure out how to break him." "And in the meantime?" "In the meantime, we stay hidden. We stay together. And we get stronger." He looked at Kettle. At Clutch. At Lexi. "All of us." The senior Ghosts exchanged glances.

Skeptical.

But also... hopeful.

It had been a long time since anyone had talked about winning.

"I'm in," Kettle said quietly.

"Same," Clutch added.

Lexi nodded slowly.

"We'll put out feelers. See who else is out there. Who might have information." She looked at D-Lo. "But this is your mission. Your theory. If it fails—" "It won't fail," D-Lo said.

"How do you know?" He thought about the threads. The possibilities. The future he'd glimpsed.

"Because I've seen what happens if we don't try. And I won't let that timeline become real."

Miles above, in the gleaming headquarters of Trust Special Operations, Director Halden studied a holographic map of New Babylon.

Red dots pulsed across the display—anomaly signatures, wired activity, thermal spikes detected by the city's sensor grid.

A cluster of red in the Marrow.

Another cluster beneath it.

Underground.

"Sir," an analyst said, approaching with a tablet. "We've confirmed multiple high-level wired signatures in the Underline. At least three Category 4 threats, plus numerous lesser signatures." "The tunnel network." "Yes, sir. They've been hiding down there for months. Maybe years." Halden studied the map.

The Underline was a nightmare—miles of unmapped tunnels, structural instabilities, and defensive chokepoints. A direct assault would be costly.

But doing nothing was worse.

"There's something else," the analyst continued. "We've detected unusual energy patterns in the same area. Something we've never seen before." "Explain." "It's like…" The analyst hesitated. "Like reality itself is glitching.

Temporal anomalies. Probability distortions. Whatever's down there, it's not just wired. It's something new." Halden's expression didn't change.

But his mind raced.

Temporal anomalies.

There had been rumors. Theories. Classified reports about a specific type of wired—one that could manipulate time itself.

If that was real…

If something like that was hiding in the Underline…

"Mobilize Siege Division," he said quietly. "Full tactical package.

Suppression units, containment specialists, and—" he paused "—the Null Squad." The analyst paled.

"Sir, the Null Squad hasn't been deployed in—" "I know how long it's been." Halden turned from the map. "But if there's an Anchor down there, we need to contain it. Before it becomes a threat we can't control."

"And the other wired? The ones hiding with it?" Halden's expression was cold.

"Collateral containment. Whatever it takes." He walked away.

Behind him, the red dots pulsed.

Unknowing.

Unaware.

That war was coming from above.

In the darkness of the Underline, in a tunnel that had been abandoned even by rats, the Janitor sat.

His coveralls were burned. His skin was blackened in patches, slowly regenerating. His shadow—that terrible, living shadow—writhed and twisted, damaged but not destroyed.

Bishop's light had hurt.

More than the Janitor had expected.

More than anything had hurt in centuries.

"Clever old man," he whispered to the darkness. "You found the cracks." He reached into his shadow.

Pulled out something small.

A shard of light—golden, warm, pulsing faintly.

A piece of Bishop's soul, consumed but not yet digested.

The Janitor held it up to his empty eyes.

"You thought you could hurt me. Weaken me. Set my prisoners free." He smiled.

That wrong, terrible smile.

"But you made a mistake." He pressed the shard into his chest.

It sank in—absorbed, consumed, integrated.

And the Janitor felt Bishop's memories.

His forty years of study.

His knowledge of the Underline.

His understanding of the Ghosts.

His love for a girl named Lexi.

"Thank you," the Janitor whispered. "For showing me exactly where they ran." He stood.

His body was still damaged.

But his mind was sharper than ever.

He knew where the secondary site was now.

Knew how to find them.

Knew how to break them.

"Rest while you can, little broken things," he said softly.

He began to walk.

Toward the east.

Toward the cavern.

Toward the hunt.

"I'm coming." *INTERLUDE — THE AWAKENING*

CONTAINMENT FACILITY OMEGA — SUBLEVEL 12

The technician noticed it first.

A flicker in the readings. A spike in neural activity that shouldn't have been possible, given the sedation levels.

"Sir? You need to see this." Dr. Harrison walked over, coffee in hand, expecting another false alarm.

The Conductor had been stable for decades. Whatever made him twitch occasionally was just residual— He dropped the coffee.

"That's not possible." The brain activity readings were off the charts. Not chaos—pattern.

Like the subject was thinking. Processing. Dreaming.

And the content...

"Is that—" "Temporal echo." Dr. Harrison's voice was barely a whisper. "He's sensing something. Another Anchor." "The Graves subject?" "Has to be. Nothing else would register like this." They watched the readings spike and fall, spike and fall. A rhythm. A heartbeat.

"Should we inform Director Halden?" Dr. Harrison thought about it.

Thought about what would happen if they woke the Conductor.

What would happen if they didn't.

"Increase sedation by twenty percent. Monitor continuously. And yes—inform the Director." He stared at the readouts. "Something's changing. And we need to be ready." In the containment tank, Isaiah Washington dreamed of a boy who could die and come back.

And somewhere in the void where his consciousness floated, something that might have been hope flickered to life.

Maybe this one will be different.

Maybe this one can end it.

Maybe this one can set me free.

CHAPTER 31

THE DEFECTOR

SIX MONTHS EARLIER

Dr. Sienna Rao had worked for the Trust for eleven years.

She'd believed in them.

She'd been wrong.

It started with a file she wasn't supposed to see.

Project Omega. Classification: Ultra Black. Access restricted to Director Halden and three other people whose names were redacted.

Sienna shouldn't have been able to open it. But she'd spent eleven years building trust—ironic, given the organization's name—and her security clearance had grown along with her responsibilities. One late night, one misplaced access code, one moment of curiosity...

And she saw everything.

The photographs came first.

A man—Black, early thirties, handsome in a scholarly way—standing in front of a chalkboard covered in equations. The timestamp read 1952.

He was smiling, pointing at something in the math, clearly explaining a concept to someone outside the frame.

The next photograph showed the same man, but different.

Strapped to a table. Eyes wide with terror. Wires running from his skull to machines that looked like something from a nightmare.

The timestamp read 1954.

The third photograph— Sienna looked away. Had to.

When she looked back, she forced herself to read the file.

Subject: ISAIAH WASHINGTON Classification: ANCHOR (Third Documented) Status: CONTAINED (Active) Designation: THE CONDUCTOR The details were clinical. Detached. The language of scientists documenting an experiment rather than people torturing a human being.

Subject displayed initial Anchor manifestation in February 1952...

Acquisition proceeded without significant resistance...

Initial conditioning proved insufficient; enhanced protocols implemented... Subject's psychological integrity was systematically reduced over a period of seven years... Core personality was successfully extracted by March 1960...

Subject currently serves as Trust's primary temporal asset...

Sienna read it all.

Every experiment. Every "enhanced protocol." Every clinical description of how they'd broken Isaiah Washington down and rebuilt him into something that served their purposes.

Seventy years.

They'd had him for seventy years.

And they were planning to do it again.

The next section of the file was labeled *PROJECT RENAISSANCE: SUCCESSOR CANDIDATES*.

The first name on the list made Sienna's blood freeze.

DARIUS GRAVES Location: Marrow Projects, District Nine, New Babylon Classification: ANCHOR (Fifth Documented) *Status: ACTIVE (Uncontained) Threat Assessment: CRITICAL Recommended Action: ACQUISITION AND CONDITIONING* There was a photograph attached.

A young man—barely more than a kid, really. Early twenties. Dark skin, tired eyes, the kind of face that had seen too much too young. He was walking through a concrete courtyard, a little girl's hand in his.

His sister, the file noted. *KIMBERLY GRAVES, age 13. Potential leverage asset.* Sienna closed the file.

Walked to the bathroom.

And threw up until there was nothing left.

She thought about going to the authorities.

But the Trust was the authorities. They had connections in every government agency, every police department, every institution that was supposed to protect people. Senators owed them favors. Generals followed their "recommendations." The President received weekly briefings from Director Halden himself.

She thought about leaking the files.

But who would believe her? The Trust controlled the media narrative.

They'd paint her as a disgruntled employee, a conspiracy theorist, a crazy person. She'd be discredited within hours and dead within days.

She thought about doing nothing.

About going back to work.

About pretending she hadn't seen what she'd seen.

But every time she closed her eyes, she saw Isaiah Washington's face.

Before: smiling, warm, human.

After: empty, hollow, wrong.

She couldn't let that happen to someone else.

Not if she could stop it.

It took three weeks to prepare.

Three weeks of smiling at colleagues who might be her executioners.

Three weeks of attending meetings about "containment protocols" and "anomaly neutralization" while secretly copying files onto encrypted drives.

Three weeks of planning an escape route that had almost no chance of success.

The Trust monitored everything. Cameras in every hallway. Sensors in every room. AI systems that tracked employee movements and flagged anomalies. Biometric locks on every door, every drawer, every classified terminal.

But Sienna had helped design those systems.

She knew their blind spots.

The AI flagged unusual behavior—but it had a three-hour learning cycle. If she acted consistently within her normal patterns for long enough, small deviations would be dismissed as noise.

The biometric locks were keyed to individual employees—but they were updated in batches, and the batch cycles created a twelve-second window when certain doors would accept any valid print.

The cameras had overlapping coverage—but they were optimized for the corridors, not the maintenance shafts. And the maintenance shafts connected to the parking garage.

Three weeks of mapping, timing, memorizing.

Three weeks of saying goodbye to everything she'd built without anyone knowing she was saying goodbye.

On a Thursday night—chosen because Thursday was Director Halden's poker night, when security was marginally more relaxed—she made her move.

11:47 PM.

Sienna walked out of her office carrying a shoulder bag with three encrypted drives and a lifetime of research.

Normal. Act normal. You're just working late. You always work late.

Her heart was pounding so hard she was sure the biometric sensors would flag her elevated vitals. But she'd been dosing herself with beta blockers for a week, training her body to stay calm even when her mind was screaming.

Normal. Normal. You've done this a thousand times.

Through the corridor. Past the break room where Agent Chen was getting coffee—she nodded at him, got a nod back, kept moving. Toward the service elevator that led to the underground parking garage.

The elevator doors opened.

She stepped inside.

Pressed P3.

Almost there. Almost— "Dr. Rao?" She turned.

Agent Kowalski—senior security, fifteen years with the Trust, the kind of man who shot first and deleted the paperwork later—was walking toward the elevator.

"Heading out?" he asked.

Normal. NORMAL.

"Just need some fresh air. Been staring at screens too long." She smiled. "You know how it is." Kowalski studied her for a moment.

Then nodded.

"Drive safe, Doc." The elevator doors closed.

Sienna let out a breath she didn't know she'd been holding.

Three floors. Ninety seconds. You can do this.

The elevator descended.

P1.

P2.

P3— The lights went red.

"SECURITY ALERT. CONTAINMENT BREACH. ALL PERSONNEL SHELTER IN PLACE." No. No, no, no— The elevator stopped.

Sienna jabbed at the buttons. Nothing.

Think. THINK.

The emergency hatch. Every elevator had one—fire code requirements that even the Trust couldn't ignore. She grabbed the railing, pulled herself up, and pushed against the ceiling panel.

It gave.

She squeezed through into the shaft, grease and dust coating her clothes, and started climbing down. P3 was only ten feet below.

Behind her, she heard the elevator start to move again.

Going up.

They're checking the elevators. I have maybe two minutes.

She dropped to the P3 landing, forced the doors open with a maintenance key she wasn't supposed to have, and ran.

Her car was in slot 47. Gray Honda Civic. Deliberately boring.

Deliberately forgettable.

She was ten feet away when Kowalski stepped out from behind a concrete pillar.

"Dr. Rao." He had a weapon drawn.

Not a regular gun—a pulse pistol. The kind that could fry her nervous system without leaving a mark.

"You know I can't let you leave," he said. Almost apologetic.

"Whatever you think you know—" "I know about Isaiah Washington." Kowalski's face flickered.

"I know about Project Omega. About the Conductor. About what you did to him for seventy years." Sienna took a step forward. "And I know you're planning to do the same thing to a kid from the Marrow

244

Projects." "Dr. Rao—" "Darius Graves. Twenty-two years old. Raising his little sister alone.

He didn't ask for any of this—he just woke up one day with powers he doesn't understand. And you want to hollow him out. Turn him into another weapon." Kowalski's grip on the pulse pistol tightened.

"The Anchor program is necessary," he said. "You've seen the projections. You know what happens when an Anchor destabilizes. Cities destroyed. Thousands dead. We're protecting the world." "You're torturing innocent people." "We're preventing catastrophe." "By creating monsters?" Kowalski was quiet for a moment.

Then: "I'm going to give you one chance, Dr. Rao. Come back inside.

Surrender the files. Undergo a memory adjustment. You can go back to your life. Your daughter—" "Don't." "Maya misses you. She asks about you every time her father calls.

She's nine years old, and she doesn't understand why Mommy had to leave." Kowalski's voice was soft. Almost kind. "Come back inside, and you can see her again. Eventually. Once we're sure you're... stable." Sienna thought about Maya's face.

About the way she laughed when Sienna tickled her.

About the drawings she used to tape to the refrigerator—stick figures of their family, the word MOM written in careful letters.

About the life she'd already lost.

"If I come back," she said quietly, "you'll do the memory adjustment.

And then you'll keep doing what you're doing. And someday, some other scientist will find those files. And they'll have to make the same choice I'm making." "Probably." "Then I have to go." She lunged.

Not at Kowalski—at the fire extinguisher mounted on the nearby pillar.

She grabbed it, ripped it free, and threw it at his head in one motion.

He ducked—reflexive, unavoidable—and in that half-second, Sienna was in her car, door slamming, engine starting.

The pulse pistol fired.

The shot hit her rear windshield, shattering it into a thousand pieces, but she was already moving—tires screaming, the Civic lurching toward the exit ramp.

More shots.

One caught her side mirror. Another sparked off the concrete beside her.

The exit gate was down.

Reinforced steel. Designed to stop armored trucks.

Sienna didn't slow down.

The emergency override. Fourth digit. FOURTH DIGIT.

Her fingers flew across the keypad mounted beside the driver's seat—a device she'd installed weeks ago, spliced into the garage's control systems without anyone noticing.

The gate shuddered.

Started to rise.

Not enough. Not fast enough— She hit the gas.

The Civic scraped through with inches to spare, sparks flying, the roof screaming against metal, but she was through—she was OUT— Cold night air.

City lights.

Freedom.

Behind her, the Trust's underground garage was already sealing. But she was on the other side.

For now.

They followed, of course.

Two SUVs, black, Trust insignia on the doors. Gaining fast.

Sienna wove through late-night traffic, running red lights, ignoring honking horns and startled pedestrians. The Civic's engine whined in protest—it wasn't built for this, wasn't designed for high-speed chases through urban streets.

But it was fast enough.

Barely.

She hit the highway ramp at seventy. The SUVs followed. In her rearview mirror, she saw one pull alongside—saw the passenger window roll down, saw a weapon being raised.

She jerked the wheel.

The shot missed—barely—punching through what remained of her rear windshield.

They're trying to kill me. After everything I gave them, they're trying to kill me. Part of her had still hoped this was a mistake. That they'd try to talk her down. That her years of service meant something.

It didn't.

She was a loose end now.

And the Trust didn't leave loose ends.

The Whitmore Bridge.

Three lanes each direction. Empty at midnight.

Sienna saw her opportunity.

She slowed—just enough for the SUVs to close the gap—then yanked the wheel hard right, sending the Civic into a controlled spin.

The SUVs tried to follow.

One clipped the other.

Both went wide, skidding toward the bridge railing.

Sienna didn't wait to see if they crashed.

She floored it, crossing the bridge at ninety miles per hour, leaving the pursuit behind.

By the time she reached the other side, there were no headlights in her mirror.

She'd done it.

She'd actually done it.

Three states away. Six hours of driving. A motel that accepted cash and didn't ask questions.

Sienna sat on the bed, encrypted drives in her lap, and allowed herself to feel.

Fear. Grief. Rage.

Eleven years of her life, dedicated to an organization she'd believed in.

Eleven years of telling herself that the Trust protected people.

Eleven years of lies.

She thought about Maya. Safe with her father in Boston. Too young to understand why Mommy couldn't visit anymore. Too young to know that Mommy had worked for monsters.

She thought about Isaiah Washington. Seventy years in a tank, consciousness fragmented, humanity erased. A weapon where a person used to be.

She thought about Darius Graves.

A kid she'd never met.

A kid who was going to be hunted, captured, hollowed out.

Unless she did something.

Unless she found him first.

Sienna pulled out a notebook.

Wrote on the first page, because sometimes you needed to see things in writing to make them real: I, Dr. Sienna Rao, hereby commit to the following: 1\. I will find the Anchor known as Darius Graves.

2. I will provide him with the information and resources he needs to survive. 3\. I will expose the Trust's crimes to the world.

4. I will not stop until the Conductor—Isaiah Washington—is freed from his imprisonment or granted the peace of death. 5\. I will not allow another Anchor to be hollowed.

Not on my watch.

She folded the paper.

Put it in her pocket.

And got to work.

The Trust was powerful.

But knowledge was power too.

And Sienna Rao knew more about the Trust's secrets than anyone alive.

Time to use it.

CHAPTER 32

THE SCIENTIST

The message came through Clutch's network.

Someone wanted to meet.

Someone who claimed to have information about the Trust.

Someone who claimed to know what D-Lo really was.

"Could be a trap," Kettle said.

"Probably is a trap," Clutch agreed.

"We should go anyway," D-Lo said.

They both looked at him.

"What? If someone knows something about my power, about Anchors, about any of this—I need to hear it. Even if it's a trap." "Famous last words," Clutch muttered.

But she agreed.

The location was a coffee shop in a gentrified part of District Nine—the part where young professionals were moving in, pushing out families who'd been there for generations.

D-Lo hated it here.

But the woman waiting for them didn't belong to this neighborhood either.

She sat in the back corner, hood up, sunglasses on, hands wrapped around a coffee cup she wasn't drinking. Brown skin, sharp features, the kind of posture that said she'd been important once and hadn't forgotten it.

"Darius Graves?" she asked as they approached.

"Who's asking?" She lowered her sunglasses.

"My name is Dr. Sienna Rao. I used to work for the Trust. And I know what you are."

They sat.

Clutch kept one hand on her coin. Kettle kept his temperature simmering.

D-Lo tried to look casual.

"Why should we trust you?" Clutch asked.

"You shouldn't." Dr. Rao's voice was tired. "I worked for the people hunting you. I helped design the systems that classify wired individuals. I was part of Project Renaissance from the beginning." "Then why are you here?" "Because I discovered something. Something the Trust never wanted anyone to know." She looked at D-Lo. "Something about what you really are." D-Lo leaned forward. "I'm listening." Dr. Rao took a breath.

"You know about the Anchor classification. Level Zero. Reality Engine potential." She paused. "What you don't know is that the Trust has been hunting Anchors for centuries." "Centuries? Project Renaissance only happened last year." "Project Renaissance was the latest attempt. Not the first." Dr. Rao pulled out a tablet, swiped to a document. "The Trust has records going back to the 1800s. Incidents of 'temporal anomalies.' People who could bend reality, reset events, reshape the world around them." "Other Anchors." "Five documented cases. All of them eventually destroyed the areas around them. Sometimes a city. Sometimes more." Her expression darkened.

"The Trust was founded to prevent that from happening again. To find Anchors before they reach full power and... neutralize them." "Kill them." "Or capture them. Hollow them out. Turn them into something useful." She met his eyes. "That's what they did to the Conductor." D-Lo felt cold.

"The Conductor was an Anchor?" "The third documented case. Emerged in Chicago in 1952. The Trust captured him at Stage Three, before he could fully manifest. They spent decades breaking him down, rebuilding him, turning him into a weapon against future Anchors." "That's what they want to do to me." "That's what they've been planning since they detected your first reset." Dr. Rao's voice was urgent. "You're not just a target, Darius.

250

You're the endgame. Everything the Trust has built for the last century is designed to capture and control someone like you."

"Why are you telling me this?" D-Lo asked. "What do you get out of it?" Dr. Rao was quiet for a moment.

"I have a daughter. She's nine. Lives with her father in Boston—I haven't seen her in two years." She stared at her coffee. "When I joined the Trust, I thought I was doing good. Protecting people. Preventing disasters. But the more I learned, the more I realized..." "You were the disaster," Clutch said flatly.

"Yes." No defensiveness. Just admission. "The Trust doesn't protect people. They contain them. Control them. And when they can't control them, they destroy them. The wired, the Anchors, anyone who doesn't fit their definition of 'acceptable'—they're all just threats to be managed." "So you left." "I tried to. They don't let you leave." Dr. Rao touched a scar on her neck—barely visible, but there. "I've been running for six months.

Living off the grid. Trying to find someone who could actually use what I know." "And you chose me." "You chose yourself. The moment you started protecting people instead of hiding, you became the Trust's priority target." She leaned forward.

"But you also became something else. Hope. Proof that having power doesn't mean becoming a monster." D-Lo didn't feel like hope.

He felt like a guy who kept dying and didn't know how to stop.

"What do you want me to do with this information?" "Survive. Grow. Become something they can't control." Dr. Rao's eyes blazed with intensity. "The Trust's models say you'll reach Stage Four within two years. They say you'll lose control, like every Anchor before you. They say you'll destroy everything you care about." "And you think they're wrong?" "I think you're different. I think whatever's inside you—whatever makes you keep getting up, keep fighting, keep protecting people—might be the variable they never accounted for." She stood. "I have files.

Research. Everything I could smuggle out before I ran. I'll get them to you. But I can't stay. They're tracking me." "Wait—" D-Lo reached for her arm.

She was already moving toward the back exit.

"One more thing." She paused at the door. "The Janitor. The thing hunting you. The Trust didn't create him, but they know what he is. An Anchor who broke differently. Who turned inward instead of outward. Who consumes reality instead of reshaping it." "How do I stop him?" Dr. Rao's expression was grim.

"You can't stop him. Not alone. Not with what you are now." She opened the door. "But if you survive long enough to reach Stage Two—if you learn to see the threads—you might find a way." "That's not very comforting." "It's not supposed to be." She stepped into the alley. "It's supposed to be true. Good luck, Darius. You're going to need it." She was gone.

They sat in the coffee shop for a long time after she left.

Clutch was the first to speak.

"That was a lot." "Yeah." "You believe her?" D-Lo thought about it.

"She didn't lie. Not about the important stuff. I could see it." "Since when can you see lies?" "Since I started paying attention to the threads." He rubbed his eyes.

"She was scared. Genuinely scared. And she believed everything she said." "Doesn't mean it's true." "No. But it means she thinks it's true. And that's something." Kettle had been quiet the whole time. Now he spoke.

"The Conductor. An Anchor they broke and rebuilt." "Yeah." "That's what they want to do to you." "Yeah." "We're not gonna let that happen." D-Lo looked at him.

Kettle's jaw was set. His skin glowed faintly—warm, not hot.

"We're not gonna let them take you," Kettle repeated. "Whatever it takes." Clutch nodded.

"What he said." D-Lo felt something shift in his chest.

Fear, yes.

But also something else.

Something like strength.

"Okay," he said quietly. "Then let's figure out how to survive."

Three days later, a package arrived at one of Clutch's dead drops.

No return address.

No note.

Just a thumb drive and a single sheet of paper with two words:
TRUST NO ONE.

D-Lo plugged the drive into a laptop Murmur had scavenged.

The files were extensive.

Project Renaissance research.

Anchor classification protocols.

Trust organizational charts.

And a folder labeled CONDUCTOR — ORIGIN AND CONTAINMENT.

D-Lo opened it.

Read.

And felt ice in his veins.

The man who became the Conductor had a name once.

Isaiah Washington.

Father of three.

School teacher.

The kind of man who stayed after class to help struggling students.

The kind of man who coached little league on weekends.

The kind of man who was good.

The Trust had found him in 1952.

Captured him in 1953.

Broken him by 1960.

And turned him into the thing that now hunted D-Lo across realities.

"They do this to everyone," D-Lo whispered.

Clutch looked over his shoulder at the files.

"They do this to everyone," she agreed.

"We have to stop them." "We will." "I mean really stop them. Not just survive. Not just hide. Tear the whole thing down." Clutch was quiet for a moment.

Then she smiled.

"Now you're talking my language, Reload." D-Lo closed the laptop.

The war wasn't just about survival anymore.

It was about justice.

For Isaiah Washington.

For all the wired they'd caged.

For everyone the Trust had ever broken.

And D-Lo was going to deliver it.

Or die trying.

Again and again and again.

They were pinned down three blocks from the cathedral.

Trust vehicles blocked every route. Snipers on the rooftops. Suppression fields making Kettle's flames sputter and Clutch's luck unreliable.

"We're not getting through this," Clutch said, coin spinning weakly between her fingers. "Too many. Even with your resets—" D-Lo had already died twice trying to force a path. Each time, he came back with less time, less energy, less hope.

"There has to be another way." "There isn't." Lexi's voice was flat. "They knew we were coming.

This is an ambush." D-Lo's burner phone buzzed.

He stared at it. He'd forgotten he still had it—Glitch's number, the one Goldmask's tech had given him months ago.

A text: *Black SUV. Alley behind you. 30 seconds.*

D-Lo looked at the others.

"Either this is a trap," he said, "or it's not." "That's not reassuring." "I know." The SUV pulled up exactly where the text said it would.

The window rolled down.

Glitch. Same flat eyes. Same hoodie.

"Get in." They got in.

"Goldmask sends his regards." The SUV wove through side streets, somehow finding gaps in the Trust cordon that shouldn't exist.

"Why is he helping us?" D-Lo asked.

"Because the Trust hit his warehouses last week. Took twelve of his people. People he needed." Glitch didn't look back, focused on driving. "He said to tell you: debts cut both ways. He gave you intel.

Now you're giving him distraction." "We're a distraction?" "The Trust has been hunting you for months. Every officer in the city wants to be the one who brings down the Anchor." A ghost of a smile.

"Right now, they're all focused on you. Which means they're not focused on Goldmask's operation." "What operation?" "The kind that works better when cops are looking elsewhere." D-Lo didn't ask more. Didn't want to know.

"Where are you taking us?" "Close to the cathedral. Close as I can get." Glitch's eyes flicked to the rearview. "You're going after the Cleaner. I saw the pattern—the kills, the soul-eating, where he feeds. He's been building toward something." "You know what it is?" "No. But my sister did." The flatness cracked, just for a moment.

"She was one of his. Taken three years ago. I've been watching ever since." Lexi leaned forward. "I'm sorry." "Don't be sorry. Be effective." Glitch pulled to a stop in a narrow alley. "Cathedral's two blocks north. Trust cordon ends at Madison—they think nobody's stupid enough to go toward the Cleaner on purpose." "They're wrong." "Usually." Glitch handed D-Lo a small device. "Goldmask wanted you to have this. Emergency transponder. If you survive—when you survive—press it. He'll send extraction." "And the price?" "He said to tell you: you already paid it." Glitch's expression shifted—something like respect. "You said no. You didn't sell out.

That bought you more than you know." D-Lo took the transponder.

"Tell Goldmask thanks." "Tell him yourself. After." The SUV door opened.

They stepped into the night.

Behind them, Glitch pulled away—back toward whatever Goldmask's operation needed him for.

Ahead, the cathedral waited.

CHAPTER 33

WHITE ROOMS

Kimi Graves was thirteen years old, and she was done being rescued.

The van ride took forever.

Or maybe it was twenty minutes—time didn't work right when you were zip-tied in a metal box, listening to other kids cry, wondering if you'd ever see sunlight again.

There were four of them in the transport: Kimi, a teenage boy with burn scars who wouldn't stop shaking, a girl with floating hair who'd gone catatonic the moment they were loaded in, and a little boy curled in the corner who couldn't have been older than eight.

Kimi focused on the little one.

It was easier than focusing on herself.

"Hey," she said softly, scooting closer despite the zip ties cutting into her wrists. "Hey, it's okay. What's your name?" The boy didn't respond at first. His eyes were too big, his face too thin—the kind of kid who'd been hungry long before the Trust showed up.

"My name's Kimi. I'm thirteen. I know this is scary, but we're gonna be okay." A lie. Probably. But lies were what you told scared children to keep them breathing.

The boy looked up.

"Marcus," he whispered.

"Hi, Marcus." Kimi tried to smile. It felt wrong on her face, but she did it anyway. "You wired?" A tiny nod.

"What can you do?" "I... I make things move. Small things." His voice cracked. "Mama said it was our secret." Kimi's heart broke a little.

"That's a cool secret," she said. "My brother has a secret too. He can come back when he gets hurt." "Come back?" "Yeah. No matter what happens, he comes back." She leaned closer, made her voice conspiratorial. "And he's gonna come for me. For all of us.

You'll see." Marcus didn't look convinced.

But he scooted closer.

And when the van hit a bump and he flinched, Kimi let him lean against her shoulder.

She couldn't save anyone right now.

But she could be a shoulder.

That was something.

The Vault was worse than she'd imagined.

They processed her like cattle—scanned, catalogued, stripped of everything she'd brought. Her phone. Her jacket. The hair tie D-Lo had given her for her birthday last year, the one with the little star on it that he'd found at a dollar store and wrapped in newspaper because he couldn't afford wrapping paper.

All of it gone.

All of her gone.

Just a number now. A file. A problem to be managed.

"Subject 7749," a technician droned, fastening a cold metal band around her wrist. "Classification: Non-Wired. Category: Leverage Asset." Leverage.

Like she was a tool. A thing to be used against her brother.

Kimi memorized the technician's face.

Someday, somehow, she was going to make him regret that word.

They put her in a white room.

White walls. White floor. White ceiling. A single chair bolted to the ground. No windows. No clock. Nothing to mark the passage of time except the flickering of the fluorescent lights overhead.

Sensory deprivation, she realized. She'd read about it in a book once—how prisons used to break people by taking away all stimulation, all reference points, until their minds started eating themselves.

They're trying to break me.

Kimi sat in the chair.

Closed her eyes.

And started counting.

One. Two. Three. Four…

D-Lo had taught her that. When things got bad, count. Keep your mind working. Stay tethered to something real.

… forty-seven. Forty-eight. Forty-nine. Fifty…

She didn't know how long she counted.

Hours, maybe.

Or days.

But she kept counting.

Because counting meant she was still here.

Still herself.

Still fighting.

The woman came eventually.

Tall. Sharp. Expensive suit. The kind of pretty that came from money and surgery rather than genetics. She smiled like a snake—all teeth, no warmth.

"Kimi Graves. Thirteen years old. Guardian: Darius Graves, age twenty-two." She sat across from Kimi, tablet in hand. "Your brother is causing us quite a bit of trouble." Kimi said nothing.

Keep counting. One thousand forty-seven. One thousand forty-eight.

"He's killed several of our officers. Did you know that? Directly or indirectly responsible for multiple Trust casualties." Still nothing.

One thousand fifty-two. One thousand fifty-three.

"Of course, they came back. His little… trick… resets things. But they remember the pain. The fear. The experience of dying." The woman's smile widened. "That kind of trauma accumulates, Kimi. Even for us." "Good." The word was out before she could stop it.

The woman's eyebrow arched.

"Excuse me?" "I said good." Kimi met her eyes. Held them. "I hope he killed a hundred of you. I hope he kills a hundred more." Something flickered in the woman's expression.

Not anger.

Interest.

"Loyalty. How touching." She leaned forward. "Let me tell you what's going to happen, Kimi. Your brother is going to come for you.

258

That's inevitable—he's predictable that way. And when he does, we're going to capture him. Break him. Turn him into something useful." "He'll never work for you." "He won't have a choice. We have methods. Technologies. Ways of hollowing out a person and filling them with something more...

cooperative." The woman's smile didn't waver. "The Conductor used to be like your brother. Full of principles. Full of fight. Now he does whatever we tell him." Kimi felt cold.

But she didn't let it show.

"You're monsters." "We're pragmatists. There's a difference." The woman stood. "I'm going to give you some time to think about your situation. When I come back, we'll discuss how you can help us bring your brother in peacefully.

Cooperation will make things easier for both of you." "I'll never help you." "We'll see." The woman walked to the door.

Paused.

"One more thing," she said without turning around. "The other children you came in with? The ones in the transport? Their cooperation is being... encouraged. The little boy—Marcus, I believe? He's been asking for you." Kimi's heart clenched.

"If you want to see him again, you'll think very carefully about your choices." The door closed.

The white room was silent.

Kimi started counting again.

But this time, she was also planning.

They let her see Marcus on the third day.

Or what she thought was the third day—time was impossible to track in the white room. The lights never changed. The meals came at irregular intervals. Sleep happened when her body gave out, not when the world told her to rest.

A guard led her through corridors that all looked the same—white walls, white floors, white ceilings—to a small room with a table and two chairs.

Marcus was already there.

He looked worse than before. Thinner. Paler. Dark circles under his eyes that shouldn't exist on an eight-year-old's face.

"Kimi!" He ran to her, threw his arms around her waist, and started crying.

She held him.

Stroked his head.

Let him sob into her shirt until the guards told them to sit down.

"Are you okay?" she asked, settling into a chair. "Have they hurt you?" Marcus shook his head. But his hands were shaking.

"They... they want me to do things. With my power. Make things move.

They have these tests..." He swallowed hard. "I don't want to do it, but they say if I don't, they'll hurt the other kids." Bastards.

"Listen to me," Kimi said, keeping her voice low. "Do what they say.

For now. Survive. That's the only thing that matters right now." "But—" "My brother is coming. I know he is. We just have to hold on until he gets here." She squeezed Marcus's hand. "Can you do that? Can you be brave for a little while longer?" Marcus looked at her.

At this girl he'd known for only a few days.

At the only person in this nightmare who'd shown him any kindness.

"I can try," he whispered.

"That's all any of us can do." The guards gave them five more minutes.

Five minutes of holding hands across a table.

Five minutes of being human in a place designed to strip humanity away.

Then they took Marcus back to his room, and Kimi back to hers.

But something had changed.

She wasn't just counting anymore.

She was watching.

Learning.

Memorizing patrol patterns. Guard rotations. Which doors had keypads and which had physical locks. The way the ventilation system hummed at certain hours. The sounds that came from certain corridors.

D-Lo was coming.

She knew he was.

But that didn't mean she couldn't meet him halfway.

The snake woman came back on the fifth day.

Same smile. Same suit. Same tablet.

"I trust you've had time to consider your options." Kimi had.

She'd considered her options very carefully.

"I want to make a deal," she said.

The woman's eyebrow rose.

"Really." "I'll help you. I'll help you bring my brother in. But I have conditions." "I'm listening." "First: you let Marcus go. The little boy. He's eight years old. He's not a threat to anyone." "Interesting. What else?" "Second: you let me see my brother. Before you... before whatever you're going to do to him. I want to say goodbye." The woman studied her for a long moment.

"And in exchange?" Kimi took a breath.

This was the hard part.

The part that felt like swallowing glass.

"In exchange, I'll tell you where the Ghosts are hiding. The ones in the Underline. I know where their base is." She didn't, actually.

Not exactly.

But she'd heard enough of D-Lo's conversations, caught enough fragments of information, to fake it convincingly.

Long enough to buy time.

Long enough for whatever came next.

The woman smiled.

A real smile this time—predatory, satisfied.

"I knew you were smart, Kimi. Just like your brother." She stood.

"I'll discuss your terms with my superiors. In the meantime..." She tapped something on her tablet.

A moment later, a guard entered with Marcus.

"Consider this a gesture of good faith," the woman said. "You can share a cell from now on. As long as you continue to cooperate." Marcus ran to Kimi.

She caught him. Held him.

Looked at the snake woman over his head.

You think you've won something.

You think I'm broken.

You have no idea what I am.

"Thank you," she said, keeping her voice small. Scared. Grateful.

Exactly what they expected to hear.

The woman nodded and left.

The guard led them to a new cell—larger than the white room, with two cots and a small window that looked out onto a concrete wall.

But it was a window.

A tiny rectangle of something that wasn't white.

Marcus fell asleep almost immediately, exhausted by fear and relief.

Kimi sat by the window.

Watching. Waiting.

I'm not broken, she thought. I'm just getting started.

The raid came on the seventh day.

Kimi heard it first—distant explosions, alarms, the sound of boots running in corridors.

She woke Marcus, pressed a finger to her lips.

"Something's happening. Get behind the cot." "What—" "Now." He obeyed.

Kimi pressed her ear to the door.

Shouts. Gunfire. The crackle of energy weapons.

Then— A voice she knew better than her own.

"KIMI!" She pounded on the door.

"D-LO! I'M HERE! CELL BLOCK SEVEN!" More gunfire. More explosions.

Then the door burst open, and there he was—her brother, covered in dust and blood, eyes wild, looking at her like she was the only thing in the world that mattered.

"Kimi." She ran to him.

He caught her, held her so tight she couldn't breathe.

"I knew you'd come," she said into his chest. "I knew it." "Always." He pulled back, looked at her face. Checking for injuries. For damage.

For proof that she was really there.

"Are you okay? Did they hurt you?" "I'm fine. D-Lo—there's a kid. Marcus. He's in the cell." D-Lo looked past her.

Saw the eight-year-old huddled behind the cot, staring at him with enormous eyes.

"Come on," D-Lo said, extending a hand. "We're getting everyone out." Marcus took his hand.

Kimi took D-Lo's other hand.

And together, they ran.

Through corridors full of chaos. Past guards who were too busy fighting to notice three figures slipping through the shadows. Toward an exit that Kimi had memorized during her days of watching and waiting.

"This way," she said, pulling them toward a ventilation shaft. "It connects to the service tunnel. I mapped it." D-Lo stared at her.

"You mapped it?" "You taught me to pay attention." She was already climbing into the shaft. "Now come on." D-Lo looked at Marcus.

The eight-year-old shrugged.

"She's bossy," Marcus said. "But she knows stuff." D-Lo laughed.

Actually laughed, in the middle of everything.

"Yeah," he said. "She does." He helped Marcus into the shaft, then followed.

Behind them, the Vault burned.

Ahead of them, freedom waited.

And Kimi Graves—thirteen years old, done being rescued—led the way.

CHAPTER 34

THE VAULT

The Trust's downtown headquarters was a gleaming tower of glass and steel—forty stories of corporate efficiency hiding the ugliest operations in New Babylon.

The Vault was underneath it.

Seven levels below street level, past security checkpoints and biometric scanners and defenses that would shred anything trying to force its way in.

Which was why they weren't forcing.

"Everyone remember the plan?" Clutch asked.

They were in a maintenance tunnel, two hundred feet below the city, the smell of rust and stagnant water thick in the air. D-Lo, Kettle, Clutch, Sparks—the team Lexi had assembled for the most dangerous mission the Ghosts had ever attempted.

Kimi was with them too.

D-Lo had tried to argue. Had tried to make her stay at the secondary site, where it was safe, where she wouldn't be in the line of fire.

She'd refused.

"You're not leaving me behind again," she'd said, jaw set. "I spent a week in that place. I know the layout. I know the patrol patterns. You need me." He hadn't been able to argue with that.

"Sparks takes out the primary grid," D-Lo recited. "Kettle melts through the wall. We move fast, hit cell block seven, grab Lexi, and get out before they switch to backup power." "Twelve minutes," Clutch said. "That's our window. After that, the suppression fields come back online and we're trapped." "Then we do it in ten." D-Lo looked at his team.

"Everyone ready?" Nods all around.

"Let's go save our leader."

The wall was three feet of reinforced concrete—military grade, designed to withstand everything from explosions to earthquakes.

Kettle pressed his palms against it.

His skin began to glow.

Orange. Red. White.

The concrete started to soften, then flow, then pour away like lava.

"Fifteen seconds," he grunted through clenched teeth. "Twenty at most." "You can do it, big man." The heat was intense—D-Lo felt it on his face from ten feet away, like standing too close to an open furnace. Sweat poured down Kettle's body, evaporating before it hit the ground.

Twelve seconds.

The wall was half-gone.

Fifteen seconds.

A hole appeared—just large enough to crawl through.

Eighteen seconds.

"NOW!" They moved.

The alarm blared the moment they entered the Vault proper.

Red lights. Sirens. A recorded voice announcing "CONTAINMENT BREACH, SECTOR SEVEN" on a loop.

"So much for stealth," Clutch muttered, pulling her weapon.

"Plan B." D-Lo scanned the corridor. "Sparks, now!" Sparks stepped forward, touched an exposed electrical conduit, and closed her eyes.

Her whole body lit up—electricity crackling across her skin, arcing between her fingers, her hair standing on end like she'd grabbed a Van de Graaff generator.

"Overloading… primary grid… NOW." The lights died.

The alarm cut out.

Emergency backups flickered on—dim red, barely enough to see by.

"That's our window," D-Lo said. "Move!"

The Vault was worse than D-Lo had imagined.

Not because it was brutal—though it was. Not because it was cold—though it was that too.

It was the silence.

Rows of cells lined the corridors, each one containing a wired prisoner.

But none of them were screaming. None of them were fighting.

They just sat there.

Staring at nothing.

Empty.

"Suppression tech," Clutch whispered. "It doesn't just block powers.

It breaks spirits. Keep someone in there long enough, they forget who they are." D-Lo looked at the faces behind the glass.

Men. Women. Children.

All of them hollow.

"We can't save them all," Clutch said quietly. "Not today." "I know." D-Lo's voice was tight. "But we're coming back. We're getting them all out." "One battle at a time." "One battle at a time." They moved deeper.

Cell block seven was guarded.

Six officers in tactical gear. Automated turrets mounted on the ceiling.

A suppression field so strong D-Lo could barely feel the threads.

"Any ideas?" Kettle asked.

D-Lo studied the scene.

The guards' positions. The turret's firing arcs. The layout of the corridor.

"Yeah," he said. "Let me try something." He stepped around the corner.

Into six rifles pointed at his chest.

"FREEZE! HANDS WHERE WE CAN SEE THEM!" D-Lo raised his hands.

Smiled.

"Okay," he said. "Let's try this a few times."

The first death was quick.

Three bullets to the chest before he could move. Pain—hot and terrible and familiar by now. Darkness creeping in from the edges.

Reset.

He came back a step to the left.

Dodged the first volley.

Took a bullet to the shoulder instead.

Pain. Darkness. Reset.

Back again.

This time he ducked right. Grabbed the nearest guard's rifle. Used him as a shield.

Made it three more seconds before the automated turret caught him.

Pain. Darkness. Reset.

Again.

And again.

And again.

Each death taught him something.

The guards' reaction times—the one on the left was faster, the one on the right hesitated a fraction of a second.

The turret's targeting delay—point-three seconds between acquiring a target and firing.

The suppression field's weak point—near the ceiling, where the emitters didn't quite overlap.

Fourteen deaths.

Fourteen lessons.

Fourteen versions of himself, erased from existence.

But on the fifteenth try— He moved through them like water.

Ducked the first volley. Grabbed the rifle. Spun the guard into the turret's line of fire. Dove under the second volley. Came up inside the third guard's reach.

Elbow to the throat.

Knee to the groin.

Rifle butt to the temple.

Four guards down in six seconds.

The fifth tried to run.

D-Lo caught him by the collar.

"Cell block seven. Which one is Lexi Ghost?" The guard pointed, trembling.

D-Lo dropped him.

Walked to the cell.

Lexi sat inside—battered, bloody, but alive.

Her eyes were closed. Her lips moved silently, like she was praying. Or counting. Or doing whatever you do to stay sane in a place designed to break you.

D-Lo pressed his hand against the glass.

"Lexi." Her eyes opened.

Saw him.

And for the first time since he'd met her, she smiled.

A real smile.

Full of hope.

"Took you long enough," she whispered.

"Had some stuff to deal with." He looked at the cell door. "How do I open this?" "Control panel on the right. But you'll need—" Clutch appeared beside him, already working the panel.

"—administrator access, which I happen to have because some idiot left his keycard in his pocket when we knocked him out." The door hissed open.

Lexi stumbled out—and collapsed into D-Lo's arms.

He held her.

She was shaking.

Felt her tears soaking into his shirt.

"I knew you'd come," she whispered. "I saw it. In the threads." "You can see them too?" "Only sometimes. Only when I'm close to someone like you." She pulled back, looked at his face. "We're connected, D-Lo. More than you know." He didn't know what that meant.

But he knew it was true.

"We need to move," Clutch said. "Six minutes until backup power." D-Lo supported Lexi's weight.

"Then let's move."

The way out was harder than the way in.

Trust security had mobilized—officers flooding the corridors, automated defenses coming back online, suppression fields strengthening with every passing second.

Kettle was spent—barely conscious, being half-carried by Sparks.

Clutch's luck was running on fumes.

D-Lo kept them moving through sheer force of will.

And Kimi— Kimi proved herself.

"This way," she whispered, pulling them toward a ventilation shaft.

"It connects to the service tunnel. I mapped it." "How?" "I was paying attention. Reading the signs. Memorizing the layout." She flashed a grim smile. "What, you think I just sat in that cell feeling sorry for myself?" D-Lo stared at his little sister.

At the survivor she'd become.

"I'm proud of you," he said.

"Save it for when we're out." They crawled.

Twenty minutes of darkness and claustrophobia.

Then fresh air.

The maintenance tunnel.

The way out.

They emerged into daylight—blinding, beautiful daylight—in an alley three blocks from the Trust tower.

A van waited.

Doors open.

Engine running.

They piled in.

The van peeled out.

Behind them, sirens wailed.

But the Trust was too late.

They were gone.

Lexi was safe.

And finally, in weeks, D-Lo felt something like hope.

CHAPTER 35

THE REUNION

They found Melo in the deepest part of the Vault.

Past the processing centers. Past the interrogation rooms. Past horrors that D-Lo would never be able to unsee—laboratories where people had been taken apart wrong, walls covered in blood writing that said things like "HE REMEMBERS" and "THE THREADS ARE SCREAMING," a human being suspended in a column of light with cables running into their skull.

D-Lo kept moving.

Because somewhere in this nightmare, his best friend was waiting.

The cell was different from the others.

No glass wall. No suppression field. Just a reinforced door with seventeen different locks and a sign that read: *PROJECT PROBABILITY — AUTHORIZED PERSONNEL ONLY*.

"They did something to him," Clutch said quietly, studying the locks.

"Something special." "Can you open it?" "Give me thirty seconds." D-Lo waited.

The longest thirty seconds of his life.

Then the locks clicked, one after another, and the door swung open.

And there was Melo.

He barely recognized him.

The Melo he'd grown up with had been loud, vibrant, always moving—hands gesturing, mouth running, energy that couldn't be contained. The kind of presence that filled a room just by existing.

This Melo was still.

He sat on a cot in the corner, head shaved, scars visible where they'd stitched his scalp back together after... whatever they'd done. His eyes were closed. His hands were folded in his lap. He looked like a monk in meditation.

Or a corpse waiting to be buried.

"Melo?" The eyes opened.

They were different.

Still brown, still familiar, but deeper somehow. Like they were seeing things that weren't in the room. Things that had never been in any room.

"D-Lo." Melo's voice was soft. Distant. "I knew you'd come. I saw it.

Every possible version of this moment—you in the doorway, that expression on your face." A ghost of a smile. "Some versions, you were crying. Some versions, you were dead. But in most of them... you were here." "What did they do to you?" "They made me better." Melo laughed—a hollow sound. "That's what they called it. Enhancement. Optimization. They took my gift and turned it into something... more." "Your gift?" "Probability sight. I could always see the angles, right? Always knew which way things would fall. But it was instinct before. Gut feelings." He touched his temple, tracing the scars. "Now I see everything. Every possible future. Every branching path. Every version of every moment, stretching out forever." His voice cracked.

"It's too much, D. It's too much."

Something broke inside him.

This was his fault.

If he'd gone with Melo that night—if he'd been there when everything went wrong—maybe they would have taken him instead. Maybe Melo would be free right now, living his life, hustling his hustles, being the loud, vibrant, impossible person he'd always been.

Instead, D-Lo had stayed home. Stayed safe. And Melo had paid the price.

"I'm sorry." The words came out cracked. Broken. "I'm so sorry. I should have—I should have been there. Should have found you sooner. Should have—" "Stop." Melo's voice was gentle. The gentleness hurt more than anger would have. "I saw those futures too. The ones where you came with me that night. You died, D. Every single version. You died, and Kimi had nobody." "But if I'd—" "You couldn't save me. Not then." Melo reached out, touched D-Lo's face—the way he used to when they were kids, when one of them was crying and trying to hide it. "But you're here now. That's what matters." D-Lo grabbed his friend and hugged him.

Hard. Desperate. The way you hug someone you thought you'd lost forever.

Melo stiffened at first—touch probably meant something different after months of experiments—but then he relaxed. Hugged back. And D-Lo felt wetness on his shoulder that might have been tears, though he'd never tell anyone that.

"I missed you," D-Lo whispered. "Every single day. I missed you." "I know. I saw that too." Melo's voice was muffled. "The versions of you looking for me. Fighting for me. Dying for me." He pulled back, and his strange new eyes were wet. "You're the only constant, D. In every future I can see. You're always there. Always trying." D-Lo wiped his face. Pretended he wasn't crying.

"Yeah, well. Marrow boys for life, right?" "Marrow boys for life." For one moment, in the middle of hell, they were just two kids from the projects again. Brothers who'd sworn to always have each other's backs.

Then D-Lo stood up.

"We're getting you out. Right now. Can you walk?" "I can do anything. I can see every path that leads to the exit. Every guard's position. Every trap." Melo's eyes focused on something D-Lo couldn't see. "There's a route—seventeen percent survival probability—that gets us out in four minutes. There's another route—sixty-three percent—that takes eight minutes but avoids the secondary response team." "Melo—" "There's also a route where we all die. Several, actually. Most of them, if I'm being honest." Melo finally looked at D-Lo—really looked, present instead of distant. "The numbers say we probably don't make it.

The numbers say I should stay here, let you escape, minimize casualties." "Fuck the numbers." Melo blinked.

"What?" "I said fuck the numbers." D-Lo grabbed his friend's hand, pulled him to his feet. "I didn't come all this way—didn't fight through all this—to leave you behind because some probability calculation says it's optimal." "But—" "No. No buts. No numbers. No calculations." D-Lo gripped Melo's shoulders. "You're my brother. You've been my brother since we were five years old, stealing candy from Mr. Kim's store and lying to each other about who ate the last piece. I don't care what the odds say. I'm not leaving without you." Melo stared at him.

Something shifted in his expression.

Something that looked almost like hope.

"The Trust took a lot from me," Melo whispered. "They took my privacy.

My sanity. My ability to look at the world and not see it falling apart into infinite pieces." He swallowed hard. "But they couldn't take you.

They couldn't make me forget you." "And you won't have to." D-Lo pulled him toward the door. "Now come on.

We've got a sixty-three percent survival route to take." "Actually, with the information I have now, I can push it to seventy-one percent." "Even better. Let's move."

Melo guided them through the Vault like he'd lived there his whole life.

Which, in a way, he had—in the futures he'd seen, in the infinite variations of this escape playing out in his mind.

"Left here. Guard in three seconds—Clutch, redirect the bullet before he fires. Now right. Kettle, there's a reinforced door in twenty feet—start heating up. D-Lo, in exactly forty-seven seconds, you're going to need to reset. Don't fight it." "What? Why?" "Because in forty-seven seconds, a sniper on the catwalk above us gets a clean shot. You're the only one he can hit, and you're the only one who can survive it." Melo's voice was matter-of-fact. Clinical. "Take the bullet. Reset. Come back two seconds earlier. Duck instead of walking." "That's... specific." "I told you. I see everything now." D-Lo counted.

Forty-five. Forty-six. Forty-seven— He ducked.

A bullet whizzed through the space where his head had been.

"I thought you said I needed to reset?" "I said in most futures you need to reset. This one—" Melo almost smiled "—you listened to me instead. Ninety-four percent survival probability and climbing." They kept moving.

Then Melo made a mistake.

"Clear path ahead," he said. "Ninety-six percent safe. No guards for the next thirty seconds." They rounded the corner.

Three Trust agents stood directly in their path, weapons raised.

Melo's face went white.

"That's—that's impossible. I saw—I saw this corridor empty—" "DOWN!" D-Lo grabbed Melo and pulled him behind a pillar as bullets sparked off the concrete.

"I don't understand," Melo whispered, voice shaking. "The numbers were clear. Ninety-six percent. I saw it—" "The numbers aren't always right." D-Lo checked the corridor. Two guards advancing, one hanging back. "You're not a god, Melo. You're a guy with a really good calculator. Sometimes the calculator's wrong." "But I've never—" "First time for everything." D-Lo pulled his friend's face around to look at him. "Hey. Hey. It's okay. We adapt. That's what we do." Melo's eyes were wild—the eyes of someone whose entire worldview had just cracked.

"What if I get it wrong again? What if I tell you something and it's wrong and you die because—" "Then I reset and we try again." D-Lo almost smiled. "That's my thing, remember? The numbers don't have to be perfect. They just have to be better than guessing." Melo took a shaky breath.

"Okay. Okay." He closed his eyes, processing. When he opened them, some of the panic had faded. "Sixty-three percent chance the left corridor is clear. Eighty-one percent if Kettle creates a heat distraction first." "That's more like it." D-Lo signaled Kettle. "Let's move." They moved.

And Melo learned something the numbers had never taught him: sometimes being wrong was part of being human.

The extraction point was chaos.

Trust reinforcements flooding in from multiple directions. Suppression fields trying to activate. Alarms screaming.

But Melo was calm.

He stood in the center of the chaos, eyes tracking things nobody else could see, calling out instructions like a conductor leading an orchestra.

"Sparks—overload that panel in three, two, one—now. Clutch—flip that coin, let it land on heads, and don't ask why. D-Lo—grab Lexi and pull her two feet to the left." D-Lo grabbed Lexi, pulled her left.

A support beam crashed down exactly where she'd been standing.

"The numbers say we make it," Melo said. "Eighty-seven percent now.

Almost safe." "And the other thirteen percent?" Melo's expression flickered.

"The other thirteen percent, someone dies. Different people in different versions. But someone always dies." D-Lo looked at his crew.

At Kettle, exhausted but fighting.

At Clutch, luck stretched to its limit.

At Lexi, wounded but standing.

At Kimi—his sister, who shouldn't even be here.

"Nobody dies," D-Lo said. "Not today." "The numbers—" "I don't care about the numbers." D-Lo reached for the threads. "I care about us. And I say we all walk out of here." He grabbed the brightest thread he could see.

And pulled.

Later—after the escape, after the safe house, after Melo had slept for sixteen hours straight—they sat together on a rooftop.

Just like old times.

Except everything had changed.

"Your mama's gonna be so happy," D-Lo said.

"Is she okay?" "She's surviving. Barely. But she'll be better now." Melo nodded.

He looked older. Not just from what they'd done to him—older in his eyes. The eyes of someone who'd seen too much.

"I don't know who I am anymore," he said quietly. "The things they put in my head... I'm not the same, D." "None of us are. That's kind of the point." "What if I can't be who I was? What if that Melo is gone?" D-Lo thought about it.

About all the versions of himself he'd lost to resets.

About the question of whether continuity of self meant anything when you could die and come back.

"Then you become someone new," he said. "Someone stronger. Someone who survived what they did and came out the other side." "That easy?" "Nothing's easy. But..." D-Lo looked at his friend. "I've died over fifty times now. And every time I come back, I have to decide who I want to be. It's terrifying. It's exhausting. But it's also a choice. I get to choose." "And you think I get to choose?" "I think we all do. Every day. Every moment." D-Lo put a hand on Melo's shoulder. "You're not what they made you. You're what you decide to be." Melo was quiet for a long time.

Then: "I want to fight them. The Trust. For what they did to me. For what they're doing to everybody." "Then fight with us." "Your crew?" "Our crew. If you want it." Melo looked at D-Lo.

At his best friend since childhood.

At the one person who'd never given up on him.

"Yeah," he said. "Yeah, I want it." They sat in silence.

Watching the city.

Two broken kids from the Marrow who'd somehow survived everything the world threw at them.

And were just getting started.

CHAPTER 36

THE CATHEDRAL

The cathedral had been abandoned for decades.

Once, it had been the spiritual heart of the Marrow—a beacon of faith in a faithless neighborhood, where grandmothers prayed for grandsons who sold drugs on corners, where weddings happened between people who'd grown up three doors apart, where funerals were held for children who'd never had a chance to grow old.

Now it was a ruin.

Stained glass shattered, the biblical scenes reduced to jagged fragments that caught moonlight and threw it in broken patterns across the floor.

Pews rotted and collapsed, the wood soft with decades of water damage.

The roof had caved in three separate places, letting in the night sky like wounds in the building's skin.

D-Lo walked through the front doors at 11:58.

Alone.

The Janitor waited at the altar.

He stood with his back to D-Lo, mop handle leaning against the ruined pulpit, eyes fixed on a broken crucifix that hung crooked on the wall.

His coveralls were faded, stained with things that weren't quite dirt.

His shadow stretched behind him, impossibly long, filled with shapes that moved when they shouldn't.

"You came," the Janitor said without turning. "I wasn't sure you would." "You gave me a choice between watching people die and facing you myself." D-Lo stopped halfway down the aisle. "That's not really a choice." "No. It isn't." The Janitor turned. "That's what I like about you, Reload. You're predictable. Noble. Good." The word dripped with contempt.

"And that's bad?" "It's boring." The Janitor smiled—that wrong, terrible smile that didn't belong on any human face. "But it's also exploitable. You'll always sacrifice yourself for others. Always choose pain over pragmatism. That makes you easy to manipulate." "Then why haven't you killed me yet?" The Janitor's smile widened.

"Because you're not just a meal. You're a masterpiece." He stepped down from the altar, moving slowly, savoring the moment. "Every fracture in your soul. Every death you've experienced. Every reset, every thread you've abandoned—it's all still there. Encoded in your essence. A library of suffering." D-Lo felt the threads pressing against his awareness—thousands of possibilities branching from this moment. Some led to his death. Some led to victory. Most led to pain.

"I've consumed two Anchors before you. The First, before she fractured Seattle. Marcus—me—before I became what I am." The Janitor's eyes glittered with ancient hunger. "But you're different. You come from here. From the Marrow. From a place so soaked in generational trauma that your power is already flavored with centuries of suffering I never had to cultivate. You're pre-marinated, Reload. The perfect vintage." "When I consume you," the Janitor continued, "I won't just get one lifetime of pain. I'll get hundreds. Thousands. Every reality you've touched, every version of yourself that's died—all of it. Plus the weight of everyone who came before you. Every ancestor who suffered in this soil. Every child who died too young in these streets." He stopped ten feet away.

His shadow writhed behind him, faces pressing against the darkness like hands against a window.

"But first," the Janitor said, "I want you to understand what you're dealing with."

The Janitor moved.

Fast—faster than anything that size should move. One moment he was at the altar; the next, his hand was around D-Lo's throat, lifting him off the ground.

D-Lo grabbed the arm, tried to pry the fingers loose. Useless. The grip was steel wrapped in flesh.

"Die," the Janitor whispered. "Let me taste—" D-Lo headbutted him.

It was stupid. Desperate. Exactly what someone with no other options would do.

The Janitor's head snapped back. His grip loosened—just a fraction, just for a moment—and D-Lo dropped, rolled, came up three feet away.

"Feisty." The Janitor touched his forehead. Black ichor dripped from a gash D-Lo hadn't even noticed he'd opened. "I like that. Makes the consumption... sweeter." He lunged again.

This time, D-Lo saw the threads.

A bright line leading left—dodge that way—and a darker line leading to the Janitor's shadow—don't let it touch you.

He moved.

The Janitor's hand closed on empty air.

D-Lo spun, grabbed a broken pew, swung it like a bat. The wood connected with the Janitor's side, splintered, shattered.

Did nothing.

"You can see them now," the Janitor observed, not even acknowledging the hit. "The threads. Celestine's work, I assume. She always did like to play teacher." He tilted his head. "Did she tell you what you're becoming? Did she tell you what happens to Anchors who learn too much?" "She told me how to kill you." "Ah." The Janitor chuckled. "Let me guess—become unpredictable.

Break my patterns. Embrace chaos." He shook his head. "Those are the words of someone who's never faced me. Who doesn't understand what I really am." His shadow swelled.

Expanded.

The faces inside it pressed forward, mouths opening in silent screams.

"I'm not just a monster, Reload. I'm a process. A function of the universe itself. Pain exists, and I clean it. Trauma accumulates, and I consume it. You can't kill a function. You can only—" D-Lo reached for the threads.

Not the ones leading to his own survival.

The ones leading into the Janitor's shadow.

The ones connecting those trapped souls to the monster that held them.

He grabbed.

And pulled.

The sensation was unlike anything D-Lo had experienced.

Not like resetting—that was death and rebirth, a clean break between one reality and another. This was reaching into something wrong.

Something that hurt to touch. Something that screamed against his grip like a living thing fighting to stay hidden.

But he held on.

A thread came loose.

And a woman tumbled out of the shadow—translucent, weeping, her form flickering like a candle in wind.

"Thank you," she gasped. "Thank you thank you thank—" She dissolved into light.

Gone.

Free.

The Janitor staggered.

"What—" D-Lo reached again. Another thread. Another soul. A man this time—young, furious, his face twisted with decades of trapped rage.

"KILL HIM!" the man screamed. "END THAT THING!" He dissolved.

Gone.

Free.

"STOP!" The Janitor's voice cracked—actually cracked, the wrong smile faltering for the first time. "You don't understand what you're doing—" "I'm opening the prison." D-Lo reached again.

And again.

And again.

Each soul he freed was a battle.

Some came easily—grateful, relieved, dissolving into light the moment they touched the real world. Others fought, confused, not understanding what was happening after so long in the dark. A few tried to hold on, terrified of what might come next, preferring the familiar prison to an unknown freedom.

D-Lo freed them all.

He lost count somewhere after fifty. Or maybe a hundred. Or maybe more—time worked strangely when you were tearing apart a monster's soul one piece at a time.

The Janitor's shadow shrank with each liberation.

His form changed.

The wrong smile cracked and crumbled. The hollow eyes filled with something—not warmth, not yet, but something human. The confidence drained from his posture, replaced by fear. Confusion. Desperation.

"Please," he whispered. "Please stop." D-Lo paused.

The thing kneeling before him barely looked like a monster anymore. Just a broken man in faded clothes, weeping on a church floor, his shadow reduced to a normal size and shape.

"Why should I?" "Because I don't want to die." The Janitor's voice was small. Human.

Terrified. "I've been alive so long. Fed so long. I don't remember what it was like before. But I remember fear. Pain. Being alone." He looked up.

His eyes—no longer hollow—met D-Lo's.

"I was like you once. A person. A name, a family, a life. Then something terrible happened, and I became this. A function. A process. Endless hunger that could never be satisfied." "What was your name?" The Janitor's face twisted. Searching. Remembering.

"Marcus," he whispered. "My name was Marcus."

"I was an Anchor. Like you. The second one." Marcus sat on the church floor, legs folded, hands clasped like a child waiting for punishment. The shadow behind him was almost normal now—just a shadow, nothing more.

"After the First destroyed her world, I emerged. A new fixed point. A new chance." He laughed bitterly. "I thought I could fix everything.

Save everyone. End all suffering." "What happened?" "I started taking it. The pain. The trauma. I pulled it out of people and put it inside myself, thinking I could contain it. Thinking I was strong enough." His hands clenched. "But pain doesn't disappear when you absorb it. It just...

moves. Accumulates. Grows." D-Lo thought about his own power.

About the deaths he'd experienced, the traumas he'd reset, the suffering he'd witnessed and carried.

"Eventually," Marcus continued, "the pain became bigger than I was.

It consumed me. Became me. And I became... this." He gestured at himself.

"A thing that feeds because it has to. A process that can't stop." "For how long?" "Centuries. I lost track." Marcus's eyes went distant. "I remember... I remember a time before cities looked like this. Before lights and cars and concrete. I remember when this land was forest, and the people who lived here knew to stay away from certain places. Places where I fed." A chill ran through him.

Centuries.

This monster had been feeding for centuries.

"That's your future, Anchor." Marcus's voice was soft. "If you keep pulling on threads. Keep trying to fix everything. Keep taking the weight of the world on your shoulders." He looked at D-Lo with something like pity.

"You'll become exactly what I am."

The cathedral doors exploded inward.

Kettle came first—his entire body blazing white-hot, a supernova contained in human form. The heat was so intense that the rotting pews near him burst into flame, and D-Lo felt it on his skin from thirty feet away.

Clutch followed—coin spinning, luck bending reality around her.

Bullets would miss her. Debris would fall away from her. The universe itself would conspire to keep her alive.

Lexi next—wounded but standing, blade in each hand, her face set in the expression of someone who'd already accepted that she might die tonight and had decided it didn't matter.

And behind them— Kimi.

D-Lo's heart clenched.

"I told you to stay back!" "I'm done hiding." Kimi stepped forward, stood beside her brother.

"Whatever you're doing, we're doing together." Clutch surveyed the scene—D-Lo kneeling, the Janitor broken, souls still streaming toward the ceiling like escaping birds.

"Looks like you started without us." "Was handling it." "Sure." She moved to flank Marcus, coin never stopping its spin.

"Let's finish."

The Janitor adapted.

D-Lo had pulled three hundred souls from the shadow when Marcus changed tactics. The mass of darkness contracted, became denser, and the threads D-Lo had been using to extract the trapped suddenly went rigid—frozen in place.

"Clever trick," Marcus said. His voice sounded different now. Older. Wearier. "But you can't free them all. There are thousands in here, boy.

Centuries of collected pain. You'll burn out before you reach them all." D-Lo tried to pull another soul free.

Nothing.

"What did you—" "I stopped letting you in." Marcus smiled—that wrong smile, but tired now. Almost sad. "I've been doing this a long time. Did you think you were the first to try? The first Anchor who thought they could save everyone?" The shadow surged forward.

D-Lo died.

Reset.

He came back two seconds earlier, already moving, already shouting: "SCATTER!" The crew broke formation as darkness crashed through where they'd been standing. Clutch rolled left, luck bending a tendril away from her spine by inches. Kettle stood his ground, heat flaring, creating a barrier of superheated air that the shadow recoiled from.

"He's adapting!" D-Lo yelled. "Closing off the threads!" "Then we need a new approach!" Lexi called back. She was bleeding from a cut above her eye, blade in hand, looking for an opening that didn't exist. "Can you see anything?" D-Lo reached for the threads.

So many futures. So many failures. Reset after reset, death after death, and none of them ending with Marcus defeated.

"Nothing. I can't—there's no path—" "Stop looking for paths." Lexi's voice cut through his panic—sharp, certain, the voice of someone who'd led soldiers into impossible situations and brought them back alive. "You're thinking like a fighter.

Think like a rescuer." "What?" "The souls in his shadow—they're not just trapped. They're connected to him. He needs them. They're his power source." Her eyes narrowed, calculating. "Kettle, what happens when you heat something up fast enough?" "It expands." "And if it's contained? Can't expand?" "It explodes." Kettle's glow brightened as he understood. "You want me to—" "Not him. The shadow. If you can heat the darkness fast enough, the souls will want to escape the heat. They'll push outward. Force him to either let them go or—" "Or tear apart trying to hold them in." D-Lo stared at her. "Lexi, that's—" "Battlefield tactics. You disrupt the enemy's resources, you disrupt their strength." She pointed at Marcus. "He's not a monster. He's a system. And every system has a weakness." Clutch grinned. "I always knew you were the brains of this operation." "Flattery later. Kettle—on my mark. D-Lo—the second you see threads loosening, pull. Everyone else—stay behind Kettle's heat barrier.

This is going to get ugly." She took a breath.

"MARK!" Kettle stepped forward and blazed.

The heat was nuclear. Impossible. The kind of temperature that existed at the heart of stars. The shadow recoiled, writhed, and—just as Lexi predicted—the souls inside began to push outward, seeking escape from the inferno.

Threads loosened everywhere.

"NOW!" Lexi commanded.

D-Lo grabbed every loosening thread he could reach and pulled. Souls poured free—dozens, hundreds—while Marcus screamed and the shadow contracted and— But there— Faint. Fragile. A thread so thin he almost missed it.

A future where Marcus didn't fight back.

"I need more time!" D-Lo shouted. "Keep him busy!" "Kettle can't sustain this—" "I DON'T KNOW, JUST—" The shadow grabbed Kimi.

His chest seized.

His sister, thirteen years old, wrapped in darkness, being dragged toward Marcus's core. Her face was pale, terrified, but her eyes— Her eyes were furious.

"D-LO!" she screamed. "DO SOMETHING!" Marcus laughed. "How many times will you watch her die before you break, I wonder? How many resets before you realize some things can't be saved?" D-Lo reached for the threads.

Saw Kimi dying. Over and over. In every future except— There.

One path. One chance.

"KIMI! DO YOU TRUST ME?" "WHAT?!" "DO YOU TRUST ME?!" Her face—scared, confused, angry—softened for just a moment.

"YES!" D-Lo grabbed the thread.

And changed it.

The shadow holding Kimi didn't disappear—it transformed.

D-Lo poured everything he had into the thread, not pulling souls free but altering the moment itself. The darkness became light. The grip became release. And Kimi— Kimi was glowing.

Something sleeping inside you, Celestine had said. *Something that might wake up if the right trigger comes along.* D-Lo hadn't understood it then.

He understood it now.

"What—" she stared at her hands, luminescent, threads of silver light dancing between her fingers. "What did you do?!" "I don't know!" D-Lo felt something tear inside him—the cost of changing reality directly, not through death and reset but through pure will. "But I think you can hurt him now!" Marcus's face changed.

Finally, D-Lo saw fear.

"No. No, that's not possible. She's not—" "She's my sister." D-Lo grinned despite the pain, despite the blood running from his nose. "And you should never have touched her." Kimi raised her glowing hands.

And screamed.

But not in attack—in terror.

The light was too much. Too bright. Too hungry. It wanted to explode outward, to burn everything, to reduce the cathedral to ash and everyone in it to memory.

"I can't—" Kimi's voice cracked. "D-Lo, I can't control it!"

It's too much!" The glow intensified. Cracks of pure radiance split the air around her.

The stone floor beneath her feet began to smoke.

"Kimi, look at me!" D-Lo grabbed her shoulders, ignoring the heat that seared his palms. "Look at me!" Her eyes were white. Pure light. Losing herself.

"Remember what Celestine said? Don't fight it. Let it come." He gripped tighter. "But you choose where it goes. You choose who it hurts.

That's the difference between power and destruction." "I can't—" "Yes you can. You're a Graves. We don't break." He pulled her close, hugging her even as the light burned him. "Think about Mama. Think about the pancakes on Sunday. Think about us. Think about home." Kimi shuddered.

The light flickered.

And then—slowly, painfully—she pulled it inward. Condensed it.

Shaped it from a bomb into a blade.

When she opened her eyes again, they were still glowing. But they were hers.

"Okay," she whispered. "Okay. I got it." "Then let him have it." Kimi turned toward Marcus.

Raised her hands—steady now, controlled.

And released.

Light exploded from her—not raw and uncontrolled anymore, but focused. A beam of pure radiance that D-Lo had helped her shape, tearing through the cathedral like a second sunrise. The shadow recoiled, burned, unable to maintain its form against the radiance.

Souls poured free.

Hundreds of them, released by Kimi's light, streaming upward through the broken ceiling toward whatever waited beyond. Their voices merged into a single sound—gratitude, release, peace.

Marcus staggered.

His shadow—his armor, his weapon, his prison—was half the size it had been. The consumed souls still trapped inside writhed, reaching for freedom, weakening him from within.

"That's..." Kettle stepped forward, hands blazing. "That's our opening." "Together," Lexi said. "All of us. Now." The crew moved as one.

Trace phased through the shadow, becoming half-solid, half-ghost, disrupting Marcus's control from within. Sparks overloaded the ambient energy, creating cascades of electricity that lit up every thread D-Lo could see. Clutch flipped her coin—heads, always heads—and probability bent, making every attack find its mark.

And Kettle— Kettle walked straight into the darkness.

His heat turned the shadow to steam. His flames purified what they touched. Step by step, he carved a path toward Marcus's core, toward the broken man at the center of the monster.

"Don't—" Marcus raised a hand. "Don't come any closer—" "You killed my friend," Kettle said. His voice was calm. Sad. "You killed hundreds of people. Thousands. You turned their souls into weapons." "I was trying to help—" "Maybe once. Maybe a long time ago." Kettle stopped in front of him.

The shadow was almost gone now, burned away, leaving only Marcus—small, ancient, tired. "But that was before. This is now." D-Lo reached for the last souls still trapped.

Pulled them free, one by one, as gently as he could.

And Marcus—stripped of his shadow, his power, his stolen centuries—fell to his knees.

Marcus looked at them.

The crew assembled against him. The family D-Lo had built from broken pieces and shared trauma. The people who'd come into this cathedral knowing they might die, because they refused to let D-Lo face this alone.

He smiled.

Real this time. Sad. Broken. Human.

"This is what I never had," he said softly. "People who came back.

Who fought beside me instead of running." "Maybe that's why you lost," Lexi said.

"Maybe." Marcus closed his eyes. "Do it. Finish it. I've been tired so long." D-Lo hesitated.

He'd freed most of the souls, but not all. There were still shapes moving in what remained of Marcus's shadow—the oldest, the most deeply consumed, the ones who'd been prisoners so long they'd forgotten there was anything else.

Freeing them would take time.

Time they might not have.

Kettle didn't hesitate.

"He killed Bishop." His flames intensified, focused, more precise than D-Lo had ever seen. "Killed dozens. Hundreds. He doesn't get mercy." "Kettle—" "NO." Heat gathered around Kettle's hands—concentrated, white-hot, like holding pieces of the sun. "Some things you don't come back from.

Some things you can't forgive." He raised his hands.

"This is for Bishop. For everyone you ever hurt." Marcus didn't resist.

Didn't run.

Just knelt there, waiting. Accepting.

"Kettle, wait—" Too late.

Kettle pressed his hands against Marcus's chest.

And released everything.

White-hot.

Star-hot.

Heat that didn't burn—purified.

Marcus screamed—not pain, D-Lo realized. Release. The scream of someone finally letting go after holding on for too long.

His body blazed.

His shadow ignited.

The remaining souls—everyone D-Lo hadn't freed—erupted outward in a cascade of light, escaping their prison as the darkness burned away.

Hundreds of voices crying gratitude.

Hundreds of lights rising toward the broken ceiling.

Hundreds of trapped souls finding peace.

And in the center, Marcus—the Janitor, the Cleaner, the monster who'd fed on the Marrow's pain for centuries—dissolved.

Not into darkness.

Into light.

For one moment, D-Lo saw him clearly.

Not the monster.

The man.

Young. Hopeful. Full of the same desperate desire to help that D-Lo felt every day.

Marcus smiled at him.

Mouthed two words: Thank you.

Then he was gone.

And the cathedral went silent.

Kettle collapsed.

Clutch caught him before he hit the ground, her luck extending to keep them both upright.

"Easy, big man. Easy." "Did I... is he..." "He's gone." D-Lo stared at the place where Marcus had been. Nothing remained. Not ashes. Not shadow. Just empty space and the lingering smell of purified fire. "You freed him." "I killed him." "You freed him." D-Lo knelt beside his friend. "He asked for it. He was tired. He wanted it to end." Kettle's face crumpled.

"I've never... I didn't want to..." "I know." D-Lo gripped his shoulder. "That's why you're not like him.

That's why you never will be." Lexi appeared at D-Lo's side. Her hand found his.

"You did it. We did it." "Yeah." He looked at their joined hands. Something had changed. He could feel it—a thread connecting them that hadn't been there before.

Silver and gold, intertwined, unbreakable. "Something happened. When I pulled the souls free, something..." "Bound us?" He looked at her.

"You feel it too?" "I feel everything." Her eyes widened. "The threads. I can see them now.

Not like you, but—glimpses. Possibilities." D-Lo studied her face. Studied the new thread linking them.

"I think we're connected now. Our fates. Our futures." "Good or bad?" He thought about Marcus. About the First. About all the Anchors who'd been alone, who'd lost themselves in the weight of their power.

"Good. It means I'm not alone. Whatever comes next, we face it together." Lexi smiled.

"I can live with that." She kissed him. Hard. Desperate. Alive.

When they broke apart, Kimi was watching with raised eyebrows.

"Y'all know we're standing in a destroyed church surrounded by monster ashes, right?" "Seemed like the right moment," D-Lo said.

"I mean, you do you." Kimi shrugged. "Just maybe save the romance for somewhere less... burnt?" Clutch snorted.

"She's got a point. Can we leave before the Trust shows up?" D-Lo looked around the cathedral one last time.

The fires were dying. The souls were gone. The monster was defeated.

And above, through the holes in the roof, the stars were shining brighter than he'd ever seen them.

"Yeah," he said. "Let's go home."

CHAPTER 37

THE AFTERMATH

They emerged as the sun rose.

Gold and pink and orange spilling over the Marrow. The first light of a new day.

D-Lo stood on the cathedral steps, watching the sky change colors.

The neighborhood was still broken. Buildings still crumbling. People still struggling.

But something had shifted.

The monster was gone.

The Trust's grip had been challenged.

And a new power had emerged—not a hero in a cape, but a crew. A family. Broken people who'd found each other in the darkness and refused to let go.

Kimi stood beside him.

"What now?" D-Lo thought about the Trust. The wired prisoners still in the Vault.

The other threats he'd glimpsed in the threads—shadows moving at reality's edges, powers waking up that made the Janitor look like a warm-up act.

"Now we rebuild. Find the other Ghosts. Get organized. Start fighting back for real." "And the Trust?" "We'll deal with them. When we're ready." Kettle joined them, leaning on Clutch.

"I need to sleep for a week." "You earned it, big man." Lexi appeared at D-Lo's other side. Her hand found his.

"The Underline is compromised. We need a new base." "Old factory in District Nine," Clutch said. "Abandoned since the recession. Big enough for everyone." "Then that's where we start." D-Lo looked at his crew.

His family.

The people he'd die for—had died for, multiple times.

"We're not heroes," he said. "We're not villains. We're just people trying to survive. Trying to protect the ones we love. Trying to make this broken world a little less broken." He squeezed Lexi's hand.

"Maybe that's enough. Maybe that's what being a hero really is." Clutch snorted.

"Getting sentimental, Reload?" "Maybe a little." "Cut it out. We've got work to do." She started walking—toward District Nine, toward whatever came next.

Kettle followed.

Then Kimi.

D-Lo and Lexi lingered.

"Thank you," he said.

"For what?" "Everything." She looked at him. At the boy from the projects who'd died a hundred times and kept getting up. At the Anchor who could reshape reality but chose to stay human. At the man she was bound to now, for better or worse.

"You're welcome." She pulled him forward. "Now come on. We've got a war to win." Into the light.

Into the future.

Into whatever came next.

The backup site was an abandoned textile factory that had closed in the '90s.

From the outside, it looked like every other derelict building in this part of the city—broken windows, graffiti, the smell of decay. But Bishop had spent years converting the interior into something defensible.

Reinforced doors. Multiple exits. Supplies hidden in walls and under floors.

A safe house in plain sight.

They collapsed onto cots.

Nobody spoke.

For a long time, nobody even moved.

They just existed.

Breathed.

Let the reality of survival sink in.

KIMI

She couldn't sleep.

Every time she closed her eyes, she saw the light.

Not the monster's darkness or the cathedral's flames or any of the horrors she'd witnessed tonight. Just the light—her light—erupting from her hands like she'd been carrying a sun inside her all along and never knew it.

What was that?

What am I?

Kimi sat in the corner of the factory, as far from the others as she could get without leaving the building. Her hands kept twitching, kept flexing, kept trying to recreate what had happened in the cathedral.

Nothing.

The power was gone. Or sleeping. Or hiding.

But she could still feel where it had been. Like a muscle she'd never used before, aching from sudden overexertion. Like a door that had been sealed her whole life, now cracked open just enough to let in a sliver of impossible light.

Something sleeping inside you, the old woman had said. *Something that might wake up.* Kimi had thought Celestine was crazy. Or mystical. Or just one of those people who spoke in riddles because they liked sounding important.

She didn't think that anymore.

The memory of the cathedral played on loop in her mind. D-Lo screaming her name. The shadow wrapping around her like cold water. The absolute certainty that she was about to die— And then the light.

It hadn't felt like power. Not the way D-Lo's resets looked like power, or Kettle's flames, or Clutch's impossible luck. It had felt like recognition. Like something inside her had been waiting her whole life for permission to exist, and D-Lo's desperate reach had finally given it.

What am I becoming?

She thought about her mother. Dead before Kimi really knew her—just fragments of memory, a voice singing in the kitchen, hands braiding her hair. Would Mama have had this too? This sleeping thing?

293

Was it in their blood, passed down through generations, waiting for the right trigger?

She thought about D-Lo. Her annoying, overprotective, constantly-dying brother who'd given up everything to keep her safe. He had power—real power—and it was eating him alive. She could see it in his eyes, in the way he sometimes looked through people instead of at them, in the moments when he seemed to be watching something nobody else could see.

Was that her future? Threads and visions and the weight of impossible responsibility?

I'm thirteen, she thought. *I'm supposed to be worried about algebra tests and boys and whether my jeans are cool enough. Not monster fights and awakening powers and whatever the hell just happened to me.* But the universe didn't care what she was supposed to be worried about.

It never had.

The Marrow had taught her that lesson early: life didn't give you what you deserved. It gave you what happened, and you either survived it or you didn't.

Kimi had survived tonight.

She'd done more than survive—she'd fought. She'd blazed with light and burned a monster and freed hundreds of trapped souls.

And it had felt...

Good.

That was the scariest part. Not the power itself, but how right it had felt to use it. How alive she'd been in that moment, more alive than she'd ever felt hunched over homework or watching TV or pretending everything was normal while her brother came home with blood on his clothes.

She wanted to feel that again.

And that, Kimi thought, is probably how monsters are made.

She stared at her hands.

They looked normal. Brown skin, short nails, the calluses from writing too fast with cheap pencils.

But they weren't normal anymore.

She wasn't normal anymore.

And she had no idea what that meant.

D-Lo found Kimi sitting alone in a corner, staring at her hands.

She looked different now. Not just older—something in her eyes had changed. A weight that hadn't been there before.

"You okay?" Kimi didn't look up. "I don't know what I am anymore." D-Lo sat beside her. "What do you mean?" "The light." She flexed her fingers, but nothing happened. "In the church, I could feel it. Like a sun burning inside me. But now it's gone. I can't find it." "Maybe it's not gone. Maybe it's just sleeping again." "That lady—Celestine—she told me something once." Kimi finally met his eyes. "She said I had something sleeping inside me. Something that might wake up if the right trigger came along." A bitter laugh. "Guess watching a monster try to eat my brother was the right trigger." "Kimi—" "I'm not sorry." Her voice hardened. "I'm not sorry I burned him.

I'm not sorry I helped kill that thing. But I'm scared of what it means.

What I might become." D-Lo thought about his own journey. The first death. The confusion. The fear. The slow process of learning to control what he'd become instead of being controlled by it.

"You become what you choose to become," he said. "That's what I learned.

The power doesn't decide. You do." "Is that how it works for you?" "Not always. Sometimes I feel like I'm drowning in it. But I keep choosing. Keep deciding who I want to be." He bumped her shoulder.

"And you're tougher than me. Always have been." Kimi almost smiled.

"I held it together when Mama died. When you started disappearing into whatever trouble you were finding. When the whole world went crazy with the flash." She shook her head. "I guess I can hold it together through this too." "That's my girl." "I'm not your girl. I'm my own person." "Fair. That's my extremely independent, slightly terrifying little sister." This time, she did smile.

"Better." They sat in silence for a moment.

Then Kimi said: "I want to learn. To control it. Whatever woke up in me." "We'll figure it out together." "Promise?" D-Lo thought about all the promises he'd made. All the ones he'd kept.

All the ones that had nearly killed him.

"Promise."

Doc arrived three hours later.

Someone had gotten word to her—D-Lo wasn't sure who or how—and she came with bags of supplies and her usual grim expression.

"You look like hell," she told D-Lo.

"Feel like it too." She checked him over. Checked Kettle, who was finally awake but weak.

Checked Lexi, whose bullet wound had been hastily bandaged but needed proper treatment.

"The big man's core temperature is dangerously low," Doc said. "He exhausted his thermal reserves. Needs rest, fluids, and no power usage for at least a week." "A week?" Kettle tried to sit up. "We don't have—" "A week." Doc pushed him back down. "Or you permanently damage your ability to generate heat. Your choice." Kettle lay back.

"The girl's wound is clean," Doc continued. "Bullet went through. No major vessels. She'll recover." "And me?" D-Lo asked.

Doc looked at him strangely.

"Physically, you're fine. Better than fine. Whatever you did in that church—whatever power you used—it seems to have healed any damage you'd accumulated." "But?" "But I'm reading energy signatures I've never seen before. Your cells are... different now. More active. More connected to something I can't measure." She shook her head. "I don't know what you're becoming, D-Lo.

But you're not quite the same person who walked into that cathedral." D-Lo looked at his hands.

They seemed normal.

But he could feel it now.

The threads.

Always visible, at the edge of his awareness.

Always there.

Waiting.

That night, D-Lo and Lexi sat on the factory roof.

Below them, the city pulsed with life—traffic, lights, the distant sound of sirens that had nothing to do with them for once. Above them, stars fought to be visible through the light pollution.

"We did it," Lexi said softly. "We actually did it." "We did something." D-Lo wasn't ready to call it victory. "The Janitor's gone. But the Trust is still out there. The Conductor is still out there. We're still hunted." "I know." Lexi leaned against him. "But for tonight—just for tonight—can we pretend we won?" D-Lo wanted to argue.

Wanted to point out all the problems still waiting for them.

But he looked at her face—exhausted, hopeful, beautiful—and decided that tonight could be about something else.

"Yeah," he said. "We won." Lexi smiled.

"I felt it, you know. When our threads connected in the cathedral. When we became... whatever we are now." "Fate-bound." "Is that what Celestine called it?" "That's what I'm calling it." D-Lo took her hand. "Sounds better than 'mystically entangled' or whatever." Lexi laughed.

It was a good sound.

The best sound he'd heard in days.

"Fate-bound," she repeated. "I like that. Sounds almost romantic." "Almost?" "Would be more romantic if we weren't covered in blood and sitting on a factory roof." "I'll work on my setting choices for next time." They sat in comfortable silence.

Watching the city.

Holding hands.

Learning what it meant to have survived together.

"What happens now?" Lexi asked eventually.

D-Lo had been thinking about that.

"We rebuild. The Ghosts are scattered, but we can find them. Bring them here or to other safe spots. Start over." "And the Trust?" "They're scared. The files Dr. Rao gave us—they show how afraid they are of what I might become. That gives us leverage." "Leverage for what?" "I don't know yet." D-Lo watched a plane cross the distant sky. "But we're not running anymore. We're not hiding. We're going to find a way to take the fight to them." "That's dangerous." "Everything's dangerous. At least this way, we're choosing our battles instead of waiting for them to come to us." Lexi was quiet.

Then: "The Conductor. He's still out there." "I know." "If what Dr. Rao said is true—if he's an Anchor the Trust hollowed out and rebuilt—then he might be the only one who really understands what you're going through. What you might become." D-Lo had thought about that too.

Isaiah Washington.

School teacher.

Father.

Monster.

Victim.

"Maybe we can save him," D-Lo said. "Instead of just fighting him.

Maybe there's enough of the person he used to be left inside that we could reach him." "Or maybe he's too far gone." "Maybe. But we won't know until we try." D-Lo turned to face her.

"That's what I learned from all this. From dying and coming back. From losing people and finding new ones. Every situation has possibilities.

Threads going in different directions. You just have to be willing to reach for the ones nobody else sees." Lexi studied his face.

"You've changed." "Yeah." "Is that good?" D-Lo thought about it.

About who he'd been before the robbery. Before the first death. Before everything.

Just a kid from the Marrow trying to keep his sister safe.

He was still that kid.

But he was also something else now.

Something he didn't fully understand.

Something that scared him.

"I don't know," he admitted. "But I'm going to find out. And I'm going to make sure it's something worth being." Lexi kissed him.

Soft.

Simple.

A promise.

"Whatever you become," she said, "I'll be there. Fate-bound, remember?" "Fate-bound." They stayed on the roof until dawn.

Watching the sun rise over a city that didn't know it had almost ended.

Knowing that harder battles waited.

But for now—just for now—they were alive.

They were together.

They were enough.

DEEP BENEATH THE CITY

In the darkness, something stirred.

Isaiah Washington had been dreaming for seventy years.

Not the dreams of sleep—those had been taken from him long ago, along with everything else that made him human. These were different.

Memory-dreams. Echo-dreams. Fragments of a life that felt like it had happened to someone else.

Maya's face on her third birthday, chocolate frosting smeared across her cheeks.

The smell of chalk dust in Classroom 4B at Harrison Elementary.

Sarah's hand in his, warm and certain, on their wedding day.

The sound of his boys playing in the backyard, their laughter rising like music.

The dreams flickered through him like old film reels, degraded and incomplete. He could see the images but couldn't feel them anymore.

Couldn't remember what joy tasted like. Couldn't recall the texture of love.

They'd taken all of that.

Left only the shell.

And the hunger.

Something had changed.

He felt it—a disturbance in the void where his soul used to be. A ripple in the nothing.

The Cleaner was dead.

Marcus—the second Anchor, the one who'd broken before Isaiah had—was finally gone. Freed by fire and forgiveness.

And a new Anchor had emerged.

Stronger than expected.

Different than predicted.

A boy from the projects who died and came back. Who saw the threads. Who was learning to choose.

Isaiah stirred in his containment chamber.

The machines that kept him dormant hummed louder, compensating.

But they couldn't stop his thoughts.

Couldn't prevent him from remembering.

Couldn't keep him from hoping— Maybe this one will be different.

Maybe this one can save me.

Maybe this one can end it all.

In the darkness, Isaiah Washington—the Conductor, the Trust's greatest weapon, the third Anchor they'd hollowed and rebuilt—began to dream of freedom.

And somewhere in the machinery, a light blinked red.

Warning.

Subject activity detected.

Status: AWAKENING.

D-Lo Graves will return

THE GUTTERVERSE
Book Two: Conductor

www.ingramcontent.com/pod-product-compliance
Lightning Source LLC
Chambersburg PA
CBHW070635260626
47161CB00007B/2706